What the critics say about THE BAD TUESDAYS:

'an excellent page turner that positively hurtles along, brimming with menace and plot twists'
Daily Telegraph

'A brisk, event-filled fantasy'
Sci-Fi Online

'An impressive debut ... that brings magic, fantasy and science together'
The Big Issue

'Very well written and consistently gripping'
Carousel

'exciting and pacy, but with a great deal of thought and thematic depth'
thebookbag.com

'An exciting read with lots of action'
Teen Titles

'fast-paced inventive writing with original plot involving strange creatures and weird science, it's guaranteed to satisfy the hunger of voracious readers everywhere'
Julia Eccleshare, lovereading.com

'Older readers will be gripped gritty, urban

Also in this series ...

Look out for ...

Visit ...

www.thebadtuesdays.co.uk

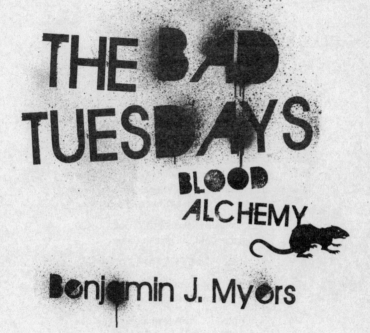

THE BAD TUESDAYS

BLOOD ALCHEMY

Benjamin J. Myers

Orion
Children's Books

First published in Great Britain in 2010
by Orion Children's Books
a division of the Orion Publishing Group Ltd
Orion House
5 Upper St Martin's Lane
London WC2H 9EA
An Hachette UK company

1 3 5 7 9 10 8 6 4 2

A catalogue record for this book
is available from the British Library.

ISBN 978 1 84255 641 2

Typeset by Input Data Services Ltd,
Bridgwater, Somerset

Printed in Great Britain by
Clays Ltd, St Ives plc

The Orion Publishing Group's policy is to use papers that
are natural, renewable and recyclable products made from
wood grown in sustainable forests. The logging and
manufacturing processes are expected to conform to
the environmental regulations of the country of origin.

www.orionbooks.co.uk

To my parents, Ted and Sybil

CHAPTER 1

The siren began to howl. This was the signal for the prison to start moving. Box flexed his arms. He knew that in moments he would be flung through the air.

'Hold on, fly head,' warned Splinter, threading his thin wrists into a pair of fabric straps that hung from the top of the metal cylinder.

'Like I wouldn't.' Box cast a sullen glance at his twin brother before gripping a strap in either hand and winding his forearms into them. He hooked his feet into the rope that looped out of the floor. 'This is because of you,' he growled.

The cylinder was about five metres long and, standing on tiptoe, Box could touch the roof. At either end and in the middle it connected with other tubes so that it was part of a network. Through the portholes that peppered its sides like gaping bullet holes, he could see the cobalt blue sky, the pan-flat terracotta earth and this unending grid of pipes which spread in all directions.

The grid was suspended high above the ground by pylons. Mechanical, pincered arms elbowed up and out of the pylons like skeletal branches, and it was these which gripped and spun the tubes, windmilling them from pylon to pylon and reconstructing the prison every time the siren wailed over the beaten plain.

Box had thought about escaping but he couldn't see how. After he and Splinter had been captured by Dog Troopers, they had been stripped to their waists, sealed in a metal crate so small he couldn't move his neck for two days once it had been opened and shipped to a planet that could have been anywhere in the universe. Or universes. They had no idea where they were. And how could they escape from a prison that hung in midair and was always changing shape? He glowered at Splinter.

Splinter ignored him and pressed his bony shoulders harder into the curved wall. His white hair was tacky with dirt and straggled down his rake-ribbed chest. His grimy feet were splayed wide apart, stick-thin shins jabbing out of narrow black trousers. Facing him, Box pulled down on the straps, thick shoulders taut and stomach hard. The fabric squeaked as he heaved up with his feet so that his body was suspended between floor and roof.

The siren cut out, leaving a phantom whistle in their ears. Box gritted his teeth, bracing himself for what was about to happen and to keep the meagre breakfast of wet bread from spilling up from his guts and out of his mouth.

'Enjoy the ride,' whispered Splinter. 'And try not to throw up.'

'If I do,' hissed Box through bared teeth, 'it will be all over you.'

The tube was wrenched up and began to spin, flat at first

like a roundabout and then up and over like a cartwheel. Box tried to keep the tension in his arms and legs but it was no use. His back was flung against the wall and then his body catapulted forwards so hard he thought his back would snap and his shoulders burst their sockets.

Through the portholes he saw the sky and the plain reverse and he saw the boundless field of tubes rotating as they were passed between the pylons, the jointed crane arms working smoothly, reassembling the vast prison.

With a pleading cry, a body slid from the mouth of a pipe that was tipping down below Box's own. It danced in the cool morning air before hitting the beaten ground, five hundred feet below. Always, there were bodies that fell. Box dug his arms and ankles into the straps until it hurt.

The tube slammed into position, flush with a new set of neighbouring cylinders and nearer to the tower at the centre of the maze; the tower from where the screaming came.

Box let his arms slip out of the straps and he slumped onto his knees and hands. 'Eight times a day,' he groaned. 'I can't stand much more of this.'

'You won't have to,' said Splinter, sliding down the wall until his legs were folded up against his chest. 'We're getting closer to the tower. It's taking us there.'

A shriek rose and then died in the still air. Box pushed himself up and lurched to a porthole. He peered out, squinting in the brilliant sunlight.

The pipe grid stretched above the baked ground in every direction but standing amongst the labyrinth of cylinders was a black tower, broad and sheer edged, its fluted ramparts studded with gates and windows and landing pads for airborne vehicles. The top storey commanded a position high above the pylons and its glass walls dazzled in the sun.

Even when they had been miles away, Box had been able to see the tower, prominent as a solitary peak within a sea of shimmering metal. He had watched the dots that were aircraft as they beetled slowly from the horizon to the landing pads and then away. At night, when the temperature plummeted and he and Splinter shivered against one another to stay warm, the drone of the flying traffic and the pinpoint flashes of landing lights glimpsed through the portholes never ceased.

They had started to hear the screaming when the cranes and pincers had spun them within the long shadow of the tower. At first they had thought it was a shrill wind, baying through the pipes. But as they drew nearer, they had listened glumly to how it cut the morning air, drifted out of the hot afternoons and pierced the freezing depths of the night. This was no wind; it was a sound that could only have been made by a living thing. Or a dying one.

Box had noticed how the screaming came at intervals. He didn't dwell on this until Splinter pointed out that it started only after a fresh tube from the prison had been inserted into the side of the tower.

Box rolled away from the porthole. 'You're such a moron, Splinter.'

Splinter frowned into a spar of sunlight that beamed through a small round window and lit his dirty face. 'We had to get away from Chess. Can't you see that?' He sighed, loudly. 'No, you can't. You're too stupid. She'd become dangerous, Box. Obsessed with her supposed power.'

'What a load of gunk. You're just jealous. Jealous that she stood up to the Inquisitor on her own. Jealous that she's different.' Box kicked the metal wall. It rang and he swore, grabbing his big toe and hopping.

Splinter looked up, wearily. 'Nice one, fly head. Now you've got brain damage.'

'We're meant to be with Chess.' Box winced as his toe throbbed and he smacked the wall. 'Whatever's going on with her and the Twisted Symmetry, she's our sister and it's our job to look out for her, 'cos whatever power you think she has, the Symmetry will come for her and they'll slab her as soon as look at her.'

Splinter smiled. 'Our little sister is a big girl. She can look after herself. She's always wanted to be in charge; now's her big chance. And she's far too *special* to be slabbed. Don't you worry about Chess.'

'If you hadn't of let go of her when she pressed the VAP, we'd have been transported with her. We'd be safe now.'

'Safe! Safe!' Splinter jumped up and stood over Box, thin as a cinder. 'Back with the Committee? Back with that crazy old hag, Ethel? How safe is that? Who keeps sending us into these death traps in the first place?'

'You got us into *this* death trap,' yelled Box. He might have been a head shorter than Splinter but he was broader and weeks of hard exercise, of press-ups and sit-ups and hanging to the straps every time the prison reconfigured, had turned flab into muscle. 'First you turn down the chance of going home ...'

'Because it was time to get away,' shouted Splinter. 'Because I was making a choice for both of us.'

'A choice!' Box's voice choked on his rage. 'What sort of choice was this? A choice to have bread and water piped to us twice a day? A choice to be trapped for four weeks in a puking drain?'

'A choice that has given us possibilities.'

'Possibilities?' Box drove his fingers into his fuzz of black curly hair. 'Of what?' A desperate wail reached out to them from the tower. 'Of a hideous and agonizing death?'

'No, fly head. Of power. Of real power.' Splinter tapped his own head with a spindly forefinger. 'For a street rat with a brain, there are always possibilities.'

'Some brain. If you hadn't started fighting with me after Chess had gone, maybe we could have hidden inside your magic box when half a million Dog Troopers turned up. You stole the portable vortex from Ethel and then didn't use it when you should of.' He remembered the tearing agony of the nerve wrenches that the troopers had used on him.

'You threw the first punch,' said Splinter, blue eyes glinting in his smudged face.

Box drew back a fist. 'Dead right I did.'

A splutter and a cough rattled out of the cylinder that connected midway with the Tuesdays'.

Box's fist remained poised to strike Splinter, but he jerked his head to look down the neighbouring tube. In four weeks they had encountered no one else, although he and Splinter had wandered through the tubular passages for days. Apart from the screams, and the bodies that tumbled into oblivion whenever the prison reassembled itself, they might as well have been alone. But somebody was near to them now.

The gloom was so thick, it seemed to smoke in the narrow

beams of light that criss-crossed from the portholes. It was difficult to see who had been coughing. Box stepped away from Splinter, arm still raised, and entered the adjoining cylinder, ducking slightly, even though its dimensions were the same as his own.

'Over there.' Splinter pointed into the shadows, although Box wasn't looking at him. 'There's somebody sitting against the wall.'

Box advanced slowly, treading lightly, fists clenched. He could see the body now; a black curve, ribbing the bottom of the wall and the floor. Tall, but human, which was a relief.

Another sharp cough and the body sat forwards, head lolling, face shrouded by long, black hair. Knees pulled up to his square jaw, the boy wrapped his sinewy arms around them and rocked, looking up at Box and Splinter, who had halted only metres away. His hair fell away from his face, revealing large, dark eyes and soft lips.

'You!' Box lowered his fists. 'You should be dead.'

Saul wiped the back of his hand across his cheek, smudging a rivulet of blood that Splinter had mistaken for a strand of hair.

'I nearly was,' he said. 'Didn't get a proper grip on the straps. Almost got thrown out.' He coughed and swallowed. 'Nearly brained myself when we landed.'

'I don't mean that,' interrupted Box. 'I mean when the General had you. The last time we saw you, General Vane was about to rip your throat out.'

'He probably will.' Saul leant back and stuck out his legs, wiping blood from his hand onto his jeans. His lean, hard chest, was beaded with sweat. 'He's waiting for us.'

'For us?' Box's question was answered by a wild scream that ended so suddenly it might have been snatched back by the tower it had broken from.

'General Saxmun Vane is feeding.' Saul turned his dark eyes on Box. They seemed less gentle than when he had helped the Tuesdays on the desert train that had been carrying them to the Twisted Symmetry's factory on Surapoor. He laughed humourlessly. 'We are in his food store. This is PURG-CT483; it's a prison planet. This maze of tubes, it covers the whole of the surface. It's not a big planet but it holds millions of the Symmetry's prisoners.'

'Why? What do they need them for?' Splinter was interested now.

'Energy.' Saul got to his feet, stooping beneath the arched roof. Box noticed for the first time how big his hands were. 'Children are better but the Symmetry will use whatever they can.'

'So that's what will happen to us?' asked Splinter.

Box couldn't understand how his brother could sound so curious when there was every reason to be terrified. 'We have to get out, Splinter. Somehow.'

Saul laughed again.

I like you a lot less than last time, thought Box.

'*We're* not here for energy,' Saul was saying. 'This part of the prison is reserved for the General's use. This is where the Symmetry send prisoners who deserve the most horrible punishments. The General comes here to feed. Prisoners are sent to him. They are locked in a small room with him, in that tower.'

Box looked at the tall black pinnacle through the

porthole, even though there could be no doubt about what tower Saul meant.

'But he doesn't attack straightaway.' Saul stood by Box, looking out. 'He waits until his treatment wears off.' Box remembered what he had seen in the factory; how the General's body began to mutate when not controlled by the treatment. He remembered how it contorted and erupted into the parts of other creatures, thrashing and twisting savagely. 'Then he tears them to pieces.'

'What have *we* done wrong?' protested Box.

'Killing an Inquisitor made the headlines,' stated Saul.

'*We* didn't kill the Inquisitor,' said Splinter, not wanting to admit who had.

'You were part of the team that did: same difference. So you get to be on the menu.'

'How long before we're in that tower?' asked Box.

Saul shrugged. 'I'd guess we're next.'

'Brilliant.' Box kicked the wall, hard, and swore as his toenail snapped back. 'We have to get away,' he grunted.

'We can't.' Saul pointed to a row of rivets on the ceiling. 'The prison changes shape so you never know where you are, and it's camera'd up.' Box looked closely and realized that some of the rivets were smoother than the others and had a glassy sheen like fish eyes. 'They can see you wherever you go, and wherever you go, they'll get you.'

'How come you know so much about what's going on?' Splinter smiled as he asked the question.

'I was closer to the General than I told you,' admitted Saul. 'He wanted a spy amongst the children that the Symmetry stole, so he would know what was going on.

He promised, kindly, not to eat my spleen if I helped him. So I didn't have much of a choice.' Saul sighed. 'Looks like he's going to get my spleen after all.'

'Why?'

'Because I wouldn't tell him what he wanted to know about Chess.' Saul paused and then looked about as if something had just occurred to him. 'Where is Chess?'

Splinter answered immediately. 'Safe and sound, back with the Committee and probably tucked up in bed with a milk drip.'

'Splinter!' fired Box.

'What?'

'Why've you told him that?'

'What does it matter? Anyway,' scoffed Splinter, 'you like Saul. You said we can trust him. Remember?'

Saul held up both his big hands. 'Don't fall out, OK? I don't blame you if you don't trust me. I'm sorry.'

Box kept looking out of the window, thinking hard. There wasn't much time. His muscles were tense, waiting for the inevitable howl of the siren. His eyes scanned the silver tubes that glinted like metal worms, seeking a way out. They came to rest on the frames of the pylons and the windings and girders of the mechanical arms. Then he noticed a cloud of dust, stirred up by a body of a couple of hundred unarmed dog-men who were trundling across the parched earth far below, escorted by a handful of fully equipped Dog Troopers.

'Who are they?' He'd spotted shabby groups like this before and assumed they were connected with the troopers, although their rough clothing and shambling bodies didn't fit with the efficient, professional soldiers he had seen on

Surapoor, or the Dog Trooper guards who escorted them now.

'The Fleshings.' Saul's face was beside Box's but Box didn't pull away. 'Bad snouts.'

'Snouts?' queried Splinter.

'It's a name for the dog people. Snouts, Dog Troopers; the same thing.'

'Snouts,' repeated Box. 'Nice one.'

'Snouts who desert their battalions, or breach military discipline, or criminals from the snout colonies get sent here as Fleshings. The Fleshings are used for target practice by trooper cadets. That's where the guards are taking them.'

'Snouts slabbing snouts.' Splinter spat grit. 'I like it.'

'What happens to them?' Box could sense a possibility.

'Most of them get killed. The few who survive get posted to the Dog Trooper penal battalions; military units used for the most hopeless battles. Cannon fodder.'

'If I could join the Fleshings,' said Box, slowly, 'I could fight my way out of here. Then, maybe, I could find Chess. Help her.'

Saul looked at Box as if he had spoken gibberish. 'They're snouts, Box; you're a human.'

'Only just,' observed Splinter. He shook his head, dismayed. 'Show fly head an army of the damned and he's the first to sign up.'

'It beats being eaten,' snapped Box.

'Even if you were capable of passing the IQ test to join the idiot squad, how are you going to get out of *this* place?' Splinter pointed at the wall of the tube.

Box smiled at his brother. 'Watch.'

The siren began to howl.

All three of them reached for the straps which dangled from the arched roof. Splinter noticed that Box merely gripped his, rather than winding his arms into them. Immediately, he guessed what his brother was planning.

'Don't be a nobwit, fly head.' He had to yell because the siren was so loud.

Box grinned back, eyes bright.

The howl stopped and silence rushed in on them; thick, waiting.

'Please, Box,' said Splinter. 'Stick with me.'

The prison broke apart, metal pipes whirling away from each other and spinning between the pylons.

Box's fingers and forearms flamed with the strain of holding on as the cylinder soared up, dragging him with it. Then, as it tipped upside down, he was smashed into the roof by his own weight, cracking his head against a rough ridge of rivets. But he didn't let go. Not yet.

Blinking because of the blood that was running into his eyes, he waited until the sky had slipped away and the cylinder mouth was gaping down at the earth. He waited until his body was hanging like a plumb line inside the tube, feet pointing at the open end. He waited until he saw another tube swinging beneath his own. Then he let go.

Box hurtled towards the ground, but he didn't shut his eyes and he didn't scream. He was a street rat. The world had taught him that he was worth nothing. So when he climbed, leapt, fought, he had nothing to lose. A jack would have screeched pitifully before smashing into the rock-hard earth, but Box focused on the curved metal roof of the tube below, the portholes, the point where the pincers curled round the shiny metal body. He would have two seconds, maybe. But two seconds was plenty when life had given you nothing else.

He struck the metal with a thud that was more painful than it sounded. Locking his fingers onto the rim of a porthole, he used the momentum of his fall to swing across the outer wall. At the same time, this tube began to tip down, vertical to the ground. This was what Box had bargained on.

He let go of the porthole and fell down the length of the tube until he was checked by a claw of the pincer. Legs apart, he slid over this and crashed into the mechanical wrist of the crane arm with a yelp. But he was alive. He had stopped falling. All he had to do was wrap himself round the arm as it worked at the cylinders, and wait until it stopped. Then he would climb up until he reached the pylon, and then he would climb down the pylon. And then he would walk up to the next batch of Fleshings and join them. And then . . . and then . . . Box closed his eyes. He was going to find Chess and, as always, he would have to fight.

When the prison had been rebuilt, Splinter dropped to the floor. He felt sick. He waited for his eyes to catch up with his body. Next to him, Saul groaned and said, 'This is it.'

At one end of the cylinder there was a bright circle of daylight, at the other, pitch darkness. Or so it seemed at first. As Splinter peered into the darkness, he realized that beyond that end of the cylinder there was a chamber, bare and dim.

Feet stamped across the chamber. Splinter didn't move.

Saul crouched by his shoulder. Two figures appeared: Dog Troopers, clad in the black combats and black body armour Splinter had seen before. On their shoulders they wore a silver awlis; the sign for infinity and the symbol of the Twisted Symmetry.

One of the troopers held a drill-nosed blaze carbine at his hip. The other unclipped the knuckleduster-shaped nerve wrench from his belt. A slash of light revealed the deranged faces; matted fur torn by strips of human skin, snarling muzzles, the eyes of one species caged in the head of another.

The trooper with the nerve wrench jerked his head towards the shadows beyond the pipe. When Splinter and Saul failed to react immediately, he bellowed at them with a grating roar, jaws wide to reveal the long fangs.

Splinter clambered to his feet. 'OK, OK,' he muttered. 'Keep your fur on.'

Saul stood beside him, taller and broader. 'Leave the General to me.'

Splinter didn't think Saul was as calm as he was trying to sound, but he shrugged his pinched shoulders and said, 'He's all yours.' Then he led the way into the chamber, limping slightly because of the ankle that had been broken by the stonedrakes' cannon shot, months before.

It was a small, square room with an open door in one wall. Splinter looked about and seeing no blood on the floor or walls, nodded to himself, satisfied. The killing didn't happen here. There was still time; time to talk.

But when he heard the thump of the iron-shod boots approaching the open door, and the sway and clink of the chains, it was hard to stop his legs from shaking. Eyes round as sapphires, he stared into the murk of the passage beyond the door, snatching at breath.

The tall, rangy frame of General Saxmun Vane loomed out of the darkness and then he was standing over Splinter. His jigsaw armour, designed to allow his body to morph when not controlled by treatment, was washed with crimson swirls like watery ink stains, and his sharp jackal snout was sticky with congealed blood. His yellow eyes stared crazily into Splinter's, the pinpoint pupils nailing him like darts. In his gloved left fist he held a cluster of silvery rods.

Splinter started back as the General swung the rods. But he wasn't swinging them at Splinter. At the end of the rods there was a ring, bearing bolt-headed spikes, and he jammed this into his right shoulder where a hollow stump marked the place at which his right arm should have begun.

The General roared at Splinter; sounds which meant nothing to him. It wasn't Chat, the universal tongue that the Tuesdays had been taught by the boxing philosopher, Balthazar Broom, on Surapoor. It was the Dog Troopers' own language, translated by a voice which droned from the plate collar worn around the General's neck. 'See what that creature you call your sister did to me?'

Unlike Box and Splinter, the General had not been hiding in the vortex when Chess unleashed the energy which had destroyed the Inquisitor, Behrens. He must have been caught in the blast that ripped through the factory. Yet he had survived, with the loss only of one arm. Splinter was amazed that the General had survived at all. But this was General Saxmun Vane: commander of the Twisted Symmetry's millions of Dog Troopers: he was murderously tough. Of course he had survived.

General Vane thrust out the rods, and now Splinter saw that this was an arm built of shiny metal, like a steel skeleton. The thick central shafts were hinged at the shoulder, elbow and wrist and between these joints ran thin metal tendons. The segmented fingers curled and uncurled silently.

Show no fear, thought Splinter. 'What happened is between you and my sister,' he said, backing off no more. He knew that a wire between the General's ear and the collar translated what he said.

'She owes me an arm,' he bellowed, but Splinter stood his ground. Then, calmly, the General cocked his head to one side and looked up and down the metal limb. 'But why should I complain? This one is much better than the last,' and he smashed it into the doorway, spraying chunks of stone until it was buried up to its elbow.

As he wrenched it free, Saul pushed past Splinter. 'General, please, listen to me.'

The General looked down at Saul and then drove his flesh and blood left fist into the centre of his face.

'My nose,' gasped Saul, clutching the front of his head and dropping to the floor.

'You're hardly worth killing,' growled General Vane, the voice translating dispassionately. 'But *you*,' he continued, turning back to Splinter, 'I will enjoy.' He stroked his bristly chin with his metal fingers. 'Not a lot of flesh, it is true, but plenty of fight.' Then, scanning the rest of the room, 'Where's the meaty one?'

Splinter said nothing, but the yellow dog eyes bearing

down on him narrowed to slits as if scrying his thoughts. The General snorted contemptuously and marched past the guards and into the tube. His boots banged over the floor and he stooped because the ceiling was low for him. At the far end, he knelt and looked out, the two Dog Troopers standing between him and Splinter.

The azure sky and the rust-ruddy earth were framed in a circle by the mouth of the cylinder. The vast grid of tubes shone white in the blistering sun. The hot air pulsed. The world was desert-still. The least movement would be visible for miles.

'I see him.' The General muttered more quietly than the collar spoke. Thoughtfully. 'He's climbing down a support tower.' He made a noise that Splinter thought might have been a chuckle. 'See how he goes? So fast. Strong. How did he escape?' A long pause and then, nodding to himself, 'By risking everything. But what does he plan to do?'

Splinter guessed that if he said nothing, he would be made to talk, and there was no point in lying. So he said, 'Join the Fleshings.'

The General grunted. 'It would be easy to kill him.' His eyes flicked towards the guard's blaze carbine before he turned his head to look back outside, still kneeling in the opening. 'But that wouldn't be fair.' To Splinter, it seemed that the General meant what he said. 'He has displayed cunning, bravery and strength. He would rather fight than die. He is not an ordinary human.'

Splinter watched the tiny silhouette as it dropped between a pair of joists, two hundred feet above the ground. 'He's a street rat,' he said proudly, and he beat back the ache in his chest that meant he wished Box was with him now.

But he was alone.

Splinter's mouth tightened. He was always alone. He was always the one who faced the greatest dangers, thought of the cleverest plans, saved everybody else. And now? Now everyone else had bailed out, leaving him to face one of the most dangerous creatures in the universe. Alone.

But he could handle this. *Only* he could handle this. He was the one who knew how to survive. He was the greatest street rat of all; the King of Rats. He would get out of this; there was a way. And from then on, it would be Splinter looking after Splinter.

He surfaced from his ruminations as he re-entered the cool darkness of the chamber, a guard pushing him in the shoulder. Saul was still on the floor, propped up against the wall and trying to staunch the flow of blood from his nose. Splinter didn't spare him a thought. Saul was as good as dead now. The only person who mattered was Splinter.

General Vane crossed to the door, walking away. He said nothing, which surprised Splinter because he was expecting something more before he was taken to be slaughtered. This was his one chance and it was slipping his grasp, vanishing into the far passageway.

Splinter had meant to bargain coolly, eloquently, displaying his formidable intellect. But now he screeched. He screeched the two words on which he was staking everything. He screeched them because his life depended upon them.

'The Traitor.'

The boots stopped. The words hung in the air like the ring of a blade.

The General turned and pointed at Splinter, the light gleaming off the two metal struts that ran either side of his left forearm; struts which carried his emergency treatment bolt.

'What do you know of the Traitor?' The bitter growl rumbled out of the shadows; the dead voice translated.

'I know who he is. I know *where* he is.' Splinter's heart was thumping. His lips were dry as ash. He swallowed what felt like a mouthful of glue. 'I can give you Lemuel Sprazkin.'

Lemuel Sprazkin; the primary warp whose failed surgery on the General had transformed the General's body into a mutating curse; who had run from the Twisted Symmetry to the Committee and remained hidden for two hundred years. The person whom General Saxmun Vane hated above all others.

'How?' The General arched over Splinter now, his rancid breath hot on Splinter's face as his snout craned down.

'He will trust me,' said Splinter. 'Trust me enough to catch him.' Now I've got you, he thought.

'Why should *I* trust *you?*'

Splinter had expected this question. 'Because it costs you nothing. Give me back my coat and my box and I will find your traitor for you.'

General Vane straightened up, gloved fingers drumming against his hip, steel fingers pulling a shred of meat from between his canines. His long, pink tongue lingered about the edge of his lower jaw and a drop of spittle ran down it and spotted the floor.

Splinter was confident now, pleased with how his cleverness had defeated the General. He allowed himself to say, 'You need me if you want Sprazkin.'

The General moved so quickly that Splinter was still standing in the same place as the metal hand grasped the mace-blade, unleashed the long steel edge with a hiss and slashed it across Splinter's arm.

Splinter screamed and crumpled to the floor, clutching his arm and kicking himself away from the heavy boots. He flapped across the floor like a drowning fish.

'I need no one,' roared the General and he pushed the tip of the mace-blade into Splinter's breast bone, pinning him to the floor.

'I'm sorry, I'm sorry,' whimpered Splinter and his body was shaking so hard he thought he would impale himself on the point. He dared to look at his arm and saw that the General had opened a wound a couple of inches long. Blood was seeping out but he knew it could have been much worse, if the General had wanted.

'I will get Sprazkin with or without your help. Using you is merely convenient. You are nothing to me. Do you understand?'

Splinter nodded, trembling.

The General knelt by his side, the metal hand still pressing down on the pointed tip of the mace-blade. Seizing Splinter's trouser leg, he tore a strip of cloth. Then he pushed this into the wound, so roughly that Splinter cried out. When the material was drenched with blood, he stood up, retracted the mace-blade and walked towards the door, the cloth hanging wet in his fist.

'Do you know what a *hungry* spook can do?'

'No,' mouthed Splinter, at the General's back. All he knew was that the Twisted Symmetry used spooks to track the people whose blood they were given. They listened across space and time for the heart that beat the blood, and always, they found who they looked for.

'If I took a blast grenade, planted it in your guts and let it blow, the mess would look like fine art compared with the damage a hungry spook would do.' The voice spoke calmly, but the General lingered over the description, pleasure rippling his throat.

'I have your blood, boy. You have ten days. Bring me Sprazkin or you will wish I had killed you now.'

CHAPTER 2

'Look, Mummy, there's somebody up at the window.'

'Don't be silly.' The woman in the woollen hat took the little girl's hand and pulled her away. 'Children!' she said to her companion, with a martyr's smile. 'Always seeing things that aren't there.'

Chess retreated from the window but she could still see the little girl in the red anorak, arms hoisted by the two women in hats and fleeces, boots skimming the ragged grass as she was directed away from the keep wall. The women's faces had been stung pink by the cold January air and the little girl's coat glowed sharp as a berry beneath the hard winter sky.

Always, it was the children who noticed her. Grown-ups saw crumbling castle walls, padlocked gates barring old stone steps, plastic screens nailed across mullioned windows and low, wooden doors marked 'NO ENTRY'. But the children saw her, sometimes, when she pressed her face up to the scratched plastic screen in the high window of the tower. They saw her because they hadn't learnt *not* to see things like her.

Maybe one of the women was the girl's mother. Her hand would be strong and hot and the girl didn't have to worry about where she was going next because her mother would know. Chess imagined that's what it would be like.

You're pathetic, she told herself. You know nothing. You don't even know who you are. You don't even know your own name.

She closed her eyes and blotted out the little family. She blotted out the broken curtain walls, the solitary ice cream van, the man in the yellow fluorescent jacket collecting litter with a stick, another groundsman with a rake, the white, stone chippings of the car park, the low, bare hills and the busy dual carriageway beyond them. She turned her back to the window, unclenched her fists, opened her eyes and saw the scrubbed, wooden floor, the humming fan heater, the trestle table with its folding chairs standing open and Jones.

Always, there was Jones. When she went to the toilet, took a shower, lay in the bunk room, Jones would be there. Jones the preactive; Jones, who according to Ethel was a kind of mathematical equation made flesh; Jones, with her long, yellow hair, skull-sunk face, blank red eyes like rubies behind dark glasses and reactions quicker than thought itself. Always watching, always waiting, supposedly protecting her; in reality, making sure she stayed exactly where the Committee wanted.

Chess thrust her fists into her loose, black, leather jacket and strode across the room, white trainers squeaking over the wooden boards. Jones's head tracked her with a mechanical jerking.

Chess pulled out her hands and smoothed back her hair.

The chestnut strands had been braided with beads at their ends. She liked their weight on her head and shoulders. It was about the only useful thing Jones had done since she had started to keep watch over her. She had been keeping watch for nearly two weeks now; ever since Chess had recovered from her trip to Surapoor.

She shivered. It was a lot colder here, in January, than in the tropical heat of Surapoor. And whenever she thought about Surapoor, she thought about what the Twisted Symmetry had done there, to the children they had stolen. How they *extracted* the energy from them. How they did this in the scream rooms. How it felt, to be trapped there, at the mercy of the enemy. How she was determined that this should never happen again. And she thought about how she had used the energy from the stolen children to destroy the Inquisitor, Behrens.

But she didn't know *why* she had been able to do this.

Chess marched over to Jones, stopping when she was standing toe to toe with the preactive. She put the palms of her hands together, as if in prayer, and pointed the tips of her fingers towards Jones's chest. Jones mimicked her, so that the ends of their middle fingers touched. They faced one another like reflections.

This was a game Chess had introduced after Jones had won a thousand contests of rock-paper-scissors and Chess had thought she would go screaming mad. At least with the new game, she might get to hurt Jones.

But she knew she wouldn't. Always, Jones's hands were pulled back before Chess's hand had begun to swing forwards, so she slapped only air. Then it was Jones's turn. Jones never missed. She might have been slapping a piece of steak. At least the stinging took Chess's mind off how much she missed Box and Splinter, how much she missed her friend, Gemma, how much she hated being locked up by the Committee for her own protection; how badly she wanted to get away from Jones.

But today, even the pain didn't help. Chess had spent her life trying to escape the locks, chains and guards that haunted every street rat and now, the people whose side she was meant to be on, the Committee, were burying her with them.

She swore at Jones and punched down at the table, hard enough to break a knuckle. But Jones's hand was there before she hit the wood, cushioning her fist; stopping it.

'You won't even let me hurt myself,' Chess screamed at the bone-white face. Jones said nothing, as usual.

Ethel stomped into the room, wrinkled her nose at how Jones was holding Chess's fist on the table, chose to make no comment about it and said, instead, 'It's all change, dear.'

Ethel, resplendent in a cheap jumper, frayed tweed skirt, hiking boots and green body warmer; nothing to reveal that she was actually the Baroness Mevrad Styx, Grand Mistress of the Outer Crescent, one of the most powerful beings in the universe. Or *universes*. She looked like a semi-respectable tramp. But Chess had learnt that that was the problem with appearances; they didn't always show you what was really there.

Standing behind the bespectacled, shrivelled figure of Ethel was Lats. Lats was a member of the snatch squad which had recovered Chess from Surapoor and he had been on guard ever since. His skinless body, with its fibrous chunks of muscle and exposed bone lurched above Ethel. Across his shoulders were slung the convoluted tubes of a plasma punch, his ribs-of-beef fist gripping the handle, elbow pointing up, muscle fanning out from his waist to his upper arm. He wore a pair of thick leggings and a metal plate across his collar bones, like the one Chess had seen on General Vane. She knew, now, that it was called a rap collar, and that it translated what the wearer said through a built-in microphone. It interpreted what was said back through the wire that hung between the collar and Lats's ear.

Lats winked at Chess. Chess nodded back. He might have looked like an anatomized gorilla but he was all right. Then she scowled at Ethel. 'We're moving? Again?'

'I'm afraid so.' Ethel sounded businesslike and afraid of nothing at all.

'But this is the fourth move in two weeks,' protested Chess.

'Don't blame me, dear. We performed a cardiac freeze on you when you returned from Surapoor, to shake off any spooks. But, spook or no spook, the enemy have developed the irritating habit of finding where you are. I'm sorry,' Ethel sounded no more sorry than she had sounded afraid, 'but it's a fact of our current life that given sufficient time, the enemy will locate this protection group, and once they have located it, they will have located you. And, my love, it is *you* that the Twisted Symmetry want more than anything in the universe.'

'Universes,' corrected Chess.

'Very good!' Ethel clapped her small, chapped hands with genuine delight.

Chess wandered to the window. 'So they are coming. Again.'

'We believe so. We don't know how, we don't know when, but we know it will be soon. So we have to move you. A.S.A.P.'

A crackle came from one of Ethel's body warmer pockets, where the stubby antenna of a walkie-talkie protruded.

'We should hide somewhere away from *everyone*,' insisted Chess, 'miles from anywhere. Not stupid places like this, where people are always wandering about. It's no wonder the Symmetry keep finding us.'

'Wrong, dear,' chimed Ethel. 'A National Heritage site is perfect. It's because we hide in places where people wander about that the Symmetry haven't got you. Yet.' Suddenly, the old lady's mouth was by her ear. 'It's because we are amongst the public that the enemy cannot just send a fleet of gunships to destroy us and take you. Nobody is meant to know what is happening. The last thing the Twisted Symmetry want is publicity. War is waged up and down and across the universes, under people's very noses, but they don't see it and they mustn't.' She brushed a fleck of her spit from Chess's hair. 'Think of the panic, dear, if people knew what was really going on.'

Stones crunched as a coach pulled into the car park. Chess switched her attention to Ethel's insomniac-pink eyes. 'We should fight back.'

'You've become terribly aggressive, dear. I don't know if that's a good thing. Is it hormones?' She looked Chess up and down as if hormones were something she wore. 'You are that sort of age now.'

'That's not *my* fault,' Chess pointed out. But she had grown accustomed to how she had aged nearly two years in just six weeks, because of the way she had travelled back from Surapoor. She had started out eleven and now she was nearly fourteen, and she liked it. She felt bigger and smarter and less like being bossed by Ethel.

'You won't let me find my brothers . . .'

'I've advised you against it,' said Ethel, defensively.

'Advised!' Chess's brown eyes widened with fury. 'Locking me up and gluing that weirdo to me is a bit more than advice.'

Jones didn't react. She said nothing. Always, she said nothing.

'It is *firm* advice,' admitted Ethel, pulling a paper bag out of her body warmer and offering it to Chess. 'Lemon drop?'

Chess glowered.

'Oh dear, bitter enough already, I see.'

'The least we could do is fight.' Chess slammed her fist against her thigh.

'The enemy aren't that easy to beat,' Ethel pointed out.

'Aren't they? I destroyed their factory *and* an Inquisitor.'

'They will recover from the loss of Behrens and the factory is already being rebuilt.'

'So? It will take them months, maybe a year,' said Chess, belligerently.

'No dear, it will take them days, maybe weeks. This is the Twisted Symmetry, not the local bricky. They build planets, not conservatories. We believe that your destruction of the factory created dimensional shock waves that scrambled the behaviour of the Fat Gobster so badly that the suck worm strike data is now inaccurate; the Symmetry have been unable to transport the children they've stolen. So your explosive activities have already saved countless young lives. Well done, for that.'

'You're welcome,' muttered Chess, anticipating the cloud of misery that accompanied every one of Ethel's silver linings.

'But,' came the inevitable jeremiad, 'before long the computer will begin to calculate fresh data. Then the enemy can transport more children to a factory that will soon be operational and there they will be consumed. Unfortunately.'

'How long?' demanded Chess. 'How long before the brain is ready?'

'How should I know? A week, maybe two, maybe the day after tomorrow. You can't find this stuff in a timetable, dear.' Ethel observed Chess's face work through frustration and gloom before returning to angry determination.

'OK,' announced Chess. 'That just means we have to act fast. We know the Symmetry need children to give them power. We know where they hide the computer that works out where the Fat Gobster can collect the children they steal. We know where they run the whole child-stealing operation.' Even now, the cerebral torus, that huge ring of brain that predicted where the suck worm would next strike, would be sitting inside the Riverside Prison, shrouded in the poison gas that nourished it. 'It's simple. We attack the Twisted Symmetry by destroying their brain *before* it starts working again.' No more children in scream rooms. No more suffering.

'Our resources are limited.' Ethel was looking out at the coach now.

'I know,' muttered Chess. 'An ice cream van and a couple of gardeners.'

'There's a couple of civilian agents at the ticket office, too. Although,' said Ethel with a sigh, 'they spend most of their time complaining that there's no running water to make hot drinks. But the Charitable Operations Executive are over-stretched, so the last thing they can do is mount a full-scale attack against the enemy. And anyway, children aren't the only source of energy. The Symmetry obtain plenty from the misery they inflict throughout the rest of the universes. You won't stop the Twisted Symmetry by stopping them from stealing children.'

'But what they do to children is wrong,' stated Chess. 'I'd stop them doing *that*.'

'Very commendable, dear. I admire your moral courage. But since you're going nowhere without us, we'll never find out if you would succeed.'

'I *hate* you,' yelled Chess.

'Sooner or later, my love, everybody does.'

Chess shoved her shoulder towards Ethel and scowled at the party of elderly passengers who were meandering off the coach. There were about twenty of them, men and women in camel-brown jackets, macs and capacious shawls. They moved unsteadily, milling like confused sheep, as they congregated by the coach doors, crowding one another and tripping over walking sticks. But what distracted Chess from her anger were the glasses. There was a variety of styles, but all with darkened lenses. It wasn't sunny, it wasn't even bright, yet every one of the passengers was wearing them.

Chess watched as the gaggle of senior citizens shuffled in a loose, unsteady group, towards the entrance to the castle ruins. Another couple of metres and they would be shielded from view by the remains of the outer wall. They wobbled, they doddered. And then, they ran.

Chess gasped, astonished, as the first of the pensioners broke right, sprinted to a shattered buttress, leapt up to the jutting stones and swung herself over a low section of wall.

'Oh no,' groaned Ethel, yanking the walkie-talkie from her body warmer. 'Muttons.'

'Muttons?' Chess had no idea what Ethel meant. Another five senior citizens were scaling the outer wall, with the rest following.

'Rogue pensioners. Servants of the enemy. In exchange for vigour and longer life, they serve the Twisted Symmetry. They are skilled in surveillance, survival and unarmed combat. They are wrinkly, but dangerous.'

'A bit like you,' muttered Chess, more glibly than she felt.

'You're all charm, dear,' bridled Ethel, before giving instructions into the walkie-talkie.

Already, two attendants wearing National Heritage sweatshirts were sprinting out of the entrance booth, towards the first of the muttons. Chess looked right and saw that running down a grassed slope from the other direction were the man in the fluorescent jacket with the litter stick and the gardener with the rake.

The first to reach the pensioners was the gardener with the rake. He wheeled it at the legs of the woman who had led the charge. Even as she ran, she jumped, hurdling the rake effortlessly. Landing square to the gardener, she kicked high and hard, straight to his jaw, felling him, senseless.

Behind her came the hoard of muttons, pounding the

turf, vaulting lumps of wall, heading for the tower where Chess was being kept.

'They're looking for you, dear.'

Chess's mouth was dry. 'What do we do?'

'We have to stop them, of course.'

The litter stick was thrust between the ankles of a man in a blue gabardine who stumbled into a broken, sandstone column. But the next thrust was parried by a walking stick wielded by a grizzled mutton who looked like an ancient sea captain. He slashed his stick across the litter-picker's arm, grabbed his lapel and butted him in the face before throwing him clear and into a nest of litter bins.

Two women whose stockings had slipped to their ankles were galloping for a door at the base of the keep, below Chess. Chess heard the thump and gasps as they were rugby tackled by the entrance booth attendants. But although they had been bulldozed to the ground, both of them began to trade blows with the Committee's agents, rolling and kicking across the grass.

'This is the advance party,' said Ethel, between exchanges on the walkie-talkie. 'Once they have pinpointed your whereabouts and assessed our strength, the Symmetry will send in the main force.

'Their eyes.' Chess had seen the bearded mutton's face after he had butted the litter collector because his dark glasses had been knocked off.

'I know. If I was an artist, I'd call it Symmetry green. Unpleasant, isn't it?' She rested a hand on Chess's shoulder and even though she didn't want to, Chess drew closer to it.

'You can't be kept alive by the Twisted Symmetry *and* keep your looks.'

Chess pushed her face against the plastic window to follow two muttons who had made it to the foot of the keep. But they had vanished in the lee of the tower.

'I don't care how desperate it is,' Ethel was saying into the radio. 'Get into position but no firing until the public are clear.'

At the same time, Chess heard the engine of the ice cream van kick into life. The van began to trundle down the drive from the edge of the car park, towards the entrance gates.

A thud overhead, and then the tread of footsteps across the ceiling.

'They're on the roof.' Ethel looked towards Lats. He nodded and swung the plasma punch off his shoulders. He held the engine-sized weapon at his hip with one hand, whilst he turned a calibrated dial on its casing with the other. The plasma punch began to hum.

The ice cream van had emerged from the castle entrance and stopped in the grassed area between the outer wall and the keep. Chess saw the hatch window slide open and two gun barrels poke out.

'Not yet,' commanded Ethel.

'No,' mouthed Chess, when she saw the bright red coat bob across the grass.

The little girl stopped, mouth agape, as she absorbed the attendants grappling on the grass with two old ladies, the litter collector sprawled across the rubbish bins, the gardener unconscious on the floor and the muttons, in their dark glasses, gathering at the foot of the ruined keep.

'Mummy, Mummy,' she shrieked, running out of view. 'The grannies are fighting.'

But as she returned with the grown-ups, nobody was fighting. One clutch of pensioners had assembled by the litter bins, masking the prone body of the litter collector and apparently listening to a member of their group describe the purpose of the nearby stones. Another group was sitting on coats, spread over the grass and over the gardener, whilst at the foot of the keep, two National Heritage attendants were gently escorting a pair of infirm ladies back to the rest of their party.

Above everyone, two muttons clung to the castle walls, still as gargoyles. But nobody saw them because nobody looked up. There was no reason to look up.

'Come on,' said the little girl's mother. 'You are seeing a lot of things today.'

'Can't blame her,' said the other lady. 'There's not exactly a lot happening, is there?'

They began to walk towards the entrance booth.

'Can I have an ice cream, Mummy? Please?'

'I told them an ice cream van was a bad idea,' grumbled Ethel. 'Stick a child at the North Pole with ice cubes down its pants and it would still want ice cream.'

The little girl started to run towards the van window.

'Not before we go in the car,' shouted her mother. 'You can have an ice cream when we get home.'

The little girl hesitated. A few steps closer and she would be staring at the muzzles of the guns.

'Now come on, or no ice cream at all.'

She turned and ran back to the grown-ups.

Everybody waited as the members of the public ambled back to the car park. Everybody waited as car doors clunked open and then slammed. Everybody waited until the tyres had crunched over the chippings and the car had trundled into the lane at the end of the car park.

'All clear.' Ethel's shrivelled lips, close to the radio.

Then everybody burst into action.

Both the attendants were down, bodies crushed beneath a pack of muttons that was attacking them on the floor. Two of the group who had been near to the bins began to hurry back to the coach. A hatch flipped open on the roof of the ice cream van and up stood a man, rifle to his cheek. Two sharp cracks from the rifle and the muttons were down.

Chess pressed her face up to the plastic window. It was difficult to see out because the plastic was fogged by her breath but she had heard the rifle shots and she could see the muttons were dispersing.

THUD.

A face slammed towards her own, upside down and on the other side of the plastic. Chess yelped and jumped back. One of the muttons must have climbed down the outside of the wall from the roof, like a bat. The livid green eyes and tiny pupils were fixed on her and a scrawny fist beat at the window.

'Lats?' There was an edge to Ethel's voice as the plastic whitened beneath the blows.

Two more faces appeared, one to the side and one at the bottom of the window. Their glasses were still in place but grey fingers scratched at the screen maniacally.

'Chess.' The name was uttered softly, breath steaming out of their heads and over the window.

One of the muttons looked down and shouted, 'Here. She's here.'

The coach engine started up with a growl.

'Now the heavy mob will come,' said Ethel.

Lats grunted and made the slurring sounds he did when he spoke. 'Ready,' said the voice from the rap collar.

The faces were pressed to the window, the lurid eyes fixed on Chess. 'They're coming for you,' moaned one of the heads.

'Stand away from the window, dear.' Ethel shoved Chess hard enough to make her stumble.

Lats stepped forwards, muscle-chunked arm extended, the blunderbuss mouth of the humming plasma punch two metres from the window.

'Knock knock,' cackled one of the demented heads.

'Bang bang,' replied the rap collar.

There was a resonating thrum that made the space behind Chess's eyes ache and vibrate. The air between the mouth of the plasma punch and the window shimmered in a huge bubble. The front of the bubble flattened against the window and it expanded from floor to ceiling before bursting with a blast that blew out the tower wall, showering the ground below with lumps of masonry and shreds of mutton.

When Chess's hearing returned, a diminishing whir came from the plasma punch which Lats slung back across his shoulders. Her eyes were watering from the heat of the explosion.

'If only everything in life were that simple,' said Ethel, wistfully, clasping her hands across her lap.

The coach was leaving. The National Heritage attendants were staggering up a brown-turfed knoll on the left of the keep and there were no muttons to be seen. Cold air swirled in through the ceiling-high hole in the wall. Chess's breath streamed white when she spoke.

'You won't tell me who I am. You won't let me look for my brothers. You won't stand up and fight. You won't do anything except hide me.' Her cheeks were cold and her voice caught in the chilly air. 'And you can't do that properly because they're coming for me, again.'

Ethel walked to where the wooden floor looked like it had been bitten off at the wall. Her little figure was dark against the white sky. She said nothing. It looked to Chess as if she was weighing things up. When she spoke, she didn't turn round.

'Lemuel would be the person to talk to.'

Chess couldn't see how Lemuel would be able to help her right now. 'Lemuel isn't here,' she said, walking round, behind Ethel. Jones moved, shadowing her.

'Lemuel hasn't been with us for months, my love; ever since I suspected him of spying for his former masters. He took my suspicions very badly.' She heaved her shoulders, wearily. 'Once he'd built our supercomputer, he moved on. Last known address: the Cones.'

Chess knew about the Cones, the tallest buildings ever, she had heard. They had been constructed at the north edge of the city, despite public protests. But the necessary grease changed hands and the Cones got built. There were six of them and they were higher than clouds. Chess had never been to them but on a clear day, if you climbed on top of the warehouses at the wharf, you could see their spires needling high above the jagged, city horizon.

'Lemuel knows a lot. A lot about *you*, dear.'

'So?' Chess tried to sound as if she didn't care what he knew, as if wanting to know the truth about herself wasn't something that stopped her sleeping, gnawed her like hunger, lurked behind all her other thoughts.

'So many secrets,' sighed Ethel.

Why are you telling me this? thought Chess. None of this would help her *now*; not with the enemy coming. All it did was make her want to find Lemuel.

'If I walked out of here, you couldn't stop me.' Chess waited for Ethel to dismiss the challenge. When the old lady said nothing, Chess repeated, more loudly, 'You couldn't stop me.'

Ethel's arms dangled by her sides. She still held the walkie-talkie. Someone was speaking, trying to get her attention, but she didn't respond.

Finding her brothers, destroying the brain, discovering who she really was; the first step to all of these things was walking out of this place.

'You couldn't, could you?' It was a statement. Chess's breath rasped in the cold air. She stuffed her hands in her jacket and blew hot air into the loose neck of the red jumper she was wearing.

Looking out across the bare ruins, at the streaks of grey breaking the vault of winter-white sky, Ethel's dry lips moved and she said, without speaking aloud, 'This is when you run.'

Ethel closed her prune-skinned eyelids. Her eyes felt hot and wet. She did not expect to see Chess again, before the end. 'You *have* to run.' So quiet, she might have been whispering to herself.

'I'm off,' announced Chess. 'I've had enough. I'll find Lemuel; I'll stop the Symmetry stealing children; I'll get my brothers. You could help but you won't. Fine. I'll do it all on my own. *You* can't stop me.'

Ethel was silent. Chess stared at the old lady's back, still as stone against the wide sky. She stared until the cold made her shiver. There was nothing more to say. She walked out of the room and away from Ethel.

Getting rid of Jones was easy; a bit lively, but easy. The idea came to Chess on the way to the main road.

Jones had followed her as she left the castle, the white face and long, yellow hair floating at the edge of her vision. Across the road, over a stile and into a field, Chess headed for the dual carriageway, following a route she had traced with her eyes for days.

Chess planned as she squelched over the freezing farmland. It was difficult to organize all her thoughts because there were so many, but one thing was clear; she had to find the cerebral torus and destroy it before the Twisted Symmetry could start to use it again. However, her thoughts were tugged from the brain to Lemuel Sprazkin and his secrets; secrets about *her*, according to Ethel.

Chess wanted answers to those secrets more than she wanted anything; the promise of secrets revealed was like a hook in her soul. And these secrets could be important, she told herself; they might give her ammunition against the enemy. That was how she justified her decision to find Lemuel before doing anything else. But she would have to find him quickly.

The city was a long way south of here but if she hitched a lift she could be there by tomorrow. Once she found Lemuel, he would tell her what she wanted to know; Lemuel was one of those people who couldn't stop himself from answering questions. Then she could turn her full attention to the enemy.

Chess stumbled on a half-frozen cattle rut. It hurt her ankle and made her feel stupid, as if people were sniggering at her as she tripped. She stopped and looked about.

As ever, the gaunt, blank apparition that was Jones was at her shoulder. It was infuriating, but Chess was sure she would work out a way of getting rid of her; she had saved Box when he had been snared by strangler vines; she had found out how to use the stonedrakes; she had calculated how to defeat the Inquisitor, Behrens. She was clever, she was powerful. She could do anything if she tried.

It was as she feasted on these thoughts that she slipped on the bank of a drainage ditch. The route that had looked so simple from the high window of the keep had revealed itself to be a tangle of woody brambles and sucking mud. Sliding head first into the sodden ditch would complete the process of getting caked from hair to trainers in filth.

But she didn't hit the black brook. Jones was there already, blocking her way with her own body, making sure no harm came to Chess. She had moved as instantaneously as only a preactive could and she had grasped Chess's upper arms with wiry strength, preventing the fall.

'Thank you,' said Chess, for Jones's help and for providing her with the solution to her problem.

When they came to the edge of the dual carriageway, Chess stood close enough to the road to feel the spray from the juggernaut tyres splash her face. Her braids whipped round her head and her black leather jacket flapped like wings. Lorry horns blared at her, warning her to back away, but she ignored them.

At her shoulder stood Jones. As usual. Watching. Waiting.

Chess didn't allow herself to wonder whether Jones would *always* move first. She didn't allow herself to wonder what she might lose in the coming moments. She closed her eyes. She listened to the thunderous rattle of the approaching lorry. Louder. Louder.

She jumped.

And felt something slam against her chest, knocking her backwards. Away from the road.

Horns blew. Tyres screamed.

Chess was lying on the stones at the side of the carriageway and already traffic was stopping, mounting up behind the lorry that had skidded but been unable to avoid hitting Jones; Jones, who had leapt in front of Chess to block her jump into the road; Jones who had been smashed out of existence.

But Chess was all right. She jumped to her feet and scanned about. Jones had definitely gone. All that remained were a pair of dark glasses that lay on the tarmac, at the edge of the road. Chess picked them up, wiped them and put them on, even though dusk was falling.

'You don't know what you are dealing with, and I have been too patient,' she said, enjoying the sound of Behrens's last words in her own mouth. Then she vanished into the fields before anyone could discover what had happened to the girl who had thrown herself into the road.

CHAPTER 3

The motorbike crunched to a halt at the foot of the steps that striped the front of the plaza. Chess swung her legs clear, straightened her jacket, shook the long, brown braids away from her face and adjusted Jones's glasses. Then she looked up. The ice-bright towers speared the metal-blue sky.

The motorbike engine was purring now, the rider leaning over the handlebars. 'Sure you don't want to hang out?'

'No. Thanks,' said Chess, not turning round. 'Here's where I want to be.' Now that she didn't have his back to keep her warm, the air chilled her neck. She stuffed her numb hands into her jacket pockets, pushing the jacket closed.

The throttle opened and the bike growled. 'See ya.'

'Yeah. See ya,' echoed Chess. The bike screamed away and she was on her own again.

Getting to the Cones had taken longer than Chess had expected; two days of hitching lifts and trudging roads, eating what other people didn't want and sharing cups of bitter coffee; two days of wondering whether the cerebral torus had already begun its fateful calculations. But at least there'd been no DVs. A DV was a divert; a lift who took you where you didn't want to go. Chess could usually spot them when they pulled up; they were too eager to get her into their car or van and sometimes there was a smell; a sweet, sweaty smell that made the skin at the back of her neck feel like it was shrivelling. On this trip she'd been lucky; she'd taken only lifts who were heading where she wanted to go, and the guy on the bike had covered half the journey in a night. And now, here she was.

There were six towers, each stretching so high that even with her hand shading the dark glasses, she couldn't tell where their aerial spires stopped and only sky was left. Their bases were broad and their glass and steel walls tapered as they climbed so that she thought they looked like upside-down golf tees. They were clustered on a field of white concrete that was broken by neat parallelograms of baize-green grass and small trees that had lost their leaves. Around the Cones, the other sky scrapers looked no more impressive than mismatched building blocks. Humbled.

Chess stamped up the wide, white steps.

Five of the towers stood in a ring with the sixth at the centre. On the lower section of the central tower a huge, elongated letter C blazed in the sunlight. Chess reckoned that the distance between the top and bottom of the C must have been at least twenty floors. Its metal surface was planed like the face of a diamond and in its centre were mounted three stars, sharp and sparkling in the hard, morning light. She had no idea to whom the C belonged, but she understood what it meant: business, grease, control. Power. It told her how big it was and how small she was.

Chess sniffed. You don't know what *I* can do, she thought. Then, for the first time, she began to wonder how she would actually find Lemuel Sprazkin.

She drifted towards a pavement café. Even with the street heaters pumping out warmth, the patrons sat deep in thick coats, chic scarves pulled to their chins. Chess heard the neat shuffle and clink of coins across steel table tops and, without having to think about it, she knew she could palm the tips that were left, as easily as a breeze turns paper. She let a hand dangle by her thigh and curved her way past the first of the tables towards a small stack of change that a departing customer had left. She looked the other way and gently swerved, hip first, past the table. Then she let her hand follow her hip. But something took hold of it and she was pulled back, sharply.

'Get off,' she shrieked, trying to snatch her hand back and hoping to cause enough embarrassment to make her captor let go.

'Sit down, Chess,' said the man in the long, black ulster coat. He looked up and, from under the wide brim of the black fedora, a large pair of pale grey eyes tilted over a crescent moon smile.

'Lemuel!' gasped Chess.

'The very same,' said Lemuel Sprazkin with a muted tinkle of delight. 'And waiting for you.' His smile intensified. 'Always, for you.'

He didn't let go of Chess's hand until she was secure between the arms of the seat he pulled up to the edge of the table. When she was in position and had taken off her sunglasses, he patted the back of her hand, pulled the sugar bowl closer and offered it to her. 'Or something to drink, maybe?'

Chess shook her head. Lemuel dipped his fingers into the bowl and plucked out a white cube, holding it between the black, tapered nails of his thumb and forefinger. He popped it into his dark-lipped mouth and sucked in his cheeks, which made his head look even longer and thinner.

'Forbidden fruit,' he said, with a sudden crunch and a smack of his lips.

'You knew I was coming?'

'Absolutely.' Lemuel produced a folded sheet of yellow paper from inside his coat and proffered it to Chess, his arm moving slowly enough to give him time to study her, observe her reactions, linger on her bright eyes and the way her white teeth bit the corner of her lower lip. Anxious.

'You are,' he paused, not wishing to sound rude, 'older.'

'I've had to do a lot of growing up,' muttered Chess. She reached for the paper but before Lemuel released it, he said, 'You've made quite a stir. Everybody's talking about it. *Everywhere.*'

'It? You mean Behrens?'

Lemuel nodded. Still he wouldn't release the paper.

Chess huffed. 'He didn't know what he was dealing with.'

'Obviously not. It's certainly shaken everything up, caused a good deal of *instability.*' He made it sound as if that was not a good thing. Then Lemuel let go of the paper and arched an eyebrow. 'Tell me, what do you plan to do now?'

Chess's hand paused in mid air as she weighed up what might lie behind Lemuel's enquiry. But there could be no harm in telling him straight. 'I'm going to keep fighting. Nobody else will fight the Twisted Symmetry, but I'm not frightened of them.'

'They will be ready for you,' warned Lemuel. 'You have to be careful. What happened with Behrens was due to the most peculiar circumstances. All that loose energy floating around.' He made little sucking noises between his teeth. 'They won't make a mistake like that again.'

'I'm going to stop them stealing children. I know what they do to children.' She couldn't stop the images; the horror of what happened in the scream rooms. 'I've been there. I've seen it,' she hissed.

Lemuel waved his hand. 'Please, Chess, not so loud. People are looking at us.'

'So? I don't care.'

'*You* might not.' Lemuel coughed politely. 'But I do. You must understand, Chess, the Symmetry are everywhere. They hide themselves. They don't all walk about with glass heads.' He tittered modestly.

'You're not with them anymore.' Chess regarded him sombrely.

'I'm not with anyone,' stated Lemuel. 'But you must be on your guard. Suits, corporations, governments; the Inquisitors' influence penetrates deep into your world.'

A blast like ice made Chess's neck prickle and a chair close by screech across the concrete.

'So much suffering in your well-ordered world; drugs, corruption, cruelty.' Lemuel whispered into the wind. 'The poison runs very deep indeed. Tell me,' he asked when he saw Chess idly staring up at the sky, affecting boredom, 'how will you stop them? How does Chess Tuesday propose to stop the Symmetry?'

'Simple. I'll destroy their computer; their brain. I'll get my friends to help.'

'Friends?'

'Yes,' snapped Chess. 'Friends.' She didn't need to hear any more about how powerful the Twisted Symmetry were.

'It arrived this morning,' said Lemuel with a flick of his fingers at the letter. 'Have a read.'

Chess unfolded it and held it up for inspection. Her eyes tried to focus on the writing. It had been done with a typewriter. The thick black print marched across the page in a knot of letters that she couldn't order, that wouldn't make sense to her. It was always like this with writing; like a code that everyone else could crack.

'Would you like me to read it to you?' Lemuel's voice was not unkind. Chess nodded. He took the paper and flattened it on the table, looking about suddenly enough to make Chess glance around as well. Then he leant forwards.

'"*Dear Lemuel,*
We trust this communication finds you well and, if not
well, alive."'

'How thoughtful,' commented Lemuel.

'"*The Committee write to inform you that you may*
expect a visit from Chess. She has left us, at last. It is
better that way. Be ready to meet her and to render
her such assistance as you are able. Tell her about

Sherevsky (Crazy Boris). She will be travelling with the preactive, Jones, but she will be in greater peril than she understands.

You know the Committee would welcome your return. Our resources are depleted, the enemy advance in every dimension and in the wake of Behrens's destruction, there is dangerous instability. We need your help. We offer you, again, our apologies and, as ever, our friendship.

Yours,

Mevrad Styx, Baroness etc . . . ,

Professor Joachim Breslaw OEB, GROS(2), ELCP, FISPR, FSRD

Julius (in absentia)

(The Committee)'''

Lemuel folded the paper, pressing it along the creases and then slipping it back into his coat.

'It's confusing,' said Chess, mulling over what had just been read to her. 'I always forget that Ethel is Mevrad. I forget who she really is.'

'She is . . .' Lemuel selected the word with care, 'deceptive.'

Chess folded her arms and frowned. 'She makes it sound as if she had a choice about me going. She didn't. I went because I wanted to go.'

'Really?' A smile danced from Lemuel's eyes to the corners of his mouth. 'Then what made you come here. To me?'

Chess thought about this. 'Well, she didn't know I'd get rid of Jones.'

'Oh no, she certainly didn't,' agreed Lemuel. 'That was all

your own work. Tell me, how *did* you "get rid" of Jones?'

'How do I know that you've read what was actually in that letter?' It seemed a good way of switching the subject from Jones. Thinking about what she had done to Jones made her feel uncomfortable.

'We must go inside.' Lemuel spoke softly and his eyes flicked left and right beneath the brim of his fedora. 'I have been out here too long.'

Chess wasn't sure if *he* was now avoiding *her* question. However, she knew that the enemy hunted him as they hunted her. But for different reasons. They wanted her so that they could control the Eternal; a weapon that would allow them to stop space, stop time and live forever. In Lemuel's case it was more simple: the Twisted Symmetry wanted revenge.

Lemuel grasped the tubular arms of the chair, preparing to stand. But Chess didn't move. Lemuel was a warp, a genetically engineered intelligence grown by the Twisted Symmetry to create the dark technology they desired. Before he had defected to the Committee, two hundred years ago, he had been the Symmetry's primary warp. By nature, he should have been as cruel and devious and brutal as every other element of the Symmetry. But he was able to change his behaviour by a machine that he inserted into his brain through a glass plate in the top of his head. He was able to make himself good, if he wanted.

'You look,' said Lemuel, half standing, 'as if you are trying to see what I have under my hat.'

'Are you still ... good?' Being blunt was the only way to be.

Lemuel pushed back the chair and stood up. He looked down at Chess. 'These days I am more like a human.'

It wasn't much of an answer. He must have seen Chess's bemusement, so he explained. 'It's like this; sometimes I'm good, and sometimes I'm not.'

That wasn't the assurance Chess wanted. 'How are you *now*?' she asked, cautiously.

'On balance, and in the knowledge that you would be visiting, I have *made* myself as good as I can possibly be.'

'Good,' said Chess, and Lemuel trilled at her inadvertent pun.

'Who's Sherevsky?' Chess hadn't risen yet. 'The letter said you were to tell me about him.'

'Follow me,' whispered Lemuel and walking quickly, he cut through the café and towards the Cones.

As soon as she entered the marble-floored atrium of the nearest tower, Chess was buffeted by warm air, pungent perfume and a thousand chattering voices making one rippling voice that said nothing. Faces flashed past.

Lemuel's arm slipped around her waist and he steered her through the crowd. 'My rooms are at the top; on the hundred and fiftieth floor, eight hundred metres from the ground.' His thin, dark lips were so close to her ear that it tickled.

They walked past the lifts that travelled between the ground and the lower levels and entered one that travelled to the top floors. The press of bodies was hot and smelt of clothes shops. Never before had Chess been in reach of so many pockets.

'I feel like an orange that's about to be juiced.' Lemuel's breath was a hot fog on Chess's neck.

'Keep breathing on me like that,' whispered Chess, 'and you'll feel like a nut that's just been cracked.'

You don't know what you are dealing with.

She liked those words. They were her words now. She had taken charge of events. For the first time in her life, *she* was in control.

They were the last people out of the lift. Alone, they trod the soft carpet that followed the curve of the glass tower wall. Lemuel was in a hurry but Chess stopped to press her face against a window. The city rolled out below her like a map. She was too high to see people or even cars, but she could trace the main roads and flyovers, look down on skyscrapers she had only ever looked up to before, follow the looping crease made by the river far to the south and beyond that, see the brown fog of the factory sector, unfolding until it met the sky. Her forehead rested against the glass. A fresh surge of longing to be with Box and Splinter and Gemma clutched her throat. She tried to see the wharf.

'Be careful when you look out of windows,' Lemuel breathed in her ear. 'You don't know who might be looking in.'

Chess drew away and let him lead her to his rooms. This reminded her of the time Lemuel had taken her to his rooms at Committee HQ, in the old city bus depot. But the similarity ended when he pushed open the door marked SKY SUITE 8. Last time, there had been a flood of sunlight; now there was a wall of pitch darkness.

'In there?' Chess stood on the threshold, her trainers not crossing the metal strip between the corridor and the room beyond. She looked back, briefly, sure that she had heard somebody cough. But there was only the empty corridor.

Lemuel stepped into the darkness and vanished from view entirely. Then there was a click followed by the hum of track lighting across the ceiling and around the walls. He was standing by a low table, just inside the doorway and was lifting a hand from a black, rubber pad that was set in the centre of the table.

He beckoned to Chess. 'Come in.' He pointed at the pad. 'A tenebrous lamp. It pumps out darkness within a programmed area. Good for hiding things.' He giggled. 'Good for hiding *me*. When I press it the lights come on and here I am.' He swept off his hat which he threw over the pliable, stubby lamp.

Lemuel opened wide his arms and closed his eyes and turned about, introducing the room. The lighting glinted over the glass panel on the back of his long, narrow, chalk-white head. 'A hidden house, in a hidden place.' He opened his eyes. 'Not my words; Albertus Magnus, 1193 to 1280 by your calendar.'

'I don't have a calendar. I don't exactly know the date,' said Chess glumly.

'Not to worry. It's the principle that matters, not the date.'

'And it's not a house,' muttered Chess, crossing the threshold. She looked about slowly, suspiciously, wondering at the purpose of the beakers and crucibles and pipes that covered the workbenches like glass undergrowth. Unblinking, she surveyed the racks of tubes containing blue and red liquids, the nests of electrodes, the wires draping the walls like frozen cobwebs, the shoe-box sized machines with dials on their faces and a tall, transparent refrigerator filled with runners on which there hung plastic packs, swollen with a purple-brown liquid.

'Don't be frightened,' beamed Lemuel Sprazkin. 'It's only science.'

The primary warp shook off his heavy coat and threw it onto a chaise longue that reclined beneath a hammock of cables. Now, he was wearing a loose, white shirt that buttoned to his throat and a pair of black trousers.

'You are perfectly safe with me.' His face broke into a white-toothed grin. 'I promise to be on best behaviour.' He adjusted his features, and pouting solemnly, he held up a hand as if taking an oath. 'Warp's honour.'

'I'm not frightened of *you*.' Then, in case she had displayed a weakness, Chess added. 'I'm not frightened of anyone. Or anything.'

'Then,' said Lemuel Sprazkin, the humour deserting him, 'if you would forgive me for saying so, you are a very foolish little girl. Everyone has to be frightened of *something*.'

'What are you frightened of then?' Chess stuck out her chin.

Lemuel's face swooped very close to her own and his almond-shaped, black fingernails rested on the top of her arm. Quietly, he said, 'I am frightened of *me*.'

Chess looked over his shoulder, at the far wall where there was mounted a long, grey spike on a bracket and next to it, a lever with a black handle. She could see that if the lever was pulled, it would drag down the spike so that it would stab the air at about the height of Lemuel's head.

'Today, Lemuel,' said Chess hoarsely, large brown eyes

fixed on the brain drill, 'you have nothing to be frightened of.'

Lemuel seemed to drink her in, through his eyes. Chess didn't flinch, even though she didn't like to be stared at like that. 'I am very proud of you, Chess. You are my greatest work.'

Chess wasn't sure what to say back although she opened her mouth. She closed it quickly at the thought of how stupid she must have looked.

From below their feet came music, rising up through the floor; the mellow strum of an electric guitar, the thrum of a base, a trumpet scatting to a swing beat. Lemuel danced across to his rumpled coat, soft-shoe shuffling in time to the floating music, thumbs and fingers clicking the rhythm.

'The people downstairs are very noisy,' observed Chess. The music sounded like it was echoing round the room below; as if it was coming from a place that was as big and empty as a disused lock-up.

'I like it.' Lemuel dug deep in a pocket with his back to Chess, all the time mimicking a hissing cymbal with his tongue and teeth. When he turned round he was holding a bar of chocolate as tenderly as a rose. He shimmied across to Chess.

'Chocolate? Children love chocolate. It always works.' He gave her a foxy smile. 'Dark chocolate; sweet and bitter. I bought it this morning, just for you.' He offered it to her and her stomach rumbled. 'There isn't a lot about children that I don't know.'

Chess took the bar, unwrapped it and broke the top off with a loud snap. She was hungry but she didn't want to have to be grateful to Lemuel. She hadn't asked him for the chocolate. She bit it, making loud chomping noises.

Lemuel crooned along with the music.

Chess had had enough of playing games. *She* was in control. 'Ethel said you knew a lot about me. And her letter said you should help me.'

Lemuel bowed. 'I am here to assist your ladyship.' A tinkle of laughter and a flash of teeth.

Chess broke off another piece of chocolate as if she was snapping a thick stick. 'I've got some questions for you.'

'Oh good, a quiz,' trilled Lemuel, clasping his hands.

Chess sat on the chaise longue and eyed Lemuel Sprazkin as suspiciously as she would have eyed a rookie lawyer who'd promised to do his best for her at the crash stop. But this wasn't a police station. This was far more serious. This was the chance to find out secrets.

She dug the chocolate away from her teeth with her tongue and swallowed.

'Who am I?' she asked.

Lemuel was disappointed. 'The problem with your ladyship is that she always asks the wrong questions. The correct question is *what* am I?'

'All right,' said Chess patiently, and tugging a clutch of braids away from her face with a click of beads. 'What am I?' She was in control. They might do this his way but she would get to the truth.

'That's better. You're a synth.'

Chess fiddled with one of the beads. 'The reason I'm no good at questions, is because I never understand the answers.'

'A synth is a synthetic being; a creature that has been

— 56 —

made artificially.' Lemuel laughed at the way Chess wrinkled her nose at him. 'Just like me.' He giggled. 'We have so much in common.'

Chess indicated her opinion by a vicious snap of the chocolate bar. She threw the chunk into her mouth and clacked her teeth.

'Well, not exactly like me,' he continued. 'I was grown. You were born, which is to say, you came from the body of a woman, as most humans do.'

'All humans are born like that.'

'I know of at least one who wasn't, but your mother should tell you about her.'

That made Chess angry. 'I don't know my mother. She can't tell me anything.' She eyed Lemuel darkly. Was he making fun of her?

'You are a girl of many parts.' Lemuel ticked them off on his fingers. 'Part human, part god, part universe and ...' he swivelled onto the chaise and spoke excitedly in Chess's ear, 'part wickedness.'

He sat back and raised both long eyebrows and pursed his lips into a dark little O. 'Only a tiny part. A grain. Barely a mustard seed. But enough; a little wickedness can go a very long way.' He placed a hand over hers and spoke confidentially, like they were sharing secrets. 'It shouldn't have got there, but there was a problem with your father. That's why all of us have to be very, very careful.'

The chocolate had started to melt in Chess's fingers and her head felt tight. She tried to organize her thoughts so that she could say something to show Lemuel that she wasn't surprised by what he said, wasn't going to believe it, wasn't feeling like a ninepin that had just been sent spinning by a cannonball.

'I'm normal and . . . and I don't have a father,' she stuttered.

'You are a synth, Chess.' Lemuel's tongue was a scalpel. 'I was given your body even before it came screaming into the world. I was the first person to touch it. I had to save it. I had to make you what you are.' He stood over her now, face electrified. 'I had to stop you becoming what the Symmetry wanted.'

Chess shook her head dumbly. She had no words, only a desperate will not to believe what Lemuel was saying.

The music had stopped. Lemuel paced before her, the heels of his boots tapping the floor. 'We had been waiting for years. It was always going to be *you*, Chess; the bloodline had been identified. But it was never going to be without complications. Your grandmother was the first mistake.' He laughed grimly. 'Mevrad's first big mistake.' Then, bitterly, 'But not her last.'

He plucked a loose cotton thread from his shirt, fastidiously, and flicked it into the air. 'I made your mother out of what the Symmetry left of hers. Your mother was very brave. She was a Blood Sentinel. She served the Committee very well. She was most useful.'

Chess's eyes stung hot but she would not cry. Not here. Not in front of Lemuel.

'But bravery is no defence against evil. Your father bided his time.' Lemuel tapped his glass cranium. 'Very clever, you see. So, when the time came, we got you, but not as we had expected.'

Lemuel shut his eyes. 'I remember when they brought you

to me. It was a room like this on a night when the frost was so hard the icicles chimed. You were still in your mother's tummy, no bigger than a broad bean.' Lemuel giggled. 'I had to make myself especially good.' His slanting eyes opened and he laughed like a silver bell. 'To think that they trusted *me* with *you*. If that isn't taking a risk, I cannot imagine what is! When I look back, it seems that all the eyes in the universe were turned on us. It was a most vital moment.' He sighed. 'And I could smell you; so rare, so powerful.'

Lemuel's eyes flicked to Chess's finger and his pupils dilated. 'The chocolate has melted.' He knelt. 'May I?'

'No, you may not,' Chess shot back, as if a glass of water had been thrown in her face.

'You're quite right.' Lemuel stood, slapped his face, stamped a foot and said, with an effort, 'The spirit inside you radiated out and forwards and backwards throughout the dimensions, just like it was meant to, just as Mevrad had predicted.'

'Some spirits are stronger than others.' Chess was reciting something that Professor Breslaw had told her, hanging on to the words because they were a link to a place far away from here.

'Yes, yes, that's right.' Lemuel spoke eagerly. 'Your raw spirit was vast. But the darkness had taken root, spreading through your blood and into your mind. We had to stop it.'

A pulse was throbbing behind her eyes. Chess made herself close them.

'Do you know anything of evolution?' Lemuel grasped her arms to snap her head up and open her eyes. 'Evolution is nothing,' he hissed, 'compared to what *I* can do. I can make millennia pass in minutes. Minutes. Do you know how?'

Chess shook her head. She didn't even know what evolution was.

'It is a delicate procedure. I call it genetic melding. It allows me to alter the genetic blueprint of a human; something that would normally take an epoch. But I have accelerated the process; in my laboratory, the slow crush of time is shrunk to a heartbeat. I used blood from Julius; one of the ancients, half man, half god; only that could stem your father's poison. Under the melding process, it replicated throughout your cells, infiltrating and mutating your genetic code. Changing you into something you weren't.' Lemuel smiled down at her, haughtily. 'I like to work with blood: to turn base humanity into gold.'

Chess couldn't stop herself from looking at the refrigerator, where polythene bags hung purple and heavy as over-ripe fruit.

Lemuel licked his lips with a dark tip of tongue. 'The process is applied to the humans who become Blood Sentinels, whose spirits can withstand a glimpse of infinity. But their spirits have only a fraction of the capacity of yours. And in your case I went further. I used amarantium, fusing it deep in the chemistry of your tiny form. Saving you, certainly, but also turning you into what the Committee wanted. Only after that did I replant you inside your mother. And then we waited. Everyone waited.'

He stepped back and appraised her huddled body, from the dishevelled braids to the muddy trainers. 'Always, there will be a struggle. But without a doubt, you are my greatest work.'

'No,' whispered Chess.

But she knew that Lemuel wasn't lying. When Julius had first touched her, she had felt his spirit so close to hers and she couldn't understand why. Now she knew. And when she and her brothers had penetrated the Twisted Symmetry's complex at the Riverside Prison, she had been able to touch the cerebral torus, even though it was enriched with so much amarantium that no living creature should have been able to do so. She had been able to do this because of the things Lemuel Sprazkin had done to her.

But she didn't want this to be the truth. She didn't want to be something that had been made in a laboratory, for other people to use.

'I'm not a synth,' Chess succeeded in croaking. '*You* didn't make me.'

Lemuel yanked her up from the chaise and pulled her to one of the long workbenches. 'I shall show you something that no one else has seen.'

Chess stood, meek as a tethered dog, whilst Lemuel marched to a crate by a wall and lifted out an object the size of a drum of cooking oil. It was draped by a grey cloth. It must have been heavy because he had to carry it back to the bench, cradled in his arms and resting against his chest. He set it down with a grunt.

'When I worked on your body, I kept a little of your blood; only a speck, you didn't have much to go round. I had my reasons.' He rested a hand on the shrouded object. 'This was one of them.'

'What is it?' asked Chess. 'What is under that blanket?'

Lemuel hadn't finished explaining yet. 'Unlike the rest

of the Committee,' he said 'the Committee' with mock-solemnity, 'I understand you, Chess. I understand what it is to struggle with yourself; how hard it is to be good when the alternatives are so much more . . .' again, the tip of his tongue darted out of the corner of his mouth before vanishing, '. . . inviting. I understand how fighting what is inside is as difficult as fighting what is outside; how easy it is to become cruel, to feed on anger, to be controlled by desire.'

'I'm not like that,' protested Chess.

'Where's Jones, Chess?' asked Lemuel in a sing-song voice. 'What have you done with her? How did you "get rid" of her?'

Lemuel patted the cloth. 'I made you something. I grew it from your own, precious blood. I wanted you to have somebody who could share the burdens that you must carry.' He smiled, and with a courtly flourish of his hand said, 'Allow me to introduce you to your closest, living, relative.'

The cloth was whipped away and Chess was staring into a large, glass jar, filled with a clear fluid. Floating in the fluid and staring back at her was a grey-skinned creature, its fat, hairless body coiled up like an unborn baby's but with the wizened face and peevish eyes of a cruel, old man. Or woman.

Chess stepped back and shook her head. 'It's horrible. It's nothing to do with me.'

Lemuel stooped and peered into the jar, his face spreading in the liquid and magnified to Chess, who stood on the other side. 'It is called a wretch. Its manufacture is not easy. I have only ever made one other, for somebody else. But this one has *everything* to do with you.'

He tapped the glass. The wretch twisted its head to look towards Lemuel and Chess saw it stick out its tongue. 'I have been watching it a lot, recently. It has started to grow. It doubled in size after Behrens's destruction. I believe a new jar will be required if you carry on like this, Chess.'

'It has *nothing* to do with me,' repeated Chess, backing away.

'Think something bad, Chess. Really bad.'

Chess shook her head. She wanted Lemuel to shut up.

'Let me tell you what happened to your mother.'

'I hate you!' screamed Chess. She felt the heat burst from her. A test tube shattered by Lemuel's face. The wretch swam round to face her and opened its little mouth, emitting a silver stream of bubbles.

'It's laughing,' cooed Lemuel, smiling into the jar like a proud mother. He brushed glass from his shirt front. 'See how it feeds on your feelings? It is a part of you, Chess. It will help you to survive what is going to happen to you. It will carry the weight of your anger, your hatred, your cruelty. Without it, there is every chance that you will be eaten by the darkness.' He drew a hiss of air through his nose and sighed with a rich pleasure. 'The two of you are unmistakable. Your smell is identical, and almost irresistible.'

Lemuel threw the cloth back over the jar.

You don't know what you're dealing with.

Chess shook her head. They were not her words; they were the Inquisitor's. *She* didn't know what she was dealing with. She didn't know anything.

'Why did you do this to me? Why couldn't I just have been left who I was?'

'For myself,' said Lemuel, modestly, 'it is enough to see the wonder of my skills unveiled. But for others your value is more functional. When the fifth node comes and the time spiral is at its most vulnerable, everything will depend on you, Chess.'

'Only if I get to the Eternal first.'

Chess knew that more than anything else, the Committee wanted to stop the Twisted Symmetry from getting the Eternal. But if she had meant to sound menacing, she had failed. Lemuel sought to put his arm around her shoulders. 'It is a terrible burden.'

She shook away his arm and retreated, jamming her fingernails into her palms until she could speak straight. 'Sherevsky.' She focused her thoughts on the name. 'Who is Sherevsky?'

'He was what you would call a "rock star"; a musician, of sorts.'

Chess tried to digest the words 'rock star'. Coming from Lemuel Sprazkin, they sounded alien.

'*Was* a rock star? What is he now?'

'Now, he is a retired rock star. He understands nothing, but he is the person who can help you meet your mother. There are things that only she will tell you.'

At Chess's confusion, Lemuel burst into a squeal of laughter. 'You silly, chocolatey little girl. I made arrangements to enable you to meet her.' He moved so quickly that he caught her wrist. '*I* didn't have to help you, Chess. I *wanted* to help you. Do you understand? I am a synth too. I know what it is like. But there is nobody to help *me*.'

Chess had lost all grip on what she thought now. One

moment, Lemuel was as hard as a warp, devious as the Symmetry, the next, he revealed his own pain and fear and she wanted to trust him.

Trust no one.

But Ethel's advice failed her. Chess wanted to trust. She needed to trust.

'Please, forgive me.' Lemuel released her wrist. 'In its own way, this has been as difficult for me as it must have been for you. I understand you, although you do not understand me. It is my appetites, they are so ...'

He lifted his hand as if to touch her hair and his eyes darted to the spike of the brain drill, pointing at him from the wall. He shook his head with a little grunt.

Chess was backing away. She wiped her face and realized that her cheeks were wet with tears. 'Why?' She hissed the word as if it was breaking her. 'Why?'

'You are very special, Chess. In the eyes of the universe, *all* humans are special. But you are *very* special.'

'Who is my father?' She clawed at her hands as if she could discover the truth by tearing the skin to find what lay beneath.

Lemuel shook his head. 'You are not ready for that. It would be most deleterious to concern yourself with him. Please, Chess.' He laughed, nervously. 'This is not what I expected. Now, wait here, there are things I must find for you. Sherevsky's address, and there is something else. Something I made for you but have mislaid. Something that will take you to your mother when the time comes.'

'My mother is alive? You know where she is?'

'Your mother is dead, Chess.' A curl of Lemuel's lip

suggested that he had enjoyed telling her this. 'But there is a way for you to find her.'

It was too much. The truth had become a maze of blades and she had to escape it. She needed time to think. She needed to be with friends. She needed Gemma.

'I'm going.' She rammed on the sunglasses, slippery over tears.

'But I haven't given you what you came for.' Lemuel's face sharked up to hers. 'I haven't given you what you *need*.'

'I'll come back. Tomorrow,' Chess managed to choke and she turned to go.

A black-nailed hand clasped her shoulder.

'Walk out of here,' warned Lemuel, 'and you walk into *them*. The Symmetry are waiting for you, Chess. Remember, you are on your own now. You have never been more vulnerable. The moment you walk through that door, the Symmetry will come for you, and they will keep on coming until they have you.'

CHAPTER 4

There was a man playing a clarinet. He sat on a suitcase not more than a spit from the main entrance of the tower and the crowds broke around him like flotsam. Chess allowed herself to be swept towards him, drawn by his stillness amongst the surging mass of people, and by the discordant tune he played; a see-saw cry to a clockwork beat.

She tried to pull her thoughts together; the certainty that time was narrowing to the point where the brain would start its work, balanced against the revelations that Lemuel had made and those he offered, cunningly laced by the promise of her mother. She knew that she would have to return to Lemuel's apartment, but not yet; not until she had grasped the fragments of the creature Lemuel had told her she was and organized them into a person she recognized as herself.

The man wore a long, drab coat. Coarse, yellow hair sprouted from beneath his tartan cap. Chess thought he might have been blind because of the way he turned his dark glasses skyward as he played, but her attention was gripped by the three, small figures who danced between his shins. They were wooden marionettes, a girl and two boys, hanging by wires from a pole that was fastened across his pointy knees. As the man tapped his heels, the children danced, limbs jerking in time to the music.

Chess couldn't stop watching the children and the notes filled her ears until it seemed that they were actually coming from inside her head. She was aware of two figures, working their way through the crowd to either side of her, collecting money in their caps, but it was difficult to wrest her eyes from the hanging children.

They used to hang children; Chess knew that bit of history. Children who stole things were made to dance on the end of a rope. Suddenly she wanted to pull away from the twitching puppets and the Wurlitzer bray of the clarinet. She looked up to where the man's head had craned down, inches above his knees and she saw that he was looking at her as he played. His face was tilted forwards so that he was peering up from beneath his deeply wrinkled brow. The dark glasses had slipped down his blotchy nose and she could see his eyes; soulless green eyes with speck pupils. The man stopped playing and smiled at her.

The throng broke open to her left and to her right, forced apart by the men who had been collecting coins. They had dropped their caps and were elbowing their way towards her. Their eyes were screened by sunglasses, but Chess recognized these creased, capilliary-webbed faces and shrivelled, black lips.

Muttons.

Lemuel had warned her that the Twisted Symmetry would come, but Chess hadn't realized it would happen so quickly. She backed into a wall of people, stumbled over her own ankles and fell, landing on her bottom and losing her glasses with a crunch beneath the feet of bystanders who scattered in a ring about her. When she looked up, the two muttons were pushing through the onlookers.

Chess was on her heels. She put down her head and burrowed into the nearest clump of people. Then she pushed her way up, until she was standing. Now she was in amongst the flowing crowd.

It was easy to make people fall over. Jacks never looked where they were going. It created mayhem and it made escape easier. Chess pushed.

Her hands felt the rough weave of a winter jacket. It fell away, somebody swore, somebody tripped, a phalanx of bag-bound shoppers ploughed into the knot of stumblers and then there was uproar, and Chess was ramming her way across the plaza, looking back to see what was following. Whoever came after her would have to get through the seething chaos that sprawled over the concrete.

She would have slowed down, picked her way with more care but for what happened next. The muttons sprang, scrawny thighs powering them over the heap of pedestrians, tatty coats flapping. They landed, firm as frogs, metres from Chess. One leered, skew-mouthed, and shook his arm. Something dropped from the cuff of his coat to the hand that hung by his side. His wrist flicked and a sliver of blade flashed clear of the handle and pointed down by his thigh like a long, silver finger.

'Stop,' croaked the other mutton.

Chess only stopped when her body was checked by the woman she ran into.

'He's got a knife,' gasped the woman.

'I haven't done anything wrong,' pleaded Chess, a standard response, even when she had. She peeled herself off the lady's glossy bags, and saw her bite the edge of her lower lip. They were nice, soft lips, but no lipstick. Chess could tell that the lady was deciding what to do, anxiously.

'They'll kill me,' stated Chess, although she knew that the Twisted Symmetry had more elaborate plans for her.

'Quick.' The lady's lips tightened. 'Come with me.' She was walking into the crowd, stepping as quickly as her smart, heeled shoes would allow. Chess pressed close, as if mere contact with this woman could make her safe. She caught her perfume; natural, unlike the nauseating essence of alcohol and flowers that jacks usually wore.

'Down here.' The lady clipped down the stairs that led to the underground parking, Chess close behind. Now that they were out of the crowd, they had to move faster.

'Just get me away. Please.' Chess could see how the lady's naturally porcelain cheeks had blanched. She didn't want her to crumble now; to leave her in the car park. 'They'll be here any moment.'

'What are they?' But before Chess could answer, they had stopped in front of a dazzling, metallic-grey jeep. Just the sort of growling, guzzling, oversized, dumb-headed tank that jacks drove, even when they were on their own. But Chess was glad to be next to it now.

The bags of shopping were shoved into Chess's hands and the lady was scrambling in her coat pocket. Keys jangled.

'I'm all thumbs,' she laughed nervously. Then the central locking clunked. Chess opened the rear door and threw the gaudy bags up, onto the back seat of the jeep before yanking open the passenger door and climbing in.

The lady slipped onto the driver's seat, pushing her tweed skirt neatly over her tan-stockinged legs. An elegant hand brushed back a strand of light-brown hair that had worked free from the tightly scraped bun, and Chess noticed her finger nails which weren't varnished but were smooth and tapered in fine crescents. She heaved shut the door.

'I'll stay low,' explained Chess, sliding off the seat and into the spacious footwell; out of sight.

'Have you done this sort of thing before?' The lady laughed uncertainly.

You wouldn't believe it, thought Chess, but she said nothing. The engine turned and grumbled into life.

'My name's Oriana, by the way. Oriana Lache.'

'Thank you, Mrs Lash,' said Chess from the gloom of the footwell.

'Dr Lache, actually. Not that it matters.' Oriana Lache adjusted the dark, horn glasses which almost distracted from her arching eyebrows and hazel eyes and as Chess looked up, she thought this: that whereas lots of people tried to make themselves look more beautiful than they actually were, Dr Oriana Lache tried to make herself look less beautiful than she really was.

The jeep jolted backwards. 'Woops!' apologized Dr Lache. Her eyes flicked to the rear-view mirror. 'Here they come.'

'I'll stay down.' Chess felt the jeep swing right and then forwards. She heard Dr Lache curse and saw her bite her lip again.

'They're getting into a car. I don't know whether they think you're in here or not.' She looked down at Chess, lost. 'I don't know what I'm meant to do with you. Shall I drive you home?'

'No.' Chess objected so vehemently that Dr Lache raised her eyebrows. Even though she wanted to go to the wharf, wanted to find Pacer and Hex and Gemma, heading for the wharf right *now* was too obvious.

'You must be in a lot of trouble,' Dr Lache observed. 'I'm not sure I'm doing the right thing.'

'Could you just drive about for a bit, until we *know* they've gone?'

'I don't know where to go,' muttered Dr Lache in her neat, precise voice.

'Just keep driving. Please.'

They had cleared the Cones now. Looking up from the footwell and through the passenger window, Chess could see high buildings flash by like windmill sails. She felt the car climbing and guessed they were heading up, onto one of the overpasses that wound between the skyscrapers, above the streets.

'I'll head west, for a bit.' Dr Lache gave a brief smile. 'I think we're not being followed any more.'

'OK.' Chess noticed a thin, silver chain that was fastened high about the doctor's neck. A tiny pendant hung just under her jugular notch, above the open collar of her blouse. The pendant was silver too; a tiny circlet maybe, or a decorative initial. Possibly an O. O for Oriana; that would make sense. But Chess thought that maybe there was too much detail for an O.

They were high above the ground and the tower blocks were flashing by more quickly now. Millions of windows were yellowing with electric light as night drew closer.

'Where are we going?' asked Chess, wondering whether she might shuffle onto the seat now.

'We're heading west for a bit, like I said.'

Chess climbed up and looked out of the windscreen. The sun was plunging into a crimson-streaked bed of cloud that was broken by the blackening blocks of the skyscrapers.

'I think they'll definitely be gone,' said Chess, hopefully, before slumping against the leather backrest. She didn't want to sound ungrateful but she didn't think it was necessary to drive any further from the city centre.

'Maybe if we drive to the Lungs?' suggested Dr Lache.

The great parks had been cultivated at the western edge of the city centre. They were dense with trees, like forests. People said they produced air to replace the filth spewed by the city. That was how they got their name. Chess thought it was more to do with giving the richest jacks, who pretended they weren't part of the city, somewhere nice to live: gathered within the trees and beyond were suburbs full of grease. Chess had never grafted out that way, but the Regulars did, when they wanted more than ordinary pickings. But you had to be smart. Plenty of the houses had dogs; big dogs. Chess stifled a shudder. These days, she didn't like dogs.

'It's not far,' Dr Lache reassured her. 'At the Lungs we can turn round without being seen and then head back.'

Chess watched the evening close; the sky sink from red into violet before the last of the colour was swallowed by a charcoal horizon. Just below the horizon, through the pale bars that were breaks between the skyscrapers, she saw the rolling blackness that was the Lungs. The blackness was broken only by occasional clusters of light, tiny as pinheads.

The highway swept down, heading west, chasing the last of the light. But Chess preferred the neon-studded night they had left behind. 'We could turn round now.' She fidgeted with a shred of fingernail.

'I think you're right. Just let me go a little further, Chess. Into the trees.'

'Good idea,' agreed Chess and she smiled; she smiled to hide the shock that jolted her belly; to hide the question that she did not dare to ask.

How do you know my name? I never told you my name.

'Actually,' said Chess, as blithely as she could manage, 'here would be good. To stop. And go back.'

Dr Lache's perfect nails whitened against the steering wheel. Chess saw the way her knuckles tightened. 'I don't think so. There's too much traffic.'

'There's turn-offs along this part.' Chess twisted her head, watching the mouth of a junction flash past. When she turned back, Dr Lache was looking ahead, rigidly. The jeep picked up speed.

It wasn't a chance meeting; that much was obvious now. Chess hummed aimlessly, as if she wasn't panicking. It didn't mean that Dr Lache was working with the muttons though; after all, she had driven her away from danger. But maybe she had driven her away to take her somewhere dark, somewhere secluded. Somewhere that the public would not see.

The trees were coming at them like a high, black wave.

'How about here?' Chess tried to sound natural. She wasn't sure about Dr Lache, not yet. And if you let them know you were frightened, they'd get you.

Dr Lache leant forwards to adjust her position and she looked at Chess, as if puzzled. 'Are you all right?'

They plunged into the trees.

'Oh yeah. Fine,' and Chess gave a little laugh as if it was ridiculous to think she could be anything other than delighted. But, by the glow of the instrument panel her eyes had caught the detail of the little pendant which had dangled free as the doctor had shifted position; a letter C, and at its centre, three sharp, miniature stars: just like the emblem on the tower at the Cones, but much smaller.

Chess didn't know what this meant, but it felt bad.

You're just being paranoid, sneered Splinter, inside her head.

Trust no one, warned Ethel.

'You were looking at my necklace,' remarked Dr Lache. There was a crack of nervousness in her voice.

Chess swallowed drily. 'It's very nice. I bet it's valuable.'

'It's just paste, a trinket, costume jewellery,' stuttered Dr Lache. Her fingers fluttered over the pendant as if brushing away a piece of dirt. 'It's worth nothing.'

The pendant was obviously *very* valuable to Dr Lache.

She's as edgy as I am, realized Chess, and with that, she knew she had to get out of the jeep. She might be wrong, but she couldn't take the chance; Chess had to trust herself.

She calculated quickly. Oriana Lache might be a doctor, she might look like a very clever schoolgirl, but she wasn't smart; not smart like Splinter. She had made too many mistakes, given too much away.

Chess squirmed in her seat.

'What?' twitched Dr Lache.

'I'm really sorry but I need the toilet.'

Dr Lache sighed. 'Can't it wait?'

Chess shook her head and gave what she hoped was an embarrassed little smile. 'I've been dying. I'm going to burst.'

Dr Lache breathed heavily though her perfect nose before deciding to stop the jeep, hard. The tyres crunched on the gravelly verge and then silence and darkness pressed against the windows.

'Go on then. Be quick.' The engine was still turning, patiently.

'Thanks.' Chess gave an apologetic grimace and jumped out.

Cold air lapped her face. Her trainers crackled over rime as she headed for the nearest bush, half hidden by the vespertine, ankle-high mist. All around were the still and silent trees. Up on the park road, the engine rumbled.

The obvious thing was to run, now, whilst she had the chance; to put as much distance behind her and the jeep as possible. But the most obvious thing wasn't good enough. Chess had to outsmart Dr Lache.

Behind the bush, Chess dropped to her belly and began to slither back up the low embankment, towards the jeep. Her fingers sank through a peppering of frost into cold mulch but she was hidden by the mist which cobwebbed between the tree boles. The snap of twigs and rustle of her body over the earth was masked by the engine noise. When she came to the road, Chess rolled square under the jeep and lay on her back. Heat from the exhaust radiated over her upturned face.

When, after several minutes, the engine was turned off, Chess shut her eyes and held her breath. This was the lively part. The wooded silence thickened and from just above her face came the ticking of cooling metal and the fuming odour of hot oil. In the darkness every sound and every smell was sharpened.

A door opened. Heels clicked onto the road. Hesitation and then footsteps alongside the vehicle. Chess turned her head right and thought she could see Oriana Lache's ballerina calves. She closed her eyes again. Swift steps to the front of the jeep, then to the edge of the road.

'Chess!' The high note of the doctor's cry died amongst the trees, the mist, the darkness. 'Chess!' Louder, but the forest still swallowed the sound. The jeep rocked and the tarmac thrummed as a line of traffic thundered by, vanishing as quickly as it had come.

A low curse and then heels came rattling back to the driver's door. A pause. The bleep of keys pressed on a mobile phone. Chess exhaled tremulously and sucked back fuggy engine oil.

'The rat has gone,' Dr Lache snapped into the mobile, bitterly. She sounded very different now; sharp, a piano wire tightened to snapping point, and immediately, Chess knew she had done the right thing. But now she *had* to get away. 'She made me stop ... for the toilet, the little snake ... Never mind slippery, you fool; if you hadn't insisted on a location so far from the centre, we'd have her by now. It's your fault ... No, I don't want excuses; this was *my* opportunity, Boulevant. My chance ... Yes, perhaps, but it must be kept low intensity; the last thing we need is reports of this operation leaking to the world at large ... I know that, and if it comes to it, they'll send the heavy mob, but not yet.'

Chess could hear Dr Lache huffing as she listened to

whoever was at the other end of the line. 'Don't flap, you idiot. We don't need to say anything yet. We don't need to tell *them*. I know where she's gone . . . north of the main road. We'll track her down before she gets far . . . Yes, the hunters, they're the experts when it comes to catching rats. But make sure they leave enough of her for the management to play with.'

Dr Lache stepped into the jeep and the door slammed like a cannon shot. The engine fired and Chess pressed her back into the tarmac and lay absolutely straight, eyes tight shut, hoping not to feel the crush of the big wheels or the cut of any low-hanging metal. The tyres rolled forwards, scattering stone chips and then the hot metal had gone. Chess opened her eyes to see the red glow of the tail lights as the jeep roared away, but she didn't move until she heard traffic rumbling towards her. Then she scurried to what must have been the south side of the long, park road.

It was pitch. She looked about, trying to see into the trees although she couldn't see more than the black silhouettes of the nearest. She had grown up in the city centre, where there was always light; the close darkness of the countryside made her pulse thump and her breaths come sharp and short. But she had to get away from the road. She turned and plunged into the deep trees, moving by touch, not sight, wading through woody brambles, scuffing against bark, feeling ice water from the boggy peat leach into her trainers.

Somewhere ahead she saw lights, although she couldn't tell how far off they were. They vanished and then shone again; a row of lamps, probably a street; one of the suburban outposts. But then Chess heard dogs, and she swerved away.

Of course, they might have been *just* dogs. But Chess knew

that not everything that sounded like a dog, was a dog. The Twisted Symmetry had shape shifters; amongst the Dog Troopers, there were some who could assume the form of dog or man as they wished. There would be no way of knowing which was which until they were upon her. Maybe they were already hunting for her in the woods. So it was best to keep moving, towards the city centre.

To her left, the forking limbs of the trees were revealed by an orange glow in the sky. That would be the way to go. She began to jog, panting, feet crunching on earth. Occasionally, she heard a yowl, but from far off now, drifting like the howls used to drift across the river from the secure yards in the factory sector, when she lived at the wharf.

After twenty minutes of slogging, she knew she wasn't being followed and with that knowledge came a surging weariness.

Chess gasped as a sapling branch stung her cheek and the darkness burst white. She rubbed her eye as she ran, but her legs were wet and heavy and she was out of breath. It was still a long way back to the city and her lungs were raw. She slowed down: she might as well stop. However much she hated this darkness, right now she was as safe here as anywhere; and probably safer if she stayed still and silent rather than crashing through the night.

The only sound was her own panting. Chess slumped to her haunches, leant back against a broad tree trunk and smelt the sweet, gingery leaf mould. The air was cold, but she felt hot from running. There were no more dog noises. She seemed to be alone. Chess drew her knees to her chest, pulled the leather jacket tightly shut and watched the darkness.

CHAPTER 5

The goalkeeper was good. Chess had never played hockey, she had never played any sport, unless throwing stones at the windows of empty warehouses was a sport, but she knew that this game was called hockey and she knew that the tall girl wearing all the pads and the masked helmet was the goalkeeper. And she knew that she was good because no matter how close the attackers came, and no matter how hard they slammed the ball at the goal, the girl always managed to block it with her stick, or her leg or her body. So, she wasn't just good, she was brave.

It was the thwack of the ball that had woken her. She was wet with icy dew and her head ached from the cold air after a night spent sleeping fitfully on the leaves at the foot of the tree. The crack of the ball was accompanied by shouts which drifted through the black saplings like ghosts. Chess had crept through the vegetation until she was kneeling behind a hawthorn bush that was only a couple of metres from the fencing which enclosed the sports pitch. She was directly behind the goal so she had a good view of what was happening. It helped to distract her from the hungry cramp in her stomach.

Red-faced, two attackers were running at the goal, panting like dogs. They were boys, as tall as the girl in goal and much broader. They shouldered past the defenders and a third attacker sent the ball skimming in from the wing. As it came to the first boy he flicked it at the goal. The keeper stepped wide, kicking out her left foot and blocking it. It rebounded, and the second boy swung his stick, hammering the ball towards the other side of the goal mouth. The ball hurtled too quickly for Chess to follow it, but the keeper threw out the arm holding her stick and the ball was smacked away from the goal. The keeper was stretched flat across the ground. As she scrambled to her feet, one of the attackers shoulder-charged her, the other elbowed her in the side of the face, hard enough to knock her back to the floor and then the girl who had first crossed the ball was there to guide it into the goal.

The chubby referee blew her whistle, ignoring cries of 'Foul' from the defenders whilst the attacking players high-fived their way back to their own half. Chess heard someone mutter about the referee being biased because she was the attacking team's coach but she noticed that the girl in goal said nothing. She just tilted up her helmet, spat out a damson-sized gobbet of blood and then hefted her stick in her fist, waiting for the next attack.

The attack came quickly, the same players wrong-footing the defence and breaking so that once more, it was the three of them against the keeper. At point-blank range, the biggest boy swung his stick, hard as a pile driver.

The keeper kicked the ball away with her wide shin pad,

like it was a football. But this time, as the other boy came in to body-charge her, she scythed her stick well above the ball that rolled at his feet, into his shins. He careered onto his shoulder and rolled into the goal. The other boy trapped the ball, but before he could strike it, the keeper had run her stick over the astroturf and between his legs so that his ankles tangled over it, he up-ended and he skidded over the artificial turf on his palms.

The ball rolled clear of the goal.

The boy at the back of the goal net was clutching his bruised shins and blubbing. The keeper looked at him through her mask and spat blood. 'Goal,' she said.

'Foul!' screamed the girl who had passed the ball. 'Foul!'

The referee's whistle shrieked and she marched towards the goal, pointing at the keeper, whistle jammed between her balloon cheeks. 'You!' she exploded. 'Off the pitch. Now.'

Chess watched, fascinated at this insight into the behaviour of jack schoolchildren.

One boy was limping out of the net, helped by his female team mate, whilst the other was blowing on his palms which looked as if they'd been sunburned. The keeper had strolled to a long bag at the side of the goal with her stick slung over her shoulder like a felling axe. She ripped off the shin pads and the body pads, snatched her hands out of the gloves and pulled off her helmet, throwing all the equipment together with the stick, into the bag.

'You, wait by the gate,' hollered the referee who looked as if she might burst her neck with rage. 'I'll speak to you after the match.'

The keeper swung her bag over her shoulder and across

her back. Her hair was black with a straight fringe that hung just above her dark eyebrows and it swung lazily about her shoulders as she turned to the referee and said calmly, 'I'm off. You can speak to my parents; explain how I got this.' She pointed towards her face and when she turned back to walk towards the gate, Chess saw a bright streak of blood running from her split lip to her chin.

Silently, everybody watched as the girl sauntered to the gate. Her limbs were slim and long and Chess thought they moved a little drunkenly, as if they were so long that the girl's thoughts hadn't yet caught up with them. But she had seen how fast they were and how strong. Her gawky gait was deceptive.

Outside the gate at the back of the pitch, the girl knelt down to tighten her laces. The game had recommenced but Chess was so intrigued by the girl that it sounded as if the game was being played a mile away.

'What are you looking at?' She was still kneeling but she had lifted her head and was staring straight at Chess. Her eyes were blue, like Splinter's, but whereas his were like slits, hers were widely spaced and as big as a cat's, and whereas his lashes were so pale as to be almost invisible, hers were as thick and black as her long, straight hair.

The girl stood up. 'What are you doing? Are you hiding? Who from?' She spoke as bluntly as a crasher.

'I've been sleeping here,' stuttered Chess. The girl looked older than her, older than Box and Splinter. Probably, she was about fifteen.

'Funny place to sleep.' She wiped her bloodied face with her sleeve, hoisted the bag and began to walk away.

Chess had liked watching the girl. She liked the way she stood up to the hockey players, and the referee. Being near to her felt good. So she followed.

The girl turned round. 'Haven't you got anywhere to go?'

Chess shook her head and without knowing why, blurted, 'I'm a street rat.'

'Big deal. What am I meant to do? Why do street rats think everyone should feel sorry for *them*?'

This was a new concept to Chess; a jack who expected pity from a street rat.

'Anyway,' continued the girl, starting to walk again, 'you don't look much like a street rat. Nicked that jacket?'

'No,' said Chess.

'What's your name?'

'Chess Tuesday.'

'I can play chess. But it's a stupid name.'

That's not my fault, thought Chess. I don't know what my real name is. But she settled for, 'I didn't choose it. What's yours?'

The girl didn't answer at first but after several long strides she said, 'Anna. Anna Ledward.'

'That's a nice name,' said Chess, hoping that would be a way of making friends with Anna. But Chess hadn't had much practice at making friends; she wasn't sure how to go about it. But she knew she *could* make friends. Gemma was her friend. Thinking of Gemma made her feel more confident.

'It's a much nicer name than mine,' risked Chess, and then felt stupid for trying too hard.

Anna was walking in front. Maybe she was walking away.

Then Chess would be alone. She quickened her step to keep up.

'You still haven't said why you were spying on us.'

'I wasn't spying,' protested Chess. I was hiding, she thought. And I'm lost; I don't know where I am, I don't know who I am, I don't even know *what* I am.

You're a synth, laughed Lemuel, inside her head, and with a stream of silver bubbles, the wretch laughed too.

Chess tried to banish Lemuel to a dark place at the back of her skull. 'You're good. At hockey.'

'Big hockey fan, are you?' Anna lobbed the query over her shoulder as the path they had taken emerged at a wood-lined street. Chess hung back, looking up and down the road, checking that it was safe. It was all right for Anna; she could march out of the wood and into the open. But Chess knew what was out there. She knew what was looking for her; what might be waiting.

Anna wasn't waiting. Long legs swinging, she strolled away.

'I'm hiding,' said Chess, rooted at the edge of the wood. 'From a big organization. They're after me, although I'm not sure why.'

Why am I gabbling like this? she thought.

'They're very powerful: more powerful than you can imagine. And they have spies; servants everywhere.'

I sound paranoid.

Anna had stopped. She stood with her back to Chess. Maybe she was listening; maybe she was deciding to walk away.

Chess swallowed to clear her throat. 'They've got a giant

brain that is really a computer and they use it to steal children. I've got to stop them.' Now I sound mad. 'But if they get me, I'm not sure what will happen.' Fatigue and desperation choked her voice. 'I'm not sure what will happen at all.'

She hated herself for sounding pathetic.

'It's strange.' Anna spoke towards the white sky. 'I wasn't meant to be playing today's match, but the first team fixture was cancelled and the second team keeper threw a sickie so they rang this morning. We were meant to be away this weekend but Dad's got too much work on so I *could* play. I was available.' She turned round then and looked at Chess with eyes that were as piercing as Splinter's. 'Do you see?'

'See what?' Chess was baffled and she shivered. She was very hungry and the cold was eating into her now.

'See that I was meant to meet you? It's like someone put me here, so we could meet.'

Chess shrugged. She didn't want to risk disagreeing with Anna, but she didn't want them to have met because someone else had decided they *should* meet. 'Maybe it's just a coincidence?'

'There's no such thing as coincidence, Chess Tuesday,' announced Anna Ledward, solemnly. 'Do you want to come to my house? Do you want some breakfast?'

Chess nodded and immediately forgot about the cold, forgot about everything: she had done it; she had made friends.

But as she was led past high laurel hedges that only partially obscured large, red-brick houses with long front lawns, she began to wonder whether she would be able to do this. Anna probably lived at home with her family as most jacks did, and they would realize Chess was a street rat and then they wouldn't let her into their house. And she wasn't sure what it would be like, seeing someone with a mother and a father; someone with parents.

Chess had clung to the scraps of memory that were her mother for so long that the thought of being close to a real mother panicked her. And there was something else that made her hesitate as they turned towards a tall, gaunt house that was partly screened by dusky-green plane trees; supposing the house was so full of loot that it was too much for her? So many enticing, sparkling items that Chess wouldn't be able to stop herself from lifting something? This was a big, jack house. Chess could smell the grease. She was worried that she wouldn't be able to help herself helping herself.

'Come on,' urged Anna, at the foot of the gravel drive. 'Mum and Dad will be fine. Just don't start nicking stuff.'

It might have been a joke but it hit Chess like a branding iron. 'I'd never,' she protested, face burning.

Anna weighed her up with those sombre eyes. 'You *are* a street rat, aren't you?'

'Never said I wasn't.'

'Come on,' she insisted.

The front door was painted white. It was panelled and there were frosted glass panes in it. Chess thought it looked very grand. It opened into a house that was thick with warmth and wealth.

'Hi, Dad, hi, Mum,' said Anna robotically, as she marched in, dropping her kit bag with a crash, in the porch. 'This is

Chess. She's a friend. Can we have some breakfast? This way, Chess.'

Chess shuffled along the gloomy hallway, avoiding the gaze of the tall, bespectacled man in a shirt, who had opened the front door. She was followed by a much shorter woman who was wearing smudged make-up and holding a glass tumbler.

'Hello, Chess,' said the lady, when they were in the kitchen. It was a bright kitchen and through the big windows, Chess saw a perfect stretch of lawn bordered by high trees and in the far corner, a green, wooden pavilion with dark windows. At the foot of the lawn there were woods. Automatically, Chess's eyes swept the edge of the wood, looking for movement, looking for shapes that shouldn't be there.

'Drink?' Anna's mother plonked the glass tumbler onto the kitchen table. A curl of liquid sloshed out. Chess smelt gin. The lady's eyes were pink and puffy. 'Tea? Water?' Chess nodded and was handed a glass of water, Mrs Ledward eyeing her hair with a mixture of surprise and interest. Then, gently, she pulled an orange sliver of leaf from it and let it drop to the floor.

Anna was opening cupboards, extracting items and slamming the doors shut. On a tray on the table she had thrown bread, a jar of jam, three doughnuts, a knife, a lump of cheese and a fistful of chocolate biscuits.

'What've you done to your lip, Anna?' Mr Ledward's voice was uncertain, as if he was worried about the reply he'd get.

'Nothing,' stated Anna, with a slam.

Nobody kissed anybody. Nobody talked very much. They just stood about the kitchen like lost boats and listened to

Anna banging cupboard doors. Chess allowed her keen, brown eyes to take in details; the hooks in the wall behind the door, the row of mugs under the wall cupboards, the chairs around the table and the settings on the table top, and she noticed that there were four of all these things.

Maybe they knew I was coming, she thought, looking at the place settings.

'Where are you from, Chess?' asked Mr Ledward. It was an innocent enough enquiry, but for the first time, Chess noticed the smears of dried mud on the arms of her leather jacket.

'She's a friend, Dad,' snapped Anna, with a glare.

'He's allowed to ask,' said Mrs Ledward, tipping a splash of gin into her glass and adding tonic water. She gulped her drink and put the glass back down, hand trembling.

'That's enough for breakfast, darling.' Mr Ledward shuffled uncomfortably.

'I'm starting lunch early, then,' bridled Mrs Ledward, grabbing the gin bottle.

'Please, darling.'

'Please nothing. Don't worry, Chess,' Mrs Ledward rested the hand without the bottle on her hip. 'This is normality in the Ledward household.'

Mr Ledward bit his lip and lowered his head. Then he walked slowly from the kitchen.

Chess couldn't understand. This wasn't how jacks were meant to be. They had everything; they had every reason to be happy. Yet, for all her years of squalor in the wharf, she had never encountered tense misery like this. She watched Mrs Ledward drain the next tumbler of gin.

'Does your mother know you're here?'

Chess shook her head. 'She won't mind,' she said.

'Come on. Upstairs.' Anna led the way from the kitchen with the tray in her hands.

A wide staircase with mahogany banisters on either side led up from the hall and halfway, where it turned back on itself, a gilt-edged mirror reached to the lofty ceiling. Chess couldn't avoid seeing her reflection as she followed Anna and for the first time, she realized what a mess she looked; pieces of leaf and twig in her hair which was unkinking from the braids like shocks of rough wool, her leather jacket daubed with dry mud, her jeans and trainers stained with peat-water. She realized at the same time that she didn't smell too good.

'You can have a wash later, if you like,' suggested Anna from the landing at the top of the stairs. 'Lose the corn rows, maybe? If that's what they were.'

Chess left her reflection and hurried up the remaining stairs and into the room that Anna had entered. It was illuminated feebly by a table lamp and it was very messy; a bed with duvet skewed, clothes carpeting the floor like crazy-paving and everywhere, wires and cables and pieces of computer; keypads, motherboards, monitors, memory packs, cards, discs, chips, switches, hard drives and CPUs.

There was a pair of folding metal tables standing side by side, and festooned with so much gadgetry that the desktop computers on both of them were almost hidden. A luminous grey seeped between the gaps from a flickering monitor.

'Is this your room?' Chess hovered in the doorway.

'It's my brother's.' Anna put the tray on the bed and looked out of a long window. Outside, there were thin trees and a sea-grey sky.

'Isn't he here?'

'No. He's dead.' The words thudded from Anna like rocks hitting earth.

'Oh. I'm sorry.' Chess shuffled into the room, very uncomfortable. She thought about the kitchen; four of everything.

'That's OK,' said Anna, fingertips on the pane of glass, still looking outside. 'It's not *your* fault.' She turned round, eyes sombre. 'But I know whose fault it *is*. I know who killed him. I know why they killed him.' She swung to the bed and picked up a doughnut. 'All I need is proof.' She bit the doughnut and jam dribbled between her fingers.

'When did it happen?' asked Chess, as gently as she could, but snatching a doughnut for herself. She was starving. 'When did he … die?' She pushed the sugary softness into her mouth and bit.

'He was killed three weeks and four days ago,' stated Anna. 'A drugs overdose, except it wasn't.' She wiped sugar from her mouth with the back of her hand. 'The police said it was, but I know it wasn't.'

Chess chewed slowly, waiting for Anna to continue.

'I know it wasn't because he didn't do drugs. None. He was too into all of this.' Anna indicated the technological chaos that filled the bedroom. 'He was killed because he knew too much. They waited until he was at a party and then spiked his drink. A massive dose of Dream, the coroner said.'

'Who's "they"?' Chess wolfed down the rest of the doughnut. She tried not to belch.

Anna ran from the room. Chess heard her pound down the stairs and wondered whether she had upset her. But then she came pounding back up and into the bedroom. She was holding a slim black rectangle, the size of a digital notebook and she was a little out of breath. She flopped to the floor.

'It was in my sports bag. I take it everywhere.'

Chess recognized it at once. 'That's a Link-me.' She knelt by Anna. 'They're illegal.'

'Says the street rat!' scoffed Anna. She flipped open the lid and held the Link-me in her hands like an open book. 'Richard built it. I can hack into anywhere with it, any network, CCTV system, phone line. It's got built-in scanners, diallers, modem, net-hooks, mikes and webcam. I'm not all that good on it yet. Richard was brilliant. He could hack into anything. Technically, that's called cracking, but I prefer hacking. Sounds better.' She fixed Chess with her blue cat eyes. 'You ever hacked into a computer?'

Chess thought about this for a moment before saying, 'Yes, but not like this.' It wasn't a lie; cutting through the cerebral torus was a kind of hacking.

'Did you use a Link-me?'

Chess shook her head. 'No. A nail file.'

'Cool!' Anna was impressed. 'Richard used this when he was hacking. He hacked into loads of different places, but by the end, he spent all his time on one group. The group that killed him. Or had him killed.'

Anna tapped the tiny keyboard that filled one half of the Link-me, like a laptop. 'My password.' The screen began to glow. 'It's my online name. Well, it was Richard's but I use it now.'

'What is it?'

Chess didn't think Anna would tell her, but she was wrong. 'Fury,' said Anna, tapping more keys.

'Nice one,' whispered Chess.

Anna handed the Link-me to Chess so that she could see the screen. On the edge of the frame, above the screen, the tiny lens of a webcam glinted like a sparrow's eye. There was a symbol on the screen, like a logo in an advert. Chess stopped chewing. It was the same symbol that Chess had seen on the tower at the Cones, and on the pendant worn by Dr Oriana Lache.

'What is it?' she breathed.

'They're called the CREX Corporation, I know that much.' Anna retrieved the Link-me but studied Chess as she spoke. 'I'm only just starting to find out about them. Just starting to hack my way in. Richard had been into them for months. He wouldn't tell me much, he said that what he'd found out was dangerous. I thought he was just winding me up.' She struck a key and the screen dimmed. 'Wrong, wasn't I?'

A winternoon darkness had gathered under the trees. It seemed to press against the window. Or maybe it was the effect of staring at the lambent screen.

'What did he tell you?' asked Chess.

'That they're an international mining and chemical company, *supposedly*. But that's not what they really are. It's all a front for a global crime network. They smuggle, they traffic people. They traffic *children*.' Anna snapped the Link-me shut, dramatically.

Chess nodded slowly although instantly her mind began

to make the connections; Dr Oriana Lache, the CREX Corporation, children stolen. Anna might have been astonished by what her brother had told her, but Chess wasn't. She knew all about children being stolen. She knew that nowhere was safe, she knew that the enemy had servants amongst powerful people and she knew that if the CREX Corporation had anything to do with the Twisted Symmetry, Anna's brother was as good as slabbed from the day he'd first hacked into them. The thought of how easily Dr Lache had manoeuvred her into the jeep made her feel sick.

'Don't do that again,' she insisted.

'Do what?'

'Don't go there. Don't look at them.' Anna didn't realize what she was close to, but Chess did. 'Listen to me. Your brother was right. I don't know about the CREX Corporation, but I know that there are people who are really bad and they can watch you, whatever you're doing. And I know that they kill. OK? I believe what you say about your brother. I believe that *they* killed him.'

Anna's eyes were shiny with a film of tears.

Chess never liked to stare into people's eyes if she could avoid it but she held Anna's gaze. 'There's only one way to be safe,' she said, breathlessly.

'Which is?'

'Trust no one. *No one.*'

'You came here,' Anna said immediately. 'You've been very trusting.'

'There's exceptions to every rule,' admitted Chess. But she didn't smile as she meant to because she had started to wonder what Lemuel Sprazkin was doing; why he was so close to the CREX tower.

'Time for you to tell me your secrets.' Anna spoke in a creepy voice that made Chess laugh.

Chess wanted to tell Anna about herself, but it wasn't something she was used to doing. 'We're friends, aren't we?' She was anxious. Talking about being friends was as exhilarating as spending a massive wedge of grease, except that she had never spent even a handful of grease. And maybe Anna might say, 'No'.

'I'm sharing my biscuits, aren't I?' said Anna, handing a biscuit to Chess. '*Chocolate* biscuits.'

Chess nodded gravely. 'I'm going to tell you everything.' She must have sounded very serious because Anna's face resumed its sombre expression.

'OK,' blinked Anna. 'Everything.'

So Chess told her. All afternoon. The sky grew dark until the trees seemed to bend under its weight. Hail rattled over the window like a thrashing chain. Anna left the room and returned with more biscuits on two occasions. And Chess spoke. Never before had she said so much for so long and she found it difficult because it was complicated and because she wasn't used to explaining.

To Chess's surprise, she found that she didn't want to tell Anna about Saul. Even as she made that decision, she thought how like Saul Anna seemed; brave and kind and able to stand up to others. She even looked a tiny bit like Saul. Saul would probably like someone like Anna. It seemed best not to mention him; he was her secret.

When Chess had finished her throat was sore.

'The Twisted Symmetry,' intoned Anna. 'The Committee. Ethel. Inquisitors. The Eternal.' She combed her fingers through her long, black hair. 'So the Twisted Symmetry are after you, right, because they think you can control the Eternal?'

Chess nodded.

'What does it do?'

Chess screwed up her nose. 'Stops time, I suppose. Which lets them live forever. That's what they want.'

Anna laughed drily. 'It's like something from a film, or a book.'

'Except it's all true,' insisted Chess.

'I believe you,' said Anna sombrely. Her eyes were intense. 'I said we were *meant* to meet. We're connected.'

Chess didn't reply. She wanted to have met by chance. That was how real friendships began. She inspected her fingernails.

Anna spoke. 'It's weird, isn't it, how we've both lost brothers?'

Chess nodded.

'How old are Box and Splinter?'

'Fourteen, I think. Maybe fifteen now. How old is Richard?' Chess corrected herself. 'Was Richard?'

'Eighteen. Three years older than me. I can't believe Ethel wouldn't help you find your brothers. What a cow.'

'She had her reasons,' said Chess, wondering why she was defending Ethel. 'Anyway, I'm going to stop the Symmetry from stealing children and then I'm going to find my brothers, whatever Ethel says.' But there wasn't much time to stop the Symmetry, if it wasn't too late already.

She realized that Anna was looking at her with eyes half-closed, as if calculating something. 'What?' asked Chess, suspicious.

'I'm thinking. If you're full of this substance that's everywhere at once …'

'Amarantium,' said Chess.

'Yeah, well, whatever it is, you should be able to do stuff, even when you're not exploding with other people's energy.'

'What stuff?'

'Special stuff. You should have special powers. That's how it works.'

Chess shrugged. 'Apart from what I've told you, there's nothing special.' Splinter had drilled that into her.

'Have you tried?'

Chess frowned at Anna. She wasn't sure whether this was a clever person's way of making fun of her. 'If you don't believe me,' she muttered, 'that's fine. I know it sounds stupid.' She got to her knees, ready to stand. 'I'll go.'

'Hey, stop being the touchy little street rat.' Anna grabbed her arm and pulled her back. 'We've both got reasons to get upset but you can't just kick off. I'm not being mean. I'm not having a laugh at you. It might sound daft, but maybe you can do things you don't know about.'

'Like what?'

'I don't know.' Anna shrugged. 'Walk through walls, fly, read minds.' She laughed and Chess laughed too. 'Seriously, if you're full of this stuff that's connected to all these *universes* and dimensions you've been going on about, you should be able to go anywhere you want.'

'Seriously?'

'Seriously. Put your hand on that table. You should be able to push it through, like water.'

It seemed a ridiculous suggestion but Chess wanted to share the joke; sharing jokes was what friends did. She shuffled to the metal table on her knees. At first she put her right hand palm down on the top but then she switched it for her left. When Anna raised an eyebrow, Chess said, 'Need to use my real hand for this. The new one won't have crystal in it.'

'Ah yes,' said Anna. 'I forgot about the change of hands.'

'Ready.' Chess had stopped shuffling. 'You really think I can do this?'

'I really do. Professor Ledward has spoken.'

'OK.' Chess focused on her hand as if it was a strange creature that had to be watched carefully. 'I'll try to push it through. I just need to find the spaces in between the metal. The spaces we can't see.'

She knew this was how it would work. But she didn't know how she was meant to do it. Chess didn't really think anything would happen at all.

She felt the pressure of the table on the pad of her thumb and her fingertips. She pushed and the resistance of the table pushed back. The skin around her nails whitened as she pushed harder.

'Nothing,' mouthed Chess, uncertain whether she was relieved or disappointed.

'We're probably not doing this the right way,' considered Anna.

Chess went to slide her hand off the table. As she did so,

her middle finger buzzed hot with pins and needles and Anna gasped before saying, hoarsely, 'Wow!'

Chess lifted up her hand and stared at the fingertips. Then she looked at Anna, both of them open-mouthed.

'Cool,' was Anna's verdict.

If Anna hadn't reacted like this, Chess would have dismissed the momentary disappearance of her fingertips into the surface of the table as an optical illusion, a mistake in her vision.

'How?' was all she could say.

Anna was surprisingly calm. 'It's because of how you've been made.' Then, with unwavering authority she said, 'It's obvious, Chess. You've been built to work in all the dimensions.'

Chess shoved her hand between her thighs. 'I'm not a machine.'

'Don't start all the poor little victim stuff again. We've all been *made*.' She snorted a stifled laugh. 'It's just that you were done in a science lab.'

'Shut up,' snapped Chess, eyes hot, but she couldn't stop a rough snigger. Anna didn't seem the sort of person who did a lot of laughing, but when she did it was catchy.

'Go on, Chess, do it again. You're going to have to practise.'

'It doesn't feel too good.' Chess eyed the tips of her fingers and then the table top. 'I'm not even sure how I did it.' But without further prompting, she put her hand back, closed her eyes and felt the cold, smooth surface of the metal and pushed. Then she remembered; she hadn't done this by pushing: she'd done it by pulling her hand away.

It was as if she had to slide it into the table.

Chess pushed down, simultaneously sliding her hand back, towards herself. Without knowing how all the dimensions might look, she imagined space separating, like a mirror shattering, all its colours and boundaries breaking apart.

Her hand began to prickle and it felt hot.

'No way!' whispered Anna.

Chess opened her eyes and saw that her fingers had sunk into the table up to where they joined her hand. She swore softly. But she had stopped concentrating. Her hand had stopped moving. Her fingers were embedded in the solid metal of the table top.

'It's stuck, Anna,' she gasped, and immediately remembered the time when Splinter had put his arm into the portable vortex, and how it had been gripped by the mortice-gate. But Ethel had been there to save him.

Her fingers were growing hotter and the prickling sensation was changing to a bursting pressure. Chess realized that the metal was crushing her fingers as the dimensions were closing together again.

'I can't get it out,' she wailed, pulling back.

'You've got to relax, Chess.' Anna placed a hand on Chess's shoulder. She tried not to raise her voice because she didn't want Chess to panic any more than she was doing already. 'Relax, Chess, relax.'

'I can't relax,' screamed Chess. 'It's crushing my hand.'

Footsteps came thumping up the stairs.

'Oh no,' groaned Anna. 'Dad.'

Chess was heaving at the table. It lifted slightly and a

precarious stack of cables and circuit boards crashed to the bedroom floor.

'Just what I need,' muttered Anna. 'Dad at the door and you with your hand stuck in a table.'

'You made me do it,' hissed Chess.

'I didn't say glue yourself to the table. I said make your hand go through it.'

'Well, it's not my fault. I've never done it before.'

'If you can blow up an Inquisitor with your mood swings, a table shouldn't be a problem.' Anna bit her lip at the approaching footfalls. 'Next time,' she growled, heading for the door, 'we practise on jelly.'

'There won't be a next time,' Chess growled back. She looked back at the table and gritted her teeth. 'There won't even be a hand.'

'Hi, Dad,' said Anna as her father entered the room.

Mr Ledward looked about. He saw the strange girl standing in front of one of the tables with her hand behind her back. She smiled, but not very happily. Her face was white and her teeth were clenched.

'Are you all right?'

Chess nodded. To have opened her mouth would have been to risk crying out in pain.

'All that noise?' said Mr Ledward.

'Sorry, Dad, Chess knocked some stuff off the desk.'

'Sorry,' mouthed Chess, as if she were sucking hot potatoes. She watched to see if Anna's father would come any further into the room. He was looking over his black spectacle frames, obviously interested in what Chess was hiding behind her back.

'What have you got there?' he asked. He didn't know this girl his daughter had brought home and she made him uneasy with her sullen watchfulness, her quick movements and her big, hungry eyes.

'She's got nothing, Dad,' insisted Anna.

'I want to see.' The tall man approached Chess.

Chess held out her right hand and then her left. 'See,' she said, in the way she spoke to crashers when she wanted them to think she was harmless. 'Nothing.'

Anna stared at Chess's bright pink hand. 'How?' she mouthed from behind her dad's shoulder.

Mr Ledward gave an embarrassed smile. 'Sorry,' he said. 'I didn't mean to be rude. It's just . . .'

'I know,' mumbled Chess. 'It's just you don't know me.'

'Chess'll be staying tonight, Dad,' announced Anna, and then, as an afterthought, 'if that's OK?'

Mr Ledward hesitated. These were not easy times for his daughter. 'Sure. That's OK, Anna. Just keep the noise down. You know how Mum is.' He pulled the door shut when he went.

'How did you get it out?' asked Anna when she had heard her dad walk away.

'I was so worried about your dad, I stopped worrying about my hand.' Chess didn't meet Anna's gaze. She was inspecting her hand although it looked unmarked. 'I guess I relaxed enough that I could slide it.'

'Cool,' said Anna.

'Yeah, dead cool,' muttered Chess dismissively.

Anna knew that she shouldn't have lost her temper when

her dad was approaching. 'Sorry. OK? I was worried about what would happen.'

'That's fine,' but Chess was more guarded than she had been. 'But no more experiments.'

'You can stay here tonight.'

'Thanks.' At least it felt safe at Anna's house. And it was warm.

'What are you going to do?'

'Go to the wharf, tomorrow. Find Pacer and Hex and Gemma. Then, probably, burn down the Riverside Prison. We're good at fires. That way the Twisted Symmetry won't have their computer brain, so they won't be able to know when the Fat Gobster will strike. Then they won't be able to take away any more children.' And, sooner or later, she reminded herself, I have to go back to Lemuel, if I want to find out about my mother, about me. But she felt nervous about Lemuel now.

'Destroying the computer won't be the end of the Twisted Symmetry,' observed Anna, bluntly.

'It'll stop them stealing children. That's what matters.' Chess wiped her nose with the sleeve of her jacket.

'Listen,' said Anna, 'us meeting wasn't a coincidence. You needed to meet me.'

'I was doing all right,' insisted Chess.

'Rubbish. We were made to meet.'

Ethel makes a move; they make a move, thought Chess. They make a move; Ethel makes a move.

'Maybe,' conceded Chess. 'Maybe we were meant to meet.' Which meant that she and Anna had made friends because that was how Ethel had planned it; which wasn't making friends at all. She scowled at her dirty trainers.

Anna shook her shoulder. 'We can help each other. I'll help you if you help me.' Chess looked at her blankly, so she continued. 'I help you destroy the computer; you help me find out who killed Richard.'

So this is how friendship works, thought Chess. The Committee twist events to make sure I meet the right person and then, it turns out, that person has a use for me.

It was just as Lemuel had said; she was there to be used.

But Chess knew what *she* wanted to do. As long as she stuck to that, it didn't matter what anyone else wanted. That was how she'd done things on Surapoor, when the Committee had sent them to spy on the Twisted Symmetry. That was how she was going to do things now. And, maybe, Anna could be *useful* to her.

'Tomorrow morning,' she told Anna, 'we're going to the wharf.'

CHAPTER 6

'There's no one watching us.' Anna was confident about this. She was sitting beside Chess on the back seat of a bus that was crawling through the centre of the city. It was slow and overcrowded but it was the cheapest way to travel from where Anna lived in the western suburbs to the seething morass of the south.

'The enemy don't wear badges to say who they are,' muttered Chess, irritably. She sank deeper into the rough fabric which smelt of burgers and cigarette smoke. She didn't look about as Anna was doing. She had learnt long ago that the best way of not being noticed was to act like you weren't there at all.

'Your hair looks a lot better, by the way.' Anna interrupted her cool-eyed surveillance with an approving glance at Chess. 'You don't want the enemy to mistake you for an electric shock.'

'I wouldn't mind,' mumbled Chess.

That morning she had showered out the dirt and the beads and braids, so now her chestnut hair was loose and curly again. Through the splashing water she had heard voices.

She couldn't hear what was being said, but she could tell it was Anna and her father, arguing. But her jeans and T-shirt had been washed and Anna had taken an old green jumper from her mum for Chess to wear.

They had grabbed some breakfast; toast, jam and tea. Anna had stuffed two packs of biscuits and her Link-me into a boot bag, thrown a fake fur-lined anorak over her short skirt and jumper and marched to the nearest bus stop, black, woollen tights keeping the freezing cold at bay, big feet in chunky, brown boots.

With a hiss and a hot whiff of brake pads, the bus halted at its most southerly stop and disgorged the remaining passengers. There weren't many. Most people who came to this part of the city had no money to spend on bus fares and the armed conductors ensured that there were no free rides.

Chess and Anna were the last off the bus. They didn't stay to watch it rattle away but headed up the hill that would take them to the ridge where the Pit began; the rambling, filthy, sweep of hovels that cascaded down to the remains of the wharf.

Anna, who had had a lot to say during the ride, fell quiet. Chess found herself clenching her fists, digging rough fingernails into her palms, as she prepared to see her home for the first time in months. There was no guarantee that Gemma would still be there, or Pacer or Hex. It would have made sense for them to have moved on, found somewhere safer to hide. Somewhere less exposed. Chess's mouth was dry. If Gemma wasn't there, she wasn't sure what she would do. It wasn't that she needed Gemma for her plans; she didn't want to risk Gemma at all. She just needed Gemma to be there.

At the top of the ridge they looked out in silence, over the Pit, the wharf, the slow, brown flow of the river, and out to the steaming factories on the far bank, all capped by a low, white sky.

'What a godforsaken mess,' croaked Anna.

But Chess sighed with relief. At least it looked no different from when she had last seen it. And when she scanned the desolation of the wharf, she picked out a plume of smoke that spiralled high from a cluster of derelict warehouses which staggered up from the sea of ruins.

'Come on,' she said with a kick in her heart, and she gave Anna a bright grin. 'I'll show you where I live.'

Walking across the rubble was a lot easier in a pair of trainers. And it was a lot warmer. Pockets of frost filled tiny crevices like old spider nests and chunks of ice sheened like glass amongst the broken bricks. This was the first winter since the hunters had smashed and burnt the wharf to a wreck. Chess bit her lip; it looked a harder place to survive than ever.

'Don't talk too much,' she instructed Anna. 'Not to start with. OK?'

Smoke churned out of the smashed frontage of the warehouses, filling the air with a stinging tang.

'Whatever you say,' replied Anna, coolly. 'I'm just here for moral support.'

You're just here because you want *me* to help *you*, thought Chess, but she didn't dwell on that because the smoke was making her nervous.

'Are they trying to *let* people know that they're hiding here?' muttered Chess, distracted. The crashers weren't the problem; normal police officers only bothered with street rats when they crashed them for grafting. But the hunters were different; they tracked and trapped rats. They exterminated. Once the hunters showed up, rats got slabbed.

'There should be lookouts.' Chess felt her nails dig harder into her palms. But as she led Anna towards the loud snapping of fire and the funnelling smoke, nobody challenged them.

It was Hex who stumbled upon them. He loped round the cracked side wall, big boots unlaced, tall figure stooped.

'Chess!' he boomed, almost bumping into her by accident.

'Hi, Hex,' said Chess, aware of how Anna was trying not to stare at Hex's hare lip.

'Chess!' repeated the tall youth and he beamed at her before turning back and lolloping out of sight, his voice echoing across the frozen rubble. 'It's Chess. It's Chess.'

'Is this part of keeping a low profile?' enquired Anna but Chess ignored her. She hurried towards the lofted shell of the first warehouse and in to Pacer and Gemma.

Anna hung back, cautious. She had seen people like the lad in the black hooded combats. They hung about at tram stops and near to train stations. They scurried in packs down alleys like dogs. Or like rats. When her dad saw his type near their house, he rang the police, just to be safe.

The little girl looked odd. Anna studied her wispy, blonde hair and soft, blue eyes and painfully bare feet and the light blue dress that would have left her freezing, even under the wrap-around sacking, and she decided that she was odd because she looked too happy; idiotically happy for a street rat who lived like a savage in a dump like this.

'Chess!' The little girl sprinted through the rolling smoke. Anna winced as she watched her pale feet skitter across the cold brick. She felt angry for a reason she didn't understand.

'Gemma!' Chess hugged her friend. 'You're cold.'

'You're bigger.' Gemma stepped back, eyeing Chess uncertainly.

'I know, but I'm still me,' Chess assured her.

Gemma couldn't hold back for long. She hugged Chess and Chess hugged her back, to give her warmth as much as to greet her. But she needn't have worried. Two bonfires blazed in the mouth of the warehouses, blasting out heat.

'Yo, Chess!'

'Yo, Pacer,' replied Chess, breaking away from Gemma but still holding her hand.

Pacer stopped short and looked at Chess without smiling. 'You look like a jack,' he said, glancing at her mostly white trainers. Then he looked her up and down, scornfully. 'Nice jacket.'

Chess shrugged. This wasn't the reception she had imagined.

Pacer cocked his head to one side and approached slowly. Hex had stopped grinning. He stood by Pacer's shoulder and chewed his lower lip anxiously. Gemma was still holding Chess's hand.

'You look different,' stated Pacer.

Chess sighed loudly. She hadn't spent days trying to get back to the wharf to listen to this suspicious rubbish. 'I'm me, OK? Stop acting like a moron, Pacer.'

That surprised him. The last time Pacer had been with Chess, she would never have spoken to him like that. His eyes switched to Anna and they narrowed.

'Who's the jack?'

'A friend,' Chess shot back, more certain than she felt.

Pacer frowned at the space behind Chess. 'Where's Box? Where's Splinter?'

Anna got ready for trouble; these weren't questions, they were accusations.

'With the enemy,' stated Chess. She noticed that Pacer still kept a distance from her, as if he was frightened to come too close.

'How?' Pacer approached slowly, eyeing Anna as if she was responsible for the brothers' absence.

Chess shook her chestnut curls. 'I don't know. They were meant to come back with me but they didn't. They weren't touching me at the right time.' She remembered how Splinter had let go of her shoulder as she pressed the VAP which would allow them all to be rescued, so long as they were all touching. 'Splinter let go of me.'

'Doing his own thing?' Pacer was in front of Chess and Anna now, eyeballing Anna who was taller than he was. Chess could tell that he was acting tougher than he felt. There'd be no trouble so long as Anna kept her mash shut.

'Sounds like Splinter,' continued Pacer. 'His hands usually stick to things; they never *slip* off. What's your name?'

Before Anna could reply, Chess said, 'Fury.'

'She don't look very furious.'

'You haven't seen what she can do with a hockey stick.' Chess peered into the white smog. 'Are you crazy, Pacer?'

She pointed at the fires. 'The hunters will come.'

Pacer looked at Chess as if she had missed something obvious. 'The hunters won't come here again.'

'Why?' Chess's forehead furrowed as she began to pick out shapes moving beyond the smoke; shapes she hadn't expected to see.

Pacer was looking at her strangely, again. Chess couldn't tell whether he was suspicious or puzzled. Or frightened, maybe. 'Because of *you*,' he said. 'Everyone knows about the battle here, when the hunters were slabbed. Everyone knows that you've got stuck into the Twisted Symmetry; that you've started killing them.'

It was such a stark comment. Chess shook her head. 'I don't kill things.'

But what about Behrens? she asked herself. Well, there was nothing wrong about that: Behrens was evil, she *had* to destroy him. What about Jones, then? Jones had been looking after her, protecting her.

Chess stopped that thought by asking, 'How do you know about what happened on Surapoor?'

'Ethel's been here,' replied Pacer. 'She's cool; for a wrinkly.'

'How many times?' demanded Chess.

'Now and again,' shrugged Pacer. 'Tells us bits, of what you've been doing. Said you might need our help.' Pacer rubbed the top of his shaved head and looked at Chess apologetically, as if she was the last person to need help.

'Can't she leave me alone?' yelled Chess, and her voice ricocheted around the ruins and across the wharf.

'She says nice things about you.' Hex shuffled, embarrassed.

'You're a scary girl, Chess,' and suddenly, Pacer grinned. It shocked Anna because it made him look so different; the slash of white smile in his black face was so friendly. So normal. But she could see that behind the grin lurked uncertainty. For all his bravado, Pacer was being very careful; as if he was handling a gun with a hair trigger.

From behind Pacer there came a slapping and scraping of feet, and then shadows wavering, and out of the smoke loomed more street rats; rats of all ages, in torn clothes, shreds of sacking, ripped boots and bare feet. They were gaunt, with grimy skin, matted hair, long wrists and bright, hungry eyes. They gathered in an arc that stretched from behind Hex and Pacer, back into the smoke and into the warehouses.

'Everybody's coming here.' Pacer shrugged again. 'They think it's safe, see?' He grinned at Chess. 'You're famous. Everyone knows the hunters won't touch us, 'cos of you.'

'I don't want to be famous,' complained Chess.

Hex thumbed at the silent army of street rats. 'They've been waiting for you.'

Gemma gave Chess's hand a terrific squeeze. 'We've *all* been waiting for you, Chess,' she said.

'This is sweet,' muttered Anna.

'I need help,' stated Chess. 'I want to stop the Twisted Symmetry stealing children.'

'Jack children?' Pacer scratched his jaw, casting a cool glance at Anna who stared back stonily.

'Jacks or street rats, it doesn't matter,' said Chess. 'It's time to stop them; it's time to kill their brain.'

'See?' Pacer smiled knowingly. 'You *do* kill things.'

Hex broke the uneasy silence. 'Best cook up a brew. Can't make plans without a proper brew.'

'Come on,' said Pacer, 'and bring your quiet friend with you. Fury!' and he released them all from the tension by laughing loudly.

'You told me to be quiet,' complained Anna, stepping over a heap of broken brick, aware of the hungry eyes that were riveted to her nice clothes, her boot bag, her warm tights, her well-cut, well-washed, long black hair. She realized that she was on her own and began to wonder whether coming here had been a mistake.

Once they had rounded the furnace-roar of the bonfires, they were into the broken warehouses.

'You've been busy,' observed Chess, surveying the jerry-built shelters that lined the shattered walls. They had been constructed from old pallets, charred timbers, sheets of rusty iron and rope-lashed polythene and they were stacked on top of one another so that the highest row could only be reached by ropes and rickety ladders.

'Looks like a massive pet shop,' commented Anna, a little too loudly.

'Sorry there aren't no gold-plated toilets,' said Pacer, leading them to a brazier that glowed with hot ash. They sat on old tyres and Hex tipped powder from a box into a pot that stood in the embers. He added water from a chipped ewer, stirred the mix with a dipstick and sniffed the steaming vapours.

Anna threw her boot bag between her feet and sized up the best route out in case she needed to get away quickly. Dozens of street rats had drifted from the bonfires to where

Anna sat in a close circle with Chess, Gemma, Pacer and Hex. They had gathered around them in silence, blocking any way out.

Hex had collected one enamel mug and three empty tins. When steam was swirling rapidly from the pot, he tipped its contents into the mug and the tins, hissing as his fingers were scorched. Then he found a lump of frozen margarine wrapped in an oily cloth and he cut off four nuggets with a penknife.

'Ain't got no milk,' he explained as he dropped the soot-smeared lumps into the liquid. He handed a tin to Chess and a tin to Anna, kept one tin for himself and gave the mug to Pacer.

Anna looked into the greasy brew. 'What is it?'

'Dried, smoked bits of leaf,' explained Hex. 'The marg gives it body.'

'Lovely,' she said, glumly.

'Cheers,' said Pacer, raising his mug, watching Anna over its rim.

Anna returned his stare and lifted the hot tin to her lips. It smelt like a car engine. She took a sip. Her lips burnt, her throat gagged and she sprayed the liquid out of her mouth.

'It's like a cat's done it,' she gasped.

The street rats erupted with laughter.

'You really drink this?' asked Anna as the laughter dampened down. Perhaps this was a trick that they had played on her. Her solemn enquiry was enough to kick-start them again.

'This is *all* we get to drink, when the graft's not done proper,' explained Pacer, with an accusing glance at a group of rats who fell silent. 'Sometimes we get tea or coffee, but mostly we don't.'

Anna opened her bag and pulled out the biscuits. Now all the rats went quiet. She threw a packet to Pacer. 'These are good for dunking,' she said, and then, looking at the mass of rats without a drink, 'or just plain eating. I'll bring some more tomorrow.'

Pacer looked at the packet and tossed it in his hand. Then he nodded at Anna. 'Thanks.'

The biscuits didn't go far. Chess and Anna didn't have any and neither did Gemma or Pacer. The street rats listened as Chess told them everything about what had happened on Surapoor, about what happened to children in the Twisted Symmetry's scream rooms; about how none of the stolen street rats would ever be coming back.

'And there'll be more children stolen, unless *we* stop the Symmetry,' concluded Chess.

'And we stop them by killing a big lump of brain.' Pacer rubbed his jaw.

'Yeah, but we have to do it soon. Before they start using it again.'

'But even that won't stop them from taking over the world, will it?' confirmed Pacer.

Chess shook her head. Behrens had told her that the Inquisitors had stockpiled plenty of energy. What they needed was a way to deliver it. That was where she fitted into their plans.

'It will hurt them though.' Chess enjoyed saying that. 'At least it means somebody is putting up a fight.' Ethel and the Committee had as good as given in, as far as Chess was concerned. 'All I need is enough of us to burn down the Riverside Prison. That's where they keep their brain.'

There was a scuffling as a rat in denim overalls, toeless boots and a trapper's hat pushed his way forwards.

'We c ... can't do that,' he stammered.

'Why not, Whizz?' asked Pacer.

'C ... c ... 'cos the Riverside Prison ain't there no more.'

'Not there?' exclaimed Chess. Of course it would be there; the Riverside Prison *had* to be there.

'They dem ... molished it. M ... months ago.' Whizz pulled up his thin shoulders when he saw the expression on Chess's face. 'S ... sorry, Chess.'

'He's right.' Hex scratched his lanky, sprouting hair. 'I remember hearing about it. The place is like this now,' and he pointed to the gaping frontage of the warehouse. The river slid past the desolation with barely a gurgle.

'Worse than this,' added Whizz awkwardly. 'There ain't n ... nothin'.'

Chess hadn't foreseen this, but it was obvious; of course the Twisted Symmetry would have moved the operation once they realized that the Committee had succeeded in infiltrating them and stealing a slice of their brain. She was angry; mostly with herself for being so stupid.

'The brain could be anywhere.' She kicked a stone which bounced off the brazier with a loud ping. 'Anywhere in the universes. How do we find it?'

Anna had pulled the Link-me out of her bag. There was a ripple of interest from the nearest street rats who recognized it, automatically, as something good to steal. She kept a firm grip on the device, and held it close to her body.

'Let's start with the most obvious,' she said, turning it on. Chess shuffled close to her and Gemma shuffled close to Chess, not very interested in the Link-me but very happy to be with her friend again.

'Be careful,' Chess warned Anna. 'We don't know if it's safe, looking in there.'

Pacer laughed. 'That's more like the Chess I know.'

'If we get into the city records office ...' Anna's long fingers tapped the keys.

Chess could see the commands on the screen but they meant nothing to her.

'I have to break in with the right rootkit,' muttered Anna. 'Hook into the city's operating system. It's not hard. There are so many sloppy users, always leaving ports open.' A luminous green bar flashed on the bottom edge of the machine.

'Password protected. Well, the jerk at the other end got that bit right.' Anna hummed to herself, studiously.

Pacer and Hex were looking over her shoulders now.

'She knows how to do this stuff?' asked Pacer, in a whisper.

'She does,' Anna whispered back. She pressed a button and a stream of letters scrolled up the screen. When it stopped, only a question mark remained flashing. 'Doesn't match any of the ten thousand default passwords,' grumbled Anna. 'Let's try something else. I can scan his phone line from this link. I can call him.' She entered a string of numbers. 'Quiet now.'

But nobody was talking, and Chess noticed how Pacer was listening to Anna. Watching her. Impressed. Chess had known Pacer for years and he had never looked at her like that. She picked at a fingernail.

'Planning office.' The male voice came clearly from the Link-me's speaker.

'Yes, can you help me?' Anna spoke in a precise, clipped, jack fashion. 'I want to know who arranged the demolition of the Riverside Prison. We are shutting down our own operation and require a reputable contractor.'

The voice grunted in the speaker. Then came the soft click of a keyboard being tapped at the other end.

'Can't help you,' said the man. 'That information is confidential.'

'What a pity,' lamented Anna. 'Goodbye.' She turned off the phone link and said, coolly, 'Got him. I installed a snare programme on his computer, to record his keystrokes.' Her fingers danced. 'Here's his password, ready for us to use.'

Chess couldn't decipher the letters before Anna had read, 'LUNCHBRAYKE2'.

Anna entered the password. 'We're in. No time to enjoy the view. Let's go straight to "Riverside".' She took time to flick through the records. She didn't say anything, but Chess noticed her breathing change and heard her make a deep noise in her throat, like a growl. Then she held the screen right in front of Chess and looked up at her, face electric in the glow of the display.

Chess saw the letterhead displaying the C and three stars of the CREX Corporation.

'What does it all say?' asked Chess.

'The demolition was arranged by CREX. The hardware was removed by lorry and airlift.'

'Where did it all go?'

Anna pressed a button. The screen switched to an image of the Cones. She homed in on the CREX tower. 'Here.'

The image started to flicker.

'Can you look in there with your machine?' asked Pacer.

'Not right now. The power's going. I haven't charged it for ages.' The screen blanked. 'Going, going, gone.' Anna looked up. 'The CREX Corporation and the Twisted Symmetry are linked, obviously,' and she accompanied her deduction with a glance at Chess that was meant to say, 'Like us.'

Chess was slow to speak, caught between the vertigo-dread of losing control now that the cerebral torus wasn't where she had bargained, and the feeling that there was a distance between her, and Anna and Pacer; a distance that *she* felt because Anna and Pacer obviously *didn't*.

'They must have moved the whole operation to the tower,' she managed to say.

'Seems so,' agreed Anna. She put the Link-me back inside the boot bag. 'It's not going to be a simple matter of burning down a derelict prison.'

'So what do we do?' asked Pacer, and Chess noticed that he said 'we' which was good. She noticed, also, that he was asking Anna what they should do.

'We need to know the layout, obviously; those towers are huge.' Anna yanked the draw cord to close her bag. 'We need to know exactly where the computer brain is.'

'How?' Hex licked his lips.

'Break into their CCTV. Or get a look at the plans; there must be plans for a building like that, somewhere.'

-[119]-

Anna shrugged. 'Maybe someone's going to have to go inside to take a look.'

Nobody had anything to say about that suggestion.

'When I get back home, I'll power-up and see if I can hack into the CREX system.'

'No,' objected Chess, too loudly. When all eyes had turned to her, she added, 'You know how lively that is. You *know*.'

Anna shrugged as if she had no idea what Chess was driving at. 'You coming back with me?'

'I don't know.' Here, she was with Gemma and her own people, even if they treated her strangely now. If she stayed at the wharf perhaps she could patch things up with Pacer. And beneath all that was her instinct that now she was at the wharf, she should stay at the wharf. She felt safer here than anywhere else. And there was no reason why she *had* to go back with Anna.

'You could help Fury bring back more biscuits,' suggested Pacer with a hopeful raising of his eyebrows.

'I guess I could,' admitted Chess, instantly cross with herself for sounding so feeble.

Pacer ruffled her hair. That was the sort of thing he used to do; she didn't like it now. 'You'll just have to suffer another night of your jack friend's fat fodder and central heating,' he teased. 'And her gold-plated toilets.'

'We'll be back tomorrow,' Anna assured her. 'We can start making some proper plans; plans to get even.'

It was the steely edge to Anna's voice that prompted Chess to say, 'OK, I'll come back with you. Tonight.'

'Good.' Anna stood up, throwing the bag over her shoulder.

Gemma stayed with Chess until she and Anna had come to the sole road that climbed through the Pit from the wharf. Their eyes itched from the vapours that hovered over the cesspools.

'You'll be all right.' Gemma squeezed Chess's hand, which she had held since they had left the warehouse. 'You'll be back tomorrow.'

To Chess, it seemed that a void yawned between now and tomorrow.

'You were away for so long,' explained Gemma, 'that you can't be away for very long again.'

'I don't think it works like that,' said Chess distantly. 'You're not wearing your glasses anymore.' Not that it made any difference; there had never been lenses in Gemma's glasses anyway.

'I think my eyes are a lot better.'

'Good.' Chess stood still.

'Come on.' Anna didn't hide her impatience.

'You'll be all right, Chess,' repeated Gemma, and she let go of Chess's hand. 'I predict that everything will be all right,' and she grinned, displaying her stubby, crooked teeth.

When they had marched up the road and Gemma was no more than a pale dash in the frozen rubble behind them, Anna spoke. 'That kid is in desperate need of a brace.'

'Shut up,' said Chess.

The afternoon was dying as they turned into Anna's road. The trees and bushes were black and solitary street lamps were flickering as if each one had a moth trapped inside.

The stillness was so deep that every sound was alive; the rustle of a blackbird in a hedge, the scrape of their feet on loose pieces of tarmac, the hardening frost.

Chess spotted an empty car, parked a couple of metres from the entrance to Anna's driveway. She slowed down.

'It's no one,' Anna assured her. 'No one to do with us.'

But Chess saw the world differently from Anna; every detail was a clue to survival; the unknown was always a threat.

'It wasn't there this morning.' She halted.

'People come and go, Chess.' Anna put her hands on her hips, elbows out.

Chess didn't take her eyes off the car. 'Do you know it? Do you know whose it is?'

Anna huffed, steam puffing past her face. 'Do you want me to go knocking on everyone's door?' She put on a snooty, busybody voice. 'Hello, I know you've lived in this quiet road for decades and I know that nothing *ever* happens here but I wonder whether you'd mind terribly checking under your beds to see if the Twisted Symmetry are waiting to catch Chess Tuesday.'

'It isn't funny.' Chess pushed her hands into her jacket and looked about; looking for signs, but signs of what, she didn't know.

'You're right.' Anna was scathing. 'It isn't funny. It's really irritating. Can we go inside now? I'm freezing. If the enemy were going to pounce, they'd do it here, not in my house.'

That made sense. Chess started to walk again, although she didn't stop watching the car. But they entered the drive without trouble and now they were approaching the heavy front door.

Chess grasped every detail; the darkness under the shrubs, the shapes in the surface of the gravel, the faint staleness of a cigarette smoked minutes before, a movement behind the wax-dull, front door window.

She knew she should be turning, running away. But Anna was sure that she would be all right.

'Does your dad smoke?' she meant to ask Anna, but Anna had already pushed open the front door and they had entered the house.

It was Anna who shouted, 'Dad, no!'

Mr Ledward grasped his daughter's shoulders and pulled her away from Chess.

'Why?' shouted Anna.

Two men stood in front of Chess. A third had emerged from the corner by the front door, blocking the way out. He wrenched Chess's arms behind her back before she could react. She tried not to wince. All the time her eyes were locked on Anna's.

One of the men in front of her stepped forwards and pulled a wallet from the inside of his jacket. He opened it to display the warrant card.

'Chess Tuesday, you are under arrest for the murder of Dr Oriana Lache.'

CHAPTER 7

Once Box had climbed down the pylon, he stood in the ring of shadow at its foot and waited. He didn't have to wait long. A train of about a hundred shabby snouts came tramping through a fog of dust. Their heads were hanging and their feet scraped across the hard sand. Beside the Fleshings, uniformed troopers walked at ten metre intervals, blaze carbines across their chests.

Box glanced back at the spires of the black tower, where Splinter would be. It felt like a thread still connected him to his brother; a thread that was suspended taut across the hot, open space. With a wrench in his chest, Box turned his back on the tower and walked towards the snouts. The thread snapped. Box was on his own now, with only one thought: to find his way back to Chess, whatever it took, however hard he had to fight.

He hadn't wondered what the guards would do when his solitary figure emerged from the shimmering heat and joined the back of the file. It turned out they did nothing and that didn't surprise him. They were there to stop prisoners escaping. If anyone was suicidal enough to join the Fleshings, that was no concern of theirs.

They walked for an hour maybe; long enough for Box's hair to have turned white with dust and his throat raw. They walked in hopeless silence, shoulders sunken, legs dragging, tracking a narrow line through the soul-sapping span of the orange plain, the maze of silver pipes above their heads.

Box didn't notice the metal hut until the snouts immediately in front of him had been swallowed by its cool shadow. It wasn't much bigger than a bus shelter, with a roof that curved up from the ground like a shell, yet it accommodated all the prisoners. When he had entered, Box saw why: this wasn't a hut, it was an entrance; an entrance to a ramp that led down.

The way was lit by luminous strips in the walls. The ramp descended in a gentle spiral. Box's vision was blotchy after traipsing beneath the harsh glare outside, and by the time his eyes had adjusted, he had come to the bottom of the slope. The nose of a blaze carbine prodded his bare chest and a Dog Trooper guard with a face that was almost human save for the nest of canines that spiked out of his jutting jaws, jerked his head towards a corridor that ended in a rectangle of dim light.

'Nice doggie,' said Box, raising a hand to reassure the guard that he would obey, and he turned to follow the bodies ahead. He was in the dogs' world now. He didn't know what to expect but he felt surprisingly calm. He just had to keep his head down and make sure he survived. As usual.

He emerged from the tunnel into an arena. It was longer and wider than a football pitch and was enclosed by sheer walls which reached to a high roof, hatched at intervals by white slits. Dust glistered in drifting clouds beneath the slits and following these upwards, Box saw that the slits were grates in the roof which allowed sheets of daylight to penetrate the gloom of the vast, subterranean stadium. The roof must have been level with the ground above.

When he walked, the way in which the strips of light from above flickered across his vision made it difficult to focus, but the rest of the Fleshings had gathered in a grumbling rabble at the foot of the nearest section of wall, where the shadow was uniformly deep. Box joined them, sitting on the cool sand. He sniffed the air which was dank with the stench of dog, and spat out a mouthful of gritty phlegm.

Now that they had settled down, some of the other prisoners were watching him and muttering to one another in the harsh language of the dog-men. Box didn't understand what they were saying, but he could smell trouble, whatever species it came from. However, since there were about a hundred snouts and only one of him, he decided the best thing would be to keep his mouth shut and his eyes from making contact.

He cast about the high space and observed the caged walkways suspended from the roof in which Dog Troopers kept guard, machine gun nests hanging at intervals like bristling gourds. And, looking across the wide floor, he saw patches of sand, flattened and darker than elsewhere and guessed that this was not shadow, but blood.

Slyly, he observed his fellow prisoners through fingers that appeared to be rubbing his eyes. They were a dishevelled, cunning, brute crew, clearly the worst of the dog-men; the criminals, the undesirables. Box snorted to himself with grim humour. Even on this planet, a universe away from the wharf, he had managed to fall in with the roughest, lowest, craftiest-looking gang that could be found. Maybe Splinter was right; maybe he could never be anything other than a street rat.

Then he noticed a long, lean, hard-bodied snout who was sitting apart from the others. He had a short-furred, black pelt and a mane of ebony hair that swept around his Alsatian face and down his back. The dark skin of his left arm and chest looked like it had been shaved and tattooed with a flesh-pink ink, but the symbols were meaningless to Box. Then, Box saw that the solitary dog-man was staring back at him, so he looked away, but slowly, to show that he wasn't backing off; he just couldn't be bothered with trouble right now.

But Box knew that whenever trouble was in the air, it was guaranteed to land on him, and now, trouble had landed in the shape of a snout with a body like a mail sack and a face like a pig. Box squinted up at him with one eye closed and sighed wearily. It was always the same; join a new gang and they tried you out, saw how hard you were, what you could do. Why should the snouts be any different?

What did you expect? Box asked himself with a shake of his head. Just like a gang of street rats, only hairier, and with teeth long enough to tear out throats.

Box knew the ritual. Beat or be beaten. Except that here, it was beat or be eaten. He looked towards the roof and saw the guards leaning on the rails and looking down, interested to see what would happen.

Thanks a lot, thought Box, standing up slowly and dusting

sand from the seat of his leggings. Don't expect mercy from me if my finger's ever on the trigger.

The snout spat at him. Box wiped the mess from his cheek and kicked his mind into gear. He remembered what Balthazar Broom had taught him on Surapoor and what he had continued to practise ever since: weigh up your opponent, calculate the likely weaknesses, plan your assault. Fight clever.

Box flexed his fingers, loosened his shoulders and took a hard look at pig-face. About his height, but heavier. Short arms, fat belly, bowed legs. Probably a good wrestler, so don't start grappling. But slow. Therefore attack with fast blows, and to the head, not the belly, which was too well protected with lard. If he could put him down quickly, that *might* dissuade others from having a go.

Pig-face thrust out his chin, inviting attack. But Box delayed.

There had been a scrape of sand and he had felt the least stirring of air against his back. Someone had moved in, behind him.

Without a flicker of his own eye, Box noted where the eyes of the nearest Fleshings were trained, on a space a bit more than a metre behind him. He noted also how a velvety tongue slipped from the jaws of one and slapped pink across his yellow fangs. From somewhere else, a hungry growl grazed the heavy silence.

The dogs were getting ready to feed.

Box sprang backwards on his left leg, powering his right in a backthrust at chest height. He felt his heel smash into something soft and heard choking. Pig-face's eyes opened wide, surprised, before Box's left fist buried itself between them, followed immediately by a stamp of his right foot into the snout's knee joint.

Pig-face staggered to the dust, howling and clawing at his kneecap.

Box shook the sweat and damp, curly black hair out of his eyes before looking at the other snout who was clutching his throat and writhing in the sand like a broken spider.

'Who's next?' he demanded in Chat, voice shaky as adrenalin pumped through his body. Did snouts speak Chat? Who cared. He had to show the dogs that there were easier ways to have fun than fighting with him.

Something the size of a grizzly bear lumbered to its feet. 'I'm next,' it rumbled in Chat, clenching and unclenching fists the size of lump hammers with a cracking of sinews.

Box had to arch his neck to meet the massive snout's glare. He swallowed although his throat had just gone as dry as the floor. The snouts nearest were panting excitedly.

Box backed away. The giant dog-man would snap his bones like twigs before he could even land a blow. He would have to deliver a head shot to stand a chance. That meant he had to find a way of getting the beast to lower its ugly, sag-skinned head.

You expect me to keep backing off, Box realized.

Surprise was the best weapon of all, and in this situation, it was Box's only weapon. The trick would be to do what was unexpected.

Box charged forwards, head down. He didn't stop. With all his strength he rammed the top of his head into the snout's stomach.

The dog-man was winded and he bent double. But, before Box could spin with a reverse hook kick to the side of his head, a pair of brawny arms had locked themselves around his body. Head down, Box was hoisted up, gripped against the snout's torso.

Box used his weight to unbalance his opponent, allowing his body to be swung up far more swiftly than the dog-man had expected. This caused the huge snout to reel backwards, crashing onto his back in a blast of sand with Box sitting astride his chest.

The snout shook the sand from his eyes. Still sitting on the slab of chest, Box wasted no time in delivering what should have been a knock-out punch to the beast's temple. But its skull was as hard as rock. The only thing to crack was Box's knuckle.

The dog-man glared at him, roared and baring his nail-like fangs, crashed his jaws shut at the top of Box's legs. Box had seen what was coming, and with a yelp, sprang up and away so that the snapping jaws closed only on the space between his legs.

Then, his arms were pinned behind his back and held fast by two more snouts. Rubbing the side of his head, the giant lumbered to his feet and shook his jowls with a flap. He stood in front of Box, clenched his breezeblock fist and drew it back.

'Stop this.'

The voice was as dry as a winter breeze and as cold. Box looked towards the arena and his mouth fell open. His arms were released and the snout with the big fists lowered his arm.

'My name,' said the creature that approached, 'is Six, and I am the Yard Master. Here is where you will train, sleep, eat, fight and very probably, die. You are mine now.'

Box knew enough Chat to understand what Six said, but he didn't process the information because he was stunned by the appearance of the Yard Master. He was twice the height of the giant snout. Parts of him were dog-man, normally sized but with grey-pink, hairless skin stretched over them. It was his spine that gave him his great height. It was segmented like a shower hose, and it connected his emaciated ribcage to his skeletal pelvis so that his body was in two parts. His legs were bowed and clicked noisily as he stalked forwards, his thin right arm hung loose like a withered stick but his left arm was tubular and metal, like his spine, and appeared to end in an oval lump of steel.

'Survive,' croaked Six, 'and you might even end up like me.' His bald, sharp-nosed dog head jerked from side to side and Box saw that where his left eye should have been there jutted a metal socket that glowed red. Below the protruding socket, his cheek and jaw had been constructed from strips of iron, overlapping roughly like the clinker-built hull of a boat.

The big dog-man with whom Box had been fighting muttered something under his breath. Without moving his crooked legs, Six's tubular waist spun round and he threw out his metallic left arm. It extended in a smooth loop and as it did so, the steel lump at the end opened revealing three, clawed pincers. Eight metres the arm stretched and then the pincers fastened round the dog-man's head.

Before the dog-man could react, Six corkscrewed the long,

thin limb and the pincers revolved so hard that the snout was whipped off his feet, and so fast that his body spun in a blur until it tore free of his neck, leaving the head clutched within the pincer-claws. Six hurled the head at the far wall of the arena as if it were a baseball. It smashed like an egg.

'Do what you like to each other,' croaked Six, 'but don't even *think* of upsetting *me*.' He coughed, spindle ribs twitching under their corpse-like sheath of skin. His long left arm retracted until the closed pincers hung to just below the protruding crest of his hip bone, where they swung, slowly.

'Do any of you know how important you are?' Six prowled in front of the Fleshings, who were trying not to look at the headless mound sprawled in the sand. 'This is the one time and the one place where you will ever have a value. As sacrificial training aids you are indispensible to the success of our masters. When the time comes, and you lie dying in the dust of this yard, you will have the satisfaction of knowing that you have played a crucial role in the training of those pan-universal warriors we are pleased to call the Dog Troopers.'

Six rested a foot on the corpse and he licked his long lips before continuing the well-practised speech. His voice barely rose above a whisper, but the Fleshings heard every word. 'You will train hard and be fed well. You will learn to use the mace-blade. At all times, the guards will be ready to shoot mutineers,' Six indicated the troopers in the roof scaffolds. '. . . If I don't get to them first. I must warn you, I have a particular appetite for mutineers,' and Box noted Six crane his long neck, like a serpent, to look at the snout with the tattoos who still sat a short distance from the others.

'When the time comes, the cadets will be brought here. In this yard, cadets will fight Fleshings, hand-to-hand, until only half remain.' The Yard Master coughed, his bony shoulders shaking. 'The cadets will have the benefit of body armour. It is unusual for any of the Fleshings to survive. Those who do will be sent to a convict battalion which will be posted to one of the Symmetry's most hopeless battlegrounds, where they will serve to the end of their days, which will come very quickly.'

Six spun three hundred and sixty degrees on his tubular waist. 'There are eight hundred Fleshing Yards on this planet. There are five prison planets administered by the Symmetry. And yet the penal battalions are very small, so few survive the Fleshings.'

'Did you?' asked Box. As one, the snouts looked at him, jaws hanging.

'Stand up,' whispered Six.

Box stood.

Six bent down, his long back arching like a spider's, his tight-skinned, pointed face close enough to Box's to breathe on him.

'I have been told about you,' hissed Six. 'There are some who have high hopes for your progress but I am not so sure. You are only a human, boy. In my experience, even the strongest humans have weaknesses that prove fatal.'

Box couldn't imagine who had high hopes for his progress. He couldn't do anything except wonder what had possessed him to draw Six's lethal attention to himself. But, instinctively, he knew how important it was for the snouts to see how he was different from them. The best fighter. The bravest. Even if it meant risking his life like this. Sometimes, risking your life was the only way to save it.

Six straightened and inwardly, Box collapsed with relief. He was not going to be killed today. But everyone had seen that he had more guts than them.

'In answer to your question, boy, I did survive the Fleshings. And, I survived my time in the battalions of the damned. But, there are not many who do; death comes quickly and horribly in the Final Starfields of the Crystal Wars.'

Six turned the top half of his body away from Box, and then the bottom half. As he began to walk off he said, 'There is a special reward for those who do survive.' He raised his thin, metal arm and indicated the arena. 'Those parts of their bodies that can be scraped up and still used are fastened together and they come to somewhere like this, with the title of Yard Master. And so our vital role in the fortunes of the Symmetry is sustained.'

He hacked out a cough like a shovelful of grit. 'I told you, boy, survive, and you may be lucky enough to end up like me.' He paused, his back towards Box. 'I think you are a little like I was. You will become more like me before the end.'

I swear that I will be nothing like you, Box promised himself. He thought of Chess; what might be happening to her now, and how much he wanted to get back to her. He would risk everything to find her; he would fight, he would kill, he would live like a snout for as long as it took. Then, he noticed the rim of a metal tube that protruded from the back of Six's skull. It glowed red, like the tube on the front of his face.

Eyes in the back of his scrawny head, thought Box. I'll have to be very careful.

And then he saw that the snout with the tattoos and the long, black hair was also looking at the back of Six's head and they caught each other's eye. Box understood the language of eyes; in one glance he could read hatred, cunning, who was safe, who was a squealer. Rat or dog, it didn't matter; you stayed alive by instinct, whatever animal you were. The snout nodded at him and Box knew that when the time came, here was someone who would back him up.

A couple of inches in either direction and Splinter would fall into eternal nothingness. But that didn't frighten him. Splinter had a head for heights, even infinite ones. His morning coat had been returned to him and he sat on the reaching like a black slash, suspended in the unending whiteness.

The reachings were the narrow, invisible paths that provided a solid passage through the vortex. It was safest to navigate them with a tesseract because such a device made them visible. But Splinter's tesseract had been lost when the Dog Troopers had kidnapped him on Surapoor. However, he had the habit of mentally recording turns and paces in routes that he took; it was useful for travelling in the dark. So, he had memorized the layout of the reachings nearest the mortice-gate from his journey with Ethel to the Riverside Prison, and from his early explorations conducted whilst he had been at Balthazar's tree house. He had discovered that wherever he put the portable vortex, the little box that he had stolen from Ethel, the reachings were almost always the same when he entered it. Sometimes there was a little slippage, but mostly it was like always starting at the same place on a map. Consequently, he could find his way without the tesseract, so long as he was *very* careful.

Splinter let his thin, black-trousered legs dangle over the edge of the reaching. Fascinated, he watched his bare feet disperse into a swathe of minute particles that dust-devilled into space. It reminded him of when he used to dip his hand into the fast-running shallows where the river broke at the edge of the wharf, trailing the slipstream from his fingers. When he pulled his finger out, the slipstream vanished.

Splinter pulled his legs up to his body and his feet shrank back to their normal, firm dimensions. He hugged his shins, stopped thinking about the wharf and what he had once been, and returned to the vastly more satisfying prospect of what he *could* be.

The unending grey span of the mortice-gate revolved slowly. He knew that it turned close to where he was sitting, although in the cold blankness of the vortex it was impossible to judge distance. On the other side would be General Vane and Saul. Splinter spared Saul no further thought, but he considered how best to track down Lemuel Sprazkin in the ten days the General had given him. And he calculated how he could best use his current, awkward position to further his burgeoning ambitions.

This was a puzzle, and Splinter enjoyed puzzles. It was a puzzle of many interlocking parts, of brain-squeezing complexity, but he could solve it. Splinter could solve anything when he put his mind to it. And he wasn't lumbered with his brother and sister, which was even better. Box's only solution was to fight his way out of problems. All Chess did was to think of herself. She was the most selfish person in the universes. Only *he* had the skill of thinking through a problem.

He forgot about the ache in his arm where General Vane had cut him. He rested his sharp chin on his bony knee and smiled at eternity. This wasn't a problem; it was an opportunity. An opportunity to transform himself into what he *should* be. An opportunity to become powerful. *He'd* be the most important person; the most special. He'd show everybody; most of all, he'd show that old hag, Ethel.

Splinter needed to consider the tools with which he would solve this puzzle. The first thing he did was to empty his coat pockets, of which there were many. He laid his possessions on the reaching, taking care to place everything in the centre of the solid surface, which was no more than a metre wide. Then he took stock:

a box, containing eight unstruck matches;

a knot of string (about three metres);

a pencil;

six marbles;

a set of lock picks;

a switchblade;

a magnifying glass (stolen from Balthazar);

a watchmaker's screwdriver (also stolen from Balthazar);

a flattened wedge of silver (taken from the stonedrakes);

a die-sized, triangular pyramid (taken from Balthazar's cave).

Idly, he extended a long forefinger and nudged one of the marbles. It glided across the reaching silently, slowing down before rolling over the edge. For a moment there was a narrowing streak of glass that trailed horizontally into the white. Then the marble had gone. Inside the vortex, gravity didn't seem to work, other than on the reachings.

Splinter smiled to himself as he imagined the glass ball falling sideways, forever, until perhaps, it emerged in the sky of an unknown universe where it struck the head of a mysterious creature, mysteriously.

Five marbles.

It amounted to a modest amount of equipment for what Splinter was planning, although he was hopeful about the miniature pyramid. He had pocketed it whilst searching through Balthazar's crates when Chess had been unconscious on the skulk rack. He didn't know what it was for, but when his fingers alighted on its plain, metal surfaces in the gloom of the cave, he knew it was worth taking. Splinter's fingers were like antennae that were attuned to interesting things.

He lifted them to where he kept his most useful item, running them through his long, white, spiky hair. This brain was what would show everyone how wrong they were about him. It could be used to work things out and within its unfathomable circuitry was locked knowledge; vital knowledge. Splinter took stock of the knowledge that would be useful to him.

Knowledge of the vortex; in particular, how to return to

his world, how to find the Committee, how to locate Lemuel Sprazkin.

Knowledge of the Twisted Symmetry; obtained from many hours in Balthazar's library, studying the Omnicon.

Knowledge of where to find the second Omnicon; Balthazar had said that there were two Books of All Things but that the second was lost. Lost it may have been, but Splinter knew where to find it. He had used Balthazar's Omnicon to discover the whereabouts of its sister volume; a very clever thing to have done. Too clever for that fool, Broom.

Knowledge of greed; the most important knowledge of all. Everybody wanted something. Find that something and you had them. Look at how he had handled General Vane. The Commander of the Dog Troopers had been brought to heel with nothing worse than a slash to Splinter's arm.

Which brought him back to the most pressing task: to locate Lemuel Sprazkin. He doubted that Sprazkin would trust him enough to accompany him anywhere; Splinter wouldn't have trusted *himself* so there was no reason to think a creature as clever and devious as a primary warp would. But that didn't matter. It would be enough to locate Sprazkin and provide this information to the General. The General would do the rest and enjoy doing it.

To locate Lemuel Sprazkin, Splinter would trace the reachings to the point where they opened at the Central Post Office; Ethel had stopped there on her way through the vortex to the Riverside Prison, which Splinter had found conclusive of her slash-dot madness. From the post office, he would find his way to Committee HQ and there he would discover the whereabouts of Sprazkin. Simple. A perfect example of his indisputable cleverness.

Only one thing jabbed his bubble of self-satisfaction. When he had delved into the secrets of the Omnicon, at Balthazar's house, he had sought to discover what it could reveal about his future. But, every time the page came up blank and this blank page hung about the edge of his thoughts like a spectre.

There was a possible explanation: Balthazar had said the Omnicon revealed only facts, that it couldn't predict the future. But when Splinter had searched for what the future held for Box or Chess, the Omnicon responded with the message 'SEARCH DENIED'. So why did *he* get a blank page? Supposing the Omnicon *was* showing him his future? Even then, Splinter didn't understand the meaning of a blank page. He locked the spectre of the blank page in the deepest vault of his mind and began to replace his possessions within the pockets of the morning coat.

As he did so, the flattened wedge of silver caught the diffuse light of the vortex, and Splinter saw himself reflected. He breathed over the metal, rubbed the surface with his sleeve and held it at an angle so that now there were five distorted Splinters, each looking back at him. By tilting the battered bowl, he could make the five Splinters change their faces, whilst his remained frozen. Aloof.

Splinter liked this. He could imagine the warped faces talking; they spoke of power. *His* power. He could imagine other faces, other people, under his control, just like the reflections. All it took was the ruthless brilliance to seize the opportunities. And, undoubtedly, this was a time of limitless opportunities.

But right now, Splinter had to focus on practicalities. He fought back the quickening flicker of ambition that clenched his chest and tucked the silver faces inside his coat.

It was time to track down the Traitor.

However, before he began, and to herald his first great act of ruthless brilliance, Splinter allowed himself to kneel on the reaching. He lowered his face until it streamed into eternity and he said, 'I'm coming for you, Lemuel.' And then, at the thought of his voice flowing through time, with every universe listening, he whispered, 'The King of Rats is coming for you.'

CHAPTER 8

With a loud click, the button was pressed and the tape started to turn.

'My name is Detective Reeves and also present is Detective Allan. The time is 10.05pm and this interview is being conducted in an interview room at Station 28. Also present is . . .' Detective Reeves nodded at Chess to indicate she should introduce herself to the tape. Chess's arms remained crossed in front of her chest and she looked at her legs which were stretched out, under the table.

Detective Allan huffed and rolled his eyes and Reeves continued. 'Also present is Chess Tuesday. Chess, you are being interviewed for an offence of murder. You don't have to answer our questions but it would be better for you if you did.'

'Saying nothing looks as dodgy as hell,' warned Allan.

'Unless you've got a good reason to keep quiet,' added Reeves encouragingly. 'This tape machine records everything that's said in here, so nobody can argue about it later. Chess, you're only eleven. Are you sure you don't want a solicitor?'

Chess sniffed at his mistake. 'I don't need one,' she grouched, still looking at her feet.

'It speaks,' muttered Allan, who was bigger than Reeves and whose corpulent frame perched uneasily on the small wooden chair. He shifted position constantly, with a rustling of his quilted parka, inadvertently knocking against Reeves, who was much slighter in build with a smart suit under his waterproof jacket and a keen flush in his face.

Chess knew the score; the bad-tempered, sour old crasher and the sharp new one. She knew the rules; she knew what they could do to her and what they couldn't. She knew that there was a button under the table where the detectives sat which activated a panic alarm. Sometimes, when the crashers had her like this, she'd reach under the table with her leg and press the button with her big toe. You couldn't hear the alarm ring in the interview room but more crashers would burst in and everyone would look at each other, startled, and then look at her. But they couldn't do anything because she was too young.

She knew that right now, there was no point saying anything because the crashers would never believe her. The only thing that mattered was getting out of this place. She needed to get out so that she could visit Lemuel, to see what information he had about the man called Crazy Boris, and what he could tell her about CREX. Lemuel's proximity to the CREX tower unnerved her, but Crazy Boris seemed to be the key to discovering about herself, so she had no alternative. And she needed to get back to Anna and Pacer and the other street rats, to find the cerebral torus; to destroy it.

But also, she had to get out because as long as she was stuck here, she was helpless. *They'd* get her. She hadn't touched Dr Lache, but it was no accident that she was sitting opposite two policemen who were accusing her of murder. However, she'd done nothing wrong. Once the crashers had checked out all the details, they'd have to let her go. So, there was no need to say anything.

Reeves opened a brown manila envelope and pulled out a glossy sheaf of black and white photographs. They flopped noisily in his hand. He placed each one on the table as if dealing cards, positioning them so that they were upside down for him and Allan, but the right way round for Chess. Chess smelt the ester haze of the photographic ink.

There were five photographs. The first two were shots of Dr Lache's jeep, pulled up by a wooded verge. The next three were taken from different angles inside the jeep and showed a body sprawled over the steering wheel. Chess recognized Dr Lache's neat clothes and the hair gathered in a prim bun. Across the dashboard was blood, spattered like the spray from a burst can of pop.

'CCTV from the underground parking at the Cones shows that you were the only person who could have been with the victim at the time of death.' Reeves spoke softly, almost regretfully.

'We've recovered the handgun used to shoot the doctor,' added Allan, more matter of fact. 'Your prints are on the grip, Miss Tuesday. Any chance of you telling us why?'

This was far worse than Chess had imagined. Being accused was one thing, but here was evidence that would nail her. She'd been set up, to make it look as if she'd killed

Dr Lache. There was no way the crashers would just send her on her way after questioning now. Whatever the Twisted Symmetry were doing, they had her cornered.

Chess looked up at the crashers. They looked back. It didn't feel like they were working for the enemy, but you could never be sure. She couldn't be sure what to tell them; whether they would believe her; whether it would be safe.

Trust no one.

Chess said the only thing she could say, 'I didn't do it.'

Allan breathed in through his nose and then snorted, like a bull. 'That's not what the evidence says.'

'I didn't,' repeated Chess, angry with herself for sounding like she was pleading. 'I just didn't.'

'We've looked at your record, Chess.' Reeves was coaxing, almost friendly. 'We know this isn't your thing. Stealing's what you do mostly, isn't it?'

Even with the ice fear that the Symmetry were behind this, Chess was a street rat; she'd never admit *anything* to a crasher.

Reeves sighed, frustrated. But not angry. Not for the first time, Chess had the strongest sense that he was sorry for her, maybe even worried. That really frightened her. Why should a crasher be worried for a street rat?

Reeves looked to Allan, the senior crasher, and Allan did something that didn't fit with him being bad-tempered or sour. He switched off the tape machine. Then, he pushed the photographs to one side and leant across the table to take hold of Chess's shoulder gently.

'Listen, love, you've got to tell us what happened, OK? I've been doing this job for too long and I've bagged dozens of killers and you don't look much of a killer, although that doesn't mean you aren't one. But you've got to tell us what happened.'

'Nothing happened. No murder. I didn't *touch* her.'

From the other side of the barred window, Chess heard noises that made her heart lurch. Engines; motorbike engines. Two of them. Rumbling and then choking into silence. Then boots, crunching over stone.

Chess's eyes flicked to the window; black uniforms, silver death's-head badges, the neon street lighting glinting off a heavy case.

'No,' she whispered. 'Not them.'

Reeves was standing now, knuckles on the table, leaning towards her. 'You have to tell us, Chess. It's the only way we can help you.'

'Listen, Miss Tuesday,' said Allan, letting go of her shoulders. 'I hate hunters. They're animals. But unless you tell us what happened, we have orders to let them take over the interrogation.'

What was in the case the hunter had been carrying?

Allan rubbed his face, wearily. 'I don't know why they have the authority,' he muttered.

I do, thought Chess, realizing that she knew so much more about how the world *really* worked than either of the detectives. And she realized something else; that the crashers were a bit like science. Lemuel had once told her that there was good science and bad science. Maybe that was how it was with crashers. To street rats, crashers were automatically bad, but perhaps it wasn't as straightforward as that. Perhaps there were bad ones *and* good ones, but the problem was always the same: how to tell which was good and which was bad.

'Aren't you listening to us?' came Reeves's voice.

'I am.' Chess's throat felt tight and her breathing was shallow. 'But I'm frightened,' she admitted.

'Then tell us what happened,' insisted Allan, thumping a big fist on the pile of photographs.

'I can't.' Chess's hands gripped the edge of the table.

She stared at her hands and the detectives stared at the top of her head until the door to the interview room banged twice, making her jump. Someone was waiting to be let in.

'So that's it?' Allan spoke tersely but received no answer.

Chess heard him and Reeves walk to the door. 'I haven't done anything wrong,' she pleaded. 'There's people who've made this look like it was me.'

'Which people?' Allan turned, a hand already on the door. He was giving Chess a final chance.

Chess bit her lip, her fingers curled and she stabbed her palms with her nails. When she spoke, her voice wavered. 'The Twisted Symmetry.'

'The *what*?' Reeves screwed up his nose.

'The Twisted Symmetry,' repeated Chess, as unconvincingly as the first time. She pulled a bunch of chestnut knots from her face and saw Reeves scratch his head and the hopeless set of Allan's mouth.

'It's a big city, Miss Tuesday,' said Allan, 'but I've never heard of a gang called the Twisted Symmetry.'

'They're not a gang.' Chess's voice was a whisper. 'They're worse than a gang.'

Allan's eyes were blank now. Chess had had her chance

and she'd blown it. 'I don't think we can help you, Miss Tuesday. I'm sorry.'

The detectives left the room, and for the first time in her life, Chess backed away from an open prison door.

The hunters marched in, jackboots cracking on the floor. Both big. Both in dark glasses. One male, with curly, red hair and the other female with a blonde ponytail and holding a large, hard-shelled case.

The hunter with the case heeled the door shut with a slam, dropped the case and headed straight for Chess. The other came round the opposite side of the table, smashing the tape machine with his fist as he did so.

'Hear no evil,' he scoffed.

They rammed Chess against the far wall and she choked as the air burst from her lungs. Ponytail pulled a short skewer from a belt pouch. Chess could see it although the gloved fist that gripped her chin blocked most of her view.

'No!' she shouted, but before she could scream again, something jabbed her sharp in the neck and her throat went numb. Now, when she tried to shout, all she could do was squeak, hoarsely.

'Paralyzed your voice box, darling,' crooned the female hunter, with her face close against Chess's. A hot smell of dog made her gag. 'Got to keep you quiet; we don't want any interruptions.' The hunter lifted the corner of her mouth to display a row of gleaming canines, sheathed neatly against one another.

A shape shifter. Dog Troopers were a jigsaw of dog and human and some of them could change entirely into human form, or dog. That was how the Twisted Symmetry infiltrated the hunters, although human hunters required little encouragement by the Symmetry; their appetite for tracking and punishing street rats was naturally ravenous.

Whilst Red kept a grip on Chess, Ponytail strode back to the case. It was grey, hard and flat-sided. A blue light flashed on the top, near to the handle. A black-gloved finger pressed a button by the light and it started to flash green. After a moment, tendrils of smoke began to issue from where the two halves of the case met, rolling down its sides and onto the floor.

'Activated.' Ponytail spoke brusquely. 'Thirty seconds and it will be ready.'

Chess was propelled forwards, Red grabbing the back of her leather jacket and frogmarching her across the room and onto one of the wooden chairs where the detectives had been sitting. There was a ratchet and a click and the familiar sensation of handcuffs closing on her wrists, and her arms were bound around the back. Her shoulders began to burn immediately. Close behind her was the table and facing her was the door. On her right, a leg's length away, was the smoking case.

Chess's throat still felt as if it had been packed with ice and when she tried to shout for help, the only sound to escape was a whimper. She pulled against the chair but her arms were held fast and she realized that all she would achieve would be to end up on the floor, still fastened to the chair, which would be worse even than this. But this was bad; like this, the hunters could do whatever they wanted.

Vapour clouded the floor and then dispersed into nothing as it drifted away. Chess was reminded of the way in which

Ethel's jewellery box smoked with ether from the vortex. Then, with a fresh surge of panic, she realized what the large case actually was.

Ponytail noticed Chess's eyes widen. 'Perhaps you know what we're going to do with you already? You know what a portable vortex is?' The hunter cupped Chess's chin to make her look up. 'Believe me, this is a kindness. It is the most efficient method of transportation. Cooperate and it will be swift and painless; until the warps take charge of you on the other side.'

Chess didn't want to listen; she had to escape. Remembering what she had done with her hand at Anna's house, she tried to relax. She imagined her left hand sliding free of the handcuff. But her heart was thumping and her muscles were trembling and relaxing was impossible. The cuff remained hard around her wrist.

A click came from the lock on the case. 'It's ready,' said Ponytail.

Red was kneeling by Chess's feet. He opened the case so that both halves lay flat on the floor, joined at the hinges. The vapours spumed up from the near half and a silver glow lit the underside of the hunter's lantern jaw.

Desperate to do something, Chess lashed out with a foot. It was a good kick, right under the hunter's chin. He wheeled backwards, one arm plunging up to the shoulder into the yawning case, vanishing impossibly beyond the level of the floor. When he heaved himself up, a trickle of blood zigzagged from the corner of his mouth and down his lower jaw.

He came for Chess. 'You little . . .'

'No,' ordered Ponytail, sharp as a whip crack. Red stopped.

'No unnecessary damage, remember? We are to deliver the girl to the warps unharmed.'

All colour had drained from Red's face except for the livid streak of blood. He pulled the stun stick from his belt and held it towards Chess like a wand.

'I'm going to lift you from the chair and you're going in there.' He pointed at the portal to the vortex with his free hand. 'Any more messing about . . .' and he levelled the stun stick at her. 'Either way,' he promised, 'I'm going to enjoy this.'

CHAPTER 9

It was as she reared back in the chair and the upper part of her arm hit the table that Chess realized there was a way out of this. She repeated the movement, rocking the chair so that it tilted forwards. As it did so, and her hands rose behind her back, her fingers scrabbled frantically along the under-surface of the table. She thought she'd never find what she wanted but then she felt the plastic button of the panic alarm and she pressed it.

The chair rocked back again.

The stun stick hummed, at the edge of her vision. Red licked his bloodstained lip as he prepared to lift her.

'Don't make this difficult,' warned Ponytail, holding down the back of the chair.

The door to the interview room slammed wide open.

Detectives Allan and Reeves saw the girl handcuffed to the chair (contrary to regulations), the stun stick poised to strike her defenceless body (contrary to regulations), and the open suitcase, smoking (contrary to what a suitcase should do). They saw the streak of blood on the hunter's face and the terror on the face of the girl.

'What the hell are you doing?' yelled Allan.

'You have orders not to enter,' stated Ponytail.

'And those orders don't apply when the panic alarm rings,' fired Allan. 'Put that thing down,' he commanded Red.

Red looked to Ponytail. 'You have no authority over us,' she said. The stun stick remained activated, inches from Chess's body. The hunter allowed herself a sparse smile. 'You know the rules, Detective. Rules are rules.'

Allan said something to Reeves who withdrew, hurriedly, with a swishing of his waterproof jacket.

'You can go now.' Ponytail dismissed the big detective with a curt jerk of her chin. 'The girl is our business. We are grateful for your concern.'

Chess tried to talk but the only sound she could make was a mute gagging. Allan *had* to stay. She couldn't be left with hunters.

Allan's face twisted. 'What have you done to her?'

'Administered a drug to keep her quiet,' explained Ponytail.

Allan shook his head with a wobble of his heavy jowls. 'In here, we're meant to get them talking, not shut them up.' He glowered at the hunter.

Reeves was at the door. He handed something to Allan.

'Go,' ordered Ponytail.

'Sure,' said Allan. Chess shook her head, desperate. 'But, before I leave, I'd like you to do something for me.'

'What?' Both hunters were looking at him.

'Smile!' said the detective, lifting a small black box. 'For the camera.'

There was a click and a flash. Allan handed the camera to Reeves. 'Store the image,' he said. Reeves left the room.

'No smiles?' asked Allan, turning to the shark-faced hunters. 'Never mind.' He smiled. 'I'll tell you what. You put your toy down, and you pack away your case and I don't put a picture of two goons tormenting a child on the front page of every newspaper, in time for tomorrow morning's breakfast.'

'You are on dangerous ground, Detective,' simmered Ponytail.

Please, please, please don't give in to them, begged Chess, grunting.

'So are you,' warned Allan. 'Newspapers? *Publicity?*'

'Nobody cares about street rats.' Red still had the stun stick ready.

'Nobody likes hunters all that much,' replied Allan. He pulled an expression of regret and whispered, 'Sorry to break the news, big fella. Now put it down.'

'Put it down,' said Ponytail.

'And get her talking.' When the hunters didn't respond, Allan said, 'I know you freaks love secrecy. The public don't know how sick you really are. But I can change that. Reeves,' he barked, 'in five minutes, I want that photo sent to every editor in this city, with my compliments.'

With a growl that Chess knew was not entirely human, Ponytail took a small plastic vial from a belt pouch, broke off the top, and drew its contents into a tiny syringe from the same pouch. She jabbed the needle into the side of Chess's neck before she had time to flinch.

The numbness in her throat was flooded with a burning that spread to her face and deep into her chest. She coughed loudly.

'Good,' said Allan. 'That's better.' Then he saw Reeves who was back in the doorway, mouth open like a fish. 'There's a lot of strangeness in the world, Reeves. We don't get the full picture. Our job is to throw up a cordon and clear up the mess; make sure the public don't get spooked. It happens, from time to time.'

'She's still under arrest. For murder.' The female hunter pointed at Chess. 'You're going nowhere, darling.'

Chess needed to speak but her throat was thick with rubbish. She coughed like a gatling gun.

'I've made a few enquiries whilst you've been busy, officer,' Allan said. 'Did you know, I can't trace Dr Lache's corpse? No record in the city morgue. No record anywhere.' He shrugged his wrestler's shoulders. 'Strange, hey?'

'There's photographic evidence,' retorted Ponytail, 'and fingerprints. There's no escaping fingerprint evidence.'

'Which hand? Which hand were the prints from?' spluttered Chess.

The crashers had told her that the handgun found at the scene had her prints on the grip. It would have been easy for the Twisted Symmetry to set her up because her fingerprints were stored in police data and had been for years. But what the Symmetry wouldn't have known was that after her right hand had been maimed on Surapoor, the Committee had given her a new one. Ethel had said that it wouldn't bleed, it wouldn't be hurt by cold or normal fire and that its fingerprints were different.

Detective Allan scowled. 'Your right hand, if that makes any difference.'

Chess felt weak with relief. 'They're not my prints.'

'Nice try, Miss Tuesday,' said Detective Allan, 'but I've scanned the prints from the gun and they match your records.'

'They're wrong. The records are wrong,' insisted Chess. 'Check my prints, now. My *true* prints,' and she pulled at the handcuffs.

More slowly than was necessary, Red unlocked the cuffs. Chess snatched her hands away before either of the hunters could touch her skin; she hadn't forgotten how the Inspector had tagged her, months ago.

The familiar ink pad was brought to where she sat and the prints of her right hand were taken.

For an uncomfortable two minutes, Reeves, the hunters and Chess waited in silence. When he returned, Allan was struggling to mask a curl of triumph at the corner of his mouth.

'She's right,' he announced. 'Don't ask me how we have the wrong prints on record, but the prints on the gun don't match the prints on Miss Tuesday's hand.'

The plastic syringe snapped in Ponytail's gloved fist. Her jaw clenched and she growled in a way that made Reeves shuffle nervously.

'No prints, no evidence.' Allan eyeballed Ponytail.

'We want her,' hissed the hunter.

'You can't have her,' said Allan slowly. 'There's insufficient evidence. Surely you know the rules, officer? Like you said, rules are rules.' He looked across to Chess. 'You're free to go,

Miss Tuesday. Sorry about the inconvenience.'

Chess was unaccustomed to apologies from crashers. She blinked dumbly, wondering whether he might change his mind. But he stood away from the door.

'Thanks,' she mumbled.

'Just following the rules.' Allan turned to face the hunters. 'You two can stay here until you've tidied up your mess and the girl is off the premises.'

'Giving her a head start?' asked Ponytail.

Detective Allan thrust his hands into the pockets of his parka and sniffed in a satisfied way. 'Just doing my job,' he said.

The female hunter walked to the door. She removed her glasses and looked directly at Chess so that only Chess could see the manic-yellow eyes and the needling pupils. 'We are listening. We are watching. Always. We will find you, wherever you go. This was your chance to come easily, darling. From now on, damage is necessary.'

Chess walked.

Out in the chilly darkness, she didn't run; not at first. First there was a job to do. A swift search in an alley down the side of the station provided her with a flat piece of stone. It was so cold it made her fingers tingle. Breath haloing her head, Chess returned to the front of the station. She could see the meagre light leaking from the interview room and the hunters occupied with their equipment. Satisfied that nobody was watching, she knelt by the rear wheel of the first motorbike, jammed the stone between the chrome and the brake cables and levered it as violently as she was able. With a wrench and a snap, she broke the cables. She repeated the operation with the other bike and then, as a final measure, she tucked the ragged cables out of sight, concealing the damage she had done. Maybe, when the hunters next slammed on their brakes, they would be hurt. Badly hurt. She liked that thought.

'You don't know what you're dealing with,' she whispered as a frost-bladed wind dragged her hair across her face. Then she buttoned the leather jacket and sprinted into the night.

'Lemuel! Lemuel!' Chess banged her fist against the door marked SKY SUITE 8. She was trying not to shout too loudly. 'Lemuel!'

It had been easy to get into the tower. At three in the morning there were plenty of drunken jacks who were over-friendly and under-cautious. Hang about the entrance, get chatting, wander in, lose the joker who'd let her in and slink to the lifts. Sometimes, it was hard to know how jacks got anything right. Then again, all of them wore shoes.

Chess kicked the door with her trainer. She was about to kick it harder when a triangular film of light wavered outwards from a pinpoint aperture in the centre of the door. Quivering, the base of the triangle extended up and down until it spanned her length. She stood still in the knowledge that this must be a body scanner. Lemuel would be observing who was kicking at his door. The light vanished and the door swung open a couple of inches.

Chess pushed the wood with her fingertips and entered. The apartment was filled with the alembic, electronic, cybernetic entrails of the warp's experiments, as it had been before. Opposite her, behind a long, central work bench, stood Lemuel Sprazkin. He was wearing the black frock-coat, criss-crossed with narrow, metal cooling strips, that Chess knew was a brain-enhancing computer. In front of him, lying on a wire rack was a cheese-green rubber glove. In one hand he held a long electrode and in the other ... Chess couldn't see the other hand; he had tucked it into the folds of his coat. His eyes were venomous.

'You're late,' he spat.

'I'm sorry,' said Chess, going no further into the room. The light was bright and it reflected off the stacks of glassware and the sprawl of cabling.

Lemuel's slanting, pale-grey eyes darted as if to look behind her. 'You said you'd come yesterday.'

'I got held up. Sorry.' Chess picked up a beaker that was standing on the low table, next to the pad of the tenebrous lamp. She swirled the pink liquid within and sniffed, trying not to show how unnerved she was by Lemuel's maleficent glare. After what had happened when she had last been here, Chess needed Lemuel to see that she was in control now.

'Are you on your own?' The nostrils of his arched, thin nose spread minutely as he tasted the air.

'As far as I know,' Chess assured him.

'As far as you know?' Lemuel squeaked back. 'As far as you know!' His long, white face split open and he tilted back his head as he cackled. Then the dark lips snapped shut and he leant forwards. Light flashed on the top of his cranium. 'You know *nothing*,' he sneered. His thin tongue licked a fleck of spittle from the corner of his mouth. Chess noticed how it was purple-dark, like a tongue stained with berry juice.

'That's why I'm here. You were going to help me find things out.'

'You were meant to come back.' Lemuel had dropped the electrode and begun to move around the side of the long bench. 'You were meant to come back and you didn't come back.' He pointed at her as he drew closer. 'But someone's been. Someone's been spying on me. I know it.'

'I'm sorry. OK?' Chess didn't know what Lemuel was talking about, and she didn't like the way he was behaving. Lemuel was always different from other people, which wasn't surprising because he was a warp. But now, Lemuel seemed different from Lemuel. She hadn't seen him behave like this before. The way he was smelling his way towards her was how the Symmetry's current primary warp, Petryx Ark-turi, had sniffed her way close when Chess and her brothers had been hiding in the Riverside Prison.

Chess knew that warps were part of the Twisted Symmetry. They fed off children just like the rest of the Symmetry. Their hunger was cruel. She had to be very careful. But she had to get Lemuel to help her; she needed to find out about Crazy Boris and she needed to find out about CREX. And then, she needed to get out; get away from Lemuel and back to the others. But she knew she mustn't show what a hurry she was in; Lemuel wouldn't like that. And she knew she mustn't show how frightened she was; he would like that too much.

'Two hundred years they've been looking for me. Have they found me now? Have they? Have they put a spook on me?' Laughter rattled. 'Have you led them to me, Chess?' He sprang forwards and pawed the lapels of her leather jacket with a hand. Then, his eyes half-fogged. 'You smell . . . fresh.'

Chess pushed him away. She looked across at the drill which he stuck in his brain to make himself be good; when he wanted to be good. 'Why haven't you been having your treatment?' She tried not to sound angry or frightened. You need his help, she told herself. But show no fear.

'Things change,' said Lemuel with a wave of his left hand. His right remained inside his frock-coat. He turned his back to her as he looked at the drill. Chess observed the minute cogs and flywheels that whirred silently inside his brain. 'They are coming for me. Somehow they have found me; someone has been watching. I am no longer safe. So, I must unsheathe my wits and take precautions. When I wanted to be good, I had to be very, very good. But now I am in danger, I must let myself be a little bit bad.' He turned and smiled at her.

'What have you done to your hand?' Chess had noticed how Lemuel's right hand had remained hidden inside his frock-coat throughout.

With his left hand, Lemuel Sprazkin pointed to the workbench, to the rubbery lump on the wire rack that Chess had thought was a glove. 'I'm taking precautions,' he explained, a little drunkenly. Then, he held up the stump of his right wrist to display where the thing on the rack had come from. Chess's eyes widened. All questions about CREX and Crazy Boris were dispelled by the raw limb.

'I'm making a grip-switch.' He seemed very pleased with his handiwork. 'Good for catching intruders; for whatever it is that's sneaking up on me. Come and look.' He gavotted to the bench.

Curiosity killed the cat, warned a voice inside Chess's head. Or the rat. But, satisfied that nothing stood between her and the way out, she stepped over a slack loop of cables and approached the hand. Close up, she could see that a pair of wires trailed from the severed wrist to the terminals of a box battery.

'Go on,' invited Lemuel. 'Have a touch.'

Chess shook her head.

'Use this.' He handed her a Perspex probe, as long as a pencil.

Chess took the probe and, very slowly, moved it close to the open palm. Nothing happened. Her large, brown eyes looked across to Lemuel's grey ones. He nodded encouragingly. 'Go on.'

She let the short rod drop to the palm. In the same heartbeat, the dead fingers with their black nails, twitched up and closed on the Perspex, snapping it. Chess managed not to gasp but she did jump back.

'Clever, eh?' Lemuel fluttered his lashes with false modesty. 'I just have to place it where I think it will catch sneaky fingers.'

'Horrible,' said Chess. 'And cruel.'

'Cruel?'

'Cruel to *you*.'

'How very interesting,' he purred, 'but not really. A new hand is easy to come by. You know that, Chess. And this is a time for desperate measures.'

'Did it hurt?'

'It was nothing,' Lemuel waved the fingers of his left hand in the air, 'compared with what the Symmetry will do when they get me.' He sighed and then leered at Chess. 'But at least, for now, I have got *you* to raise my spirits.'

'Nobody has "got" me.'

Lemuel glided closer. His left hand moved towards her hair.

The slap was as sharp as a gun crack and Lemuel reeled to one side. Whatever he was, he was no preactive. Chess lowered her hand as Lemuel rubbed his cheek.

'Ouch,' he complained. 'But, thank you. That was necessary. The shock!' he tittered. 'It's fairly brought me to my senses. Or one half of me, at least.' Then he smiled ruefully. 'The nice half.'

Chess rubbed her palm which was stinging. 'Perhaps you can be good without that thing,' she said, with a nod at the drill.

'Perhaps,' considered Lemuel, 'but do we both want to stay together long enough to find out? I rather think not. I'll be all right for a little while, long enough to give you what you've come for. But, I feel somewhat wobbly in my passions, if you see what I mean.' He laughed hollowly. 'If I start to slide, if I can't keep inside the me that's trying to get out, you must go. Whatever I do, whatever I say, get out.'

Chess nodded.

'I have two items for you.' Lemuel had returned to the workbench. He pulled open a drawer and his good hand scrabbled within. Chess looked askance at the dead hand lying on the rack. Now was the time to dig for information, whilst Lemuel was distracted. Before her nerve broke.

'What's the CREX Corporation?' she asked.

'It's taken you a remarkably long time to ask me about that.' There was shuffling of papers and a rattling of cylindrical objects from within the drawer.

Chess said nothing. Sometimes, leaving a silence made other people talk; particularly people who liked to talk.

Lemuel grunted as he burrowed deeper. 'Calyx Research and Exploration. C.R.E.X. From the earthly perspective, it is a vast and wealthy commercial enterprise; a global mining and pharmaceuticals business. Rocks and pox, you might say.' He looked up with a cascading giggle. 'That's rather good, isn't it?'

Chess looked back blankly.

'Oh well, suit yourself. From a *universal* perspective, CREX is a crucial limb of the Symmetry's earthly operations.'

'Not very helpful,' muttered Chess, meaning Lemuel's explanation and wishing bitterly that Anna had not used the Link-me to open a connection that might lead back to CREX. She noticed him push aside a bundle of bank notes.

'Crystal is mined in the Calyx nebula,' enlarged Lemuel, 'hence *Calyx* Research and Exploration, although there is no commercial connection between your planet and the amarantium mines. Behind its respectable front, the Symmetry use CREX to promote activities that assist in increasing the sum total of pain and suffering which humans have such a capacity for inflicting upon themselves in the first place: organized crime, drugs, revolution. You know the sort of thing.'

'For energy,' suggested Chess. 'Energy from pain?'

'Don't start me off,' warned Lemuel, with a dangerous little smile.

Chess picked up a fountain pen that Lemuel had rested on the bench top. She unscrewed the cap. 'Who's Dr Oriana Lache?'

'Have you met her?'

Chess nodded.

'Pretty, isn't she?'

'Pretty weird,' muttered Chess.

'Jealousy, jealousy,' tutted Lemuel. 'CREX is administered by a board of twelve directors. Business types. Professionals. Some are even admired for their charity work.'

'I bet Dr Lache isn't.'

Lemuel laughed. 'Dr Lache is regarded as nothing less than an angel. Don't you read the papers?'

'No,' grunted Chess. It wasn't a kind question; Lemuel knew she couldn't read.

'We call the twelve directors the Crystal Priests,' said Lemuel.

'*We?*' Chess dabbed an ink spot on the pad of her thumb with the pen.

'The Symmetry, I mean.' A nervous chuckle from Lemuel. 'Twelve Crystal Priests to oversee the Symmetry's earthly work.'

'There's twelve of everything,' observed Chess. 'Twelve Crystal Priests, twelve Blood Sentinels.'

'Equals and opposites,' nodded Lemuel.

'And twelve suns,' mused Chess, remembering what Balthazar had told her: *Where the twelve suns are one, that is where you will find the Eternal.*

'No,' corrected Lemuel. 'There are an infinite number of suns, but,' and he spoke with a hungry urgency, 'there are only twelve that matter.'

'They tried to say I murdered Dr Lache.'

'Did you?'

'No. I was set up. And she isn't dead; there wasn't even a body.'

'It is a time for games and struggles; for fugues and subterfuges. Ha ha!' he tinkled. 'I like that; fugues and subterfuges. I am on top form today.' He rocked the drawer shut. 'Drawers are so much easier with two hands,' he grumbled. 'Behrens's destruction has caused an aftershock that heralds change; change within the Symmetry. Great instability. And perhaps, for some, a great opportunity.' The corners of his long lips curled up to his inclined, tear-drop eyes. 'Chess, you have created a vacancy in the Inquisitor line of work.'

He waved a crumpled piece of paper over the bench. 'Found it.' He read aloud, "Boris Sherevsky, 18 Mendoza Row".'

'Where the grease-jacks live.' Chess dropped the pen and stuck out her hand. 'I'll have the paper. I'm not stupid.'

'I never said you were, but "thank you" would be nice.'

'Thank you.' Chess snatched the paper, screwed it into a chunk and pushed it into her jeans pocket. 'Why are you here then, so close to CREX, if you want to hide from the Symmetry?'

'I would have thought that was obvious.'

'I would have thought it was stupid,' retorted Chess.

'People don't see what they don't expect to see.'

'That's what Ethel's always saying.' Chess scowled.

'Then she and I agree on that at least.' Lemuel continued. 'Who would think that Lemuel Sprazkin, the Traitor, would be *here*, right under the noses of his friends?' He coughed. 'I mean, of course, his former friends. And also,' lowering his voice now, 'above this place there is a way out.' He pointed a black-nailed finger upwards.

'In your ceiling?' Chess eyed the ceiling panels skeptically.

'No, silly. Higher. Above the Cones.' Lemuel winked in a way that made Chess note the quickest way out. 'Why did CREX want to build the Cones here? What was so special about this location?' Lemuel was talking very quietly. 'Up there, in the space above the radio masts is a gap, a dimensional hole; like in a portable vortex, but much larger, hundreds of metres wide. Not visible to humans, but a gap that lets things in and lets things out. A sink hole. And, for me, an emergency exit, if necessary.'

'How?' asked Chess. 'How do you go through it?'

'You just climb up a radio mast and step into space.'

Chess imagined shinning up one of the javelin-thin spires and then jettisoning herself into nothingness. Even for a street rat, it was a gut-lurching prospect.

'It's a good place to hide,' explained Lemuel, with a devious glint in his eyes.

'There was something else you had for me.' Chess spoke quickly, sensing it was time to leave.

'There's no hurry,' Lemuel assured her.

'Anna's waiting for me,' lied Chess.

'Anna?'

'Anna Ledward. She's my friend.' Chess meant to sound defiant, as if invoking the word 'friend' might be a charm that would protect her.

'A friend?' Lemuel rolled the word around his mouth as if tasting it. Already, Chess was regretting mentioning Anna's name to Lemuel. But now, she didn't want him to think she was alone.

'Does she know you're here? With me?'

'Yes. She can see everything I do,' boasted Chess. 'Apart from in here.'

'She has remarkable eyesight, your Anna.'

'She's got a Link-me and she can hack into the CCTV in the Cones, so if I don't . . .'

'That is very foolish, Chess. Very, very foolish.' Lemuel sat on the chaise longue. He stroked a loose brocade fringe with a fingertip. 'Let me give you a piece of advice. I touch this fabric, see?' Chess nodded. 'But the fabric touches back. Do you understand? Whatever I see or taste or hear, the universe is seeing and tasting and hearing back. When you open up secrets with something like a Link-me, it is *you* that is opened up in return. When you sense the universe, the universe senses back. And where the universe senses, so will the Symmetry.'

'Like the skulk rack.' Chess mouthed the words, barely audible.

'I have a gift for you,' announced Lemuel, taking a cardboard carton the size of a small box of sweets, from under the chaise. He opened the lid and licked his lips. 'It is very pretty. I made it for you.' His eyes sparkled over the top of the box. 'It will take you to your mother.'

'Let me see.' Chess leant forwards although her feet remained rooted.

'In another life,' contemplated Lemuel, 'I would take up fishing.' A scherzo of laughter made Chess jump. 'I think I'd have the knack, don't you?'

'I don't like fish.'

'You are hardly characterized by the catholicity of your tastes, are you?' Without waiting for a reply, he held up a bracelet for Chess to see. She came closer, struck by the obvious value of the item.

'It looks very beautiful,' she admitted.

The milky glass hoop was full of swirls like a creamy gas, and tinged with purple. Skin-side it was plated with gold and it fastened by a gold catch and a delicate, golden chain.

'As you know,' confessed Lemuel, 'when they first brought you to me, I took a speck more of your blood that I should have. But it wasn't for myself, although the call of that precious fluid was positively siren-like. I was thinking of you.' He sighed heavily. 'Always thinking of you. I took the blood and locked it within this ornate device.'

Chess studied the bracelet, captivated by the ethereal patterns within the glass body.

'It is a parallax bangle,' explained Lemuel. 'A thing of beauty, yes, but also a thing of extraordinary utility.' Breathing heavily, he slipped to his knees and closer to Chess's face. 'If the blood in your body mixes with your blood in the bangle, you will travel backwards in time. Because of the amarantium in your blood, this is possible. And the clever thing is, that if you mix the blood in the appropriate geographical location, you will travel back to when you were last at that place. An extraordinary triangulation of now, then and there.'

'How does that help me find my mother?' Chess drew away from Lemuel's face, although her gaze remained fixed on the bangle. She knew she should go.

'Sherevsky is the key to that.'

'You don't know?'

'Mevrad did not reveal that detail to me. I realize, now, that she has never really trusted me.' He pursed his lips as if to contain the tongue that was trying to escape. 'Perhaps she was right.'

'How does it work?' Chess needed that information before she could leave.

'Hold it,' ordered Lemuel. Chess did so, discomforted at the unexpected warmth of the glass body. 'See this catch, where it fastens?' Chess nodded at where Lemuel's fingers pinched a minute golden cusp. The fingers twisted. All around the inside surface of the bangle, needle-thin points projected.

'These will pierce the skin of your wrist. Pull this catch round,' he indicated a circular movement from the top to the underside of the bangle, 'and the blood in here will mix with the blood in there,' and he prodded Chess's arm. 'And you will travel.' He turned the cusp back and the needle teeth retracted. 'Its effect will last only minutes.'

Chess slipped her left hand through the open bracelet and then fastened it round her thin wrist. It was warm and tight.

'Will it break, by accident?' She started to retreat from Lemuel, slowly, to make it look as if she wasn't really edging away.

'It is much tougher than it looks.' His eyes traversed from her crown to her feet. 'As are many precious things.'

'I'm going.'

'Don't.' He swung up to her from the chaise longue. That was how it felt to Chess.

'Get off,' she demanded as his left hand clutched at her arm.

'I want you to stay, a little longer,' insisted Lemuel.

'You're hurting my wrist.' Chess spoke as calmly as she was able, watching the struggle behind Lemuel's eyes. I am sorry, they said. But at the same time they were saying something else: I am a warp; I need to feed.

'I need money.' Chess stopped pulling away. 'To get to Mendoza Row.'

'Of course you do,' smiled Lemuel, dropping her wrist and heading for the work bench. 'I suppose I can have the pleasure of your company whilst I look for it? I might have guessed you would smell the notes in my drawer. All of us sniff out the things we most desire.' He chuckled and then he heard the click of the door.

When he turned, rage pinched his eyes; but only for a moment. Then, Lemuel Sprazkin smiled bitterly at the space where Chess had been standing.

'Clever girl,' he whispered.

CHAPTER 10

It was bright and the brisk chill of the air stung Chess's sinuses like a punch to the nose. Huddled under the cardboard boxes and wraps of polythene, deep inside the industrial bin where she had hidden to sleep, Chess knew that something had changed. She surfaced through layers of rubbish until her fingers touched metal. Then she slid back the curved tin lid and looked out, blinking at what had happened.

Chess liked snow. The city was simpler to look at when it was cast in black and white. Almost nothing escaped the pure gleam of the winter sun. The crook-backed heaps of rubbish that lined the alleyway were softly crusted. Fire escapes were etched and every rung carried its own, perfectly balanced finger of snow. Scooped drifts softened the feet of buildings and blotted out the gutters. Only the solitary rear windows of the cheap restaurants and one-night hotels which backed onto the alley remained untouched; hard, black, unblinking in the coruscating light.

Chess looked one way and then the other. The alley was long and narrow and traffic flashed past at either end. But between the high, snow-dusted brick walls, there was nothing to be seen. It was very quiet. She swung her legs over the lip of the bin and landed in the snow with a crunch. She made sure to pull the lid shut; to keep it dry for whoever else might need to sleep there tonight. Then she rammed her fists into her pockets and marched away.

Mendoza Row formed one side of a square, with a small garden at its centre. The shrubs and miniature willows had bent to the ground under the sudden fall of snow and were frozen still. A notice on a chain said that this was a public garden but Chess didn't think there was very much public about it. It was enclosed by a fence of icy javelins and patrolled by keepers dressed in a way that made them look like crashers. One of the keepers smiled at Chess as she kicked past and she smiled back.

The houses were tall; at least four storeys above their basements. They were built from red brick and had thick, honey-coloured steps and coping stones. There were lots of railings and some of the windows had old-fashioned, panelled shutters on their insides.

Already, the big, black slates of the roofs were wet and the eaves dripped with melting snow. Looking at the sky, Chess guessed it must have been nearly ten in the morning. She climbed the steps and pressed the buzzer on the blue door which carried a brass 18.

When the door was pulled open, she realized that she hadn't thought about what she would say so she said, 'Hello. Are you Crazy Boris?' Warm air gushed over her.

The man wore a pair of jeans, a white vest and nothing on his feet. The jeans looked old and hung baggy on his thin legs. His hair was curly and straggled to his collar bones like it had never been combed. It was a mixture of dark grey and light grey but his stubble was almost white. It made a rasping sound when he rubbed his hand across his chin.

'You must be Chess Tuesday.' His voice was deep and had a weary brogue that Chess liked immediately. His eyes were sunken in sockets that were ringed tired purple and they looked up and down the road as he leant past her.

Chess nodded, unsurprised that he knew her name. Ethel must have warned him about her visit.

'You'd better come in.' Crazy Boris took a final look outside. 'How many more have you got coming?'

'There's only me,' Chess assured him. She entered and the door thudded shut, blocking out the cold. Under her feet was a thick, cream carpet which stretched down a short hallway. On one side of the hall were two closed doors and on the other, a gloss-white staircase going up. At the far end there was a doorway full of light. A pair of chunky, brown boots sat on the floor beside her. They looked familiar.

'Shoes off,' said Crazy Boris. 'I like my carpets clean and fluffy.' But it wasn't said nastily.

'It's a very nice carpet.' Chess wiggled her bare toes on the soft pile. 'It's a very nice house,' she added, unaccustomed to genteel conversation but doing her best.

'It's a very busy house,' said Crazy Boris, '*this morning*. And I was on the verge of watering my plants; of communing with the silent brothers and sisters of the vegetative world.'

Chess liked the way the man sounded as if he was a bit puzzled by everything. But it meant also that he might not know why she was there. She sensed that just saying, 'Tell me about my mother,' might spook him, and then Crazy

Boris might not tell her anything at all. She couldn't risk getting this wrong. So Chess followed his thin, ungainly figure to the doorway, calculating how best to discover the useful information he possessed.

When she drew level with him, he placed a hand behind her shoulders, guiding her into the kitchen. 'You'd best be greeting your friends. They've been here for over an hour.'

'Yo, Chess,' said Pacer, sullen, in his black, hooded combats.

'Hi,' said Anna, subdued, in a red duffle coat, a short skirt and thick, hooped stockings.

They were sitting next to one another on a lemon-coloured sofa. Opposite them and adjoining the kitchen was a huge conservatory, radiating light and full of plants.

'How come you're here?' Chess's face was blank despite her surprise. She guessed now how Crazy Boris knew her name.

'Don't sound so pleased to see them.' Boris Sherevsky walked behind her and across to the steel work-surfaces. 'Anyone for some herbal tea? Or fruit juice?' He ignored the silence and made himself a mug of tea. Then he sat in a fan-backed wicker chair and observed his visitors through a plume of steam.

'It's Monday. Shouldn't you be at school?' Chess asked Anna, sharply.

'Burst pipe over the weekend,' replied Anna, patiently. 'School's closed for at least a week.' She looked at Chess in a way that Chess knew was meant to say that this was not a coincidence; that somebody, somewhere was making sure they were together. But Chess didn't want to be controlled by somebody, somewhere. She pursed her lips.

'Look, I'm sorry, Chess,' said Anna, and then, more firmly, 'But it wasn't my fault, OK? I didn't know.'

Chess didn't have the words to say why she wanted to hold Anna responsible for her arrest by the crashers so she scowled at the floor. That was when she saw Pacer's feet.

'Why are you wearing granny slippers?' she asked, wrestling the edges of her lips taut at the spectacle of the luxuriously tufted footwear.

'*He* made me wear them,' grumbled Pacer, with a jerk of his shaven, ebony head at the man who sat sipping herbal tea and watching them.

'Like I said,' Boris reminded them, 'I like my carpets.'

'Here.' Anna dug into her boot bag which was propped between her feet. 'A peace offering.' She held out an unopened packet of chocolate biscuits, blue eyes solemn, long, black hair framing her white face.

Chess's tummy rumbled. She didn't know when she had last eaten. It must have been when she had stayed at Anna's house. She took the biscuits and said, 'OK.'

'Wow! Wow! Not crumbs!' Crazy Boris bolted off the chair as if electrocuted. Herb tea slopped down his vest and onto his lap. 'Now look what you've made me do,' he wailed. 'I'm practically scalded.' He deposited the mug on a circular, glass-topped table and dived for a cupboard from which he produced a hand-held vacuum device.

'Biscuits,' he warned, 'are the enemies of the tidy house. You,' to Pacer, 'fetch her a plate. From over there. I'm not taking any chances.'

Bemused, Pacer did as he was told, shuffling on the shaggy slippers.

'You're not very crazy,' observed Anna, 'for someone called 'Crazy Boris'.'

'The name's stuck from the old days,' explained Crazy Boris. 'I used to take a lot of risks.' It sounded like he was scraping sandpaper as he scratched the bristles on his jaw. 'Truth is, I used to take too much of everything.' He sat down, rested the vacuum cleaner over his narrow thighs and held up the mug of herb tea. 'These days, I prefer to play it safe. Now, mind the crumbs.'

'Where d'you get that?' asked Pacer with a glint in his eye, spotting the bracelet Chess was wearing as he handed her the plate of biscuits.

'Found it.' Chess stuffed a biscuit in her mouth and chomped noisily.

'It's purgatory,' groaned Crazy Boris as the crumbs rained down.

Chess continued to crunch. 'How come you're here?'

'Lemuel Sprazkin contacted me.' Anna watched Chess's jaws freeze. 'On the Link-me. Don't ask me how he knew who I was. He told me to tell you he was sorry. Very sorry.'

Chess swallowed like she was swallowing sawdust. Anna continued, 'He said you'd be here and you'd need help.'

'Fury came for me,' interrupted Pacer, 'as back-up.' He stuck out his chin and glanced across at Crazy Boris, to show that he wasn't someone to mess with. Crazy Boris raised his eyebrows at the fluffy slippers.

'This Lemuel of yours sounded nice.' Anna reached for a biscuit. 'Is he OK? He said he could meet up with me some time. There wasn't a picture but he sounded funny. Friendly.'

'Stay away from Lemuel Sprazkin,' warned Chess.

Anna eyed her warily.

Chess could tell that Anna thought she was trying to keep Lemuel to herself. 'He's a warp. You know what a warp is, I told you. He'll kill you. Just stay away from him. Don't even speak to him again.'

'OK, OK.' Pacer stood between Chess and Anna. 'Chess is right, Fury. I don't know a Lemuel. Just avoid this guy.'

'Sure,' shrugged Anna. 'He's not that important; to *me*.'

Boris Sherevsky had gone to the glass door which led into the conservatory. 'Snow's melting,' he reported. 'Anyone going to tell me what you're all doing here? At *my* house.'

But before Chess could answer that question and ask questions of her own, Anna had interrupted. 'What happened? With the police?'

Are you really bothered, or just curious, Chess would have liked to say. But she knew she might need Anna before all of this was over, so she said plainly, 'It was a fit up,' which meant she had to explain what had happened with the crashers, how the hunters had nearly taken her, how Detective Allan had scared them off with a camera. She lowered her voice as she began to tell Anna and Pacer what Lemuel had told her about the CREX Corporation.

'Don't mind me,' called Crazy Boris, and then, almost dreamily, 'All this wacky stuff, it's a bit like the old days; having so much fun your mind starts seeing things your eyes don't know about.' He shook his tangled hair wistfully. 'Takes me right back.' Then he looked at Chess, thoughtfully.

'So, CREX and the Twisted Symmetry are the same, in a way.' Chess noticed the way Crazy Boris was staring at her. He began to whistle to himself.

'We *were* meant to find each other.' Anna wouldn't let Chess look away from her.

'Maybe. Where's Gemma?'

'She's OK,' Pacer reassured her.

'She was checking that the little rats . . . the little ones were warm when I was at the wharf this morning,' added Anna.

'You've been to the wharf a lot whilst I was gone?' Chess snapped a biscuit.

'You were away for less than a day,' Anna snapped back.

'Nobody minds?' Chess asked Pacer. Nobody minds a jack coming and going in our territory, was what she meant.

'Fury's cool, Chess,' replied Pacer. 'She's off-grid.'

Chess looked at Pacer as if he'd pinched her.

'What?' Pacer hunched his shoulders, perplexed.

'What's off-grid?' asked Anna.

'Not like a jack,' muttered Chess. 'Different.'

Anna smiled. 'Off-grid. I like that.'

Chess sighed. They couldn't spend all day complimenting Anna. But *she* couldn't spend all day trying to think of how to ask Crazy Boris about her mother.

'We don't have long, Chess. The brain might start at any time.'

Chess shook her head as if Anna's voice was water in her ear. 'We don't even know where it is yet,' she bridled.

'Or how to kill it,' added Pacer.

'That's easy: we turn off its gas,' said Chess. The cerebral torus was nourished by a gas that was lethal to humans. 'Kill the supply and we kill the brain. But we've got to find it first.'

'I don't know what you're planning,' interjected Crazy Boris, breaking off from whistling, 'but it doesn't sound strictly legal, and worse than that, it doesn't sound safe.' He began to whistle again.

'There's loads of the rats as will help,' said Pacer.

'Great,' mumbled Chess, listening to the tune Crazy Boris was whistling. It was a bit aimless, but it also seemed a bit familiar.

'And the Regulars are interested too. The grown-up crooks,' Pacer added in answer to Anna's questioning glance. 'The Bank gripped me down by the water last night. He'd heard that we're planning something. He'll help us, if we help him.'

'Meaning?' asked Anna.

'The Bank does money. He says that CREX will have loads of useful financial information; he can help us break into the CREX tower, if we get information for him.'

'Splinter always says not to work with the Bank,' warned Chess. 'And anyway, we don't know enough about CREX, yet; we don't even know where the brain is.' But she was only half-listening to Anna and Pacer.

Anna cleared her throat. 'I've been doing a little research,' she said, modestly, but now Chess wasn't listening at all.

'What are you staring at?' asked Crazy Boris, a long-spouted, tin watering can in hand. 'You look like you've seen the proverbial.'

'That tune you're whistling,' stammered Chess. 'I know it.'

'You and a good many others,' and Boris whistled to the end of the phrase and then sang, in a grating base, '*I am a young soldier that never done wrong.*'

'My mother used to sing it.'

'Does she have a pretty voice? It needs a sweet voice to give it soul.'

Chess thought how best to say what she felt. 'I think her voice is beautiful.' She sought words and blurted, 'I was told you can help me.'

'I was wondering when we'd come to the business of the day. And you,' pointing the spout of the watering can at Pacer's slippers which were shuffling on the floor, inches from the crumb-strewn plate, 'watch your feet.'

'You know about my mother,' insisted Chess, standing up. 'You whistle the song she sang to me, when I was a baby.'

'There's a lot of people who might whistle that song, but I doubt they all answer to the name of Mrs Tuesday.' Boris saw Chess's face sink. He put the can down. 'All right, all right. But listen, Chess, I don't think I know your mother and let's face it, you're too young to be calling me Daddy, if you see what I mean. I'm old enough to be your grandpa.'

'You don't look like a grandpa,' observed Anna.

'Thanks,' said Boris, with a big smile and a display of teeth that had seen better days. 'But the thing is, Chess, I'm not your grandpa, although,' and here, he came closer, 'there's no denying you have a look of someone I once knew.'

'But I've been told you've got information. Information about my mother.'

Boris rubbed his chin. 'Tell me this, then. Who would have given me such information?'

Lemuel had said that he had made the arrangements for Chess to meet her mother. So maybe he had given the information to Boris. 'A man with a long, white face and dark lips.' And then, just to make sure, she added, 'and maybe, also, an old lady.' Lemuel hadn't mentioned Ethel, but Chess knew that Ethel was behind everything.

'After I quit the band, I didn't get a lot of visitors,' reminisced Boris, 'but they were the strangest pair. Turned up, one night, nine years back. They asked me to look after something; said the time might come when a girl rather like yourself would come calling for it. They said nothing more about the girl or about what they had given me but the old lady whispered a name in my ear, a very special name. And it all made sense, in a crazy sort of way.' He cleared his throat. 'Pardon my quizzing you, but it's always best to be careful.'

'Trust no one,' intoned Chess, gravely.

'Yeah, well, that's putting it a bit high. Carry on like that and you'll end up with no friends.' He laughed until he saw the grim expressions on the visitors' faces. 'OK, OK, enough of the party atmosphere. Let me show you what they left. And no messing the place up.'

Chess, Pacer and Anna followed Crazy Boris up the stairs. Pacer was alert for loot but he found that whilst the tall house was well painted and lavishly carpeted, it was devoid of pocket-sized items of value.

'It's a bit big for one person, isn't it?' assessed Anna from the back, long legs traipsing up the third flight of stairs.

'It's a bit small for four,' lamented Crazy Boris, at the front.

At the top, they came to a landing where the ceiling sloped under the eaves and there was a door.

'Now, if we were in a film or a book,' announced Boris, 'I'd warn you of the terrors that lurk behind the locked door. But, I'm pleased to say the door's unlocked and there are no terrors. Only memories.'

He opened the door and walked into the room.

It was huge and it filled the whole of the space under the roof. Thick wooden beams ran between the walls and light streamed in through sloping panes overhead. The room smelt of paint and dust and the wooden floorboards were scrubbed and clean. All around the floor, propped on their stands, were electric guitars and against one wall, a row of amps and a stack of speakers.

The walls were hung with glass-cased posters announcing dates and venues and headed with the name DINOSAUR RIBCAGE in red, electric, slash lettering. In between the tour posters were framed photographs; photographs of smoking stages surrounded by tens of thousands of people, screaming and waving their arms; photographs of four men in lizard-skin waistcoats and leggings, chests naked and matted with sweat-drenched curls; photographs of one man, with hair like gorse that cascaded to his hips, a moustache like a bandit and straddling a guitar like it was a stallion. The spray from the man's shaking head and tossing mane sparkled in a neon halo.

'Of course,' said Crazy Boris, apologetically, 'this was all a long time ago.'

'When you were crazy?' enquired Anna, archly.

'Are all these your guitars?' marvelled Pacer.

'You need the right axe for the right gig. Sometimes you need a couple,' explained Boris. 'And believe me, when the Ribcage powered up, I'd bust an axe a night.'

'Hard to believe,' muttered Anna, taking off her coat and tossing it at the foot of the nearest wall.

'You're right,' agreed Boris. 'These days I get enough

excitement from busting an egg. And I'm happy with it. Rock and roll; it's great, but it's risky.' He saw Chess studying one small, framed photograph. 'Ah, I thought you'd find that one.' He stood by her side, smiling at a picture of Crazy Boris nearly forty years younger than himself, with an arm around the waist of a young woman whose solemn eyes were as dark brown as the hair which hung in a bob to her jaw. The garish reds and yellows of a Ferris wheel looked tawdry behind them.

'Beautiful, isn't she?' said Crazy Boris, tripping back in time. 'Her name was Esme.'

Anna pushed her face between Chess and Boris, looked at the photograph, looked at Chess and studied the photograph again before giving Crazy Boris a long, cool look.

'I know, I know,' he shrugged. 'It's the eyes.'

'And the rest.' Anna's hands were on her hips, her head on one side. 'It could be you, Chess. A bit older, with shorter hair. And a bit less miserable. But she's the spit.'

'Trust me,' insisted Boris, 'it's not your mother, Chess.'

'Grandmother, then?' suggested Anna.

'It can't be. Esme never had children. She never had time.'

Chess's mind swam back to the room, high in the Cones, where Lemuel lived with only the wretch for company. He had told her that he knew of at least one human who hadn't been born from the body of a woman. When she thought of his words and looked at the woman in the picture, she felt a crippling fear, a sense of being cornered and the darkness closing all around her. Terror. Then nothing.

She never had time.

'Chess?' Anna was shaking her shoulder, gently, coaxing her away from the photograph. 'Hey? What's the matter?'

'Sometimes,' said Chess, 'I see what other people feel.' The scream rooms; the pain. The photograph; the terror. All ending in darkness.

'I don't care what he says,' Anna whispered in her ear. 'You're related to her. It's obvious.'

'I bet these are worth a bit of grease.' Pacer was on the other side of the room, moving between the guitars. He'd been drawn to the bright, pearl-shot scratch plates and the glinting, chrome bridges and machineheads. His fingers stopped on a guitar with a long neck and a metallic-green scratch plate. A lead hung from it like a dead slowworm.

'In the great stable of electric guitars, that one's a mustang,' warned Boris. 'What you need is a pony. Kindly remove your hand.'

'I wasn't going to do anything,' muttered Pacer.

'All right,' complained Boris, 'but you lot are all over the place.' He dragged his fingers through his frosted-slate locks. 'So much activity, I can't keep track of you all. It's like you're going mad in here.'

'She's been looking at a photograph,' objected Anna, 'and he's touched a guitar. It's hardly going mad.'

'Yeah, well you don't know how quiet it usually is,' protested Boris, 'and those tights of yours are a public disturbance on their own.'

'Where's the stuff they gave you?' asked Chess.

'Stuff?' Crazy Boris scratched his head.

'The stuff that the old lady and the man brought.'

'Oh, that stuff. It's over here.' Boris knelt by a white floor-chest behind the door. 'I haven't moved it since the night they gave it to me.'

Anna and Chess looked over his bony shoulders as he dug into the detritus of old concert programmes, electric leads, crumpled T-shirts and loose photographs.

'Here,' he said, sticking an arm out behind him. There was an envelope in his hand. Chess took it. 'There's something else.'

Boris dug deeper. 'Got it. And I haven't got a clue what it is or what it's for.'

He was holding a cylinder. It was the size of a scroll and was striped black and white. Anna took it, tilted it one way and then the other. Inside, something slid with a clunk.

'Is it plastic?' asked Chess.

'No.' Anna rolled it in her palms. 'I don't know what it's made from. It feels pretty tough, though. I don't know how we're meant to open it.' Her hand worked at either end. 'It won't unscrew.'

She held it up to catch the light from the big windows in the roof. 'It's covered with tiny lines, like a grid.' She rubbed the tips of her fingers over the black and white surface. 'They're kind of cut into it.'

The bank of speakers whistled and then screamed, the air buckling with a shrill howl.

'Would you put it down?' Crazy Boris pulled himself up, kneecaps clicking. A loud hum came from the speakers.

Pacer put the guitar back on its stand. 'All I did was pick it up.'

'Yeah, and the rest; turning on switches and waving it about like it was on fire.' Boris turned off the power.

'It must be broke,' groused Pacer. 'That wasn't hardly

music.' His voice had an edge which meant he wasn't there for Crazy Boris to snap at.

'That was feedback, you dunce. Some time, when we're not taking a trip down memory lane, I'll show you how to make a noise that doesn't waken the dead.'

'Show me how to play the guitar?' The idea of really being able to play a guitar hit Pacer like a new taste.

'Well, not all in one go. A couple of chords. Enough to hum to.'

'Nice one.' Pacer rubbed his head with a thoughtful smile.

'What's in there then?' Anna reached for the envelope.

Chess hesitated, but there was no point hanging on to it. She didn't want Anna to watch her not being able to read. She let Anna take it.

Anna put down the cylinder and ripped the envelope open. Chess flinched. 'It's OK,' Anna assured her. 'I won't tear what's inside. It's just an envelope.'

But to Chess, this was not *just* an envelope. Her mother might have touched it, kissed it even. As soon as Anna dropped the riven slip, Chess snatched it up and thrust it into the inside pocket of her jacket.

'They're instructions.' Anna regarded Chess sternly over the top of the sheet of paper, as if Chess had been behaving childishly.

It's all right for you, thought Chess, you've got a mother. But then, Chess remembered the suffocating grief at the Ledward house. Anna's brother was dead, and maybe the Twisted Symmetry were responsible for that. She shuffled on her shins until she was next to Anna. She could see the typescript on the yellow paper Anna had taken from the envelope, like the typescript on the letter sent to Lemuel by the Committee.

'Go on then.' Chess nudged Anna, gently.

'OK,' said Anna, holding the paper so that it would be easier for Chess to see, even though she knew that Chess couldn't read.

Speaking slowly and clearly, and loudly enough to silence Pacer and Boris, Anna read:

'"INSTRUCTIONS FOR USE OF THE VAULT
1. ACTIVATE THE VAULT.
2. PRESS THE CORRECT SYMBOL TO OPEN.
3. PROMPT : WHO AM I?
NOTE:
THE VAULT CONTAINS A MINUTE THERMO-NUCLEAR DEVICE. IN THE EVENT OF INCORRECT OPERATION THIS DEVICE WILL DETONATE, DESTROYING THE CONTENTS OF THE VAULT AND ALL MATERIAL WITHIN A RADIUS OF 150 METRES".'

'Get that thing out of here.' Crazy Boris was pointing at the cylinder, stricken. 'A thermo-nuclear device in *my* house. It's unsafe. Think of the mess.'

'It's not unsafe at the moment.' Anna picked up the striped container and tossed it in the air, catching it.

'Are you mad, girl? What are you doing?'

'It's been knocking about in your attic for nearly ten years.

It's not going to go off now. Unless we do something wrong.'

'Just put it down, OK, whilst we decide *what* to do.' Crazy Boris ran his fingers through his hair. 'A bomb, in my attic, and me downstairs thinking I was safe, drinking herb tea.'

'I bet crumbs don't seem so bad now,' suggested Pacer.

'Don't you believe it. It's just a question of degree. It starts with folk taking liberties by way of scattering crumbs, and before you know it, they're leaving thermo-nuclear devices in your attic.'

'First, we have to activate it,' Anna said. 'Then we open it. Then we get what's been locked inside.'

All four of them were kneeling about the cylinder, which lay on the floor.

'Activating it should be OK,' continued Anna. 'We have to be careful after that.' She looked over at Chess. 'Any idea what's inside?'

Chess shrugged. 'Something to help me find out about my mother, I suppose.'

'Don't take this the wrong way, OK?' Anna's words came as delicately as if she was walking on nails, 'But do we really need to do this, Chess? I mean destroying the brain, fighting the Twisted Symmetry, finding your brothers; none of them depend on this.'

'*I* depend on this.'

Chess's brown eyes were intense, like those of the young woman in the photograph, thought Anna. But angrier. Unpredictable.

'*I* don't,' muttered Boris.

'And Lemuel said there were things she has to tell me,'

added Chess. 'So, maybe, there's information that will help us all.'

Boris winced when Anna picked up the cylinder. 'It's safe, until we activate it,' she reminded him.

'Is there a button?' asked Pacer.

'Too simple.' Anna smiled. 'This has been designed to make things difficult.' She held it up to the light, sighting along the linear cracks in its surface. 'There are eight stripes; four white and four black. The surface is cut so there are grooves, along the edge of each stripe and all the way round the cylinder too.' Anna lowered it.

Pacer pushed his nose up close. 'It's like the surface is lots of little squares.'

'Yeah,' agreed Anna, 'and see here?' She pointed a long, white finger at one end of the vault. 'There's a gap.' Where one of the black stripes ended, there was a square depression, as if one of the little surface squares had been removed.

Now that Anna had focused on the grooves, she saw the surface of the cylinder as squares, not stripes. She calculated quickly; sixty-three little squares and one space. Perhaps the space meant that she could move the squares, shuffle them around the outer surface of the cylinder, rearrange them; rearrange them into a pattern that meant something.

She looked up, blue eyes bright with satisfaction. 'It's a chess board,' she said.

Everybody looked at Chess.

'So?' Chess hunched her shoulders as if she'd just been accused of a crime. 'That's just what they called me at the orphanage.'

Anna placed a finger on a white square above the space

on the surface of the vault. She pushed. Boris twitched. 'This is just to activate it, OK?'

The little white square didn't move until Anna pushed hard. Then it slipped into the gap with a click. Now there was one white square at the end of a black stripe. Anna grinned. 'See?'

Patiently, she manoeuvred the surface squares, the empty space working its way around and across the vault until the whole cylinder was chequered black and white. Then, the last square was slid into place and the empty space became the final black position.

A loud snap came from inside the vault.

'What the hell was that?' flapped Crazy Boris.

'The bomb's glowing.' Pacer shuffled away from Anna.

'It's OK.' But Anna was holding the vault as if it had suddenly become very hot. She rolled it in her palm, gingerly. 'And the whole thing's not glowing. Just some of the squares. And there's shapes marked on them. Look.'

Chess looked. Spread about the cylinder were five squares that were marked with glowing crimson symbols: two crowns, a pointed hat, a horse's head and a castle tower.

'What's that lot mean?' Pacer was baffled.

'They're chess pieces.' Anna indicated the squares in turn, taking care not to press any of them. 'The two crowns are kings, that funny-shaped hat is a bishop, the horse is a knight and the castle's a rook. Although you can call it a castle too.'

'So there's four, maybe five possibilities?' confirmed Boris. 'We have to press the right one, yeah? Chose the right one and it opens; chose the wrong one and we turn into talcum powder. Great.'

Anna put the vault on the wooden floor and everyone stared at it.

'We can't guess,' said Pacer, as if he had genuinely toyed with the possibility. 'Too lively.'

'You're dead right we can't guess,' croaked Boris.

'But it could be any of them,' complained Pacer.

'What was the other bit on the paper?' Chess asked Anna. 'The third thing.'

Anna picked up the paper and read aloud, '"PROMPT: WHO AM I?"' She looked at Chess. 'This is all to do with you, Chess. You tell us what it means. Who are you?'

Chess tugged a strand of hair. What was she? A human? A synth? A tool for the Committee to use? A real person? 'I don't really know,' she admitted. 'I don't even know my proper name.'

Anna clicked her fingers. 'No, but you've got that stupid one.' She was excited. 'At the orphanage, why did they call you Chess?'

'Because when I was left there, I was holding ... a chess piece.' Chess looked at Anna and Anna looked at Chess, and Boris and Pacer looked at both of them.

Very slowly, Anna asked, 'Which chess piece?'

Just as slowly, Chess replied, 'I don't know.'

'How don't you know?' cried Anna, exasperated.

'Because I was three,' fired Chess. 'How am I meant to remember what I was holding? What were you holding when you were three?'

'That's a stupid question,' Anna snapped back. 'It doesn't even make sense.'

'Well, I don't know.' Chess shoved herself away from

Anna. Her heel caught the end of the vault and sent it windmilling across the wooden boards. It began to spin more slowly until it caught a guitar stand. Then it rolled, inch by inch, to the foot of the far wall where it came to rest with the shapes still glowing.

Boris let out breath like steam from a pressure cooker. So did everybody else. 'Wasn't that a stroke of luck? Now, listen, arguing solves nothing.' Then, to Anna, 'If she doesn't remember, it's not her fault.'

Anna folded her arms.

'Right, Chess.' Crazy Boris put a hand on Chess's shoulder.

Why do people always grab my shoulder when they speak to me, she thought. She shook the hand off.

'Sorry,' said Boris. 'But what was the name of the orphanage?'

'The Elms.' Just saying the name made Chess feel sick with unhappiness.

'In the Graveyard?' asked Pacer.

'What's the Graveyard?' asked Boris.

'The old city,' explained Chess. Then she said to Pacer, 'I wish you wouldn't call it that.'

'Everyone calls it the Graveyard.' Pacer shrugged. 'Apart from you and Box and Splinter.'

There were parts of the old city that held bad memories for the Tuesdays; like the place where the Elms Orphanage was located. Calling it the Graveyard only made it feel worse.

'Who runs the Elms?' asked Boris hesitantly, watching Chess closely.

Chess had locked these memories in a special box inside her head. Cold rooms. Hard beds. Beatings. Figures that crept about the corridors at night. Bad grown-ups. She shut her eyes, but turning off the memories was more difficult. 'Mrs Elms.'

'OK,' said Boris, rumpled voice patient, gentle. 'If you want to open that container, Chess, we're going to have to pay a visit to Mrs Elms.'

'No.' Chess drew away from him. 'I'm not going there. Never. We ran away.'

Who came creeping through the rooms at night? Chess didn't want to know. She didn't want to remember.

'Listen, Chess. You say you want to find out about your mother? Well sometimes, good memories and bad memories go together. You can't have one without the other.'

Chess shook her head. Then, to her surprise, she felt the warmth of Anna's hand over hers. 'I'll come with you, Chess. You won't be on your own.'

'They upset you again,' warned Pacer, 'anything bad happens; me and the others will torch the place.'

'I think we have to go, Chess.' Boris's voice grated wearily. 'Sooner or later, some things *have* to be known. And maybe somebody, somewhere, is going to answer for the bad stuff they've done.' He wasn't looking at Chess; his sleep-ringed eyes were fixed on the small photograph, where he smiled back from forty years ago, with his arm around Esme.

'Shoes on and slippers off,' he announced. 'I'll get my shades, and we'll take a trip to the Elms. And don't worry about the taxi fare. Crazy Boris will be driving.'

'Shades?' smirked Anna. 'It's not the south of France.'

'I'm a rock star, Fury.' Crazy Boris stood with a clicking of knees and brushed back his grey locks, 'and this is a public appearance.'

CHAPTER 11

Pacer stamped his boots in the slush, enjoying the way they made the brown ice spurt. 'Hex does this,' he grinned. 'But I've got laces in mine.'

'You'll never undo them,' observed Anna, breathing into the collar of her red duffle coat. 'You're meant to tie them in bows, not Gordian Knots.'

'I'll just cut them off.' Pacer jumped on a rust-stained mound.

'Pacer!' shouted Anna, whose hooped stockings were now spattered with freezing mush. It was no good shouting, 'Haven't you worn boots before?' because he hadn't. Crazy Boris had given him these old black boots because it was so cold outside. Pacer had said that he didn't want them but Anna could tell that he did and so could Boris. Now they were waiting round the back of 18 Mendoza Row; waiting for Boris and his car to emerge from the basement garage. The vault had been left on the floor in the attic. Crazy Boris was adamant that that was the safest place to leave an activated thermo-nuclear device.

'I needed these.' Chess was stuffing the last of the

chocolate biscuits into her mouth. 'I was starving.'

'Thought you would be,' said Anna. She huffed and stamped her foot. Slush jetted across Chess's jeans. 'Sorry. But how long are we meant to wait for Cautious Boris? What's he doing?'

'Being cautious, I suppose.' Chess kicked her foot to shake the flakes of ice from her jeans.

With an electric whine, the door of the garage tipped up. A flat bed of oyster-grey cloud had pulled itself over the city but a solitary spar of sunlight flashed across silver as the mouth of the garage opened. With a low, cool rumble, the car crested the hump of the short driveway and rolled towards them, red and chrome and confident.

Pacer whistled. 'This jack must be dripping.'

'Dripping?' Anna screwed up her nose.

'With grease,' explained Chess. 'You know, got loads of money.'

'So?'

Chess shrugged. 'So nothing. It's only an observation.'

The car crunched to a halt beside them, engine turning idly. Crazy Boris lowered the window and poked his head out. He was wearing a rough charcoal jacket with a thick purple scarf wound tight up to his chin. Chess thought that with the dark shades on, his hair didn't look so old, just messy.

'Are you planning on getting in?' he asked them.

Pacer laughed, tipped back his head and let out a yell. 'Cool! I've never been in one of these before.' He admired the long, red body trimmed with silver, the clear, lozenge headlights and he shook his head at the white rings on the tyres which circled the star-inlaid wheel hubs. 'Hex'll wish he'd come.' But as he put his hand on the chrome passenger door handle, it was slapped away by another.

'Longest legs in the front,' said Anna.

'The back'll take two.' Boris leant across. 'But if she tries to get in there, I'll have to put her legs in the boot.'

Anna opened the door and the passenger seat flipped forwards. 'Midgets in the rear,' she smiled, with a wave of her hand.

'I don't actually want to go, anyway,' muttered Chess as Pacer led the way.

'Watch what you do with them filthy boots,' warned Boris. 'This is in mint condition. If it's all right with you, I'd like it to stay that way.'

Chess was cramped in the back of the car, and it was made worse by Pacer who was leaning forwards, into the space between the front seats, so that he could talk to Boris.

'It's a Mercedes Benz 280SL,' explained Boris, in answer to Pacer.

'The steering wheel's really thin, like what's left on a burnout,' observed Pacer.

'Classic styling,' Boris enlightened him.

'Don't the keys get in the way, hanging like that?' They jangled as the car rolled over a pothole.

'There speaks the man who prefers his cars without keys,' replied Boris. 'No offence. But I bet you've done a fair bit of driving yourself?'

'A bit,' admitted Pacer. There was an uncomfortable pause. 'Mostly in other people's cars.'

'Yeah? Well keep your thieving mitts off this person's car.'

Pacer dossed back into the rear well with a smirk and watched the streets change from places to live into places to do business. They widened, filled with jacks, all elbowing each other so they could splash more grease. The buildings began to climb, ribbing themselves with steel girders and breaking out into glass and interlocking walkways where music droned to pretend it was a good place to be. He watched the press and file of crowds, the open jackets, the thick outside pockets, the careless display of a well-stuffed wallet. He sighed and closed his eyes. Today would have been a good day to graft.

'As I was saying,' commenced Anna who hadn't been saying anything at all, 'I've been doing some research, on the Link-me. Into CREX.'

'What kind of research?' asked Chess, tensely.

'Not *inside* CREX, so keep your knickers on.'

'What did you do?' Chess didn't want to sound angry but she'd asked Anna not to use the Link-me. She knew how easy it would be for the Twisted Symmetry to feel its way towards them if they let it. It was as if she was the only person who appreciated how dangerous this was.

This is what happens when you use other people, Chess told herself. This is the price you pay.

'All I've done is to look through information that's up for public access; magazines, investors' brochures, stuff like that. And I've hacked into the city records to try to find out more; about the layout of the CREX tower.'

Pacer clicked his tongue against his teeth, impressed.

Chess pursed her lips and stared at the back of the seat in front.

'OK,' continued Anna, 'we know that the Symmetry relocated their child stealing operation to the Cones, yeah?'

'Child stealing?' groaned Crazy Boris.

'What we *need* to know is where the cerebral torus is,' said Chess.

'And what's a cerebral torus?' enquired Boris.

'The Twisted Symmetry steal children,' explained Chess wearily. 'The cerebral torus is the computer which predicts where the Fat Gobster will strike, to take the children away. We think it isn't working yet; but it will be, in days. That's why we have to destroy it as soon as possible.'

'The Fat Gobster?' Boris shook his head. 'Who's the Fat Gobster?'

'It sucks up children and transports them to where the Twisted Symmetry extract their energy.' Chess spoke as flatly as is if she were describing how to catch a bus.

'This Fat Gobster bloke must be pretty big.'

'It's not a bloke,' said Chess, 'it's a suck worm.'

'I'll just drive.'

'So? What've you found out?' Chess slouched deeper into the back seat, as if she wasn't all that interested, even though she was.

'Well, the CREX Corporation is massive.'

Chess said nothing. They already knew that CREX was massive.

'And their headquarters are in the CREX tower.'

'With the big C on the front?' confirmed Chess.

'Correct. Now, given that everything was taken from the Riverside Prison to the Cones, it's a fair bet that your brain will be inside the CREX Tower. It certainly looks as if they're running the operation from there now. It's where CREX's chairman is based; someone called Fenley Ravillious'.

'How can we be sure the brain is there?'

The roadster swung left and began to climb a six-lane highway that took traffic east, towards the old city. The carriageways levelled out high above the streets. They cruised in the slow lane, between blocks of skyscrapers.

'Doesn't this go faster?' Pacer asked Boris.

'It does,' replied Boris. 'But I don't.'

'If I was driving a car like this, I'd drive it fast.'

'If you were driving a car like this,' said Boris, 'you'd be arrested. Pacer, I've driven off several hotel terraces and I've driven into a fair few swimming pools and it's not only expensive, but it's a lot less fun than folk will admit.' Then he leant round with his head between the seats and leered at Pacer. 'Believe me, fella, I've got so little to prove, I sometimes wonder why I bother getting out of bed in the mornings.'

The car lurched towards the edge of the highway. In unison, Pacer and Anna yelled at Boris to watch the road. He swivelled back to face the way they were travelling. 'Just livening things up a bit,' he complained.

'But we can't be sure the brain is in the CREX tower, can we?' stated Chess, oblivious to the drop that hurtled beneath her window.

'At the moment, no,' admitted Anna, 'but from hacking through the architectural plans lodged in the city records, I've got some helpful information. The towers are a hundred and fifty floors high.'

'Eight hundred metres, yeah, I know.' That was what Lemuel had told Chess.

'OK,' continued Anna patiently. 'There's a concrete superstructure with a hyper-reinforced glass and aluminium sheath. The central area is marked on the plans as the 'core'; it's where the lifts are and there are car parks too.'

'Car parks?' Pacer roused himself. 'Inside the Cones?'

'I said they were big, there's even lifts for the cars. The CREX tower is the heart of a global mega-corporation. More than fifty thousand people work there. But the thing is,' and now Anna allowed herself a little smile at Chess and Pacer, 'there are no plans for the hundredth floor.' She let Chess and Pacer digest the implications and then, to be sure, she added, 'There are plans for the core up to the ninety-ninth and plans up from the hundred and first to the hundred and fiftieth, but nothing for the hundredth. It came up as "RESTRICTED". I wonder why that was? I wonder what CREX are hiding on the hundredth floor?'

'But we can't be *sure* the brain's there,' repeated Chess truculently. 'And even if it is, we need to know more if we're going to be able to get in safely and destroy it.'

'Don't be too grateful,' said Anna hotly. 'There's things I want to find out as well, you know. I want to get in there just as much as you do.'

Chess scowled at the backs of her hands, but inside she felt a blistering guilt. She was so eaten by her own part in all of this that it was easy to forget that Anna carried her dead brother with her. Tracking down his killers was what drove her. She and Anna might have been thrown together by somebody else but both of them had their reasons for taking on the Twisted Symmetry; they had that much in common, at least.

'I know you do,' she said to Anna. It was a way of saying sorry.

'Everybody friends again?' Pacer snorted, keen to return to practical matters. 'The Bank might be able to help. He said he's got someone on the inside, at CREX Headquarters. Someone who owes him a big favour.' Pacer laughed drily. 'Most people who owe the Bank favours that big end up as slab-jobs, but he said he'd kept this one alive 'cos he might come in useful one day.'

'Never work with the Bank,' stated Chess. 'It always gets messy.'

'Says Splinter.' Pacer gave Chess a cool stare. 'But he's not here. And we need to find out more before we try to destroy the brain. So what's your idea, Chess?'

'Given that you've banned us from using the Link-me to break in,' added Anna.

'Maybe someone's going to have to go in and take a look?'

Chess's suggestion was met by total silence.

The highway curved downwards, diving between the skyscrapers. It curled round the base of a rise, studded with concrete blocks of flats before merging at an interchange controlled by high banks of traffic signals. Chess pulled her jacket round her body, stuck her chin into the collar and stared at the leather back of the seat in front. They were heading into the old city; into the Graveyard.

Even though she didn't want to look, Chess's eyes were drawn to what was outside the car. She had been to parts of the old city plenty of times before. She was familiar with the rust-brick walls, the gutted warehouses, the weed-bound railway sidings, the decrepit, grand civic buildings. She'd been here with Box and Splinter to scavenge, although it was so well scavenged already that they had spent most of their time prowling the barren streets in search of the few remaining windows they could smash. And the bus depot that was the Committee's HQ was in the old city, and so was the dog track and the gutted flats where she and her brothers had hidden after they had first left Ethel and the Committee. But the old city was big; it was *this* part of the old city that Chess wanted to avoid.

'Are you OK?' Anna looked round the front seat.

Chess's palms were itchy with sweat and her breathing was shallow and quick. There were street rats from rival gangs who lived in the sewers in the old city, but it wasn't them that made her feel like this.

'You'll be all right. OK?' Anna knew what was wrong from Chess's grey pallor and snatched breaths. 'We *have* to go to the Elms. You're with *us*. Nothing bad is going to happen to you. OK?'

'OK,' mouthed Chess. But Chess knew that bad things could always happen.

They rolled past a file of high-rise flats, buff concrete as miserable as bone. Behind the flats rose two ornate, ceremonial arches much older than anything else in this part of the city and built to commemorate battles about which Chess knew nothing. Although the triumphal arches loomed high behind the tower blocks, their feet were mounted on plinths in a dip of desolate waste ground far below so that as the car coasted down the hill, the perspective made Chess feel dizzy and even more sick.

'This place is weird,' said Anna.

'Does nothing to lift the spirits,' Boris agreed.

'The Graveyard.' Pacer put on a ghostly voice.

'Shut up,' hissed Chess, teeth clenched.

At the bottom of the hill, strands of wire strung with little triangular flags and pieces of rag had been nailed to the lower storeys of the apartment blocks. They were wrapped around the walls and straggled loosely from building to building. Probably the cloths had once been gaudy, but now they were a variety of fuscous shades and they hung like dead bats, twitching in the wind.

Chess knew that the people who lived in the flats had strung them with these pennants so that there could be something pretty in this part of the city. But this was the Graveyard and nothing here could stay pretty for long. People still lived in the flats though, quiet and watchful as ghosts.

'OK, Chess?' Anna gave Chess's knee a squeeze.

This was the place. A low, multi-storey car park on one side of the street, a row of security-grilled offices on the other, and facing them, at the far end, the Elms Orphanage.

'They keep children in *that*?' Boris drew up beside the empty car park and ratcheted the handbrake. He shook his head. 'It looks like a place for executions.'

It wasn't a tall building, only five storeys, and it was narrow. The front was bowed like the prow of an ocean liner, with a tier of balconies that had tall, narrow windows, metal rails crowned with spikes and long white security cameras that angled downwards on support pillars. The rest of the orphanage was faceless brick, except for the entrance which had a concrete facade and hard, wooden, double doors. The building stretched back further than they could see.

'You three stay here, to start with,' said Crazy Boris. 'Once they open the front door, come in and join me.'

'Why do we have to stay here?' asked Pacer.

'They might not want to open the doors if they see us all milling about outside.' Crazy Boris swung out of the car. 'I don't imagine they welcome visits from the public. Here are the keys, Anna. You lock it.'

Chess wasn't listening. She was staring at the front door, trying to remember what had happened when she had been left there with Box and Splinter. But she couldn't get back to it. Then there was a feeling of shadows and coldness and being on her own, and she stopped trying to remember, as if she was quickly closing a door on something she didn't want to see.

'Chess, come on.' It was Anna. 'Quick.'

Automatically, Chess clambered out of the car and followed Anna to the front door. Pacer pulled her inside and the door was closed behind them. The orphanage was dark, cold, cheerless as a hospital.

'You didn't say there were four of you,' said a girl in a black dress. She wore strappy, clunking black shoes and her greasy black hair hung down one side of her head in an oily plait. Chess guessed that she was a couple of years older than Anna. 'I wouldn't of let you come in with four of you.'

'Sorry about that,' said Boris. They moved like puppet

silhouettes in the dark of the corridor. 'We've come to see Mrs Elms.'

'Are you from the government?' The girl twined her fingers in front of her lap and her hollow eyes were big as coals. 'We won't have nobody from the government. And anyway, Mrs Elms won't see nobody at all.'

'We're not from the government,' Boris assured her.

'Didn't think you were,' said the girl, with a glance at Pacer. Pacer smiled brightly and the girl's pallid cheeks coloured.

'I wonder whether you'd tell Mrs Elms we have a reward?' Boris's voice echoed in the corridor. 'A reward for information.'

The girl looked over her shoulder, down the gloomy passage that smelled so strongly of bleach it made Chess's eyes itch. Then she looked back at Boris. 'Money?'

Boris nodded.

'I'll see what she says.' The girl clopped away.

'A reward?' asked Anna.

Boris shrugged. 'You don't think the Mrs Elms of this world do favours for free?' Then he rubbed Chess's shoulder. 'I'm not surprised you left,' he said.

'Why do the rooms have metal doors?' Anna peered along the passageway. 'They've even got shutters on the doors to spy on the children. Or, should I say, inmates? It's like a prison.'

It's like the factory, realized Chess, the Twisted Symmetry's factory, with its steel corridor and doors with little round windows that led to the scream rooms.

'We make it so easy for them,' whispered Chess.

'For who?' Anna slid open the shutter on the nearest door. She swore under her breath. 'Correction; it's more like a lunatic asylum. Thank God, this one's empty.'

'For the Symmetry,' breathed Chess. 'We make it so easy.'

Anna slid the shutter back, very hard. The loud clack echoed down the corridor. 'When I get my chance,' she stated, '*I* won't make it easy for them.'

The girl in the black dress returned, a phantom at first and only solid when she swam out of the murk, a couple of metres in front of them. 'This way,' she said, sunken eyes lingering for a moment on Pacer.

Chess walked beside Crazy Boris and her head was full of banging doors and angry voices. I'm hearing feelings, she thought; years of misery calling to her.

'Are there actually children here?' Anna spoke too loudly. 'It's so quiet.'

'Not many now.' The girl was defensive. 'Not since Mr Elms...'

'Not since Mr Elms what?'

She's like a lawyer, thought Chess, glad of Anna's hard voice. She's like a prosecutor.

'Nothing.' The girl wouldn't speak any more.

They stopped at a door. A smudged, brass nameplate was stamped with letters. Chess knew that the letters spelt, 'Mrs Prittle Elms'. The girl tapped at the door with her knuckles.

'Enter.' A sharp, snapping voice.

They entered.

A small office, wood panelled, windowless, rows of empty shelves covering one wall, the alcoves filled with dust and cobwebs. A desk with a telephone and an old-fashioned computer as big as a microwave oven. By the desk, an electric fire with one, poker-orange bar glowing. And, looking over the top of the desk, tiny in a wing-backed, red leather armchair: Mrs Prittle Elms.

Mrs Prittle Elms, her sparrow features squeezed into the centre of her face; bright black eyes; peevish little mouth, shrivelled and pursed as if ready to peck; tiny nose; skin floured with lavender compact powder; her body perched in the chair like a doll's and wrapped in a green astrakhan rug. And, over it all, a luxurious fondant of cloud-white hair, rinsed with a hint of tangerine.

Why does everyone have desks? thought Chess, staring at the floor and using that thought to block all the others that came hammering.

'You didn't mention that there were children, Marion,' sniped Mrs Elms, her button nose wrinkling at the word 'children' as if it was accompanied by a foul odour.

'Sorry, Mrs Elms, but I thought you'd want to know about the reward and . . .'

'You are dismissed, Marion. Get out of my room.' With a drowning glance at Pacer, Marion left the room.

'Who are you?' Mrs Elms tightened her mouth towards Crazy Boris. Her tiny chin bobbed just above the top of the desk.

'Boris Sherevsky, miss. And I take it you are Mrs Elms?'

'Mrs Prittle Elms, yes. And there's just me, only me. Ever since Mr Elms got put away, there's only been me.' Mrs Elms shifted position with a little shake and a smooth swish of the hairy rug that enfolded her. 'They put him away because of the children. Because of what they did and then because of what they said. Children got Mr Elms in trouble and he'll never be let out again.' She chewed her mouth bitterly. 'I run the establishment alone now. But charity is cold without funds, Mr Sherevsky.'

She shuffled forwards in her deep seat. '*You*, lift your face so I can see it.'

Years of discipline had taught Chess to respond to that voice, however she felt. She looked up and discovered that when her eyes locked with Mrs Elms's, she didn't feel fear. Her head filled with a searing, roiling hatred.

'Chess Tuesday.' Mrs Elms spoke as if the name alone was a vile crime. 'Older and bigger, but still as rude, hiding your devious plans behind those big, brown eyes.'

'I don't see any need for that, Mrs Elms,' interrupted Crazy Boris.

But Mrs Elms wasn't to be silenced. She smiled as if she had been licking vinegar. 'Where are your brothers? Not here, I see. Come to no good? Of course they have. And you, you sly little madam, have managed to save your own snake-like skin.'

Chess was halfway across the desk before Anna and Pacer had wrestled her back.

'Hell, Chess!' exclaimed Boris.

'Take it easy, Chess,' panted Pacer, gripping her leather jacket hard enough to keep her on the floor.

Anna knelt by Chess's heaving body. 'Chess,' she whispered, 'let's get through this bit, OK? Just switch off, like it isn't happening. Please.'

Chess nodded. Eyes glistening. Anna could see that now, after nine years, the tears were coming.

'Ingratitude, Mr Sherevsky,' proclaimed Mrs Elms, raising a miniature hand to reposition the lavish wig that had been knocked askew. 'I am perfectly used to it. I take them in from the gutter, try to civilize them, and as soon as they are able, they chose to return to the gutter.'

She couldn't see Boris's eyes behind his sunglasses and she couldn't see over the other side of the desk where the sobbing was coming from, but she could see how Boris Sherevsky was shocked by what had just happened.

'If I didn't look after these ragbag remnants of society, Mr Sherevsky, who would?' Mrs Elms sniffed and settled more comfortably. 'She'll get over it. She's got an audience, that's all. A cunning little rat, aren't you, Miss Tuesday?'

Boris drew in a long breath. 'We've come for some information, if you'd be kind enough to help us.'

'Kind enough!' snorted Mrs Elms, as if insulted. Then, leaning forwards, 'What information?'

'Do you remember the day that Chess and her brothers came to you?'

'Vaguely.' Mrs Elms waved her hand. Anna noticed how short the fingers were; fat where they started and thin at their tips. 'A banging on the door and they were there. Either deposited or they'd found their own way. They never said where they'd come from. Withholding the truth, you see, Mr Sherevsky. Even at that age, they were cunning.'

'They had some possessions . . .'

'*I* don't have any of their possessions.'

'I'm not asking you for anything apart from some information,' Boris was quick to say.

'I've had to auction nearly everything I have.' Mrs Elms

indicated the barren shelves. 'Charity costs, Mr Sherevsky.'

'Mrs Elms, is there any chance of you recalling what possessions they had?'

'One of the brothers had a box, full of toy soldiers.' Mrs Elms sniffed. 'Hardly appropriate. Violence breeds violence. I took the soldiers away and he cried for a week. It was a pleasure to behold, I assure you.'

Chess had stood up now, shielded from the desk by Anna and Pacer. Her nose was wet so she pulled up the front of Anna's mother's jumper and wiped it.

'What about Chess?' asked Boris. 'What did she have?'

'She had a chess piece, hence the convenient name.' Mrs Elms tightened her little mouth. 'There was mention of a reward, Mr Sherevsky.'

'The fact is, it's the chess piece we really need to know about. We need to know what piece it was.'

Mrs Elms clenched her little fists and her face blanched. 'How am I meant to remember that, you stupid man?'

Anna cursed quietly.

'Mind your tongue, young lady.' The currant-black eyes turned on Anna. 'I've ignored your lip so far. These aren't your type of people. I don't know what someone like you is doing here. More to the point, I don't imagine your parents know, either.'

Anna stared back belligerently.

'Oh, very good, young lady. You set your standards by this pack of rats and see where it takes you.'

'I'll pay for the information.' Boris lifted his wallet from his inside pocket.

'You'll pay for the information I've already given you,' snapped Mrs Elms. 'As to chess pieces, I can't help. It's a ridiculous enquiry.'

'OK, OK,' murmured Boris; tired, patient. He opened the wallet.

'Boris!' Anna was incensed. 'Make her tell us.'

'She can't remember, Fury. Fair's fair.'

'Yes, fair's fair, miss,' chirped Mrs Elms.

Anna glared back, but Mrs Elms ignored her. She had eyes only for the wallet. She pushed herself off the chair and landed with a heavy clunk. Anna found herself looking down on a woman half her size. Mrs Elms walked round the desk jerkily, waddling slightly from leg to leg. The rug remained on the chair and as the midget approached Boris, Anna saw the metal bands of the callipers which enabled her to walk. They started at her ankles and disappeared under her long skirt.

Anna looked away, unsure now of what to think about Mrs Elms.

Mrs Elms held up her hand, like a child, begging.

'You do a difficult job, Mrs Elms,' said Crazy Boris, peeling three notes from a thin sandwich. 'Make sure you do it kindly.'

Mrs Elms licked her lips as she inspected the money. Then she hobbled back to her chair and eased herself onto it.

'If you do remember the piece ...' began Boris.

'I won't remember the piece, Mr Sherevsky. It wasn't important.'

'Come on, Chess.' Pacer had his arm round Chess's shoulders and they turned to leave.

'Thanks, anyway.' Boris began to hum, to ease Chess's exit from the room.

'Marion will show you out.'

Anna was the first to leave. Boris was behind Chess and Pacer. Very low he sang, *'When I was on horseback, wasn't I pretty.'*

'Wait.'

They stopped in the doorway.

Mrs Elms folded miniature hands. 'It was a horse, Mr Sherevsky. A horse's head, made of wood. That was the piece.'

'A knight,' whispered Anna. 'There's a knight on the vault.'

Chess closed her eyes, tracing the outline in the darkness of her thoughts, trying to feel the shape of the wood. A knight. She wasn't sure whether she could really remember it, but just knowing what it was made her feel a warmth, where before there had been only a dead chill.

Mrs Elms nodded towards Boris Sherevsky. 'Your song brings it to mind. Not that you're much of a singer.'

Boris smiled. 'I'm a little out of practice, that's all.'

For several minutes after the visitors had been shown out, Mrs Elms hesitated. Her bird eyes rested on the telephone as her fingers turned the money in her lap. If it wasn't for the money, things would be simpler. But running the orphanage cost money. A fall of dust made the electric fire spark and buzz. Her lips worked silently. She sighed and lifted the handset. She dialled.

'Good afternoon,' said Mrs Elms to the voice at the other end of the line. 'Could I speak to Mr Ravillious please? Mrs Elms. Mrs Prittle Elms. He said I was to be put straight through ... Thank you.'

There was a pause.

'Yes. And very nice to speak to you, again, Mr Ravillious.' Mrs Elms cleared her dry little throat. 'You may recall that you made mention of a reward ... for information ... I know, it has been a very long time.' Mrs Elms listened, smiled and settled back into the depths of the armchair. 'Well, she's been back ... this afternoon ... no, she left a quarter of an hour ago ... That's very kind of you ... Descriptions? Yes, of course. I'll tell you everything.'

CHAPTER 12

'How the hell do you do that?' Crazy Boris snatched off his shades and pushed his bristly face close up to Chess's hand. Chess burst out laughing and on the other side of the diner table, so did Anna and Pacer. 'Go on,' he said, deadly serious. 'Do it again.'

Chess pushed a strand of brown curls behind her ear and looked about the café. They were sitting in the front window and the red Mercedes was parked in the street, right opposite. It was busy, outside and inside the café; the street was narrow and cluttered but skewed off one of the city's main arteries. However, there were so many people crammed into the rows of tan, bench seats that nobody appeared to notice Chess and her friends; she liked it when crowds made her invisible.

'OK,' she whispered.

Anna sniggered. Pacer elbowed her, gently. 'Shut up. She's concentrating.'

Chess placed her left hand on the top of the table. Boris was next to the window and he swivelled where he sat so that his body obscured Chess's arm from view. Pacer glanced around to make sure that they were unobserved.

Chess relaxed. That seemed to be the key to getting this right. She looked forwards, at the table, but was actually looking through it, as if it wasn't there. She didn't push; she didn't try to move her hand in any way. The trick was to feel for all the space that was in the same place as the plastic table; the boxes inside the boxes as Ethel had once described it.

It's more like being on a wall of bars, Chess thought to herself. Other people can only see the bars, but I can see that it's actually a climbing frame, with spaces for me to climb up and down and backwards and forwards.

Maybe it was the amarantium that Lemuel had fused into her cells, which allowed her to be in different places, different universes at the same time. Maybe it was because, according to Lemuel, her raw spirit was so powerful that it radiated throughout the dimensions. Chess wasn't sure how it worked, but the narrow dimensions of the table had opened and now her hand was on the other side.

'Crazy!' gasped Crazy Boris and he threw his shades back on. 'And you can't do it with your other hand because your other hand isn't a real hand at all? It's made of metal, right?'

Chess nodded, eyes wide, face solemn. Boris lurched back in his seat and raked his tangly, steel-streaked hair. Then all of them laughed.

'The other hand will catch up in a bit, I think,' said Chess. 'Once all the parts of me begin to mix.' That's what had happened to her old clothing, which had remained with her when she had crawled through the cerebral torus.

Pacer tipped a stream of sugar into his glass and drained the pink milkshake with a sink-hole gurgle.

'You're disgusting,' complained Anna. She pulled the straw out of her own glass and gulped the frothy liquid quickly.

'You've got a pink moustache,' grinned Chess, when Anna had banged the glass down like it was a tankard.

Anna wiped away the milk residue with the back of her hand. 'So who's going to check out the CREX tower?'

Chess blinked back.

'It was your idea,' Anna reminded her. 'There isn't any other option. We've got to get a better idea of what it's like inside; see if we can find where they keep the brain. And, I'd like to find where they keep their records.'

'Records of what?' Pacer asked Anna.

'Records of who they assassinate.'

Boris's hands flapped like startled pigeons. 'Wow! Keep the noise down, Fury. Words like that draw attention.' They all looked over their shoulders.

'I've been thinking about this,' said Anna, a lot more quietly. 'You can't go in, Chess. But if someone could go in, say as a potential wealthy investor, and demand an interview with the chairman, Mr Ravillious, before trusting CREX with their cash, it would be the perfect opportunity to snoop about. And to take a look at the inside of his office. I bet there are some interesting records kept there.'

'Go on.' It was obvious to Chess that Anna had already thought this out.

'It needs to be an adult. I can set up false records, a false person, just like an avatar; it's really easy. When CREX make enquiries it'll check out. I can do the bank accounts and biographical details this afternoon.' Anna patted the boot bag which sat between her and Pacer. 'I'll use Richard's account but hack in fresh details.'

'Who's going to do it?' Pacer drummed his fingers on the table. 'It'll be lively.'

'Whoever goes in will need guts, and they'll have to be able to play the part. Act flash and stay sharp.' Anna looked about the table, inviting suggestions.

'Well, all of that counts me out,' Boris was quick to establish.

Chess thought through the possibilities. There was somebody who might have the brains and the nerve for this. Somebody she could use. 'What about Klinky Mallows?'

'Who's Klinky Mallows?' asked Anna.

'Who's Klinky Mallows?' laughed Boris. 'Everybody knows Klinky Mallows.'

'Well, if everybody knows Klinky Mallows, there's not much point pretending she's somebody else, is there?' said Anna, tartly.

'OK,' elaborated Boris, 'everybody who's ever scraped a living on the underbelly of this city knows Klinky. Those suits at CREX won't know her. But she can scrub up smart. They'll think she's the genuine article.'

'So, tell us about when you had a taste of the city's underbelly?' enquired Anna, archly.

'That's another story, for another day.' Boris gave an infuriatingly knowing smile.

'Well, where do we find her?' Anna asked Pacer, who was chewing a straw. 'And stop doing that, it makes you look even more stupid.' She snatched the straw from Pacer's teeth.

Pacer grabbed Anna's forearm to wrest back the straw.

Chess looked out of the window. A long, black limousine had pulled up behind the Mercedes.

'Hey, cut it out.' Boris leant forwards. 'Let's not draw attention, OK? Save the wrestling for another occasion.'

Anna flushed and glared at Boris. 'If we were wrestling, I'd break his nose. We weren't wrestling.'

Pacer replaced the straw between his teeth and chewed with a smile.

'Slack Harry's.' Boris took a sip of weak tea. 'If she's not working, that's where you'll most likely find Klinky Mallows.' He smiled reflectively. 'I haven't visited the bar in a while, but it's always been the place to go when you've no place in particular to be.'

'It's where you go to find the Bank,' added Pacer. 'And the Night Porter.'

'It's a hotel?' Anna was surprised.

'Not that sort of night porter,' muttered Chess, looking out of the window. There were shapes moving in the blanked-out rear window of the limo.

'He's a hit man,' whispered Pacer. 'His real name is Mr Fazakerley. He's OK.'

Crazy Boris spilt his tea on his jeans and cursed. 'First it was crumbs, now it's hit men; are you addicted to danger?'

'Klinky will be there tonight?' asked Anna. 'At Slack Harry's?'

'If she's got nowhere else to be.' Boris was blotting his jeans with a paper napkin. He cursed again. 'It looks like I've wet myself.'

'If Klinky will do it, I'll go with her.' Anna waited until Chess had turned back from the window to look at her.

'It'd be better with two and *you* can't go. I could be her PA.'

'PA?'

'Yeah. I'll make her a wealthy divorcee and I'll be her personal assistant. With two of us there, we'll remember the layout better. We can pretend to get lost and have a snoop about.'

'It's really lively,' warned Chess.

Don't get soft, said a voice in her head. You need her to do this. But Chess didn't want to see Anna hurt. She remembered how Anna had stuck up for her at the Elms.

'I know that, but I've got my reasons so I don't care.' Anna's blue eyes narrowed, just like Splinter's would.

'Remind me not to get on the wrong side of you,' muttered Boris.

'We'll go to the CREX tower tomorrow morning, if Klinky will help and if I can set up a meeting with Mr Ravillious.'

'And why would the chairman of this global mega-corporation desire to meet you so soon?' enquired Boris.

'I'm going to create the kind of financial opportunity Mr Ravillious dreams of meeting,' said Anna confidently. 'He'll see us as soon as we want.'

'Here come the all-day breakfasts.' Boris nodded towards the waitress who was navigating her way through the maze of tables.

'At last.' Pacer wetted his lips, hungrily watching the approach of the tray bearing three steaming plates of sausages, bacon, eggs, hash browns and beans, and a smaller plate of crumpets.

The plates were set down in a haze of fried oil, hot butter and sizzling bacon fat.

'Fodder,' breathed Pacer, rubbing his hands.

'Of course, I've had a lot of all-day breakfasts in my time,' explained Crazy Boris, 'but these days I stick to crumpet,' and he smiled in a way that made the waitress smile back patiently, as she retreated, and Anna roll her eyes.

Cutlery clattered in Pacer's and Anna's hands as they set to work. Boris scraped excess butter from the first crumpet and then asked Chess, 'Why aren't you eating?' He followed where she was looking, out of the window.

'It's just a car,' he assured her. 'Just another stretch limo. I've had a lot of stretch limos in my time . . .'

'There's someone in it.' There was a tremor in Chess's voice that made Pacer's fork of scooped beans halt two inches from his open mouth.

'Of course there's someone in it,' said Anna. 'It's a car.'

Pacer shovelled in the beans, but he was also looking through the widow now.

'Really, I can't see anything wrong, Chess,' insisted Boris.

No one ever does, thought Chess, until it all *goes* wrong. She tried to pick out details from the vague outline behind the darkened glass.

'There's no reason to think the Twisted Symmetry know where we are at the moment.' Anna rolled up a bacon rasher, skewered it and drove it into her mouth.

'They always know where we are,' hissed Chess.

'Shut your mash, Chess. You're spooking everyone.' Pacer could see that people were developing an interest in them.

Chess stared at the rear window as if her eyes could strip away the darkened glass. She *could* see an outline of a person within, she was sure of it; a person with a large, craggy head, streaming hair and a beard. A person who was much bigger than a normal person was meant to be.

'Trader,' whispered Chess, shuffling away, towards the aisle.

'What?' Boris swung his head from Chess to the window and back to Chess.

'Trader.' Her lips were dry, catching on gluey spit. 'His name is Jerkan.' The traders worked for the Twisted Symmetry; they caught children and worked the slaves in the Crystal Mines. They had bulbous bodies but long arms and legs which made them much taller than ordinary people. Jerkan was a trader chieftain. Chess had seen him before, in the Riverside Prison and then at the Eastern Airfield, when the Symmetry had nearly cornered her and her brothers. She remembered the bone-crunching hands and the cruel eyes.

So far, Jerkan, if it was him, showed no sign of leaving the car, which was odd; his sole task was to catch her. However, if he knew where she was, others would come for her, even if he didn't. She had to get away, now.

'You're just all stirred up, Chess, what with the Elms and everything.' And then, for an instant, Crazy Boris caught sight of a huge head pushed up against the car window, and a rock-knuckled fist studded with rings, close to the glass. 'On the other hand, maybe you'd better go. Out the back.'

Chess was ready to run but she stalled. 'What about the vault?'

'Come to mine,' said Boris, 'but not tonight, OK? They might follow any of us. Come tomorrow night. Have you got that, Chess?'

'Yeah.' Chess turned to go.

'I'm coming with you.' Anna grabbed her boot bag and climbed over Pacer.

'No. Just me,' said Chess. 'Don't risk yourself.'

'I'm your friend, you dimwit.' Anna's brightly stockinged legs were free and she clambered out of the table space. 'We're in this together.' And suddenly, Chess felt a lot stronger.

Pacer considered the sausage that drooped on his fork, stuffed it into his mouth and then snatched up a heavy glass ashtray. He flipped out of the seat.

'Not you too, Pacer,' said Anna.

Pacer weighed the ashtray. 'A diversion. Whilst you two give it long legs, this is going through the windscreen; let them think about that whilst you get away.'

'Wonderful,' groaned Crazy Boris. 'I'll just drive you from the scene of the crime then.'

'Anna, let's go.' Chess began to push through customers, towards the door marked KITCHEN.

'Go on,' said Pacer as Anna hesitated, looking at him. He gave her one of those grins that was so unexpected on the hard face of a street rat. 'Go!'

The best way to lose a car was by block-hopping. If you just ran down the street, they'd catch you. But if you went like a bullet, puncturing your way through shops and offices, from one city block to the next, there was no way a car or bike could keep up. That was why, after pinballing her way through the steaming kitchen, Chess waded across the rubbish-crammed back yard, leapt up to the rear wall, rolled over it, tumbled into the next, slush-pooled loading area and cannoned through the clothing racks of a gift-wrap scented, haute couture boutique.

Behind her came Anna, new to the art of street running. Swearing loudly and panting like a dog, she collided with onlookers, crashed through shop displays and grazed her hands and knees on walls. But she kept going. After the second block, Chess had to slow down for her, and she had to sling herself back over one of the walls she had just vaulted to drag Anna up, but even with the knees of her stockings torn and stained ochre with blood, Anna didn't stop. Chess managed a grimace of encouragement. Anna was a good block-hopper, for a jack.

'Definitely off-grid,' gasped Chess, with approval, as Anna crashed to her knees in the subway that led to the West and Red Line metro station. Slush had collected and melted into shallow, sour-smelling pools of brown water but they were beyond caring. Gulping breath, they squatted on their heels, backs against the subway wall, oblivious to the passers-by who were equally oblivious to them.

'I need to use the Link-me to create the accounts.' Anna wiped her running nose with the cuff of her filth-speckled red coat. One of the straps of her boot bag had snapped and it slipped off her shoulder.

'How long?' panted Chess.

'Couple of hours,' wheezed Anna. 'Do you do that often?'

'Block-hopping? Only when I have to. People always get out of the way, apart from security guards and wrinklies.' Chess stretched back her head and wiped the sweat off her forehead, where her chestnut curls had stuck flat.

Anna laughed, a clear peel that broke the murk of the subway like a stream of silver. 'It was fun.'

'It beats getting caught,' said Chess, who frowned as if fun was an alien concept.

Anna looked Chess up and down. 'How come you look OK?'

'Years of practice.' This time it was Chess who burst out laughing, short coughs that were swallowed immediately by the subway and its surging bodies. 'You look a mess.'

'Thanks.'

'We could go to the library,' suggested Chess. 'For you to use the Link-me.' She saw Anna glance at her torn knee. 'Wait for me outside. I'll get you some new stockings, and I'll get some stuff to eat.'

'You've no money,' Anna pointed out, and then, when Chess pouted at her angelically, 'Oh yes, I forgot, you get things without money.'

'Inside the library, we can use the toilets to tidy up.'

Anna nodded. 'You're much better in a crisis. You're the wrong way round to normal people.'

'Thanks.' Chess sucked her lip, hesitant. 'You could always go home now. I bet you've got loads of clean clothes, *and* you could eat.'

'And leave you on your own?' Anna looked sidelong at Chess, one eyebrow raised.

Chess wiped sweat from her cheek and smiled.

'Anyway, it was hard enough getting out this morning.' Anna made a ring in a puddle with the toe of her shoe. 'Nobody knows how to be after what happened to Richard. Now I'm out it's easier to stay out. I'll call them, say I'm OK, say I'm stopping with you today. Tonight, too.'

'They won't mind?'

'Of course they'll mind, but it's only for one night. And I'm doing this for them as well, even though they don't know.' Anna stood up. Liquid dripped from the hem of her coat, where it had been trailing in the water. 'You think it will work; going in with Klinky Mallows? Spying on CREX or the Twisted Symmetry or whoever they are? You think we'll get away with it?'

Chess wanted to say that it would work, that of course they'd get away with it; but for once, she found it difficult to lie. 'Can you think of any other way?' she asked.

CHAPTER 13

Chess and Anna were walking the last two streets to the bar. It was a little before ten o'clock at night and it was freezing cold, although the snow had gone. Under the orange street lights, their breath steamed about their heads. Their footfalls were soft.

They had spent the afternoon and early evening in the Central Library, where Richard Ledward's bank account had been transformed into the account of a lady called Rachel Leeward. She was forty-eight years old and had further accounts in the Seychelles and Zürich, a yacht in Biarritz and an ex-husband who had made a fortune in shipping, a large chunk of which he had had to transfer to the fictitious Mrs Leeward on their divorce. Chess thought that Klinky was older than forty-eight, but Anna assured her it was better to go for a lower age if they wanted Klinky to come in on this. When Chess observed that it seemed a ridiculously easy way to make money, Anna pointed out that they couldn't actually spend any of it; it was only there for show. Any attempt to use the dummy accounts would be traced immediately. It just had to appear as if Rachel Leeward, a.k.a Klinky Mallows, was an enormously wealthy potential investor in CREX.

'I've been thinking,' Anna was saying, quietly, 'about you and the Twisted Symmetry and the Eternal.'

Chess grunted to show that she was listening.

'The Twisted Symmetry need the Eternal to use all this energy they've stockpiled, right?'

Chess grunted again. They'd talked about all this before.

'And the Eternal is something that only you can control because of how strange you are?'

'I'm not strange,' objected Chess.

Oh yes you are, said Lemuel Sprazkin's voice, inside her head. You're a synth.

'OK, not strange,' conceded Anna. 'Special.'

'Splinter would go mad if he heard you say that.'

'From what you've told me, your brother, Splinter, goes mad about anything. He sounds a little over-sensitive.'

'He's all right,' said Chess. He'd know what to do now, she thought, as the small, illuminated white sign with the thin red letters that she knew spelt 'Slack Harry's', came into view.

Anna stopped walking, a stone's throw from the low door that was reached by three concrete steps. 'The thing is to find the Eternal.'

'And then?' asked Chess lamely.

'Break it.' Anna set her jaw defiantly.

'Break it?' It was such an unexpected suggestion. And the Eternal had been such a constant presence for Chess for so many months that the thought of breaking it felt as alien as blotting out the sun.

'If you broke it, the Twisted Symmetry wouldn't be able to use it and they'd leave you alone. Oh yeah, and time and the world as we know it would be saved, etcetera.'

'It's probably difficult to do,' observed Chess. But inside, Anna's suggestion had buried itself like a bullet. The idea of finding the Eternal for herself ricocheted through Chess's thoughts. She barely dared to consider the possibilities.

Now Anna was looking at her own legs disapprovingly. 'Pink stockings, Chess? I can't believe it. I look like a five-year-old ballerina.'

'You didn't complain about the crisps, or the bread rolls,' sniffed Chess. The cold air thumped inside her head.

'OK, OK, let's go.'

Chess rapped on the wood and the door was opened by a muscle-head in a black suit.

'Hello, ladies,' he said with a gap-toothed smile.

Anna walked straight in, but as Chess followed, a figure in jeans and a hooded tracksuit top pushed his way out. He was taller than Chess and she thought he had dark hair, although the umbra cast by the hood masked his face. Chess was knocked part-way round.

I know you, she thought, as she watched him walk into the night. There was an ache in her chest. She felt close to the receding figure but far away at the same time and she realized that she didn't want him to walk away, whoever he was.

'Chess, come on.' Anna pulled her jacket arm.

'Are you in or out?' asked the doorman.

'She's in.' Anna gave the jacket a yank.

They didn't have to pay any money but they had to

sign an entrance book. Anna signed it for both of them;
Batman and Robin, in bold letters. The girl chewing
gum behind the counter said nothing. Music thumped
out of the darkness at the end of the entrance corridor
and Chess smelt cigarette smoke. Then she felt Anna
shove her forwards and heard her say, 'Once more unto
the breach.'

The two of them stumbled down a short flight of iron
stairs and onto a balcony. The balcony extended around the
circular wall of the room and there were booths off it, all the
way round. Most of the booths were empty. Leaning over
the metal handrail which vibrated with the thrum of the
music, Chess looked down onto a circular floor space filled
with chairs and round tables. Groups were gathered,
smoking, drinking and playing cards. Gold encrusted fingers
shunted stacks of money back and forth, clinked on glasses,
reached for hidden aces.

There was a long bar against the far wall, under the
balcony. Chess could pick out the dark cavities of more
drinking stalls with wooden bench seats like church pews,
leading off the central area. There was movement within
some of these stalls. Figures.

'We need to go down there,' she shouted to Anna.

They descended a spiral staircase, jerky as a pair of storks,
unnoticed by the gamblers, drinkers, fences and cutpurses.
At the bottom, Chess scanned about the lower booths and
saw, seated at one, the wide, ox-back of the Bank.

'Over there.' Her voice was obliterated by the music, but
Anna nodded and followed.

Chess stopped just behind where the Bank was sitting.

There were four other people seated along the table, two on each side, and at the far end, orange hair coiled like a portrait and with a smile as cool as the first shot in a gunfight, sat Klinky Mallows.

When Klinky Mallows saw Chess, her smile widened and she beckoned her into the booth. The back of the Bank's thick neck creased as he turned to look up. His bald, grizzled bullet-head carried a pair of thick-lensed spectacles and his door-broad shoulders threatened to burst the seams of his jacket. His smile made Chess wonder whether she should back out now, whilst she still could.

As soon as she had entered the deep cubicle, the sound of the music dropped to a murmur.

'What a relief,' said Anna, pushing in behind Chess.

'It's a sound screen,' explained an elderly man who wore a tweed suit and yellow-grey, lank hair. He pointed to the mouth of the booth. 'A row of minute speakers and microphones around the entrance creates negative interference which reduces the amplitude of the incoming sound waves.'

'Which means we can talk,' said Klinky. She beckoned to Chess. 'How are you, honey? Come and sit by me. Bring your friend with you.'

Chess negotiated one side of the table whilst Anna worked her way up the other.

'Is she OK?' grunted the Bank with a nod at Anna.

'You'll have to forgive the Bank, girls,' said Klinky, once Chess and Anna had settled down. 'He and I have been having a little disagreement about my investments.'

'What Klinky don't understand,' rumbled the Bank, 'is

that in the world of investment capitalism, interest is king. And I want my interest.'

'This is Shelf,' said Klinky Mallows, introducing the others at the table. A cliff-chinned bruiser sitting on the Bank's right nodded. 'This is Johnny Long Legs.' A pock-faced, knuckle-cheeked man on the Bank's left, younger than the others and skinnier. 'This is Bloody Madeleine,' whose long, milky hands were placed flat, either side of a glass of red wine and the bone-handled cutthroat razor that lay beside it. 'And this is Croot.' The elderly gentleman smiled pleasantly.

'Croot?' asked Anna.

'Short for crouton,' explained the man, 'on account of my dandruff. Terrible flaky scalp.' He brushed his fringe and a fine snow descended on Anna's coat. 'Sorry.'

The Bank waved over the waiter. 'No good,' he complained as the waiter dropped his tray and then began to take an order from another table first. 'New on tonight. He don't know what he's doing.'

After a brief delay, the drinks were ordered: beer, gin, red wine, whisky and a vermouth for Klinky Mallows. Anna asked for an orange juice and Chess for lemonade.

'This is a bit out of your way, isn't it?' enquired Klinky, crossing her legs and slapping down her short skirt as if it had done something wrong. 'You've grown up since I last saw you. Still got my nail file?'

'We've got to get into the CREX tower, at the Cones,' began Chess, 'and we need you to help us.'

'One step at a time, girl,' said Klinky.

'We've got to check the layout of the tower and check the chairman's office, for information,' enlarged Anna.

The Bank nodded at her with approval. 'This one's got the right idea, Klinky. Ready to help, see?'

'She didn't say she'd help *you*,' muttered Chess, too quietly for the Bank to hear.

'She's got her priorities the right way round,' continued the Bank. 'No need to *kick* 'em into place.'

Johnny Long Legs snorted a laugh.

'Clamp it, chicken boy,' snapped Klinky.

The Shelf prepared to stand. Bloody Madeleine picked up her razor and flicked it open. Johnny Long Legs slammed a dagger onto the table. Croot pulled a revolver from inside his jacket. The Bank extracted a machine pistol from inside his.

'Drinks,' announced the waiter. He set out the glasses in silence and then withdrew.

'Settle down, boys and girls.' Klinky took up her vermouth. 'Life's too short to end it now.' She lifted the glass to her bright red lips. 'Here's to Slack Harry.'

The dagger was swept from the table, the razor was folded, the guns were holstered and everybody reached for their glasses. With a murmur of 'Slack Harry', they drank.

Chess glugged down the lemonade and immediately, felt her stomach cramp. She looked across at Anna who had downed most of her juice, but Anna seemed fine. She had taken the Link-me out of her bag and powered it up. Her fingers tapped buttons and then she was pointing at the screen and talking animatedly. Klinky shuffled close to her and Chess heard her laugh and say, 'At last, I get to be a billionaire.'

It was hard to pay attention because her stomach hurt so

badly; like a paddle was turning in her guts. More drinks were ordered but Chess just shook her head and now everyone was crowded round Anna. Klinky leant over Anna's right shoulder, the Bank loomed over her left and the others were gathered up close to view the screen which sculpted their faces black and silver in its goblin glow. All the time, confident explanation streamed from Anna.

'Forty-eight again!' bubbled Klinky with delight. She kissed Anna's temple. 'I love you already, honey.' Then, more reticent, 'But I'm not sure this is my thing.'

'This is good.' The Bank chewed his words like tobacco. 'You should work for me. We could do great business.'

Chess closed her eyes as she began to feel sick. She heard the Bank say, 'Me and Pacer have been having words. I can help. I've got a contact inside CREX; a squealer who needs his debts settling.' His huge frog-face split in a grin. 'He blabbed to the crashers eight years back. He owes us *big*. But, he was more use as a long-term investment than a slab-job.' He tossed his chin towards Klinky. 'Go on this little scouting trip tomorrow morning, and you can consider *our* debt settled.'

'But there's nothing in it for you,' Anna said to the Bank. She knew that Chess didn't want him to get involved. This had nothing to do with him.

'Not yet. At this stage I'm just speculating.' Then he patted her on the shoulder a little too hard. 'But there's information in CREX that will be useful to me. And you'll need my help before this is over.'

'I go with Fury here, and we're even?' Klinky asked the Bank.

'You go with her, find out how and where the chairman stores his data, and I might even make you a member of the board.'

'Are you OK?'

It took Chess a moment to realize that it was Anna who was talking to her.

'Are you OK, Chess?'

Chess shook her head. 'I need to go to the toilets.'

Anna screwed up her face. 'Will you be OK?'

'I think I can handle the toilets.'

'That way.' Klinky pointed.

'Thanks.' Chess left them planning the visit to CREX.

The pain had eased, but she still felt sick. She needed cold water and her own space. Chess crossed the bar, trudged down some uneven, wooden steps and came to the door with 'Ladies' marked on it. There was a round, brass handle. She put her hand over it and then gasped, snatching it back as if the brass had been ice. As she had touched the handle, she had seen daylight; she had seen the bar empty and flooded with light.

Looking back, up through the drop of the steps, she saw that the windows, high in the walls of the bar, were full of night.

Probably she had seen the bright light because of her upset stomach, she decided. Chess had heard that people saw flashing lights when they had bad headaches. Maybe stomach aches could so the same thing.

She made herself take hold of the handle again and this time it didn't feel like ice.

You destroy Inquisitors for breakfast, she told herself. You can handle the ladies' toilets.

She entered the chamber and the door swung shut behind her. On one side there was a row of cubicles with doors open, on the other, basins facing a long mirror. Cracked, white tiles covered the floor. A white, fluorescent tube flickered along the ceiling. Everything was white, which made Chess blink and feel more nauseous.

She squared up to herself before the wall mirror. She wasn't used to her reflection and she spent a couple of minutes looking at it. Her long, brown hair was tangled. Her face had lost its Surapoor tan; it was pale, apart from her eyes which had dark smudges under them. She licked her lips and practised pouting them in the way Klinky did. She rubbed them with a finger to see if that would make them redder.

'You could make more of yourself, honey,' she drawled, in the way that Klinky Mallows would have drawled. 'Wash your hair. Get some sleep.' She smiled and then grimaced at what she saw. 'Clean those teeth, Chess. You can't fight the Twisted Symmetry with teeth like that. Not unless you want to breathe them to death.'

She leant forwards and exhaled so that a thin mist sheened the mirror. CHESS, she wrote, with absolute concentration. Then she rubbed it out with a squeak of her palm. At least the sickness was going.

She ran a tap, bent over the basin and splashed water over her face. It tingled in a freezing foam. She splashed some more and then, she realized that she didn't want to look back up, into the mirror. She had an overwhelming desire *not* to see what was behind her.

Chess froze. Water dripped from her downcast face.

Look up, she told herself. Look up, you stupid girl.

Slowly, she looked up.

In the mirror there was an open door and a cubicle with a lavatory inside it. Nothing else.

Chess exhaled slowly, easing the tension. 'You're too jumpy, honey,' she said, before leaning back over the basin and splashing more water on her face. Maybe it would put some colour into her cheeks.

It was when she next looked up that she saw him; an old man, thin, with long hands and a face like melted wax. The Narrow Man. His tall body was naked and as featureless as his molten face, as if the flesh that hung on it was collapsing. He opened his arms and the space behind Chess flexed and then curved into the toilet cubicle like a funnel. Even before she had screamed, she had been swallowed by the convex walls of space, the door slamming shut and imprisoning her.

Some things were more ancient, more powerful than the Inquisitors, Balthazar had warned her. The Narrow Man was one of these things. He had come to her when she had used the skulk rack but had been warded away by her mother's song. But now, Chess was locked inside a cubicle at Slack Harry's and the Narrow Man had her to himself; this time, nobody was singing.

I am ending this now.

Chess had her back flat against the door and was heaving in breath. The Narrow Man's voice was inside her head, as dry and quiet as a stirring of dead leaves in a winter breeze.

There is no purpose in prolonging this game.

His long hands hung wide open by his thighs in an absurdly peaceful gesture. His tallow flesh drooped in folds from his face to his feet, so loose it was like a shapeless robe.

Chess threw herself back against the door, to force it open. The Narrow Man lifted an arm and crabbed his hand. Yellow bone broke out of the sagging fingertips and caged itself around Chess's head. She felt her neck jolt as she was wrenched from the door and onto the toilet seat. Her hands clawed at the bone. Its rough, cold hardness scraped her face and neck.

The time for the Eternal is now.

Chess felt the weight of the bone against the top of her head. She pushed back, the resistance digging into her crown. Then something seemed to give within her spine and she felt her neck sinking into her body and she knew that she was being compressed into the space that other people couldn't see; her body shifting into other dimensions.

Her eyes felt like they had been injected with hot silver and the brightness was blinding. She tried to relax, to sense the hidden dimensions for herself and climb back out of them. The squeeze of bone tightened on her head and she imagine herself sliding out of it, like her hand had passed through the table in front of Crazy Boris earlier.

A hiss of wind through skeletal branches; laughter.

You poor, beautiful, doomed creature, you are fighting yourself.

The laughter stopped. The bone brace vanished. Chess was surfacing back into her world. But as the inside of the cubicle shimmered into focus, Chess realized that the Narrow Man's grip had not been released because of anything that she had done.

Mevrad.

'Bael,' said Ethel, climbing over the top of the cubicle partition, her tweed skirt riding up and her stockings wrinkling down to her ankles.

You should not be here.

'Neither should you. You know the terms of engagement, and trying to cut through the formalities by stealing the girl for yourself isn't amongst them.' Ethel hung down the chipboard wall, clinging to the top by her fingers before dropping to the floor.

'Goodness!' She smoothed down her skirt, pulled up her stockings and patted Chess on the head. 'Hello, dear.'

'Hello,' said Chess, who was still sitting on the toilet seat.

'How are you?'

'How does it look?'

Ethel waved a chilblained finger in front of her face. 'This is how you wanted it, my love. You wanted to do it your way.' But she put herself between Chess and the Narrow Man.

How did you know I was here?

'It doesn't matter,' said Ethel, and Chess could tell from the way the old lady's voice trembled that she was very, very angry.

It was easy to find her. It will be easy for me to find her again.

'You will do no such thing,' roared Ethel, and for a moment her body expanded, unfurling from the husk that was Ethel and into the form of the Baroness Mevrad Styx; tall, with lustrous jet hair, lithe milk limbs and a voice that cracked open the dimensions. Then, she shrank back into the bag lady, Ethel. Moderately, she repeated, 'You will do no such thing.'

Chess saw that Bael stood unbowed, but she felt his aura withdraw, flickering.

'You may *use* whom you like,' continued Ethel. 'And so may I. We can plan their moves, position them how we wish, but *we* cannot interfere further. They make their choices and we live or die by the consequences. You have a time for action, Bael, but it isn't now.'

You intervened when she was first caught by the hunters.

'Of course I did. I knew you'd do something like this, so I got my cheat in early. I borrowed five minutes, just as you've done. I exercised a little influence at the detention unit. I was keeping the balance, albeit in advance of you trying to unbalance it. But I did no more than that.

'Now we're even, Bael.' Ethel spoke as if addressing a silly boy, just as Chess had heard her speak to Box so many times before. 'Prevent them from making their own choices and we cease to exist at all. Remember that, Bael. The final choices must always rest with them.'

The Narrow Man said nothing. Whatever was taking place between him and Ethel, Chess sensed his defeat. But already her mind was elsewhere. The Narrow Man had known where to find her. But the decision to come to Slack Harry's had only been made when she and the others had been at the café. Somehow, the Narrow Man had known this; or had found it out. Or, maybe, he had been told.

Then, Chess realized why Jerkan hadn't come after her. He hadn't been waiting outside the café to catch her. He'd been listening. She knew that the Twisted Symmetry used spy technology; there was no reason why they couldn't have used a listening device, the car had only been a couple of metres away from them, on the other side of the café window. Somehow, the Symmetry had learnt where they were, after their visit to the orphanage and then, instead of closing in, they had waited to gather information. Which meant that they would know all about the planned visit to the Cones tomorrow. Chess needed to get back to the others, to tell them not to go.

'You should not have come here, Bael. This was not your time.' Ethel sighed. 'How to undo what you have done? This meeting should never have happened.'

We must put her back; back to the moment before she entered this room.

Ethel hesitated.

Instinctively, Chess did not like the Narrow Man's suggestion. The fact that it was *his* suggestion meant that it would be treacherous. 'Ethel,' she began, but an abrupt flick of the old lady's hand silenced her.

'You are right,' agreed Ethel. 'The moment before she entered the room is the right time.'

When she first touched the handle of the door.

The ice cold handle. The flash of daylight. Chess knew that this was wrong.

'Exactly.' The old, grey head nodded.

'No,' gasped Chess, and then, clutching at the next feeling which drove through her chest. 'Stay, Ethel. Please.'

The old lady turned to look at her and smiled a little sadly. 'As I told you, dear, you made your choice, and I can't say I blame you. I'd have done exactly the same. But I can't interfere now.' She faced the emaciated form of the Narrow Man, again. 'Back to before she entered, Bael.'

The Narrow Man raised his hand and circled it, a gesture as lazy as the skin which sagged from his long limb.

Chess would have yelled out, begged Ethel one last time not to allow him to do this, but she was standing outside the door to the ladies' toilets. Slack Harry's was illuminated by moted shafts of daylight from the high windows and a man in an overall was sweeping fragments of broken glass into a dusty pile.

'Where've you come from?' He peered down the stairs, suspicion and astonishment wrestling for control of his face.

Chess's stomach was spinning. She recognized the sensation of having travelled through time but this felt different from the other two occasions, when she had experienced reverse-time. Which meant, probably, that this was forwards-time.

'Where is everyone, the people, Klinky Mallows and everyone?' she babbled.

'Klinky Mallows was here last night,' explained the man, holding his brush like it was a spear. 'She was with the Bank and a gang of others.'

'What time is it now?'

'Ten o'clock in the morning.' The man scratched his head, perplexed. 'Where'd you come from? You shouldn't even be here.'

Chess fought back a surge of panic. Somehow, the Narrow Man had laid a trap, a time trap, knowing that Ethel might come, knowing that she would want him to blot out his intervention. It was like he had dug a hole through time so that when he put Chess outside the door, she would fall through to the following morning, too late to warn Anna and Klinky that the Twisted Symmetry would be waiting for them at the Cones.

Ethel had made a mistake. Again.

Chess sprinted up the stairs, knocking the man out of the way.

'You're locked in,' he shouted after her.

But Chess couldn't be locked into any place that didn't have bars on the windows.

Before the cleaner guessed what the girl planned to do, she had charged up the spiral staircase to the balcony, taken a chair from one of the booths and hurled it through a window. She punched out the remaining triangles of glass before climbing through and jumping down to the sign which said Slack Harry's. From there, it was easy to drop to the pavement.

Out on the street, she sucked in cold air, filling her lungs, preparing to run.

'Please, get there late, Anna,' she whispered. 'Give me time. Please.'

CHAPTER 14

They were waiting in a loading bay, five metres from the mouth of one of the tunnel-like service entrances at the foot of the CREX tower. Chess had been running so hard, she could feel the blood pulsing in her eyes. She had pounded through the streets, skanked on the trams and buses until she'd been kicked off, and raced the final mile until the Cones were only a couple of hundred metres ahead. Now, as the group in the loading bay came into view, she allowed herself to slow down.

Shading her eyes against the sun and towers of glinting glass, she could see the Bank's diesel, flatbed truck. The solid figure of the Bank filled the driver's seat and there was somebody in the passenger seat, but from where she was, Chess couldn't tell who. Pacer and Hex were sitting on the back, legs dangling, along with three other street rats she didn't recognize. There were two more rats lounging against the front grille. All of them were waiting. Chess's pace quickened slightly. Anna and Klinky must have still been in the CREX tower.

None of them had noticed her, yet.

'Get out, Anna. Get out,' panted Chess as she jogged towards the waiting party.

A figure stumbled out of the low entrance of the service corridor. It was Anna. Chess stopped and watched, heart thumping.

Anna had been running. Chess could tell that by the way she was bent forwards, slumping slightly. Anna turned to look back the way she had come and for a moment, it looked to Chess as if she was laughing. Chess took a step forwards. It felt as if time was slowing. She was so focused on Anna that it was like she was staring down a telescope.

Anna stopped laughing. She started to walk backwards. There was a bang from the service entrance. She staggered. Another bang and this time, Anna's tall, strong body was blown off its feet, crashing into the door of the truck cab before collapsing to the ground.

Chess's mouth hung open. Her chest felt as if it had just been smashed by a piston.

'No,' she gasped. 'No, no, no.' She knew what gun shots sounded like.

She backed away from what she had just seen. She didn't want to be there. She didn't want to stay staring at what had just happened.

'Look where you're going,' said the first man she ran into. The next one shoved her in the shoulder, hard enough to knock her off balance so that she banged her knees on a stone bench.

'Clumsy tart,' he spat.

Chess ran. She ran until the plaza was behind her and she had found a shop yard full of bins and refuse sacks that was enclosed by high walls which shut out everything else. There, she dropped to her knees and choked back the sobs that came so hard it made her throat ache.

But, even if she had got to the Cones earlier, Chess wasn't sure she could have done anything to stop what had just happened. As she took control of herself and dwelt on this thought, she began to wonder if she *could* get there earlier. Time was just another dimension, that was what Ethel had said. Wasn't she learning, slowly, to open the dimensions; to travel through them?

Ethel could do it, Behrens could do it, the Narrow Man whom Ethel called Bael could do it. I'm a synth, thought Chess. I'm not normal. They made me strange. They made me able to do things that aren't normal.

Supposing she learnt to *use* her strangeness?

'None of you know what you're dealing with,' whispered Chess, feeling the invigorating surge of anger which burnt away grief.

But she understood her limitations. She was new to the science of the dimensions. It was a challenge to move her hand through two inches of wood. She was a long way from what Ethel and the Inquisitor and the Narrow Man could do. But she didn't want days or even hours; minutes would do.

Chess closed her eyes, relaxed, imagined her body merging with the space around it as if there was no boundary between her own form and what lay beyond. She felt for the gaps in space, the soft contours, the way that everything was actually one thing.

There were so many dimensions. She could feel them

opening around her. She held this feeling and opened her eyes and saw that the dustbins and rubbish bags were streaming like rays, iridescent, projecting forwards and backwards in what was called time as well as what was called space. But those names didn't apply any more because these radiating shapes had extended into everything at every time. They had become part of one thing that was more complex and more beautiful than her mind could stand.

Chess didn't try to open the dimensions further. Just shifting them apart like this was a mind-crunching effort, like trying to lift a heavy drain cover with her fingernails to get a glimpse of what lay underneath and only moving it a couple of millimetres. But a couple of millimetres were all she needed; a couple of minutes.

Chess closed her eyes again. Calm. She let her body project forwards and backwards with the rest of the city, which streamed through the dimensions for as long as it had existed and as long as it would exist. She merged with this stream and sought a way back; back to where the city was before she had reached the Cones; back to the moments before she had seen what had happened to Anna; back to the seconds before the gun had been fired.

The appointment with Mr Ravillious had been running smoothly. Klinky Mallows and Anna had transformed themselves into the wealthy Rachel Leeward and her PA at Klinky's apartment earlier that morning; Anna in make-up, a black skirt and jacket and a white blouse, and Klinky in a fur-collared coat, a short red dress, long black gloves and a pair of huge, brown-tinted sunglasses. So far, they had had no opportunity to explore the layout of the CREX tower. They had been met at reception by a smartly suited but flustered young man called Marcel who had escorted them directly to the chairman's bowling-alley sized office on the tenth floor.

Mr Ravillious was courteous and he had a deep, sonorous voice matured by long business meetings and strong cigars. With effortless grace he told Mrs Rachel Leeward (recently divorced) that he was 'delighted' and she inclined her brassy-blonde head (recently dyed) and said she was 'enchanted'. His steel-grey hair was slicked precisely and his skin was tanned like leather and scored with deep lines that spoke of fierce negotiation and pitiless living. Sitting opposite Anna and Klinky, he reclined in his desk chair with liquid ease, as if nothing could have given him greater satisfaction than this very meeting. Anna concealed her bitterness under a demurely blank face; if this was the person behind her brother's death, he was very relaxed about it.

She took notes of their discussions in a small, black notebook in which she had also scribbled down what she had seen of door codes, security personnel and the keys pressed by Mr Ravillious to access the computer and data stack on his desk. These codes were valuable, to her and to the Bank. They would be the gateway to the information they wanted. She knew that Chess had warned against teaming up with the Bank, but Anna was realistic; for a job like this, they needed whatever assistance they could get.

Right now, Anna was listening dutifully to Klinky's recital of Mrs Leeward's financial requirements whilst making a mental note of the contents of the chairman's huge office. There appeared to be no CCTV; that would be helpful. Surreptitiously, her eyes glided to the far wall on their left. According to the Bank, who had already made some enquiries, there should have been a door there; a door which gave access to a stairwell which led onto a staircase that descended to the service entrance where he would be waiting for them, if required. An emergency exit. But Anna couldn't see a door, although there might have been the outline of a panel in the wall.

Klinky seemed to be enjoying herself, but Anna was realizing that it would be more difficult than they had imagined to 'accidentally' wander up to the hundredth floor and look for the cerebral torus. And also, she was unnerved by how patient Mr Ravillious had proved to be. Anna had expected him to be polite, but brusque; after all, he was the chairman of a global mega-corporation. To have arranged a meeting like this at such short notice must have been inconvenient, however promising it appeared. Yet, Mr Ravillious's courtesy was accommodating to the point of becoming leisurely. It was because he was so generous with his time that Anna began to realize that something was wrong.

'Tell me again,' Mr Ravillious was saying in his casual, stately voice, 'how you plan to fund the investments in off-shore mining? It is a highly risky enterprise, Mrs Leeward, which means there is a good deal to be lost, as well as gained.'

Not for the first time, Anna noticed how his eyes looked behind them rather than at them, whilst his strong, neat fingers remained interlinked on the top of the broad, walnut desk.

He saw Anna watching him closely and without smiling asked, 'Can I get you anything, young lady?'

She knew that he expected her to be embarrassed into saying, 'No, thank you.' So she pointed to a side table that stood in front of the wall-long window and asked for a glass of water.

Mr Ravillious cracked a little smile, creaked out of the leather chair and strode to the table. He was dark and thin against the expanse of white sky. He stood with his back to them and poured a glass of water from the carafe which sat on the table top.

'What do you think of the view, Mrs Leeward?'

'I like it very much, Mr Ravillious,' said Klinky Mallows, casting an experienced eye up and down the chairman's neat figure.

Anna glanced over her shoulder, at the door through which they had been conducted into the meeting. It was wooden, with fogged glass panels at the top and bottom. She frowned as she saw tall shapes move on the other side of the glass; very tall shapes, like people but with unnaturally long legs.

She jabbed Klinky's upper arm and pointed.

Mr Ravillious was setting down the carafe, his back still towards them. Klinky took a look at the door and all semblance of ease vanished from her face. 'Traders,' she mouthed.

'What?'

Klinky shook her head. 'We have to get out. Right now.'

Fenley Ravillious returned to the desk, a tumbler of water in his hand. He passed Anna the tumbler and as he did so, she caught sight of the motif on the silver signet ring he wore; a decorative letter 'C' and three tiny stars. She hated that symbol but she hid her hatred behind a polite smile and her unblinking, crystal-blue eyes. 'Thank you.'

Mr Ravillious turned his attention back to the wealthy Mrs Leeward. Anna stretched her neck one way and then the other as if easing the tension cranked up by her diligent note-taking.

'Are you sure you are comfortable?' asked the chairman, a burr of irritation at the edge of his voice.

'Yes, thank you very much,' smiled Anna. *Killer*, she thought. But she was sure now that there was a panel in the far wall. The staircase had to be behind it.

She waited until Mr Ravillious had begun to converse with Klinky again before throwing the contents of the tumbler into his face. Then, just to be sure, she hurled the tumbler into it too.

'This way,' she shouted, pushing back her chair so hard it keeled over and onto the carpet with a soft thud. She didn't know whether Klinky was with her until she had reached the wall with the panel. Then came the sound of people bursting into the office through the wooden door and by her shoulder, Klinky's voice cursing the stilettos she had chosen that morning.

There wasn't a handle, so Anna threw her weight against the panel. She heard it click and when she stepped back, it swung open, towards her. She threw it wide and was out on a cold, concrete stairwell that squared downwards with a ten floor drop at its centre.

Klinky was bending down, loosening the straps of her shoes and kicking her feet free. 'Don't wait for me, honey,' she drawled, face by her knees. 'There won't be a runners-up prize in this race.'

Anna didn't stay to watch the wild-haired, stilt-legged figures who charged towards them, long coats flapping, savage faces snarling. She galloped onto the hard steps, footfalls reverberating up the hidden height of the well.

From above came a crash of footfalls and angry howls, echoing.

'Go, go, go,' Anna chanted to herself, taking the stairs three at a time and only slowing down when she crashed into the wall at the end of each flight.

'You still there?' she managed to shout at one point, although her lungs felt like they'd collapsed.

From somewhere between her and the tornado descent of the traders came a hoarse cry of, 'Not for much longer,' and Anna knew that for the time being, Klinky was with her.

She was gasping so loudly and her feet were pounding so hard that she didn't notice that the traders had broken off their pursuit until she heard Klinky yell, 'Would you slow down, for goodness' sake?'

Still, she didn't stop her downwards charge until she had crashed into three more walls and the fire in her legs had burnt out the final shreds of energy. Then the volleying footfalls slowed and a hard silence filled the stairwell, broken only by wheezing from Klinky.

'Come on,' urged Anna. 'About four more floors to go.'

'We're OK,' coughed Klinky, leaning over the handrail, several flights above Anna, the heel straps of her shoes looped over her left hand and her sunglasses gone. 'If you don't mind, I'd like to reinflate my lungs.'

But Anna was on her way down again. 'The Bank said they'd be waiting for us outside the north service entrance. It's not far from the bottom of these stairs.'

'It's OK, honey,' insisted Klinky, who was dizzy from the helter-skelter descent. 'They only wanted to chase us off. Those freaks could have had us if they wanted. Slow down.'

'We're not out yet,' warned Anna. She knew what CREX did to people who got in its way. Merely chasing them off was not its style.

Her eyes scanned the remaining flights and she listened out for the least scrape of a foot, or creak of one of the doors or service hatches onto the stairs. But she heard nothing and now she had hit the ground floor with Klinky not far behind.

Up ahead, there was a sharp square of light where the service corridor ended and outside began. It was far enough away to look no bigger than a stamp. Anna waited for Klinky by the bottom of the stairwell.

'Home and dry,' said Klinky Mallows as she staggered down to Anna, shoes still swinging from her hand. She sneezed loudly on the concrete dust that floated in the gloomy corridor.

'Come on.' Anna set off at a brisk walk.

'You're too panicky, honey. And too fit. I don't know what species you are, but I'm a human; I need to breathe every now and then.'

'I don't want to end up dead,' Anna said through her teeth.

She could see the truck now and figures around it.

'You were off like a rabbit.' Klinky laughed and her voice bounced off the concrete. 'Nearly ran through the office wall.'

Maybe it was because the tension was easing, or maybe it was because Klinky's raucous laugh triggered her own, but Anna realized that she was laughing too. And, now that she came to think of it, it was funny, the way that she had just run into the office wall, hoping somehow that would open the door.

'I can't believe you stopped to take your shoes off,' she said, and then she really did start laughing hard. 'Four or five traders coming for us and you start undressing.'

'It was an emergency.' Klinky snorted back her laughter, walking beside Anna.

'It's just as well ...' gasped Anna, 'the traders didn't think it was an emergency ... I wouldn't want to see them ... getting undressed ... and chasing us down the stairs.'

Her eyes were wet and she bent double. Klinky rested a hand on her back. 'Go on, honey,' she said. 'Tell the boys to saddle the horses. We're out of this place.' She dropped her shoes to the floor. 'I need to slip into something less comfortable.' Bending down, she dug her foot through the straps.

Anna walked ahead. She was almost out of the tunnel-like corridor. 'I'd like to see the traders giving it long legs in stilettos,' muttered Klinky, loud enough for Anna to enjoy.

'What's so funny?' grouched the Bank from the driver's seat in the truck cab. Anna was going to tell him but the deadpan faces of Pacer and the street rats reminded her that this was serious. And their visit had only been partially successful; they knew all about the chairman's office and where the data was stored but they were no wiser as to the whereabouts of the brain.

'Who's that with Klinky?' The Bank nodded his wide, bald head towards the service exit.

Anna turned round; there shouldn't have been anyone with Klinky.

But there was someone; someone closing in behind her with unnaturally long strides, someone whose thick, knotted hair streamed over his shoulders, whose beard was plaited and whose trailing grey coat swirled open revealing a broad belt into which there was tucked the barrel of a heavy handgun.

Anna was looking at Klinky, and Klinky who had just stood up from fastening her stilettos, looked back. She read Anna's face and she knew that something bad was coming for her. Anna saw how Klinky's red lips began to part, her eyes widened and she started to turn round.

Diamonds of hatred glinted in the dark eyes of the trader. His cudgel fist grasped the handgun and he levelled it at Klinky.

Klinky Mallows didn't turn round. Her eyes locked on Anna's and she opened her mouth. Anna saw her shout, 'Run,' but what she heard was the thunder-clap of the handgun.

Klinky dropped to her knees, a dark stain spreading quickly in all directions across the front of her red dress.

And now the barrel of the gun was pointing at Anna. Anna tripped backwards, but although she knew she should run, her mind didn't seem to send the message to her body.

The gun flashed and roared.

Anna expected to take the blast in her chest but instead, something hit her in her right side. She was driven sideways by a body that slammed into her own. Her feet were off the floor and then her left shoulder and hip struck the hard ground. She felt her ribs give and she began to cough as she tried to fill her lungs with air again.

'Chess,' she managed to choke. 'Where'd you come from?' She clambered onto her hands and knees.

'I did it,' panted Chess, lungs working like bellows. She had sprinted across the plaza as hard as she had ever sprinted, her head was sore from where it had banged off the flagstones, but she had done it. She had saved Anna. But she had nearly been too late. 'Lucky . . . he missed you . . . with his first,' she wheezed.

'He didn't miss.' Anna lifted her face from the floor, black hair fringing it. 'He got Klinky,' and she stared at Chess darkly.

'I didn't know,' shouted Chess. 'It's not my fault. Stop looking at me like it's my fault.'

Anna pushed herself up and swayed towards the truck. Chess followed a couple of metres behind.

The Bank was out of his cab, standing by the freshly dented door with his machine pistol by his side. His jacket hung open revealing his string vest and heavy belly. Pacer and the other street rats were standing on either side of him.

Opposite, and in the mouth of the exit, a body lay on its side in a dark pool, one white arm neatly curved above its head. Looming over it, gun still in hand, was the huge, gnarled figure that Chess recognized as Jerkan, the trader chieftain. Behind him, three more of the snake-haired, long-legged stalkers had gathered.

'You not come back here,' shouted Jerkan, mauling the words which echoed across the plaza. Then he pointed at Chess, who had stopped in front of the others. 'But you, we will get.'

Chess ignored him. She didn't even look at him. All she saw was Klinky's lifeless body and the spectres of Ethel and Splinter, standing on either side of it and looking back at her.

'This is how you wanted it, my love.' Ethel wagged a finger at her. 'You wanted to do it your way.'

Splinter stabbed her with a dagger of spite. 'You always get it wrong, Chess.'

Chess shook her head to shake away the memories. Now, Klinky lay there alone, with the traders standing over her.

'I'm sorry,' whispered Chess. 'I'm really sorry, Klinky.' It was hard, using people. It hurt them.

She started to walk towards the body. Anna was going to pull her back but Pacer blocked Anna with an arm. 'Look,' he said, and she saw that as Chess advanced, the three traders at the rear retreated.

The other street rats saw this also. They didn't know that the quickening in their chests, or the energy bursting through their limbs was what jacks would call pride, but without thinking about it, they put back their shoulders, lifted up their chins and followed Chess.

As Chess knelt by Klinky's body, she heard Jerkan say, 'We will get you. When you are alone. Listen for the whistling.'

Then a door slammed on the truck and a slow and heavy boot tread came from behind. Chess hadn't looked at Jerkan, but when she saw the steel toecapped boots crunch to a halt, she looked up at the man in jeans and a donkey jacket, who had stopped beside her. He patted her twice on the shoulder.

'You stay away from here,' rumbled Jerkan, remorseless.

The Night Porter knelt and slipped his arms under Klinky's body. When he stood, he cradled it as if it weighed nothing. One pale limb hung loose, like a drowsy child's. By Chess's face, a swathe of yellow hair unfurled, now dyed red.

Chess shut her eyes to block it out so she didn't see how the Night Porter met the trader's glare with his own executioner's gaze. But she heard his voice, cool and steady. 'You've made a bad mistake, big man.'

CHAPTER 15

It was a big fire and it crackled and spat in a way that filled the silence comfortably. Dozens of rats had gathered round it for warmth. It streaked their grimy faces and made their eyes glint. Behind them, the shattered backdrop of the wharf was silent in the winter night and the broken warehouse walls stood dark as the edge of a forest. The river was a wide tongue of black and far away, across the frozen rubble, pinpoint yellow lights speckled the Pit ridge like a band of fallen stars.

Nobody had said that it was Chess's fault. Nobody had said that Klinky had died because Chess had made her fight their fight. Nobody spoke to her at all; they just kept staring at her and the smallest street rats had come to sit near her.

'Even the traders are frightened of Chess,' she heard one tiny boy say, before elbowing his way to her ankles.

Gemma said nothing. She just sat by Chess, keeping her company.

Chess kept on telling herself that this was how it had to be; stopping the Twisted Symmetry would be hell, there were bound to be casualties; she warned herself that there would be more before this was over. For the first time, she had a prickling of what it must be like to be Ethel; planning, predicting, weighing up who to use and how to use them: living with the consequences.

But she wasn't Ethel. Tripping back in time merely ten minutes had drained her. Chess kept wondering if she could have travelled back further, or repeated it to save Klinky as well as Anna, but in the hours that followed, her strength was exhausted and as her time slipped forwards, relentlessly, Klinky's slipped into the past and beyond any place that Chess could reach.

'What are you stewing about?' Anna had been sitting on a lorry tyre, close to Chess, hands dangling idly over her knees and silent, until now. Chess had explained to her what she had done to try to save Klinky and how she had saved Anna, but still, Anna's eyes lingered reproachfully on Chess. 'What are you thinking?'

'We don't need *him*,' muttered Chess. 'You shouldn't of got him involved.'

'Don't be stupid, Chess.' Anna knew that Chess was talking about the Bank. 'We're out of our depth without some help. We haven't any choice.'

Opposite them, in a collapsible, metal gardening chair, sat the Bank. His corpulent thighs and buttocks were crammed into the seat so that they bulged out under the thin arm rests and the sunflower-patterned fabric. Beside him, on up-turned oil drums, sat Pacer and Hex. They conferred with one another, sage and deliberate as generals.

'In ten minutes' time, Johnny Long Legs will be here with the information you need,' said the Bank. 'Information about the hundredth floor in the CREX tower. If you want me to give it to you, you've got to do that little job for me.'

'The data?' confirmed Anna.

The Bank rummaged in an outside pocket of his jacket and held up a cylinder, two inches long, minute between his bulbous fingers. 'It's called a FAT-dump.'

'A what?' Pacer raised his eyebrows in mock shock and then grinned at Hex.

'File Analogue Transfer,' stated Anna, still leaning over her long legs. 'It copies data from where the data's stored, in bulk and very quickly. Ravillious's data stack is free standing; data is uploaded regularly but it isn't part of the network so you couldn't hack in, even if the thought of hacking in didn't make Chess wet her pants. But I've got his password, I saw him type it in today. I can transfer the data once we're in his office.'

'I'm not that bothered about the data,' protested Chess.

'No, but *he* is,' said Anna with a nod at the Bank, 'and there's the information I'*d* like to access. *Remember?*'

'Good girl. Stick it in the right place and press SAVE.' The Bank laughed thickly. 'By tomorrow night all those CREX accounts will be at my disposal. I'll be creaming billions.' He tossed the FAT-dump across to Anna. She snatched it out of the air with a snap of her arm and zipped it inside the top pouch of her boot bag.

'Won't Ravillious be in his office?' Chess wasn't trying to be difficult but it seemed an obvious problem.

'That's where the distraction comes in,' said Hex, with a wink at Pacer. It was clear that there had been a lot of planning without her involvement. Chess knew that she should have been grateful that the others were in on this with her, but she felt distant from them.

Guilt, diagnosed Splinter inside her head.

Chess had been thinking more and more about Splinter and Box. The further she felt she was from everyone else, the more she wanted to be back with her brothers. And she was starting to think that there was a way to find out where they were.

'We're going to need a distraction if we're going to get the data from the office and then sort out the brain,' Pacer was saying.

'Which is where you need me again, Miss Tuesday.' The Bank smiled his rubbery smile. 'The boys are thinking smoke bombs. But whereas they're thinking the stuff you get from a joke shop, I'm thinking military ordinance. I've got my contacts, and I can get you so much smoke those jacks in the CREX tower will be out like rats.'

'How will you get the smoke bombs in?' asked Chess.

'There's a gang of us will use the drains,' said Hex, very pleased to be ready with an answer. 'The Bank can get us plans of where to go inside the building.'

'Good lad,' smiled the Bank.

'We can't do this without his help, Chess.' Anna was definite.

'All I want is my data.'

'Stop going on about your data,' snapped Chess. Total silence broke out around the fire. 'This is about stopping the Twisted Symmetry from stealing children, not you making money. And we don't even know how to disable the brain yet. We need to find the poison that feeds it. There'll be a supply and we could kill the brain by cutting off the supply, but we don't know where anything is. Do we?'

There was a crunch of boots in the darkness. 'Bang on cue,' announced the Bank, as Johnny Long Legs emerged from the night and into the jumping orange circle of the bonfire, a cardboard roll under one arm.

'Sorry I was late, boss. Got lost.'

The Bank reached up and patted his hip. 'No grief, Johnny. You're here now. And just in time. Little Miss over there was about to blow a fuse.' He smiled at Chess indulgently and then laughed in a way that made her regret snapping at him.

'The squealer says he hopes this settles his debt,' relayed knuckle-faced Johnny.

'It'll make me forget about him, for a while,' chuckled the Bank, 'until I need him again, or get bored.'

He extracted a sheaf of tightly rolled plans. They had been drawn on tissue-thin sheets which rustled loudly as the Bank shook them open.

Johnny continued, breathlessly. 'He says that the day after tomorrow, the CREX tower will shut down because they're starting up a *special* operation.'

Chess looked at Anna: she knew which special operation the squealer was talking about.

'So, we've got one clear day before they start the computer.' Anna's blue eyes flashed in the firelight.

Pacer sniffed and spat into the flames. 'Seems we've got a lot to do, all of a sudden.'

Chess chewed her lip. She needed more time; time to see crazy Boris. It wasn't just that there might be vital information within the vault. Attacking the brain would be very, very lively. There was no guarantee that anyone who went would be coming back. Chess knew that if she didn't discover what the vault contained *before* they attacked the brain, she might *never* discover what it contained.

Johnny was excited. 'The squealer says that up at the top of the tower, they've been building something out of biological material.'

'He says a lot,' observed Anna.

'That's his *problem*,' muttered the Bank, slapping the plans flat over his sagging chest and curved stomach so that the others could see them.

'He gave me a list of some of the material, if you're interested.' Johnny tugged a piece of rumpled notepaper from his trouser pocket. He held it towards the fire and read falteringly. 'Adrenaline, PGK, Magbol-X, Fulger's enzyme. It's technical. I didn't write any more down.'

The Link-me was flickering into life. Anna searched for information about the substances on the list. 'Maybe useful to know what these are for,' she explained. But after a minute during which everyone watched her as if she were an oracle, she shook her head and said, 'Something to do with steroids and chemicals for muscle growth. Nothing about brains.'

'He says that there's something up on the hundredth floor; something *unnatural*.'

'That sounds more like our brain,' said Anna.

'He says these are the plans we need, but he has to get them back tonight.'

'No worries, Johnny. Now calm down.' The Bank patted his paper-coated belly. 'Time to look at the detail, ladies.'

The diagrams were so finely drawn and so intricate that Chess and Anna had to scuff their way round to where the Bank sat, beaming like a generous emperor.

'OK,' said Anna, pointing with a long finger. Actually touching the paper would have involved prodding the Bank's hump of a stomach and she didn't want to do that. 'Good, we've got the top of the lift shaft on the ninety-ninth floor, here. See?'

Chess and Pacer nodded.

'And these tramlines are actually pipes.' Anna's finger traced the meticulously drawn details. 'They pass between the top of the shaft and the core on the hundredth floor. They're exposed, probably so that they can be worked on. Yeah, because,' and she put her face as close to the plan, as close to the Bank's body, as she could stomach, 'there's breaks marked on the pipes. It's written here; valve wheels to control the supply.'

'Yeah,' Pacer's dark face was right by Anna's pale one. 'And here, the supply goes up, through the core floor. Just above the lift shaft.'

Anna placed her hands on her hips. 'There's the supply for your poison gas; piped into where the brain must be, in the core of the hundredth floor. Turn the valve wheels and we turn off the supply.'

'Bye bye, brain,' said Pacer and he held out his hand.

Hex slapped it. 'Nice one, Pacer.'

'Yeah, well, we haven't actually done anything yet,' Chess reminded them.

'We will,' Pacer assured her, jauntily. 'Climb out of the

top of the lift, up the lift cables to the pipes and turn off the supply.'

'I'll provide you with the climbing gear,' said the Bank.

'And head torches. It'll be dark.'

'It'll be a dark day for you, Pacer, if you don't come out with what *I* want.' The Bank scratched an armpit at length. 'And maybe you'll need a cryosaw, for cutting your way out of the lift if you can't force the roof. Now, Hex, time for me and you to find the best exit points for this little distraction operation you're going to mount, before the others go in.'

Hex and the Bank began to look through the plans, discussing them solemnly.

'You're coming with us?' Chess asked Pacer.

'Of course. I want to help you, Chess. Don't you get it?'

'Chess thinks she can do it all on her own,' interjected Anna.

'It's not that.' Chess didn't want to start arguing, but being friends with Anna wasn't always easy. 'It's just I don't *expect* anyone to help me.'

'Chess, you're so paranoid.' Pacer ruffled her hair but she slapped his hand away. She wasn't being paranoid. Chess recalled how, not so long ago, she and Box and Splinter had been shown dermacarts, plans made from human skin, before Ethel had sent them into the Riverside Prison to steal a piece of the cerebral torus. Things hadn't gone how they were meant to. There had been complications. You could never be sure what to expect with the Twisted Symmetry. It was important to know as much as possible beforehand.

'What's up with you now?' Anna asked her, bluntly.

Chess knew she sounded as if she was whining but she

said, 'It's just that we don't know for sure that the brain *is* in the core. The plans don't *actually* show it.'

Anna folded her arms and glowered at Chess. 'There's an easy way to find out, isn't there? Assuming there's CCTV in the core, we can look. We can take one very quick look to stop you bleating about where the brain actually is.'

'It's not bleating,' protested Chess. 'It's being careful. Going in blind is stupid, but *you* don't seem to be bothered.'

'Because *you* won't let me look,' retorted Anna. 'You seem to think the only thing the Twisted Symmetry are interested in is you.'

Chess didn't know what to say to that. To have agreed would have sounded big headed. To have disagreed would have been wrong.

'Anyway, we're not going in blind. We're ninety-nine per cent sure it's there, from the information we have.' She picked up the Link-me which was still on. 'But one quick look can make it one hundred per cent, Chess. Just one look. What harm can that do?'

More harm than you can imagine, thought Chess. She knew that the Twisted Symmetry were always watching, listening, waiting for any opportunity to feel their way closer. But all the street rats were looking at her. She'd look stupid if she objected. Chess didn't want to look stupid.

But it wasn't looking stupid which made her hesitate, grind her nails into her palms and then, eventually, mutter, 'Suit yourself.' It was her desire to find the brain; actually find it so she could touch it. Chess *needed* it.

The cerebral torus was a universal quantum computer. Its amarantium core meant that it could calculate data across

—[267]—

multiple universes; that was how the Twisted Symmetry would use it to predict the worm strikes, to transport stolen children to the rebuilt factory. Chess was sure that if the cerebral torus could do that, it could tell her where Box and Splinter were. So, even if she and Anna and Pacer could kill the brain without approaching it, simply by shutting off the poison gas, she had to find it before it died. That was why she needed to be sure that the brain was there. That was why she agreed to one, quick look.

Anna gestured to Pacer to get off his oil drum which he did, very slowly. Then he stood behind Anna and watched.

'I'm using a virus that Richard wrote. He called it the monkey-trap virus.' Anna hit the return key and a time bar appeared on the screen. 'It's really clever. He planted it in the CREX operating system before ... before they stopped him from using it.' She scowled and cleared her throat with an angry cough. 'It attaches itself to the security programme and then does nothing. It lies dormant; until I type in the command.'

The time bar flickered off and now a cursor was flashing, black on the white screen of the Link-me. Chess could feel the bodies pressing about her, eager to see what she was looking at.

Anna typed in a string of letters, fingers jabbing the keys in a blur. 'When I enter the command, the virus triggers a security alert throughout the system. Naturally, the system starts to repair itself. But because the virus is embedded in the security programme, the repair process spreads it to every part of the system. The harder it tries to repair, the more the virus spreads. By the time the all-clear is given, the system is riddled with holes that will let me in. So now, I just have to find their internal surveillance net. They must have one.'

Anna rattled through menus, harrumphing occasionally until she said, 'Aha!' and struck the return key.

The street rats swelled forwards. Chess leant over until her face was next to Anna's.

'Your hair's tickling me,' complained Anna.

'Sorry,' said Chess.

There was a rapid succession of images; corridors, doors, security guards reading newspapers and security guards watching CCTV screens. Then Anna found a black and white image of a dark room, cavernous, full of cables that were shiny and unusually thick.

'This is on the hundredth floor. In the core.' Her voice was husky. Everybody held their breath, as if the least noise would give them away.

The image jumped and then returned to the original view.

'We're here now. Just a quick look. It's a big room. It could be anywhere.' Anna's breath steamed over the screen.

But Chess wasn't only looking for the cerebral torus; she was searching also for the primary warp who looked after it. She hadn't forgotten how horrible it had been to be trapped in the cable cupboard at the Riverside Prison, as Petryx Ark-turi had smelt her way close. Wherever the Twisted Symmetry had hidden the brain, Petryx Ark-turi would be nearby.

Again, the image jumped.

'Why's it doing that?' asked one small street rat who was jammed between Chess and Anna.

'It looks . . . wet in there,' said another.

'Let's see if I can move the camera.' Anna sucked her lip. 'It's a big area. The brain could be anywhere.'

The image jolted as it had done before. 'It keeps doing that,' muttered Anna, and then, mulling this over, 'at regular intervals. Don't know why.'

'Talking to herself,' Hex whispered to Pacer.

'The only person who never gets tired of listening,' Pacer whispered back.

Anna worked the keys, fingers moving faster and faster, striking harder and she began to grumble, increasingly agitated.

'What's wrong?' asked Chess.

'It's not working. We're jammed here. Like it's crashed.' Anna shook her head, frustrated. 'It won't do anything.' Then, the picture flicked off and the screen filled with text, scrolling upwards in a luminous wave.

'What's happening now' asked Chess.

Anna was clicking the keys repeatedly; the Link-me wouldn't respond to her. But it was responding to someone. Someone had wrested control away from Anna.

'It's hacking back,' whispered Anna. She looked up at Chess. 'Something's got inside and taken control.'

The flood of letters and symbols rolled upwards swiftly.

'Well turn it off,' flapped Chess.

'I can't.' Anna had stopped trying to work the keys. 'It won't let me.'

The Link-me blanked. The web-cam flashed white as if it had just blinked. Then the cursor appeared at the top of the screen, flashing, waiting. It moved forwards and words appeared, simple enough for Chess to read.

HELLO CHESS.

Someone gasped, but Chess held her breath.

WE CAN SEE YOU.

The cursor returned to the next line. More words followed.

WE ARE COMING.

Anna read out what was written next.

LISTEN.

'Turn it off,' shouted Chess, her voice cutting the frozen night so sharply it bounced back from the far ridge of the Pit.

'We've seen enough now.' It was Gemma. She had pushed her way between Chess and Anna and she reached over and snapped shut the open mouth of the Link-me.

'Who was it?' asked a little boy, squeezed against the oil drum. 'Who's coming?'

They are coming, warned Lemuel inside her head. And they will keep on coming.

Chess didn't want to listen to Lemuel, but she *was* listening. Whistling, Jerkan had said. She strained her ears. There was no whistling. Yet. Beyond the fire-circle of the street rats and the spectral walls there was only the surging silence of the night.

'I have to go. To see Crazy Boris. Now,' she announced, barging her way out of the gathered rats.

'Now's the worst time.' Anna pushed after her, stuffing the Link-me into her boot bag as she did so.

'Now's the *only* time,' snapped Chess. 'By tomorrow ...' She didn't want to talk about what might have happened by tomorrow.

'Chess,' pleaded Gemma, trying to grab her friend's arm.

Chess was already crunching towards the outer shell of the warehouse.

'Don't be stupid,' Anna tried to reason. 'The Twisted Symmetry have got a fix on you.'

'That's a good reason to get away from here.'

'You'll be walking right into their hands.'

'Whose fault is that?' Chess shouted from the darkness. 'I told you not to use the Link-me and you wouldn't listen.'

'You said we couldn't go in blind,' stormed Anna, stamping after Chess.

'Whoa, whoa, whoa!' Pacer stood between Chess and Anna. He held out his hands, to keep them apart. 'It's nobody's fault, OK. But, Chess, you've got to stay with us. We won't let them take you.'

'And if they come, well, we'd like them to come.' Hex had loped across with a pick helve in his hand. 'They owe us. They owe Klinky.'

'Don't go, Chess.' Gemma stood beside her, feet shuffling in their sack wrappings.

The five of them stood twenty metres from the bonfire but the flames were bright enough to streak their nearest sides yellow. All the other street rats were watching. Only the Bank left the circle and began to lumber towards them.

'There's no need to go.' Gemma squeezed Chess's hand. Her grip was strong even though her hand was small. 'Look what happened last time you went.'

Chess didn't want to go, but she had to; she needed to see what was inside the vault. She needed to see her mother, if she really could. There might not be another chance.

The parallax bangle was hot on her wrist.

Chess looked down and smiled at the little girl with the wispy blonde hair. Gemma smiled back, snaggletoothed.

'They're so clever,' Chess whispered to her. 'It's like they know I've got to see Crazy Boris. They know there's this chance. This is what they've been waiting for.' She laughed hopelessly. 'This is when they'll come for me.'

'But you're going to go anyway, aren't you?'

Chess nodded. 'I have to.'

'That's OK,' said Gemma. 'I'll still be here when you get back.'

'Good,' Chess tried to say, but her throat was tight.

'You can't go on your own.' Anna spoke gently, not bossy. 'I'll come with you. I've got to go home, anyway. They only expected me to be away for a night.'

'Home,' echoed Chess. She cast her eyes about the shifting shadows of the wharf before returning to Anna's fire-patched face. 'I'm doing this bit on my own.'

'I still need to get home, anyway.' Anna tried not to sound wounded by Chess's rejection.

'I'll drive you both.' The Bank had parked his truck at the place where the road through the Pit stopped at the edge of the wharf. It was safe there, because it was *his* truck.

'Thanks,' said Anna.

'Don't mention it,' scoffed the Bank. 'I'm just protecting my investments.' A bunch of keys jingled in his hand. 'I'll be here tomorrow, Pacer. And you, Hex, pick your boys and girls; little ones, good for crawling. I'll bring the equipment. You lot just have to deliver.'

He turned to Chess. 'Two pm tomorrow, we're going in. You'd better be here an hour before then.'

'Two pm?' Chess gulped. 'So soon?'

'We don't have long, Chess,' said Pacer, carefully.

'But I don't know how long I'll be.' Chess looked at the flaming faces that were all looking back at her. 'Can't you just wait until I get back?' She didn't want to let them down by not being there; all of them, except the Bank, were doing this for her. And if the brain was destroyed before she could get to it, she didn't know how she was ever going to find Box and Splinter.

'The party starts at two,' the Bank jabbed a finger at her face, 'and I'm not waiting. If you're late here, we'll be at the storm drains, below the Cones plaza. If I have to come looking, you'll wish these other freaks you've upset had got there first.'

CHAPTER 16

Crazy Boris had opened the door before the Bank's truck had turned out of the square. Chess was bolting up the stairs to the attic before he'd closed it.

'Hello, Boris, nice to see you, would be polite,' he shouted after her vanishing heels.

He found Chess kneeling on the floor of the attic room with the vault in her hands. She was turning it slowly, trailing a finger over the crimson outlines of crowns, mitre, the horse's head and the tower. She looked up at Boris as he entered, as if startled that he should be there at all. Then she brushed a clutch of chestnut curls from her face, which rippled with a smile.

'You look like you've got a surprise birthday present.' Crazy Boris sat opposite, cross legged, knees cracking in unison. 'Except,' he added with a note of caution, 'the surprise birthday present happens to contain a thermo-nuclear device.'

'You don't have to stay here while I do this.'

'Chess, if that thing goes off, I might as well be sitting on it as three floors under it.'

'OK,' said Chess, noticing the way Boris's lanky arms poked out of his white T-shirt and his strong, vein-webbed hands rested over his chicken-bone thighs as if they belonged to a different body altogether.

'The horse's head, right? The knight?' confirmed Crazy Boris, anxiously smoothing the hair at the back of his head.

Chess nodded. You're a bit like Balthazar, she decided. But safer.

'What do you think's inside?' he asked, before Chess pressed the square with the red horse's head.

Chess's brown eyes glistened with excitement. 'Answers.'

'That's good.' Boris nodded contemplatively. 'We all want answers.'

Chess pushed the square. It depressed and the glowing outlines faded. The vault fragmented between her hands like a piece of shattering china. The pieces tinkled onto the floor and amongst them landed a key and a tiny metal box meshed in wires. A radiation sticker had been plastered over one side of the box.

'That'll be the thermo-nuclear device then.' Crazy Boris picked it up as gingerly as if he were lifting a large slug between finger and thumb. 'I guess I'll just have to drop it in the sea. Or maybe down a drain.'

'Not down a drain,' said Chess, earnestly. 'You don't know who could be living there.' She picked the key up. It was tobacco-brown and metal, with a shaft about three inches long and thick, squared-off teeth. A yellowing luggage label had been tied to the head with a piece of string. There was writing on the label.

'Is that your answer?' Crazy Boris was dubious.

'It must be an address.' Chess tried not to sound disappointed. What had she been expecting? Her mother was hardly going to drop out of the end of the vault. But she had expected something more than this.

'11A Knott Street,' read Boris, after he'd nipped the swinging label. 'I guess that's where you'll find your answers, Chess.'

'I guess,' sighed Chess. 'Where is Knott Street?'

Boris went downstairs and returned with a digimap. He keyed in the address and turned the palm-sized device round for Chess to see. She looked up. 'I can't read.'

'No worries.' Boris knelt beside her. He tapped the screen and they zoomed out. 'Right now, we're on this side of the city, OK? Follow my finger. The city centre's here. If you cut straight through, you come to what's called the Undergrove.'

'Where the flyovers start?' Chess knew where the Undergrove was; a densely packed, three-block grid of derelict terraced houses and apartments that had survived the flattening development of the city and now huddled amongst the skyscrapers, hidden from the sky by rings of overhead highways.

'That's it.' Boris zoomed back in. 'Here, near the edge, is Knott Street. Down at the south end.' He scratched his chin. 'Have you slept any time in the past week, Chess? I hope you don't mind my asking. It's just that you look awful, that's all.'

'Thanks,' said Chess. 'There's been a lot going on.' She hadn't slept properly for days.

'Perhaps you can have a nap now?'

'I've got to go,' she said with a weight like a ton of sick in her stomach.

Crazy Boris looked at the black window panes. 'It's the dead of night, Chess. What's the hurry?'

'I've got an appointment at the Cones tomorrow afternoon,' was all she would say. She yawned.

'I was a teenager once,' said Crazy Boris. 'In fact, I was a teenager for much longer than most people. I know what it's like, having things to do.'

Not like these things, thought Chess.

'Let's go to the kitchen. I'll make you something to eat. You could snatch thirty minutes kip on the sofa whilst I work magic with two slices of bread, a lump of cheese and a pickled onion? Nothing fancy, I promise.'

'OK.' Chess headed for the stairs. 'Maybe you'd keep an eye out for me?'

Boris was talking to the photograph when he said, 'Maybe it's the least I could do.'

Morning rush hour and Chess's feet were pounding the pavement, anger banishing fear for the time being at least. She hadn't felt tired until Crazy Boris had told her how tired she looked and then nights of not sleeping properly had hammered the inside of her head, driving down her heavy eyelids.

You silly little girl, said Lemuel's voice.

A thirty minute kip? When she awoke to find daylight leaking around the kitchen blinds, Chess had left 18

Mendoza Row without a sound, without even whispering goodbye.

Now she really was short of time. The others would be wondering where she was.

But perhaps this wasn't all bad. Perhaps it had wrong-footed the enemy. To be amongst crowds, flanked by vehicles, lost in the rush hour chaos was to be safe; certainly safer than cutting across the city at night. And Boris had only been trying to help.

The traffic was jammed in smoking columns. Yellow hoardings by the thoroughfares and the flashing overhead signs meant roadworks. There was an ocean of a diversion around the central square.

Not far ahead, the roads looped up, circling the steel and glass mountain range of architecture that rolled out in all directions from the city centre. And not far beyond that, on the far side of the central square, beneath the aerial mayhem of the flyovers, lay the tiny, cramped district of the Undergrove.

That was where she would find her answers.

Chess sniffed the cold, oily air and walked faster. Always, she was racing time. Not bad going, she thought, for someone who couldn't even tell it.

But 2pm was still some hours away and she wasn't all that far from Knott Street. Perhaps her late start really had worked to her advantage.

'You're just much smarter than you realize,' Chess dared to say to herself.

She became aware of yellow lorries and scaffolding poles and the hammering clatter of a road drill. The stream of waiting traffic swung left, joined by another road-full coming in from her right. But Chess was on foot so she didn't have to worry about the diversion. She jumped over the roadworks barrier and began to jog down the avenue that led to the central square.

The avenue was lined with high buildings. There were seven wide avenues that radiated out from the huge central square. The square itself was surrounded by grand, civic structures: museums, mausoleums, government offices, churches, temples, commercial headquarters, embassies. Outside the square and about its aerial perimeter was a maelstrom of traffic, but the square was quieter, less frantic, more peaceful than the rest of the city.

But usually there was *some* traffic. However, this morning, the central square was almost deserted. Chess assumed that the traffic must have been funnelled around it because of the roadworks. There were a handful of people scattered about the buildings; business-types in suits and long coats and with hard, serious faces. Otherwise, she was alone.

The chill air tingled against the back of Chess's neck. She stopped at the centre of the square and turned about. Behind her, a man in a suit stood beneath the great gothic arch of the Architects' Mausoleum and was looking her way. But that didn't mean that he was looking at her. Splinter would have laughed and called her paranoid. But how many times had Splinter got that wrong?

Chess squinted back down the long avenue she had taken. She didn't realize how far she'd come, until she stopped to look. At the far end, where the roadworks had been, a banner had unfurled between the high buildings. Through the fabric she could decipher the outline of a colossal athlete, probably advertising running shoes to the traffic on the other side.

At the foot of the banner, a scaffold barrier had been erected, barring the way into the street. Or the way out. It must have been erected in the time it had taken for her to jog up the avenue and into the square, but the workmen had gone. However, there were people there and when she saw them, Chess's heart jolted and began to thump. The figures were a long way off, but there was no mistaking the black uniforms, the jackboots, the dark glasses and the glinting skull insignia.

Stumbling over her own feet, Chess turned to face the north edge of the square and saw another banner drop down the mouth of one of the roads that led back to the city. Men in blue overalls and hard hats slung scaffolding poles across the street, hammering and locking them into place before withdrawing. In their place came more hunters, streaming out of the adjacent buildings.

So, this was it. The Twisted Symmetry had been fooled by nothing. They were coming for her. Now.

Panic crawled under her skin. Everywhere that Chess looked, the routes were being sealed, the city shut out, leaving her and the hunters and a cold winter wind. She turned on the spot, frantically guessing at the way to go. But the hunters weren't moving. Maybe she had time; time to go down, into the drains.

She was stopped by a smell. It was a smell like alcohol, but finer, sharper, striking her right at the back of her nose. She had smelt this once before, when she had been in Ethel's kitchen with Box and Splinter. Ethel had given it a name. She had said it was called mist and it came whenever a passageway had been opened into the deep vortex.

Chess knew that there were bad things within the deep vortex; things that should never come out. She turned her head, slowly, to look into the wind, to see where the mist was coming from.

All about, the hunters, the suits and the hook-faces of the stone beasts high on the more ancient buildings looked back. But the hunters and the suits stood as still as the gargoyles.

A shape flitted between two walls at the edge of her vision and Chess jerked round but saw no more. Another, to her right, vanishing behind the balustrade that swept up to the wide, Doric frontage of the Ministry of Justice. She had an impression of tawny, muscular flesh.

Then she heard the whistling.

It was low at first, swooping into a high screech. It came from the area where the mound of flesh had just disappeared and it was answered by another plaintive squeal, to her left. The final note of the screech echoed around the empty square. There was a momentary hush and then, from all about, the whistle was answered by others.

Chess stood still. She breathed slowly to control the panic and to prepare herself for what she had to do.

The enemy had used their power and cunning, had extrapolated all the dimensional probabilities to this point and calculated that *this* was the moment to come for Chess, in force.

But so had Ethel.

Remember, dear; a loose brick behind the rubbish bins at the central post office.

It was months ago that Ethel had taken a detour from their trip through the vortex to the Riverside Prison. It seemed so random at the time; another example of Ethel's craziness, according to Splinter. She had used Box's knife to dig out a brick in the wall of the loading bay at the rear of the central post office, and inside she had hidden a mobile phone. The phone stored one number in its memory: a number to contact Julius.

You will be alone and in danger. He will be ready to help you.

The whistling came from all around her. Chess was alone and the enemy were coming.

This time, Ethel had been right. She needed Julius. Now.

The mist had blown away. The creatures were emerging from gaps between the grand buildings, from behind statue plinths, advancing slowly. They walked on all fours with whale-backed bodies and were as big as horses. Their tan flesh was muscular but whilst their backs bulged like barrel chests their undersides were flatter, as if their bodies were the wrong way round. Where their bellies should have been there was a flat grille of interlocking rib bones, white against the darker flesh of their flanks.

They had no heads, but at the front of their huge chests, where a neck should have been, there was a rough, baleen-plated mouth. When they expanded their chest-backs and blew out, the lipless flesh drew clear of the striated plates and they made the whistling sounds, sometimes deep, sometimes shrill, sometimes shrieking.

There were at least ten that Chess could see and as they

slunk closer, Chess realized that their limbs were all arms; hulking shoulders, crunching biceps, blades of triceps. It looked as if the arms had been attached messily to their bodies by dark staples; the work of a drunken carpenter, not a surgeon. Their hands and fingers were long, like apes'.

It was over two hundred metres to the post office and there was no way that Chess could make it by running straight.

She ignored the wind, ignored the eldritch howls, forced herself to look away from the titan beasts and she focused on what she had to do. She concentrated on walls, windows, handholds and rooftops. She read the route.

To her right was the Ministry of Justice, opposite that and to her left was a high plinth supporting a giant bronze of a judge in a regal seat. Back on her right and adjacent to the Ministry of Justice was the Palatine Hall. Steps rose to the nearest wing, and then came the main building with its double row of ornate balconies and the flagpoles that projected from the wall above the balconies and over the principal entrance. Beyond the Palatine Hall and out of sight was the Central Post Office. At its rear would be the loading bay.

Box used to tell her that when he had to run like this he filled his head with the loudest, most thumping beat he could imagine. Chess closed her eyes, drew in breath and filled her head with sounds.

They were running towards her now, whale-backs rolling. The air was full of their cries, but the only noise Chess heard was the beat in her head. This wasn't about what Lemuel had done to her; about the universe or spirits or crystal. This was about being a street rat. Only a street rat could do what she had to do now. Chess kicked off her trainers, felt the cold stone under her feet, rocked forwards and back like an athlete waiting to explode. Then she opened her eyes and started to run.

She sprinted towards the statue with one of the creatures bounding behind her and another charging straight at her. But she wasn't distracted by the headless mound of muscle that came shrieking. As its front arms reached for her body, she jumped off her right foot onto the side of the plinth and pushed off the stone with her left, flipping her body in an arc over the back of the creature, which skidded in a semi-circle as it turned to give chase.

Now, she broke right across the square, towards the near wing of the Palatine Hall. A chain of pursuers swerved after her, screaming and screeching. Chess didn't hear them. Her head was full of her own sounds and her mind was racing ahead of her body, assessing height and distance, oblivious to risk.

She sprinted the steps with the nearest creature an arm's length behind, and raced for the corner where the side wall of the main hall emerged from the wing. She ran at the wing wall as hard as she could and drove herself up it, bare feet pushing against the brick. She heard the creature thud into the wall with a bellow of air, but already she was using her momentum to run into the next wall and kick up, before gravity pulled her down.

Her fingers closed on the lower ledge of a balcony and she heaved herself up, climbing onto the top of the ornate balustrade. It was hard on her arms but she had to keep going.

She had to get up to the second row of balconies and then round the corner and across the front of the hall.

Chess sprang forwards and up, at the patch of wall before the next balcony. She kicked off, flung her left arm high and as her hand gripped stone, swung up her right arm. She hoisted herself and now she was at the level of the second floor. The square was a bone-shattering drop below but she had no time to think about that.

Her pursuers had located her and three had begun an ascent like her own, negotiating the balconies with the fluid power of chimpanzees.

Forget them. Focus on the route.

A drainpipe ran down the front corner of the hall. Chess had logged that around the corner and across the frontage, there were sixteen second floor balconies, each separated by a gap of about two metres, with a six metre gap at the centre where the flagpoles were set.

She could do this.

There was the thump of a heavy body landing on the balcony immediately behind.

She *had* to do this.

Chess dived off the end of the balcony top and caught the drainpipe with both hands, swinging round the corner and landing on the first of the second floor balcony ledges, on both feet, neatly. She sprang up to the balustrade. Ahead stretched fifteen more balustrades broken by the gap above which there jutted the central flagpoles.

It was just a matter of balance and speed and a little bit of luck. Chess turned up the music and ran. The hunters and the suits watched from all around the square, speechless.

She didn't break her stride. Legs stretching and powering, she sprinted across the balconies, hurdling the gaps between. The stone hand rails were barely twelve inches wide but her feet dashed square along the centre of them as her arms pumped.

The enemy were behind, bounding in her wake and as she came to the flagpoles, she saw one of the headless beasts clambering onto the furthest balcony. It started to gallop towards her.

She leapt from the eighth balcony, both arms stretching up. A cold metal pole struck her palms and now she worked her shoulders, monkey-barring the flagpoles. Adrenalin flooded pain but by the final pole her fingers were numb.

Clumsily, she dropped to the ninth balcony, grazing her ankles. A hump-backed, four-armed mound of muscle was charging her way with two more swinging in behind her. She needed speed.

Chess ran as hard as she could and timed her clash with the oncoming beast. They leapt their adjacent balconies simultaneously, Chess diving high and over the clutching creature. As she rolled into the next balcony bay, she heard two bodies collide behind and turned to see them crash to the floor, the underside of one opening its ribs as it fell to reveal that inside it was hollow; a human-sized cell within its body with ribs for bars.

These were people-catching beasts and more were coming. Chess vaulted onto the balustrade and ran for the end of the building.

Now, the Central Post Office was in view, its flat roof

higher than where she was but lower than the roof of the Palatine Hall. She had to cross between the buildings but from the balconies that wouldn't be possible.

She came to the last balcony and edged round to where it met the wall, not far from the corner. She reached round the corner and her groping fingers found what she had hoped would be there; a drainpipe, as on the other side. She let herself fall forwards and with a purchase on the pipe, swung into the wall before climbing up the pipe with both hands, feet scurrying up the brickwork.

The landscape of the roof was broken only by glass skylights, like small greenhouses, and shiny, worming exhaust funnels. The wind cut over the low parapet, catching Chess's hair. From up here she had a view across the high places of the central square, and she shared in the isolation of the skyscraper fields as they began their Euclidian ascent to the white, streaking cloud base.

The edge of the post office roof was about six metres below and separated from the Palatine Hall by a four metre chasm. It would be a big jump and she'd be lucky not to break an ankle even if she made it to the other side. But the alternatives were climbing up the drainpipe immediately below her and also slinging themselves over the gutter wall, onto the far side of the roof. So she had no choice; she had to jump to reach the phone.

Chess could see the wide loading bay at the rear of the post office, with a row of vans drawn up to the depot shutters. There were high walls on two sides of the bay and it was open to the rear. Down the furthest wall was a line of tall, tin, cylindrical bins. The phone was in the bricks behind the bins. Chess knew how she would reach it, if she made the jump.

She jogged back from the drop, muscles beginning to ache now that she had paused. She saw three creatures galloping over the roof towards her, but turned her back on them and took two deep breaths. From here, she had lost sight of the post office. All she saw was the edge of the stones ahead and the jagged city horizon; she would jump for that.

Arms driving, legs pumping, she sprinted at the end of the roof. It came at her in seconds and she leapt, legs carving through the air, arms circling. Her leather jacket flapped behind her and she realized she was plummeting down, forward momentum spent. She reached for the post office roof and then it was hurtling up at her, slamming into her feet and she threw herself headlong into a roll to deaden the impact.

She didn't stop to see whether any of the creatures had made it across. She dashed over the roof, swung her legs down to where wire screens protected the top windows above the shutters in the loading bay, rattled down the mesh, fingers and toes clinging to the gaps in the wire, and sprang down to the roof of a van below.

Her heart and lungs were burning and her thigh muscles leaden as she ran across the van roofs to the far wall, where, at last, she hit the ground.

She had seconds.

Her eyes raked the bricks behind the bins as frantically as her scrabbling fingers, and then she found it; a brick that was loose.

'Come on, come on.'

Boots were crashing towards the bay, mixed with the pounding thuds and the shrieking of the creatures.

She pulled out the phone and it slipped through her sweaty fingers onto the floor. Chess was on her knees. She snatched up the phone and flipped it open.

'Come on.'

She pressed dial. The command came; 'SELECT NUMBER'. She pressed the function button, finger feeling unwieldy as a marrow.

'Please, please.'

One number appeared. She pressed dial.

Hidden behind the bins, Chess couldn't see what was entering the loading bay, but she could hear them.

The phone rang. She closed her eyes and then a voice spoke. 'The person you are calling is temporarily unavailable. Please leave a message or call back later. Please leave a message or call back later.'

There was a long bleep.

'Please,' choked Chess, pushing the phone against her mouth. 'If you're there, *please*, help me.'

She stepped out from the bins. The mouth of the loading bay was filled with hunters, drawn up in three ranks with rifles mounted. As Chess came into view there was a metallic crunch as dozens of safety catches clicked off, and the rifle muzzles swung towards her.

In front of the hunters were the creatures, fifteen of them, shrilling raucously.

In the midst of the hunters stood one whom Chess recognized by her blonde ponytail. She was the shape-shifter, the one who had come for her at the police station. Even as she felt her knees weaken, Chess noticed that Red was not amongst the hunters. The left side of Ponytail's face was livid, crusted with a bone-deep graze. That was the trouble with severed brake cables. But Chess didn't feel so clever now.

At the moment, Ponytail looked as human as the other hunters. She put a loudhailer to her mouth and her reverberating command filled the loading bay.

'Lie face down, with your hands behind your head.'

The nearest creature's cage-ribs began to open and it loped forwards, followed closely by two more.

The phone was still against Chess's mouth.

'Please,' she begged. 'Help me.'

CHAPTER 17

The Bank sat on a wooden crate stamped FRAGILE on the back of his flat-bed truck. Gathered before him and level with his toes was a gang of wiry little street rats. Pacer sat on the edge of the truck, next to the crate and Hex stood on the other side of the Bank, arms folded as he surveyed his scruffy team of drain-crawlers.

'In the cab of my truck, are ten smoke bombs; enough for one each.'

The rats looked up at the Bank with silent adoration as if he had promised them sweets.

'Hex has told each of you where to go after I've dropped you off at the main drain?' Ten pairs of eyes were unblinking. 'Can they speak?' the Bank asked Hex. Hex nodded. 'You know where to go?' barked the Bank.

Some said yes, some nodded their heads and one screwed up an eye and scratched his head.

'It's your funeral,' the Bank muttered to Pacer. 'Now, listen,' he said to the rats. 'You're going up the main pipe, inside the wall of the north stairwell. You come out at the service hatches, one of you for each of the first ten floors.'

A thin arm went up.

'What?' growled the Bank.

'What if there's a load of stuff in the drain pipes? What if there's a lot of flushing all at once?'

'Hold on tight and keep your mash closed,' was the Bank's advice. 'Now, once you're on the stairs, make sure you're under your own particular smoke sensor, what Hex has shown you, on the plan. Then you rip off the pins in the heads of the smoke bombs. The smoke comes out quick. The alarms will start. You lot go back through the hatches before anyone sees, into the shaft and down the pipe. And take the bombs with you; always remember the golden rule: leave no evidence. Pacer, Fury and Miss Tuesday will be going in by the same route after you lot have cleared the place, so don't mess this up. Any mistakes,' he added, 'and I'll be waiting, ready to snap fingers.' For the first time he smiled. Then his attention was caught by a red coat that was approaching quickly, down the road that cut through the Pit. He wiped his thick spectacles on his jacket, replaced them and then looked at the wristwatch strapped to his log of a wrist.

'Only one of them, and gone eleven already.' He shook his head with disappointment.

'Chess not here yet?' panted Anna, when she reached where the truck was parked, on the Pit road by the wharf.

The Bank gave a pantomime look-about. 'Nope. Unless she's hiding. But she's still got time. Just.'

Even though she was breathless, Anna tried not to breathe in too hard because the stink from the cesspools was sharp. 'You've got the stuff we need?' she panted.

The Bank shambled off the truck, the street rats scurrying

back as if a boulder was coming their way. He yanked open the dented cab door. 'Three head torches, one cryosaw and three of these.' He reached into a tool bag and pulled out an item that he held up for everyone to see.

'It looks like a baseball glove,' said Pacer.

'It doesn't,' said Anna. 'It's got wheels on it.'

'It's an angel glove,' announced the Bank. 'They're used by the monkeys who are stupid enough to work in construction in this city.'

'My dad used to work in construction,' mumbled Hex. 'I got put away after he fell.'

'Genetics is cruel, Hex,' commiserated the Bank. He thrust his hand into the glove, holding the hard leather fingers open so that the two small metal wheels on the palm were clear to see. 'See the grooves in the outer rims of the wheels?'

Anna and Pacer nodded. Anna could see tiny metal teeth within the grooves.

'Line up the wheels on either side of the cable, so the cable sits in the grooves. Then squeeze your hand shut.' The fist bunched shut so that it was the size of a boxing glove. 'The wheels turn, climbing the cable and pulling you up, so long as you hang on, or the glove don't come off. The harder you squeeze, the faster you go. Stop squeezing and you stop climbing. Just pull the wheel away from the cable when you want to get off.'

'How's it powered?' asked Pacer.

'Battery pack in the back.' The Bank tapped the bulge. 'That's why it's so big. That and the reinforced frame, binding the wheels to the glove.'

'What about the saw?' asked Anna. 'If we need to use it?'

'It's a beauty, this is,' said the Bank as he replaced the glove in the bag and took out a silver tool, the length of a pen, but thicker. Everybody pressed close to see it. One end widened into a bevelled cap and at the side of the other, there protruded a small button.

'This is a cryosaw,' explained the Bank. 'When it's turned on it freezes the air in a *monofilament* beam.'

'What's monofilament?' asked Pacer.

'Very thin. For cutting.' The Bank grinned his frog smile. 'It's used for surgery; because it's so cold, it seals as it cuts. But it's so small see, it's perfect for this job, if there's cutting to be done.'

He pressed the button and a laser-thin needle of blue light appeared instantly, extending eighteen inches from the top of the saw. The street rats drew back, gasping, as if it were a wand. The Bank waved it through the air, and it crackled, leaving frosty trails of vapour in its wake.

'Where'd you get everything from?' asked a tiny girl with copper hair and a barbed wire tattoo down one cheek.

'Favours.' The Bank used the word as slyly as bait. 'When you work for me, you get proper stuff.' He clicked the saw off and ruffled her hair. 'You know how to use torches?' he asked Anna.

She put her hands on her hips and pursed her lips.

'No pretty little skirt today?' lamented the Bank.

'It wouldn't suit you,' replied Anna.

'You've got the FAT-dump?'

Anna patted her jeans front pocket. Her hand slipped round to check her back pocket where a folded envelope was secure. It had arrived at her parents' house that morning, addressed to 'Miss Anna Ledward' in a cursive script. She hadn't read it yet. She'd stuffed it in her pocket before pulling on her trainers and coat and running from the house.

'Everything's set then.' The Bank scowled. 'We'll give it another hour before we leave. We need time to get into position at the other end.'

Everybody except the Bank looked up the Pit road expectantly.

'I hope Chess is OK,' ventured Anna.

'She's probably knee deep in cappuccino with her friend, the rock star,' sneered the Bank. 'I can see her now, taking it easy whilst we do all the graft.'

'Cooperate and you will be hurt no more than necessary,' echoed the loudhailer. 'Now lie down.'

The three closest creatures quickened, loping towards Chess. The wind blew and she caught a stench of the animal musk. But she didn't lie down. She looked about for any final means of escape and realized that there was none.

At last, the Twisted Symmetry had got her.

The first beast sprung with a shrill screech, its ribcage parting to reveal the dark cavity within, arms and ape fingers extended for Chess. As it bore down, Chess was aware of a shape on the bay wall to her left. Then there was a thud and the creature erupted in a swirling mass of flame. It shrieked with a tooth-cracking intensity as it burnt. The second leapt but before it closed on her, it also burst into a roaring ball of fire, its massive carcass skidding over the ground, squealing and blackening.

At the same time, Chess heard an engine roaring. It was like a hunter's motorbike engine, except that she couldn't see a motorbike and this noise came out of the air, directly above the hunters.

Chess saw some of the hunters lower their weapons and turn their dark glasses skywards, uncertain of what was coming their way. But she didn't look at them for long because charging towards her like a horse was the third headless beast. Its ribs cracked open. Chess stumbled backwards and it leapt.

Because she was looking up, she saw the motorbike scream out of the blank air, as if it had just jumped the hunters. It arced over the loading bay, wheels spinning and exhaust roaring, before landing with a crunch between Chess and the leaping creature.

The rider braked, pulling the rear wheel round in a skid and stopping side on. He pulled two flintlock pistols from under his jacket. One he levelled at the creature. The other he levelled at Chess.

There was a crack and then a boom as he discharged one of the pistols. It spat a ball of flame that expanded immediately, engulfing the monster in a roaring sheet. The beast crashed to the ground, air whistling from its body for several seconds before the crackling of the fire drowned it out. The fire burnt with a vicious intensity, but Chess's attention was riveted on the barrel that pointed straight at her.

The rider had a short, solid body made even thicker by

his black leather jacket and stumpy legs in oil-streaked denim, with scuffed brown boots that only touched the ground because of the low-slung seat of the chopper motorcycle. His face was mostly hidden beneath small, dark glasses, a greying horseshoe moustache, like a bandit's, and a matt black, half shell helmet.

His arms remained outstretched, cruciform, Chess and the hunters in his sights.

'Sometimes you win and sometimes you lose,' he stated flatly, in a voice that was as rough and cracked as the rumbling engine of his bike.

Chess nodded. She understood. If she was dead, the fight was over and everybody lost. The Symmetry wouldn't want that. That was why the dwarf on the bike was giving them no choice.

'You got my message then?' Chess said to the barrel of the gun.

The dwarf nodded. 'We were busy. Killing stuff. Hope you're not next, sunshine.'

'Me too,' gulped Chess.

Everybody was waiting: the hunters, nervously sighting down their rifles; the eight remaining creatures immediately in front of them; and the two, black-skinned figures that Chess now saw, one on each of the loading bay's side walls, draped in trench coats that flapped as they caught the wind, long recurve bows in their hands.

Everybody waited.

At first it looked as if shreds of mist were catching like loose cloth in the open space in the middle of the loading bay. The mist collected in strips that fluttered and then it grew darker and then there was the outline of a man, tall and wearing a black leather coat that hung to his ankles.

Chess felt her heart beat harder, felt her limbs strengthen and felt the heat of Julius's presence.

The mist blew clear, leaving the lone, dark figure with the long yellow hair in the centre of the bay. Chess scrambled to her knees and caught a glimpse of the flesh side of his face as he leant forwards, resting easily on a body-long pole, that bore glinting sickles at either end. His silver hands clasped the haft lightly. Strands of cable extended from the cuffs of his coat, hanging beside his wrists and suspended in the air.

'You may depart.' Julius's voice was smooth and sonorous and it filled the air. 'Humans I do not choose to hurt. Therefore, if you are human, please withdraw now.'

The headless creatures were snorting and whistling, flexing their limbs and fingers, limbering up as if preparing to charge. The hunters shuffled, rifles not as level as they had been, murmuring to one another.

Chess heard Julius say, 'I won't need further munitions, Carl.' He spoke quietly, as if talking to someone by his side, and the loose strands of cable twitched and then retracted into the cuffs of his coat.

'They are outnumbered,' crackled the loudhailer. 'Attack!'

The ranks of hunters remained undecided, but the creatures skidded into action, arms pounding as they charged in a flexing, rolling, sand-brown wave towards Julius, the motorbike rider and Chess.

Chess saw the two archers nock arrows to their swan-necked bows, from quivers at their waists, in perfect unison. Julius spun the hooked pole between his arms and braced himself and the dwarf turned the flame-throwing flintlocks towards the oncoming beasts.

Two of them hurled themselves at Julius. He dropped to one knee, swinging the pole-hooks in one silver fist, the crescent blades spinning between the creatures and ripping their flanks effortlessly. Air screamed from the deep tears. The heavy bodies tumbled to the floor like dead-weights and as a third bore down on him, he stood and swung the pole forwards and up with both hands, smashing the hook through its ribs and into its body. As if the beast was no heavier than a pillow, he slung the weapon back with one arm, long coat cracking about him with the speed of his action. The horse-sized body spun off the hook and crashed into the bins with a long squeal of rushing air.

Then Julius held up his free hand, with silver fingers spread, bowed his head and Chess thought she heard him say, very quietly, 'Stop.'

Everything stopped.

Of the remaining nine creatures, three froze in midair, metres in front of Julius, two were immobile as statues, caught in a gallop towards Chess and the rider and three more were stationary in a line, ahead of the hunters who were similarly stone-still. The final one stood in a petrified charge, on the other side of the bay.

Julius turned round. Chess could see the blue eye glitter in the pale flesh half of his face and the red eye burning in the silver half. He beckoned her towards him and she discovered that she could move as easily as he could. It was like walking through a photograph.

When she was standing beside him, he placed his free

hand against her cheek. 'Chess,' he said, and she felt the power surge through every fibre of her body. 'Chess.' He smiled more gently than she imagined a demigod could and said, 'You know so much more than when we last met.'

'I know about *us*,' replied Chess.

'Then you should be even stronger.' He swept an arm about them. 'This was too close.'

'Ethel was ahead of them.' There I go again, defending Ethel, she thought.

'Good luck and good judgement are sometimes difficult to tell apart,' was Julius's response.

'What are they?' Chess pointed at the nearest of the beasts, suspended motionless in the air above their heads.

'Whistlers.' Julius pointed to the gaping mouth between its shoulders, with a hook. 'They sense by sound, like bats. That is why they make the noises they do. Their lungs are huge. That is why they scream with escaping air when pierced.'

He swung the blade into the side of the whistler's hump-back, heaving open a deep wound. The whistler remained where it was and there was no scream of escaping air. The only sound was Julius's mellifluous voice, although Chess noticed the archers moving slowly. She saw them both draw their bows to their cheeks and then release arrows which were bulb-tipped and which flew smoothly into the two whistlers that had stopped metres from the motorbike rider.

Julius strode to the whistlers in front of the hunters and remorselessly windmilled the sickle blades into their backs, before walking back to where he had first stood, only feet from the airborne creatures.

'Maybe you feel this is not a fair fight?' probed Julius, a glimmer of a smile across the two halves of his face.

Chess said nothing. She wasn't sure what to think.

Julius took the pole in both hands, his coat parting to reveal the chunky machine-pistols hanging from his belt. 'But, the interesting question is this: has time slowed, or have we simply speeded up?'

And before Chess could think about replying, the loading bay exploded in flame and squealing and the blurred slash of Julius cutting two springing whistlers out of the air, whilst a detonating arrow brought down the last as it came in on his flank.

Chess was on her knees with her arms over her head. The air was hot and sickly with charred flesh, and burning carcasses lay about the loading bay, air escaping from them and those unburned in long, shrill peals.

Julius faced the hunters again. When Chess looked, she could see how pale their faces were, how loosely they held their weapons, how they wanted to retreat.

'There is nothing you can do here,' echoed Julius. 'The girl will not be yours today. Go.'

He turned away.

'Kill them,' screamed Ponytail and Chess saw her launch herself out of the ranks of uniforms, human face snouting into a fanged muzzle, talons bursting from her shortening fingers, neck thickening with strands of tendon.

In a black swirl of coat, Julius spun round, half crouching, a heavy machine-pistol in his silver hand. The pistol coughed, ejecting a stream of cartridge cases, rounds smacking into the Dog Trooper as she sprang out of the hunters. Her body curled, before hitting the tarmac with a dull thump, only metres in front of the nearest jackboots.

'Go,' commanded Julius. 'This is no place for humans.'

In silence, the hunters withdrew.

'We are ready, Carl,' said Julius, to no one that Chess could see. The rear of an armoured vehicle materialized close by, the reinforced, grey metal door wide open and a man in combat pants and a grimy vest leaning half out of the doorway.

'All clear, boss?' asked Carl. He had short, fuzzy black hair and the white skin of his solid shoulders was daubed with oil streaks.

'All clear,' replied Julius, clearing the firing mechanism of his machine-pistol.

'You must be Chess,' said Carl, with a grin that was all the brighter for his dirty face. 'Pleased to meet you.'

'Hi,' said Chess, leaning to one side to look for the front of the wagon but seeing only the space of the loading bay. It was as if there was only a slice of armoured vehicle present.

'You know how it is; the nose of the Ops Wagon in one place and its back side in another?' laughed Carl.

'Yeah, I know how it is,' said Chess.

'Seren, Étoile, let's go,' he shouted.

Chess saw the two archers jump from the high side walls of the bay. They did so simultaneously and for a moment, it looked as if the ground curved up to meet each of them, before they hit it at exactly the same time. They approached the wagon from the opposite sides of the bay, walking in step, long coats swinging, recurve bows by their sides.

'How was the phosphorus?' asked Carl.

'Unnecessary.' Julius pointed at a smouldering whistler carcass. 'Puncturing them is sufficient, Chess. But we have come fresh from fighting the Plague Breed. Only fire can destroy *them*, hence the phosphorus munitions we used here.'

The archers were high-cheeked, hair plaited tightly in long pony tails, shrewd-eyed. Under their coats they wore black trousers and black T-shirts. Their ebony faces were expressionless. As the first walked past Chess and ducked through the doorway and into the wagon, her hand flicked her coat from her hip, whipped a bulb-nosed arrow from the quiver and tossed it behind her. The other archer had stopped to speak with the motorbike rider, her back to the doorway, but she turned and snatched the arrow out of the air when it was only inches away. She dropped it into her quiver and continued her conversation.

Julius saw Chess's astonishment. 'Seren and Étoile are Cartesian twins; one mind, two bodies. They work together perfectly because one mind thinks for them both.'

'Complicated,' murmured Chess, as the second twin marched past.

'You have one mind, four limbs, twenty digits. You can work them in symphony. It is no more complicated than that.'

'Where are you going now?' asked Chess, who felt empty at the thought of Julius leaving.

'Back to the Seventh Panhedral Sector,' replied Julius. The wind caught the long, yellow hair which trailed from his skin and silver cranium. 'Out there, an assault by the Fifth Wave of the Plague Breed is being repulsed by the Committee's forces. But our forces are weak. Always our forces are weak.' He slammed the machine-pistol back in its holster.

Chess looked the way he pointed. Through the doorway, she could see that the interior of the Ops Wagon was huge, much bigger than looked possible, with portals and corridors leading off the central pod. She felt Julius's hand on the back of her skull.

'Look again,' and as he spoke, the space between her head and the slit window in the front cabin collapsed. Her face was against the reinforced, riveted glass and she was looking at a black sky, torn crimson as if ripped by claws. Beneath the sky was a smoking plain of broken rock, filled with figures and gouting flame.

'This is the state of the multiverse,' she heard Julius say. 'Total and perpetual war. It rages at all times and in all places. But your world is special. It can be a beautiful place. And it is full of energy, full of possibilities. That is why the battle for it is fought so hard. When this breaks through, into your world, bad things happen.'

Then she was standing in the loading bay, looking at the rear doorway of the Ops Wagon again.

'How long have they been fighting, out there?'

'We have been defending the Skarp 6-Titan sink hole for three hundred and forty-seven years.'

'That's a very long time for a battle,' observed Chess.

'Compared with the Crystal Wars,' replied Julius, 'this is a skirmish.'

He sat down, on the lip of the wagon door.

'Here, boss.' Carl's arm emerged from the opening to hand him a chipped, enamel mug. Julius put it to his lips and as he sipped his face was lost in a swirl of steam.

Chess wasn't sure what demigods drank, but it looked hotter than anything mortals could handle. 'Is it from this universe?' she asked, curious, but not wanting to sound ignorant.

Julius frowned. 'It's tea.' When he observed Chess's bewilderment, he almost smiled. 'Tea is a generous drink, it gives much and takes nothing; a rare quality.'

Chess watched him enjoy an impossibly long draft of the boiling liquid. It was easy to forget that underneath the metal and the divine, there were parts that were human, even if they seemed immune to heat.

'Do you know why you could walk with me back there, when we fought the whistlers?'

'Because of how I've been made?' suggested Chess. That seemed to be the answer to most things.

'Not entirely. You know what Seren and Étoile and Jake are?'

'Jake's the motorbike man?'

'The GTBD, most people call him.' Julius saw Chess's incomprehension. 'The Gun Toting Biker Dwarf.'

'It's an unusual name.'

'He is an unusual dwarf. But do you understand what they are?'

'They're Blood Sentinels.'

'Yes. My blood runs in them, but not even they could walk with me as you did.' He set down the empty mug. 'You are more powerful than any of us, Chess.' He looked at her keenly, the fire and the ice searing through her thoughts. 'Whatever was done to your body by others, *that* is how you *are*. That is your essence. And when the time comes, what you do will end all of this, for better or for worse.'

'When I find the Eternal?'

'If that is how Mevrad has put it.' Julius tightened his lips. 'Yes.'

'How do I find it, then?' asked Chess.

'How you find it is part of what will happen,' was the reply she received.

'Great,' she grumped. She saw one of the twins drinking from a bottle of water. 'Do they count as one or two?'

'One or two what?'

'Blood Sentinels?'

Julius smiled. 'One mind; one Sentinel.'

'That's good value,' decided Chess. 'It's like having one extra.'

'We are still one Sentinel short,' said Julius.

He looked at Chess in a way that made her say, 'After my mother?'

Julius nodded. 'But the new Blood Sentinel is coming closer all the time. Closer to me. Closer to you.'

'To me?' echoed Chess.

'I can sense it. You feel nothing?'

Chess shook her head and wondered who it was that Julius could sense through her.

'We must find the new Sentinel before the time comes.' The blue eye and the red eye both burnt. 'The time for the beginning of everything. Or the end.'

'To be honest,' ventured Chess, after digesting Julius's proclamation, 'I don't feel all that strong.' She couldn't imagine stopping time the way that Julius had.

'Jake will take you to where you need to go before he leaves.' Julius stepped into the wagon.

'Will I be all right?' asked Chess. Why shouldn't she ask that?

'The Symmetry have worked tirelessly. This was where they believed that, finally, they would catch you.' Julius tossed his head towards the loading bay. 'This was their great opportunity, to take you by force. They failed.' Chess thought this must be a good thing, but Julius's face darkened. 'Unless you are foolish enough to walk into their arms, they must now pursue a different strategy. It will be less obvious, but it will be no less dangerous. They will work from within. And that is when the Inquisitors are most powerful.'

And with that, the last of the Nephilim turned away. The door to the Ops Wagon closed and faded, and the wind blew cold through the loading bay.

'Time to go, sunshine,' rasped the GTBD as if his throat was sandpaper, and he kicked his engine into life.

CHAPTER 18

Knott Street was a bleak terrace of tenements that stretched in a line until the end blurred into an asphalt smog. Natural light was blocked by the skyscrapers that towered around the Undergrove like cliffs and by the belts of highway that criss-crossed overhead. The steady drone of traffic was loud enough to smother the GTBD's growling exhaust.

'I'll wait,' said Jake without turning round, as Chess clambered off the back of the chopper.

Chess forgot to say anything back because she was looking at the graffiti-scrawled steps that led to the front door, just as countless other graffiti-scrawled steps led to countless other front doors, all along Knott Street. The windows were blanked with steel security shutters and the paint on the iron railings was peeling, their feet orange with rust that streaked the steps. The street looked fit only for demolition. Chess's hand traced the outline of the key in her pocket before her bare feet took her up the steps.

Black plastic numbers were screwed one above the other beside the front door: 11, 11A, 11B, 11C. The door was padlocked but the padlock had been smashed open, some time ago judging by its condition. She pushed the door inwards and entered.

It smelt sour. She breathed shallowly through her mouth and stepped over the discoloured patches on the hall floor to reach the stairs. They were narrow, with a thin, metal banister that zigzagged up. There wasn't much light but there was enough to find her way up to the door on the first floor that was numbered 11A. She tried the round handle but it was locked.

'OK,' Chess whispered to herself, tugging the key from the pocket.

She put the key in the door. It turned easily and the door opened silently.

Chess padded into a narrow, gloomy passage. It smelt musty but not as foul as the entrance to the flats. A spider's web tickled her lips; she wiped it away, feeling dust and flakes of plaster crunch under her feet. There was a doorway ahead, framing feeble daylight, so she headed for this, hands open and held out; she didn't know what to expect.

Enough light pinpricked the metal window shutters to reveal a square room with a fireplace in one wall. There was a dilapidated armchair inside the doorway and strips of browning paper peeling off the walls. Otherwise, the room appeared empty. Even the light fittings had gone, revealing naked flex in the centre of the ceiling.

But this felt like the right place.

Chess walked to the centre of the room and twisted the tiny cusp of the parallax bangle.

Her wrist stung as the minute teeth on the inside of the bangle pierced her skin. Then she pulled the cusp round as

Lemuel had instructed and the blood in the bangle jetted through the teeth to mix with the blood in her body.

She stood still but inside her head it felt as if she was hurtling backwards. The room rushed in a strobe-flicker of night and day. Chess put her hands over her eyes to block the overload and then it stopped. She opened her eyes and her arms dropped to her sides and she was kneeling in the centre of the room. It was lit by a standing lamp behind the armchair that was still beside the door, but no longer mildewed or baring springs. In the armchair there was a lady.

The lady had short, black hair and was wearing black trousers and a black T-shirt and her body looked slim and tough but tired. She had one large, brown eye, sunken in a washed-out face and a black eye-patch where the other eye should have been. Chess thought that her face would have looked neat and strong, and sharp as a jewel, if it hadn't been so drained.

'That's better, baby,' said the woman who Chess knew was her mother. 'You've got to be brave. No good hiding that pretty face. You *have* to go. But you'll be taken by a *very* nice lady.'

'But I don't want to go,' protested Chess. She wanted to stay, to stay here forever, with the soft light and her mother's face smiling down at her.

'Baby, it's dangerous now. There are very bad people in the world and they've done horrid things to Mummy and we don't want them to do horrid things to you.'

'I'll protect you,' promised Chess.

Her mother leant forwards and down and put out a hand. Chess felt it touch her cheek, warm and sweeter than any touch she could remember. She put her hand over her mother's, but it was too big and far too strong to clutch. Her mother sat back in the armchair with a weary sigh and began to hum the tune that she always hummed.

And now Chess realized that she wasn't kneeling. She was standing and she was a little girl of three years; she was being that little girl and being *inside* that little girl at the same time, reliving something that had happened years ago.

'I'll be all right,' said her mother, and then speaking to herself, 'They've finished with *me* now.' She turned the one, bright eye on her daughter. 'Let me tell you something, baby.'

'Tell me who I am,' babbled Chess. Lemuel had said the effect of the bangle was short-lived.

Her mother smiled. 'Always, such serious questions.'

'Hug me,' said Chess, thinking of the sweet touch, knowing that in minutes it would be gone, forever.

'Up here, then.' Her mother opened her arms and Chess climbed up to them. 'Sometimes the universe makes something, very special. It just happens. Your grandma was very special.'

Chess wanted to listen but she wanted also to be as close as she could be, so she burrowed into the crook of her mother's arm, noticing dark, purple bruises on the inside of her mother's elbow as she did so.

'Are you listening?'

'Yes,' said Chess earnestly, enjoying her mother's body heat.

'Your grandma was called Esme.'

Chess stopped burrowing. She sat up and said, with astonishment, 'The girl in the photo?' It had to be. Anna and Crazy Boris had both remarked how Chess looked like the girl in the photograph, whose name was Esme.

'No, silly monkey. You haven't seen her in a photo.' Her mother squeezed her nose and continued. 'The bad people wanted to stop Esme from doing all the good things she was meant to do and they hurt her so badly that she couldn't live any more. And, do you know what? She didn't even have any children. But, and this is the amazing bit, a really clever person called Lemuel Sprazkin came along and did some unusual science and made Mummy out of Grandma. And he made your uncle Phoenix, who you don't know. Isn't that clever?'

I made your mother out of what the Symmetry left of hers, Lemuel had said.

'It's horrible,' said Chess.

'It's science,' replied her mother with a shadow of a frown. 'You wouldn't be here without it.' She rubbed Chess's hair. 'After what happened to Esme, the clever people said the next special thing would come from Mummy. Mummy just had to meet the right person. But she didn't; she met your daddy.'

'My daddy.' Chess repeated the words; maybe this was the first time she had ever used them.

'Your daddy wasn't a very nice person and Lemuel helped to put that right.'

'Who is my daddy?'

'You'll never meet your daddy.' Her mother hugged her more tightly. 'A nice lady called Mevrad has promised me that.'

'Promises get broken,' declared Chess.

'Don't say that, baby,' and her mother looked at her in a way which showed that Chess was right.

Her waist was held firmly and then she was standing on the floor again, looking up at her mother.

'Mummy's very tired. The doctor says she'll go on feeling more and more tired until, eventually, she just keeps sleeping forever.'

Chess felt a wave of sickness surge through her and her feet seemed to slip away, momentarily.

'Don't get upset, baby.'

But Chess didn't want the bangle to stop working; she didn't want to leave her mother; she didn't want to be taken away. Perhaps, if she could stay with her, everything that was going to come afterwards wouldn't happen. Everything would be all right.

'I want to stay here,' cried Chess.

'They have to take you away.' Her mother's voice tremored.

Chess heard the door open, but she didn't turn to look. She wanted to keep looking at her mother, drinking in every expression, every wrinkle, smelling her, clutching every sensation.

'It's time, Clarity.'

I know that voice, thought Chess.

'If you say so, Mevrad.' Her mother was so weary, so resigned. So trusting.

I will never trust like you, thought Chess.

'Please, Mummy, no. Please don't let her take me. Please don't make me go away.'

Somebody was walking towards her.

'I'm not going. I'm not. I don't want to.'

'Please, baby, please,' begged her mother. 'It'll be OK.'

Chess tried to think of something that would scupper the plan to take her away. 'What about my brothers?' she shouted. 'You can't take me away from my brothers.'

Her mother looked towards the door, face aghast, and then back to Chess. '*Brothers*? Don't be silly. You only have *one* brother, and you mustn't trust him.'

Questions crashed in on her now.

'What's my name? My real name?' she shouted. A pair of arms had taken hold of her body, the floor was slipping away.

'Stop it,' pleaded her mother. 'You know your name. Mevrad, you said everything would be all right?'

'It will be, dear,' came the familiar voice. 'Eventually.'

Chess fell silent now because she knew that she was utterly helpless against what was about to happen and because she wanted to spend these last seconds looking and hearing and focusing only on her mother, storing it up for the emptiness that would follow.

'Have you hidden the piece?' asked Ethel.

Clarity nodded and swallowed. 'Under the hearth tiles. But how will she find out about it?'

'You know me, dear. I've thought of a way of keeping its location secret, yet ensuring that she finds out about it at the perfect moment. It will be as if she is back in this very room, and you will be telling her yourself.'

Clarity laughed, weak as winter sun. 'That wouldn't be possible, Mevrad. I don't have time.'

'Leave what's possible to me, dear. I'm an expert in that department.'

'Mummy,' said Chess, wanting to use the word whilst she had a mother to say it to.

'You have to be very brave, my little love,' said her mother, throat tight. 'OK? I'll always be with you. No matter how bad the darkness, I'll always be with you. Remember that, if you remember nothing else. Remember my voice.'

Chess reached out with a hand that looked tiny and cried. Her mother hummed and then began to sing:

'When I was on horseback, wasn't I pretty?
When I was on horseback, wasn't I gay?
Wasn't I pretty when I entered Cork city
And met with my downfall on the fourteenth of May?'

The voice was still in her head as the years deluged back and then she was in the barren room, with the gutted fireplace and the empty, collapsing armchair.

Chess sniffed and wiped her nose and looked about as if her eyes could penetrate the layers of time to see what they had blotted out. Her gaze fell on the hearth of the fireplace; cheap yellow tiles decorated with faded willow leaves. Holding back the tidal wave of all she had seen and heard, Chess dropped to all fours and tested the tiles, seeing which would give. She took off the parallax bangle, which left a row of dots as if tattooed in red round her wrist, and used the nub of the cusp to work at the tiles, scraping furiously. She found a loose tile on the right-hand side. She threw away the bangle and worked the tile free.

Underneath, there was a cavity in the cement, as if a small wedge had been scraped out. Sitting in the dip was a chess piece. Chess recognized the shape now; a knight. She picked it up and it felt cold but it quickly grew warm in her hand. It looked as if it might have been made of a bright metal, but it didn't feel like metal. Its texture was more like resin, but very hard. She held it tightly and closed her eyes, trying to imagine how the chess piece she had been left with at the orphanage had felt, but that was a memory that she could not reach.

Still clutching the chess piece and wondering what she was meant to do with it, Chess shambled from the room with the armchair, and into the narrow hall, her mind starting to sink under what she had just experienced. She didn't look at where she was going, or notice the stink of the stairwell or hear the hollow thud of her feet on the stairs. She was clinging to the memory-shreds of her mother and the things she had told her.

She repeated the names Esme, Clarity, Phoenix, over and over again, using their sounds to hold back the thing she didn't know how to think about.

You only have one brother and you mustn't trust him.

But she had two brothers, Box and Splinter. She *had* to have them because having two brothers was something she could be certain of. But her mother wouldn't have been wrong. So even this certainty had been stolen from Chess. And in its place?

Which one? Which one was her brother? Which one *shouldn't* she trust?

Numb, Chess slouched down the last few steps and towards the front door.

Was it Box? Box looked more like her. But Box could be

trusted, she was sure of that. Splinter? Splinter wasn't much like her, not to look at. But did she trust Splinter?

Trust no one.

She blinked her way into the street. A motorbike engine fired up; the GTBD's face was fixed ahead, as expressionless as Chess's.

She needed to find the cerebral torus more than ever now. She needed to get to it before it was dead.

'The Cones,' she said flatly, to the back of Jake's helmet.

He opened the throttle and the bike roared out of Knott Street.

When he had slammed to a halt, a knife's length from where the others were standing by the low wall above the storm drain, the GTBD offered Chess this piece of advice: 'None of us will live forever, sunshine. Don't forget that. It makes things easier.' Then he was gone in a scream of tyres.

'Who was that?' Pacer gazed after the bike.

'Glad you could make it,' said Anna. She raised an eyebrow at Chess's bare feet. 'You forgot to put your shoes on. Good timing isn't your thing, is it?' She must have seen how that hurt Chess because immediately she asked, 'Are you all right? You look sick. Didn't things go too well with the vault?' She was trying to sound compassionate. 'Some secrets are best kept as secrets, Chess.'

Chess gave her a bitter glance.

'Two minutes to go,' said the Bank, tapping the face of his chunky, metallic wristwatch. 'Thought I'd have to come looking for you.' He slapped a head torch and an angel glove in Chess's free hand. 'They'll explain how it works.'

'What have you got in your hand?' Pacer had noticed her clenched fist. He never missed a detail, particularly when it might be valuable. 'I only asked,' he replied to Chess's hellish look. He caught Anna's eye. Anna shrugged and shook her head.

Chess slipped the horse's head into her jeans pocket.

'Right.' The Bank stood in the middle of them and turned to Chess. 'You can stop pulling faces, little miss. Get your swede on the business. My business. Keep on mooning like that and you might as well slab yourself and your two friends here and now; save someone else the trouble.'

'Are you sure you're up to this, Chess?' Anna threw her coat into the truck cab, straightened her polo neck sweater and knelt to tighten the laces on her trainers. Pacer pulled on his head torch and tucked the angel glove inside his jacket. He tossed the cryosaw in one hand, casually.

'Yeah, 'course I am.' Chess looked over the wall, down to where Hex was squatting by the arched culvert that led to the CREX tower main drain, waiting for the return of ten scrawny street rats.

'Shouldn't be long now,' called Hex, not sounding convinced. He peered back into the narrow gap of the tunnel.

'You've got a couple of minutes.' The Bank's pink jowls wobbled. 'Once the alarms start, in you go. You won't have long. But get my data, or else . . .'

'We *know*.' Anna tested the strap of her head torch. 'Ravillious will use the north stairwell to get out. It's the quickest way from his office.' Then, she fell silent, recalling what had happened in the corridor at the bottom of those stairs.

'They shouldn't of hurt Klinky.' Pacer clenched his jaw. Chess said nothing. Thinking about Klinky felt like thinking about Jones.

In minutes they would be inside, on enemy territory. Pacer and Anna both seemed cool, yet they must have been a bit nervous; Chess was. But although Pacer and Anna might have had reasons of their own for being here, they were also here for her. And they weren't the only ones; right now, Hex's team of rats would be emerging from the drain, ready to trigger the alarms and create a diversion. All because *she* had decided that they should take the fight to the Symmetry.

Ethel might have thought this wouldn't make any difference, but Chess knew it did. Destroying the cerebral torus would hurt the enemy, and more than that, it would show them that in *this* world, there were people who were prepared to strike back: children. Street rats.

Her head was clearing. There would be time for more thinking; thinking about Esme and Crazy Boris, thinking about her brothers, or her brother; but that time wasn't now.

She heard Pacer asking her if she was OK. She knew him so well that she could see that he was bracing himself for what they were about to do.

'I feel better, now I'm here,' and then she managed a smile. 'Now I'm back with you lot.'

Pacer winked at her. 'That's what friends are for.' Then he fastened his combat jacket and cracked his knuckles.

Anna was next to him, long black hair sleek, blue eyes

bright, and Chess knew that she was thinking about her own brother.

For a moment, Chess let herself remember the scream rooms and the horrors that she had seen there. She thought of the children, stolen by the Twisted Symmetry, and felt anger stir, but it was mixed with a cold stream of fear; she knew how much could go wrong in the coming minutes.

'It could get lively up there; they might come after us. You know that, don't you?' she said to Pacer and Anna. She didn't actually say that they didn't have to do this, but she owed them this last chance to turn back.

Pacer sniffed and spat on the floor.

Anna's face was stone. 'I'm after *them*. They'd better be ready for that.'

From across the plaza, an alarm began to scream.

'OK.' Chess turned to face the dark slit of the tunnel. 'Let's go.'

CHAPTER 19

Trick emerged from the service hatch onto the tenth floor of the north stairwell, a furtive shadow. She clicked off the head torch and pulled the cold tube that was the smoke bomb from inside her jumper, which she had tucked into her ripped tracksuit bottoms for this purpose. Then, she placed herself directly beneath the sensor screwed under the stairs which followed the square walls up to the eleventh. On every floor below, one of her friends would be doing the same, waiting for her signal.

The main drain hadn't been as wet as she and the rest of the gang had expected, although the smell was raw. They had followed a raised walkway, in the wall, above the sewer that ran under the plaza, head torches pricking the darkness like a team of miners. It had been easy to climb the drain into the tower because an iron ladder ran up the outside of the huge sewage pipe. The rungs were treacherous with freezing water and the cold numbed their fingers and made their breath phantom up through the yellow beams of the torches.

At each floor, one of the rats had unslid the bolt on the

wall hatch and slipped across from the ladder, to the stairwell, ready to vanish back into the drain if footsteps approached. After the ninth floor, Trick was climbing on her own, her heart thumping as she gulped the chilly air. But she kept thinking of how Chess had done things like this. Trick had heard all the stories; about Chess and the giant child-catchers, about how Chess and her brothers had stolen the computer brain, how Box and Splinter had gone to war against dog-men whilst Chess had fought a demon on her own. Trick imagined her hair was brown, not copper, and she imagined she didn't have a barbed wire tattoo on her face. She imagined she was Chess. That made her feel stronger and a lot older than nine.

Satisfied that she was in position, she whistled and heard the whistle repeat down floor after floor, like a fading echo. Then she pulled the ring from the top of the smoke bomb.

The speed at which the white cloud billowed out took her by surprise. She let go of the cylinder which clattered on the concrete, and staggered back, trying not to cough, and screwing up her eyes which were stinging furiously. Immediately, the alarm began to shrill like a braking train, up and down the massive stairwell. The noise was so harsh that Trick could feel it in the roots of her teeth. She would have covered her ears but she had to retrieve the smoke bomb and get out.

She dropped to the floor and eased her eyelids enough to see light. The canister was right by her and had stopped smoking. Throwing it back inside her jumper, she staggered to the wall where the service hatch hung open, felt her way back into the cold darkness of the drain, pulled the hatch shut, secured it and clung to the ladder, waiting for her eyes to stop hurting.

Even through the wall, the fire alarm wailed deafeningly. Trick allowed herself to cough. As she cleared her chest, she caught the volley of spluttering from below. But her eyes were so sore that she didn't descend immediately.

A rolling noise came from the stairwell, like tumbling boulders. She guessed this was the sound of people galloping down the tower, following the fire drill. By the time the galloping had stopped, she was ready to climb down, but an exchange of raised voices on the other side of the hatch caught her attention.

'Everyone is leaving the building, Mr Ravillious. Why should I have to stay here?' The man was shouting to compete with the alarm.

Trick had heard Pacer talk about someone called Mr Ravillious. She knew he was important so she listened.

'Your job is to do whatever I tell you, Marcel,' Mr Ravillious shouted back. 'You must stay, to keep an eye on the office.'

There was coughing. 'This isn't a false alarm, Mr Ravillious. Look at the air.'

'Some kind of gas leak. It's probably *not* a fire.'

'But supposing it is, sir?'

'Then, Marcel, the Corporation will pay for your funeral. Security are staying in the building and so are you. Stop fretting. I'll be back in half an hour.'

Excited, because she had managed to use the smoke bomb properly and relieved that she hadn't been caught, Trick scuttled down the ladder and ran along the walkway at the bottom to catch up with the others. There was a lot of laughing and hand slapping amongst the street rats, although they fell silent as Pacer, Chess and Fury flickered out of the darkness.

'Good luck,' whispered Trick, along with the other rats, as the big ones moved through them, like apparitions. Her eyes were on Chess whose pale, grim face softened slightly at the sight of Trick.

'Well done,' whispered Chess, and Trick thought she would explode with pride. It was only when she had wiggled through the culvert at the end of the sewer and into the light, that Trick realized she had forgotten to say anything about the conversation she had overheard.

The alarm had stopped. The north stairwell was silent.

'There's no CCTV in here,' whispered Anna, once they had all climbed out of the drain, 'but there's cameras all around the lifts. And there's bound to be security; they won't have deserted the whole building.' Head torches were pulled off and wrapped round wrists; the angel gloves were still tucked inside their jackets. Chess was carrying Anna's.

'So what do we do, after you've got the data? We need the lifts to get to the pipes.' Pacer leant over the hand rail and looked up. The stairwell went higher than he could see. Then he looked down and let a short string of spittle plummet ten floors from his mouth to the bottom of the well. A tiny smack bounced back. He smiled to himself. 'Nice.'

'I'll think of something,' mulled Anna.

Chess leant over, next to Pacer, and looked up and down the concrete chasm. Without warning, images rushed at her; she was charging down the stairs, the steps and walls spinning up at her, jerky as an ancient film. She pressed her eyes shut but heard a skull-splitting bang. A gun shot.

'Are you OK?' Pacer shook her arm gently.

Chess opened her eyes, the bang still reverberating inside her head. 'Yeah. Fine.'

Anna had crossed to a wooden panel in the wall. 'The office is on the other side of this.' She put her ear to the wood. 'Empty. I think.'

The panel was as tall as a door but wider. There wasn't a handle and when Pacer pushed, it remained secure.

'Maybe it has to be pushed from the other side.' Anna remembered how it had swung free when she had thrown her body against it.

'So we're stuck already?' Pacer shook his head. 'Great.'

'Just use the saw, you dimwit,' said Anna.

'I was about to think of that,' bristled Pacer. He took out the cryosaw and clicked the small button. A blue needle of light crackled into life.

Chess stepped back. 'What is it?'

'Very cold,' explained Anna. 'Cold enough to cut its way through things.'

'Through bodies, according to the Bank.' Pacer waved the cryosaw left and right, enjoying the swathes of icy mist it left in its wake.

'Having fun?' jibed Anna, as if talking to a little boy. 'We haven't got long.'

'It's called getting ready,' muttered Pacer. 'It's called *being*

--[326]--

professional.' He raised the tip of the laser-thin beam towards the centre of the panel.

'No. Do it at the bottom,' directed Anna. 'And only a tiny cut. Just enough for fingers. Don't make it obvious.'

Pacer huffed but he knelt down. He lanced the bottom edge. Then he looked up and grinned. 'It's like cutting butter.' A coating of frost whitened the bare wood. He pulled the cryosaw out and clicked it off. 'Cool,' he breathed, giving it a further turn on and off, before stuffing it into his combat jacket. He slid his fingers in the gap between the portal and the floor and gasped. 'It's cold.'

'I'll do it if it's too painful,' scorned Anna, hands on hips.

'I don't want you to hurt your soft, jack fingers.' Pacer winced as he pulled the frozen edge of wood. There was a click. Pacer withdrew his fingers and shoved the panel. It swung into the room, swishing over the carpet. Anna strode past him as he knelt. Pacer watched her go. 'I hope there aren't traps or anything,' he muttered.

Anna dropped into Mr Ravillious's chair and switched on the data stack. She had the password written on a piece of paper.

'We've got to be quick,' Chess reminded her.

'I know, but any mistakes and it might shut us out. It might even give an alert.' Anna pressed the keys slowly.

'How d'you learn this stuff?' asked Pacer, watching how Anna moved the grey arrow around the screen, clicking buttons, revealing page after page of script.

'Picked it up as I went along.' She produced the FAT-dump from her pocket. 'Time to use the fat lump's FAT-dump.' She felt round the side of the data stack for the right port and slotted the cylinder into the interface. 'Once we're transferring the Bank's data, I can check out the records for myself.'

'For what?' asked Pacer.

'For Richard,' stated Anna.

Chess had ceased looking at the screen. She was watching the translucent glass in the office door in the wall opposite, to reassure herself that nothing was on the other side.

Satisfied that everything was in place, Anna hit the action key.

'OK,' she said, reading the message on the screen. 'This will take three minutes.'

'Three minutes,' groaned Chess.

'It gives me time to look. I'm getting the Bank *his* data and I'm helping you with what *you* want. If it's OK with everybody else, this bit's for me.' Anna began to work at the keys, sifting through the records and searching for her brother's name.

Pacer squatted by the chair and his fingers closed on the edge of the single, shallow drawer under the top of the desk. 'Never miss an opportunity.' He winked at Chess.

Anna shuffled the chair to one side to give Pacer and Chess more space, whilst she remained rooted to the screen. Pacer pulled the drawer open. Inside, there were two items.

Pacer tut-tutted as he lifted out a small, silver revolver. 'Mr Ravillious must be expecting trouble.'

'Don't point that this way, you jerk,' hissed Anna.

'Just 'cos you can't find what you're looking for,' Pacer observed.

Chess took hold of a slim, blue notebook. It was long,

with gilt-edge paper and the leather binding was soft to touch. She opened it and riffled the pages. There were lists of names inked in small, black letters. Some of the names had been scored through with a thick line. Chess didn't try to read any of them.

There was a click from the gun.

'Pacer,' hissed Chess and Anna simultaneously.

Pacer shushed them. He had opened the cylinder of the revolver to reveal the chambered bullets. Pointing the snub nose towards the ceiling, he tapped the cylinder in his palm. The bullets clicked out and into his hand. He grinned at Chess. 'Don't want anyone to get hurt, do we?' Pacer pulled the carpet free, where it met the wall behind the desk, and slipped the bullets underneath, before replacing the carpet. 'I'd like to see what happens next time Mr Ravillious goes for his gun.' He placed the pistol back in the drawer.

Anna swore but restrained herself from thumping the desk. 'It'll take forever, if it's there at all. I can't find it.' Then she saw what Chess was holding and she knew she needed to look inside it.

'It's probably an address book, or something like that,' said Chess, not wanting to raise Anna's expectations. Chess couldn't read what it was.

'It's alphabetical,' was all Anna said as she leafed through.

Chess watched Anna closely but couldn't work out what the expression on her face meant when she stopped turning the pages. Then Anna turned the notebook round so that Chess and Pacer could look inside.

'It's a list,' she said quietly, 'of people. Most of the names are crossed out. It's only names, see? This page is L. Look at the last name.'

Chess took the little book and studied the name at the bottom of the list. It was too long for her to read, but she could see that it began with the letter R. A thick line had been drawn through the name; job done.

'It's your brother,' guessed Chess.

Anna retrieved the book, shut it with a snap and tossed it back into the drawer, which she closed.

'Don't you want to take it, for proof?' asked Chess, cautious, as anger whitened Anna's pale cheeks and forehead.

Anna's blue eyes levelled at her and it was like being stared at by Splinter, at his most dangerous. 'This isn't about proof any more, Chess. This is about revenge.'

The main door to the office swung open.

A young man in a suit and a cloud of Eau de Cologne entered, holding a sheaf of paper files. He opened his mouth and dropped the files with a crash.

'Oh,' he said, looking from Pacer, to Chess, to Anna. Pacer began to move his hand towards the pocket where he kept his knife, but Anna gently pulled it away.

For the seconds that it took for the FAT-dump to complete its download, nobody said anything. Then Anna said, 'Marcel, we won't hurt you,' and Chess was amazed at how, knowing what Anna now knew, her voice had switched from granite to honey.

'What are you *doing*?' gasped Marcel, flicking a louche tongue of blonde hair from his forehead and taking a step back.

'We're stealing data,' replied Anna, calmly. 'That's *all*. And now we've got it, we're going to go. Information's all we wanted. We've finished, OK? We're going.' She reached round and retrieved the FAT-dump.

'But you can't do that. You can't steal. I can't let you.'

'Marcel.' Anna skewered him with her bright eyes. 'Of course we can steal. You must know how wealthy CREX is?'

Marcel shook his head.

'Trillions.' Anna raised her eyebrows. 'Why shouldn't a big, greedy company like this learn to share a little?' A suggestion of a smile moued about her lips. 'It's very easy to transfer, say, a couple of hundred thousand without anyone ever knowing.' The smiled revealed itself, enticingly. 'Say they ended up in *your* bank account? It wouldn't matter to CREX, but it would transform your life.'

Marcel was struggling, but he stammered, 'No. No.'

Chess surprised herself by saying, 'Marcel, do you think they're bothered about you here? You squeal on us and what happens? We get crashed and you get nothing. How smart's that?' She spoke bluntly, caustically, but hitting home with every word; hitting home because what she said was true.

Pacer and Anna watched, astonished, as Chess padded towards the young man, coolly. 'Straight up, what can we offer you? The best clothes, the best apartment, the best holidays.' Chess sniffed the air. 'And a lifetime's supply of that gorgeous scent.'

'Thank you,' said Marcel, bashfully.

'You deserve it, Marcel,' said Chess, hearing Behren's voice inside her own head. 'We're only offering you what you deserve.' Then, she smiled.

Marcel licked his dry lips, resistance broken. 'Go on then,' he gabbled. 'Do it. Quick. But nothing ridiculous. How about half a million?'

Anna called up the account menu on Mr Ravillious's computer. 'I need your account number and your employee ID. And we've got to be fast.' When Marcel was by her side, she rested her hand on the arm of his suit and cooed, 'And we need to get out. No one must know what's happened. Best for you, as well, yes?'

'Yes.'

'So, when I'm done, you take us out to the lifts. And make sure you kill the CCTV out there. Nobody must see us go to the lifts.'

'But you might run into people downstairs,' quailed Marcel.

'Trust me,' Anna promised him. 'Once we're in the lift, we know exactly where we're going.'

'Since when did you become the saleswoman from hell?' Anna was leaning against the mirrored wall of the lift that had stopped at the ninety-ninth floor, watching Chess who was sitting on Pacer's shoulders with the cryosaw in her hand. 'All that stuff about holidays and apartments?'

'Just something I heard somebody say, once.' Chess didn't want to confess that she had found the Inquisitor's words creeping into her mind and then into her mouth. Also, she was concentrating on what she was doing with the cryosaw. In seconds she had cut a rough circle the size of a manhole cover, out of the roof. She leant aside as the burred disc of metal clanged down, missing Pacer's bare toes by a nail's breadth.

'Chess, you nobwit,' complained Pacer. 'You nearly decapitated my foot.'

'Head,' Anna corrected him. 'Only heads get decapitated. You probably meant amputated.'

'I *meant* decapitated,' snapped Pacer.

'Touchy, touchy.' Anna unwound the strap of the head torch from her wrist and pulled it over her black hair. 'Better put that saw away, Chess, before you decapitate any more feet.'

Chess put the pencil-sized torch in her jacket, took out an angel glove and dropped it for Anna. Then she slipped on the head torch and her own glove; Pacer had told her how to use it on the way up in the lift. She turned on the yellow beam and aimed it into the darkness beyond the hole.

'I can see cables and a lot of dark space,' she said, screwing up her nose. Cold air swirled through the hole, together with the smell of oil and brick dust.

'Can you see the pipes?' came Anna's voice from below.

Chess swivelled her head, angling the beam.

'Can't you sit still?' asked Pacer. 'Your butt's bonier than it looks.'

'Sorry,' muttered Chess. But she couldn't see anything. 'I need to get up there.'

Pacer supported her ankles as she clambered onto his shoulders. Taking care not to catch herself on the rough edge of the hole, she pulled herself onto the lift roof and stood with her ungloved hand holding a thick cable for support.

'OK.' Chess shouted, her voice was almost swallowed by the shaft. 'It's dark.'

'You're kidding!' exclaimed Anna, sardonically.

'There's two cables,' continued Chess, 'and they go up to a pulley or something, about twenty feet up. The pipes are just under it; I can see them now. There's two, with wheels sticking out, like on the plan.'

'OK,' Pacer called up. 'Let's shut them off.'

'Then I need to find the brain,' Chess shouted back.

Anna rolled her eyes and shook her head at Pacer.

'She's always been a bit like this,' he whispered, tapping his temple. Then he pulled a piece of wire from his pocket and inserted it in a key hole at the bottom of the control panel by the lift door. 'Turning it off,' he explained to Anna. 'We don't want the lift to start running whilst we're up there; it could get messy.'

Chess leant in and helped Pacer up, and then both of them pulled up Anna. Head torches were clicked on and angel gloves fastened tight.

'When the valve wheels are shut off, the brain dies, right?' checked Pacer.

'I think so,' said Chess. 'And then I'm going in, through the hatch that should be up there.'

Pacer latched the glove wheels onto the cable. 'Time to fly.' He grinned before squeezing shut his fist.

There was a buzzing whirr and a scream of spinning wheels and then the sound of a head hitting a large metal pipe, followed by a howl from Pacer. 'That hurt,' he moaned.

'Don't squeeze too hard,' advised Anna.

Chess found that with only a gentle pressure, she began

to rise. Hanging from the glove hurt her shoulder and when she got to the top it was a relief to take the strain with her free hand, and by wrapping her legs tight around the cable.

The cables ran up to the fastenings above the pipes and alongside these fastenings, Chess could discern the square edges of the hatch that should open into the core of the hundredth floor.

Pacer was suspended on the cable next to hers and right by his head was the first valve wheel.

'Come on, then,' hissed Anna, who had stopped immediately below him.

Chess saw Pacer lean out, feet and angel glove clinging to the cable, the yellow torchlight reflecting from the shaft wall and glistening off the sweat that beaded his dark face.

'The first wheel's easy.' Pacer spoke between clenched teeth as he pulled the metal rim round as far as it would go.

'You're sure that's off?' questioned Anna.

'Sure.' Pacer leant out further and a foot slipped down, catching the top of Anna's head.

'Sorry,' gasped Pacer.

'Nearly *decapitated* me,' muttered Anna.

Chess could hear Pacer grunt and swear. 'I can't reach the second. I can't get my arm between the pipes.'

She saw Anna's body rise with a gentle hum of the glove. Anna leant out with her trainers pushing into the cable, arm extended to full stretch.

'Stand on my shoulders,' she offered.

Pacer stepped onto them and now he could get to the second valve wheel. Chess could imagine how much strength that must have taken, how Anna's muscles would be burning and her joints aching.

'OK.' Chess could hear the relief in Pacer's voice. 'Job done. Brain dead. Or dying. And you've got the Bank's data. Time to give it long legs.'

'I'm going up there, remember?' said Chess. The others were silent. 'With the supply turned off it should be safe. I need to find the brain, before it dies.' When no one said anything back she added, 'This bit's for me. You can go. Honestly, I don't mind.'

'Don't be stupid, Chess,' came Anna's voice and Chess thought she meant it was stupid to go up, until Anna added, 'we're in this together, remember? Aren't we, Pacer?'

'Er, yeah ... Sure,' replied Pacer, a little gloomily.

'You're not going on your own, Chess.' Anna's voice was definite.

'Unless you *really* want to,' added Pacer.

'Shut up, Pacer,' snapped Anna.

'Only joking,' muttered Pacer, resigned. 'I love doing stuff like this.'

Chess was the first through the hatch. The core stretched in all directions like an underground car park and it was illuminated by a rosy glow. She turned off the head torch. The spread of the core was so wide that she couldn't see where it ended, and it was pierced by the massive concrete and steel pillars that supported the tower, as well as the thicker structures of the lift shafts which passed through it. But Chess could only stare at the source of the glow.

'What is *that*?' gasped Pacer.

The two pipes which arced up beside the hatch ran straight

into a scarlet screen that was suspended between the girded ceiling and the gritty floor. This screen extended for more than thirty metres either side of where the pipes entered, after which it curved away, so that the sides were out of sight. It had the translucent sheen of rubber.

The screen shook and a dull thump resounded across the core.

'It's in there,' Chess said to Anna and Pacer.

Again, the screen quivered with a thump.

'You want us to go through *that*?' Pacer was incredulous.

Chess walked forwards and Anna followed her, ceremoniously handing her angel glove to Pacer.

'Great,' muttered Pacer, stuffing two angel gloves down his combat jacket.

Where the pipes entered the rubbery wall, the material was wrinkled and white, like chewed leather. Anna touched it, gasped and hurriedly withdrew her hand.

Pacer stood by, with a wise and knowing face.

'It's warm, that's all,' she said. 'And soft, like skin.'

Close up, and lit by the glow from within, Chess could see the convoluted, snaking outline of tubes within the body of the screen. She stroked the surface and thought it felt tight, like the outside of a balloon, but warm.

There was a thud; not as firm as before, and the pink covering twitched across its massive surface.

'It's beating.' Anna spoke slowly, with disbelief. 'Chess, this isn't a brain; it's a heart.'

'OK,' said Pacer. 'Wrong body part. Now, before this gets any more slash-dot, why don't we *go*?'

'The brain will be inside,' said Chess, switching on the

cryosaw. She slashed open a strip of the heart wall. It collapsed outward, hitting the floor with a slap, like a huge, limp tongue. She stepped inside. Silently, Anna did the same and so did Pacer, opening the lock-knife that he kept inside his jacket.

As soon as Chess entered the humid, crimson cavern, she saw at its centre a nest of rubbery tubes that snaked up from the moist floor, open mouths gathered about a circle of empty space; a space that matched the dimensions of the ring-shaped cerebral torus. In the space was the bed of steel stanchions and struts upon which the cerebral torus had rested. But the torus wasn't there.

The vast sack shook with a faltering beat and Chess's bare feet slipped on the quivering membrane and she fell, arms and legs slithering over the slimy surface. Pacer landed on his face beside her and Anna bowled over his prostrate body. Pacer wiped the moisture from his skin. 'Where's your brain, Chess?'

'It should be here.' There was a pleading edge to Chess's voice. 'It has to be here; it's all set up for it.'

The heart tremored and a section of the membrane above their heads collapsed inwards, revealing the girders in the roof space above.

'Just think, Chess.' Anna was calm. 'CREX have grown this heart; that must be what they needed all those chemicals for. The heart pumps the stuff that the brain needs, right? Those tubes, there, are like blood vessels, except it's not blood; it's brain stuff. And you can see how they would feed into the brain, if it was here.'

A beat, more feeble than before, and a swathe of cardiac

tissue unpeeled from the high, curving wall opposite.

'Well,' announced Anna, 'the heart's dying, whatever we've done to the brain.'

'The brain will be dying,' despaired Chess. 'But I have to get to it, before it's dead.'

'Why?' insisted Anna, frustration breaking through. 'What's so important about *finding* the brain.'

'I need it to find my brother.'

'Brothers,' corrected Pacer.

'*Brother*,' said Chess, coldly.

'You're getting stranger, Chess,' warned Pacer. Then he looked back at the ring of metal and the surrounding, open-mouthed tubes. 'It's like the brain is there, but invisible; like it's all been set up, but the brain has been lifted out and put somewhere else.'

He rubbed the top of his shaved head, perplexed, but Chess clicked her fingers. 'Of course,' she blurted. 'After what happened at the Riverside Prison, why would the Twisted Symmetry leave the brain where anyone could get their hands on it? They need all of this to run it, but they don't actually need the brain to be *here*. It can be somewhere else, but *connected* to here at the same time.'

'She's lost it,' Pacer said to Anna.

'No, listen,' babbled Chess, 'it's how things are. You can't see everything that's there, and sometimes things can be in different places, in different dimensions, but still close by. Like Julius's Ops Wagon.'

'Remind me again, who's Julius?' asked Anna, patiently.

'What's an Ops Wagon?' wondered Pacer.

'It doesn't matter,' replied Chess, excitedly. 'I know where

[339]

the brain is. I know where the Symmetry have hidden it. But I have to get there, fast.'

'You go nowhere, fast or slow.'

Chess knew who had said that even before she turned and looked; before fear had time to cramp its way through her guts and into her chest.

Jerkan stepped over a collapsed sheet of cardiac membrane. Behind him came four more traders, towering over Chess, Anna and Pacer. With a knotty, jewel-encrusted finger, he pointed up at a small box that nestled on a discrete A-frame on the far side of the heart. His craggy, bearded head cracked a stone-toothed leer.

'CCTV,' he chuckled.

CHAPTER 20

The trader chieftain folded his arms and his smouldering eyes flared triumphal as he looked down at Chess, Anna and Pacer. From behind him came the neat clicking of four extendable coshes opening in the fists of the other traders.

'You see,' gloated Jerkan, 'when it comes to catching children, *I* am the expert.' His merciless gaze rested on Anna. 'I enjoyed to kill your friend,' he sneered, his cave of a mouth mauling the language that was foreign to him. 'And now, my friends enjoy to kill *you*.' He unwrapped a very long arm and pointed at Pacer. 'And *you*.' Then, he smiled at Chess through the spittle-smeared moss of his beard. 'And this time, you come with me.'

Unless you are foolish enough to walk into their arms, Julius had said.

You idiot, Chess screamed at herself, inside her head. This was her choice, and her friends were right here because of *her*.

'You need a shave.' Pacer pushed in front of Chess and Anna, knife in hand.

'Don't, Pacer.' Chess knew that however frightened he

was, Pacer would use the knife before he'd let the traders lay a finger on her or Anna. But she knew, also, that he didn't stand a chance.

However, Pacer wasn't going to back down. 'Last time I met your boys, they were the ones giving it long legs, so don't give me a load of big-mash now.'

Jerkan looked down at the boy standing a couple of feet in front of him. A growl crackled in his thick, corded throat and his fist hovered over the handle of the gun that was thrust in his belt.

'I'll count to three,' announced Pacer, 'and you can go.'

Jerkan hesitated and for a count of three, he looked genuinely puzzled. Then his squat torso shook and a hissing sound escaped from his spasming gullet.

'Very good, little man.' Then the hissing laughter died. 'Kill them.'

Whilst Anna skidded through the convoluted tubes to the metal torus bed, Pacer dived to the floor, rolled past Jerkan and thrust his knife into the calf of the first trader who came towards Chess. With a howl, the trader grasped his bleeding leg, losing his balance on the other and up-ending. But before Pacer could scramble clear, his belly was pounded by the boot on the end of a long leg and he was on his back.

At the same time, Chess saw Anna grab the rim of the bed and swing her legs underneath, kicking out one of the long, metal struts with the flat of both feet. The resounding clang as the pole broke free froze everyone apart from Anna, and the trader who was lying on the floor, grasping his wounded leg.

Anna gripped the pole with both hands. Two traders advanced and she skated to meet them so that she was standing over Pacer. She swung the strut high, blocking the first cosh strike, then thrust one end of the metal into the other trader's thigh with such ferocity that she floored him. Wheeling full circle with the strut in both hands, she smashed it against the knee of the trader who had first struck at her with his cosh. Both she and the trader lost their footing on the slimy membrane, but Anna was the first back on her feet, long black hair straggling down her face, her mouth savage.

'Where d'you learn to fight like that?' gasped Pacer, gaining his knees.

Anna whipped the hair from her blazing eyes. 'Hockey,' she snarled.

'Enough,' barked Jerkan. His hand closed on the grip of the heavy handgun.

Chess knew that what the traders wanted was her. If she let them take her, they would have little interest in Anna or Pacer. It would mean the Twisted Symmetry could do what they wanted to her: but it would also mean her friends might live. Chess wasn't prepared to stand by and watch her friends die. And if the traders wanted her, they would have to catch her.

'I'm off,' shouted Chess and she started to run towards the gap in the heart wall through which the traders had entered. Her aim was simple; to get to the top of the tower. It would take her away from the traders and, hopefully, closer to her brother.

The way was blocked by Jerkan and the two who hadn't

been taken out by Pacer and Anna. They towered over Chess as she ran at them. But, with only inches to go, she threw herself down and onto her side, skidding over the slushy membrane and past their feet. They couldn't snatch the slippery street rat before she had slid off the membrane and out, onto the hard, rough surface of the core. Then, Chess was on her bare heels and running like crazy with three traders snarling in pursuit.

There was a door open in the wall of the core, thirty metres away. Chess knew how swiftly the long, stork legs moved; she had tried to outrun traders before. And if they had their whips ... she felt the back of her neck tense, waiting for a lash-crack, or the sharp bite of a thong round her ankle. But she was through the door before they had her.

There was no time to think. She pelted down a narrow corridor. After her, pounded Jerkan and his shock-headed lieutenants, long, grey coats billowing behind them. On her left, a staircase flashed by and she was aware of at least one of her pursuers galloping onto this. Dead ahead, the corridor ended in a pair of lift doors.

'Please be open, please be open,' Chess repeated to herself as she sprinted.

She was running so fast, the lift doors seemed to come at her. Chess punched the open button and then snatched an extinguisher off the wall. Years of messing about with fire safety equipment meant she knew what to do. Pulling the pin out, she smacked the heel of her angel-gloved palm down on the top lever and turned round with the hose held out.

The trader grasped the front of her leather jacket as the jet of gas sprayed into his face. Chess directed the hissing stream at his eyes and he staggered backwards, roaring but keeping the grip on her jacket.

The doors parted behind her and Chess retreated into the lift, blasting the trader with the gas. The doors swished shut but couldn't close because a long arm was in the way, reaching between them and into the lift, still gripping her jacket. Chess raised the heavy cylinder and bashed it down on the wrist to which the big, grasping hand was attached. It released her and was pulled out of the lift. The doors shut.

Chess swore as she began to descend; she needed to go up, not down. A bell pinged and the doors opened.

'Go away,' she screamed at the two secretaries who had returned from the fire drill and were waiting to enter the lift. They reared backwards, the doors shut again and she thumped the button for the top floor. Doing her best to decipher the numbers on the control panel, Chess worked out that the lift would stop at every tenth floor; she could tell that from the zero after every figure. So, hopefully, the top floor would be the hundred and fiftieth. But back at the hundredth floor, the lift halted.

The doors opened and the same trader thrust his head in, eyes cracked crimson from the gas, flared nostrils streaming and fingers with thick, dirty nails, clawing at her throat.

Chess drew back the cylinder. 'Get out,' she screamed before slamming it into the trader's slab of forehead. There was a loud clang and Chess's elbows felt like they'd jarred out of their sockets as the base of the extinguisher bounced off the trader's skull. But he crashed onto his chin like a dead-weight.

Chess heaved the senseless body from the lift, feet first,

ditched the fire extinguisher and hit the button for the top floor again. Then she collapsed, drained, against the mirrored wall as she was carried, smoothly, into the sky. But the lift stopped climbing sooner than she had expected. On the panel, the number that was glowing was halfway between the hundredth floor and the hundred and fiftieth. She pressed the top button, and kept pressing, but the lift went nowhere.

She paced around the cubicle, wondering whether the lift might start moving if she jumped up and down, as if that might dislodge whatever had made it stick. Then, she heard a thump on the roof. Something had landed on it. Or someone.

There was a sharp bang on the metal overhead followed by another. With the third blow, the head of a fire axe tore through. The gash was enlarged until fingers worked their way onto the ceiling, and with the assistance of the axe, began to peel open the lift roof like a sardine tin.

A head peered in; big, gnarled, hungry, with grinding stubs of teeth and a lump-boned forehead crowned with tangled black hair. The head snorted and a baseball glove-sized hand heaved up the metal, its squeals filling the lift shaft as it bent free.

Chess punched the door-open button but the doors remained closed. Above her head, the roof was tearing, the trader yanking it up so that there was a gap large enough for him to enter. She saw his eyes, glittering, and heard him grunt with excitement. In moments, he would be through.

She took the cryosaw and, shielding its glow with her body, knelt on the floor. The hair's-breadth beam cut the steel without effort and Chess was able to draw a rough circle directly beneath the hole in the roof. She left an uncut hinge to support the loose floor so that it appeared whole, and jumped back to the edge as the trader dropped down.

Chess saw the wide-eyed shock as his feet hit the floor, which opened, allowing him to pass straight through, the circle of metal giving like a trapdoor. He yelped and flung out an arm, catching the front of Chess's jumper as he plummeted by. It didn't brake his fall but Chess lost her balance and as she hit the floor, she lost her grip on the cryosaw which rolled over the lip of the hole. The saw disappeared into the black well, together with the trader's yowling wail. Chess pushed herself away from the edge and made herself stand.

She had to get out of the lift and up to the top of the tower. She could see the cables, taut in the darkness above. She just needed to reach them. One jump could take her to the edge of the tear in the lift roof. However, if she slipped or let go, there wouldn't be a floor to fall on. But she *had* to get up there. Now.

Chess sprang forwards and up, clasping the rough metal. The angel glove protected the fingers of her left hand but she felt the skin of her right rip away, the jagged edge cutting in until it was stopped by the metal beneath the skin.

When Chess had hoisted herself onto the roof, she held her right hand out to see the damage. The hand shone through the ragged skin in silver tiger stripes and she thought it was beautiful. But this was no time to admire the Committee's replacement. Wearily, she attached her left hand to the cable, squeezed and let the angel glove carry her up into the freezing pitch of the shaft, her tiny figure hanging.

When she guessed she was near the top, Chess turned on

the torch and looked up. It took a little while to decipher the winch windings but as she rose, she saw a large safety cage and the skeletal outline of steps up to a door, flat in the roof. The shapes moved in the torchlight, casting shadows which crept away from her as she drew closer.

The cable ran through the safety cage and that was where Chess stopped. Her left shoulder was beyond pain; her arm so numb she couldn't disconnect the angel glove. She used her other hand to ease the straps and she pulled herself free, leaving the glove attached to the cable. It was agony as she lowered her arm and the sensation began to return.

'Not much further,' she told herself. 'Come on. Come on.'

She staggered up the stairs, feet stamping clumsily. When she reached the flat door, she pushed but it was closed.

'Come *on*,' she growled, ramming her shoulder towards it. But before she made contact, the door flew open, daylight poured into the shaft and her scalp was on fire.

Chess was suspended, her bare feet kicking a metre above the roof and her hair gripped in Jerkan's fist. He lifted her so that her face was level with his and spat at her, saliva mingling with the charnel stench of his breath so that she wretched. Then he swung her clear of the shaft and onto the roof.

Chess scrambled away from his feet, but Jerkan didn't move. He didn't have to. There was nowhere for Chess to run. The top of the tower was no larger than a couple of tennis courts, and the level surface was broken only by several service doors like the one Jerkan had dragged her from, and the pylon-spire of the radio mast; the mast that Chess had to climb.

She stood and saw that although there were clouds overhead, there was also a bed of thin cloud below the roof. About her, piercing this faint, drifting sea of white, were the pinnacles of the other Cones, lonely and splendid in this gap in the clouds.

'You have no choice. You have to come with me,' stated Jerkan.

You always *have a choice*. That was what Ethel had once said.

Chess turned her back to Jerkan and walked to the edge of the roof. Eight hundred metres below was the ground, hidden by cloud. Hopefully, Anna and Pacer had got out. She knew that the little rats were safe. So it was just she who was left.

Anna had said that the way to beat the Twisted Symmetry would be to destroy the Eternal, but Chess could think of another way. The Symmetry needed *her* to control the Eternal. Without her they were lost. She remembered what Jake had said:

None of us will live forever, sunshine.

The clouds parted long enough to uncover the ant-crowds that filled the plaza below. Chess turned to face Jerkan. Her heels were in the air, her back to the clouds. This would be like sleeping, forever. She was so tired. Chess let her mind return to Knott Street, to the sound and smell and touch of her mother. She closed her eyes and relaxed. But the song she began to sing was interrupted, the words literally choked from her throat as a leather tail lashed itself around her neck and yanked her away from the drop.

Jerkan knelt at her side, but didn't release the tension of

the whip. 'You sleep,' he whispered. He pulled the whip tighter. 'Just enough to make you sleep.'

Chess couldn't work her fingers into the wound cords. She couldn't breathe. Her eyes felt like bursting and her vision began to blur. She thought the last thing she would see was Jerkan's huge mouth, opening wide and laughing.

Then there was a bang, the top half of the chieftain's head burst red and the whip went slack.

The Night Porter eased the trigger of the sniper rifle, breathed in and rolled onto his back. It had taken a long time to position the cross-wires in the centre of the trader's cliff of a forehead but his work was all about patience. Throughout his training at sniper school, he had always been told, 'Let the target come to you.' And, amazingly, the target always did.

Even within the thermal blanket, screened by the base of an aerial mast, the freezing cold had seeped in. All day he had lain here, having got into position whilst dawn had still been dark. But patience was a virtue, particularly for a hit man. He had bargained on Jerkan presenting himself at some point during the day, but had expected to have to pick him off in the crowd below. The chance of that seemed to have vanished with the appearance of the low cloud. But by appearing on the roof of the neighbouring tower, Jerkan had rewarded him with a perfect opportunity, although it hadn't been easy because things had happened so quickly; the trader had dashed from where he'd emerged to another door, out of which he'd pulled Chess and then it was a dance between Chess, Jerkan and the cross-wires.

The Night Porter dismantled the rifle, rolled the parts within the blanket and packed it all inside the yellow tool box that matched the hard hat he pulled on. Satisfied that he had left no trace of the job, he made ready to leave the rooftop. He cast a last glance at the tower where the girl was climbing up the high mast. At its top she stepped into space and vanished, just as he had seen a man in a long black coat and a black fedora do from a different mast, minutes before.

The Night Porter contemplated the empty space left by the girl. He knew enough about the world to know that there were mysteries he would never understand. Then a chill wind stroked his neck and he knew it was time to go.

'Sleep tight, Klinky,' he whispered, before turning his back on the CREX tower.

Chess hadn't stopped to wonder which guardian angel had intervened. She didn't have time. As soon as her breath had returned, she ran to the pylon and climbed, scaling the crossbars easily. The mast ended in a cluster of antennae, but Lemuel had told her that where it ended, there was a vast sink hole. Chess guessed that it would lead into the vortex, or maybe another universe. It didn't really matter what it lead to; it was the conviction that it was where the Twisted Symmetry had hidden the cerebral torus that drove her up the high needle. At its top she didn't hesitate; any fear of falling had been erased by the reckless desire to find the brain, whatever the risk.

Chess stepped off the top of the mast . . .

. . . And into the white blankess of the vortex. She shut her eyes and felt for the cerebral torus with her mind.

'There you are,' she said, opening her eyes and knowing exactly where to look. The ring of brain was an arm's length away, no longer purple but mottled grey, and no longer firm and vibrant, but sunken, collapsing, the tissue hanging from the metal restraining hoops like damp, sagging canvas.

You again.

Chess recognized the presence of the cerebral torus in her thoughts.

'Yes. Me again.' She approached and stroked the surface, tracing the punctures that were cross-dimensionally connected to the snaking tubes in the heart; tubes that no longer sustained it because she and Anna and Pacer had shut them off.

Why?

'Because you are part of the enemy,' replied Chess.

That was not my choice.

'Find Box and Splinter for me.'

You are stronger now. But I am so much weaker. I have minutes.

Chess was not prepared to wait any longer. She thrust her left hand into the softening flank of the torus and let a little of her mind burst out, into the brain. She felt its pain but felt no sympathy. It was part of the enemy and she needed information.

'Find me Box,' and she burnt the brain with her spirit.

Images flashed so fast she saw nothing but flickers. When the kaleidoscope stopped she was looking into a gloomy stadium with a sandy floor, a vented roof and the smell of sweat and dog.

There were two snouts pitted against him, both armed with wooden training blades. Box held a training blade in each hand; his skill with left and right had been identified by Six in the first training session. His hair had been cut short so that it wouldn't get in his eyes when he fought and his body was hard from the fierce physical training and the blade drill that Six had already inflicted upon the Fleshings. He stood lightly, legs tensed, one wooden blade poised across his chest to defend his head and vital organs, the other by his thigh, ready to strike.

Chess could barely recognize the fighter that the cerebral torus revealed.

The snouts attacked together, both striking at Box's head but at different angles, planning to beat the single defensive blade.

Be flexible, Balthazar had instructed him. React in whatever way is necessary.

Box's attacking blade became defensive. He blocked the incoming blows with both of his blades and then kicked his left foot square into the stomach of the snout to his left, before spinning on his right foot and smacking the other snout hard across the face with the flat of the left blade.

Both dog-men were in the dust, with Box standing over them, wooden points at their chests.

There was a moment's pause and then Box was laughing, lowering the training blades. The two snouts were up and they were laughing too, although the one whose face Box had struck was bleeding heavily from between his yellow fangs.

To Chess's horror, they slapped Box on the back like comrades, and now she saw more snouts, dozens of them, who had been sitting in a circle around her brother, if it was her brother, and they were cheering him. One of them, a lean dog-man with a mane of long, black hair and a spray of tattoos over his left arm and chest, sprung to his heels, squeezed Box's arm and Box grinned back at him, before throwing down the wooden blades and clenching his fists above his head like a champion.

He would train with the snouts. He would fight with the snouts. He would die with them, if it came to that. This was how it had to be if Box wanted to get back to Chess.

'No!' Chess shut her eyes, struggling to accept what she had just witnessed. 'Why, Box? Why?' she shouted at the dying brain. 'What are you doing?'

Box was amongst the Dog Troopers, laughing with the enemy.

'He's joined them,' gasped Chess. 'He's joined the Twisted Symmetry.'

'You have *one* brother and you mustn't trust him,' her mother had said.

'Show me Splinter,' demanded Chess. When the brain didn't respond immediately, she twisted it with her mind, sensed its final agony and hissed, '*Splinter.*'

He was standing like a dark switch of willow, head on one side as he idly ran his fingertips over a wooden workbench. There was something familiar about that bench, but it took Chess a couple of seconds to work out what it was. And then she realized, Splinter was in Lemuel's laboratory in Sky Suite 8.

The tenebrous lamp had been turned off. Splinter was casting about, casually moving from bench to bench, handling Lemuel's apparatus with absent-minded insouciance. Lemuel was nowhere that Chess could see.

Chess's thought raced in one direction. Wherever Splinter had been, he had come back. He had no business with Lemuel that she could think of. But following her tracks *would* have led him to the laboratory. Chess felt her spirit quicken.

Splinter must have been in the laboratory because he was looking for *her*.

Chess felt as if her head had been wrenched so that it was looking at things from a completely different direction. Maybe she had been wrong about Splinter. He was hard and selfish and could be cruel, but maybe that just distracted from how much he actually cared for her.

You only have one brother and you mustn't trust him.

Which one was it?

Which one had thrown his lot in with the Twisted Symmetry? And which one had returned to look for her, probably risking everything?

Yet again, Ethel had got it wrong. Maybe Chess *could* trust someone. Maybe she could trust Splinter. Which meant that, probably, he *wasn't* her brother. But that no longer mattered.

Box was her brother. That made sense; she and Box even looked a bit like each other. Chess realized now how much she valued Box, his simple friendship, his selfless courage. She needed him. But he had obviously forgotten about her, betrayed her, and it ripped her heart. So she would have to forget about him, however much that hurt.

Chess pulled her hand out of the brain which was already dead. She gave it so little thought, it might have never existed. She had to find Splinter, now, before he left the room.

There had to be a way from the brain to the Cone where Lemuel had his laboratory; just as the CREX tower had led to this part of the vortex, via the sink hole. Chess knew that she wouldn't see the way with her eyes, but that didn't matter. She was learning to know the world through other senses.

She opened her mind like a hand, feeling for a connection with the sink hole, like fingers might feel for the fingers of a glove. There were so many ways to go; along the reachings, through the reticular matrix of the deep vortex, even by the stream of dimensions that might be called time but which she appreciated now, was nothing more than the relationship between different points in the universes. There was far too much for Chess to process and before her own mind fragmented into the maelstrom, she drew back, and cautiously probed the near vortex.

She felt cold and light and saw the city. She was looking down at the Cones and saw the one where Lemuel lived. As swiftly as thought, Chess reached with her mind and then actually felt the burning-cold sensation of icy metal. She allowed the dimensions to shrink back and drew her extended self back into her body.

I am getting good at this, Chess allowed herself to think, before descending the soaring radio mast. Once on the rooftop she found a door that opened onto a flight of stairs. She clattered down so fast she nearly fell and she banged her bare toes so sharply near the bottom that her eyes watered. But that didn't matter; all that mattered was getting to Sky Suite 8 before Splinter had left it.

When Chess eventually found her way onto the quiet corridor, high in the Cone, she discovered the door to the suite ajar. Beyond that gap there was total darkness; the absorbing blanket of the tenebrous lamp.

Caution began to catch up with her. She opened the door slowly. It was impossible to see into the room, but she could listen. However, she heard nothing. Maybe Splinter had already gone. That thought drove her into the stygian mouth of the laboratory. Fortunately, Chess knew how to turn off the darkness.

She reached out her left hand and felt for where the pad of the lamp would be.

In the darkness, a hand grasped her own, its cold fingers sliding between hers and interlocking fiercely. Chess yelped and tried to pull away, but couldn't. The clutching hand was rubbery but the nails on its fingers were like knives as they dug into the back of her own hand. Chess could imagine them; neat, almond-shaped, black nails. This was Lemuel's hand.

This was the grip-switch, placed where curious fingers might stray.

'Splinter,' called Chess. 'Splinter!'

There was no response, at first. Then Chess was aware that somebody had come to where she knew the door was; somebody who paused long enough to taste the air with little sniffs. The tenebrous lamp prevented her from seeing who it was, but when the cold, nasal voice came spearing out of the darkness, Chess's gut melted with terror.

'At last, the rat is trapped.'

And, with that, Petryx Ark-turi, the Twisted Symmetry's primary warp, entered the room.

CHAPTER 21

The footsteps were soft and they were accompanied by a noise that Chess knew was the warp's computational gown swishing over the floor. They stopped right beside her, close enough for Chess to hear the tremulous, ecstatic breathing.

At the same time, the music started in the apartment below; the scat of the trumpet, the *ts-ts-ts* of a cymbal swinging the beat, the syncopating thrum of a bass, a saxophone singing and then a voice. Chess couldn't hear the lyrics although the easy tone crooned blithely behind the primary warp's cheese-grater voice.

'This is unexpected.' Petryx Ark-turi's face was inches from her own. Even though it was pitch, she could recall the long, sunken-cheeked head, the shaved, black hair, bristling on top, the sharp wedge of nose with the pince-nez spectacles clamped to it, and the club of a box-jaw that strained to contain whatever was hidden behind her lips.

'There have been such enormous efforts to secure you, every ruse has been employed, only for you to trap yourself at the end.' The warp sniffed and swallowed. 'How fitting that it should be the Traitor's own work that should give you to us; that he should present you to us by his very own hand.'

'How did you know I was here?' asked Chess. She had to delay the warp, to give herself time to escape the grip-switch; to pull her hand *through* it if she couldn't pull it out. But to do that, she had to relax. Chess remembered the sound of Ark-turi's face cracking open, and the glimpse of bone and wriggling flesh within; the face that was right next to hers, now. Her heart was jumping against her ribs and her breathing was so shallow, it snatched at nothing. She couldn't relax.

'I monitor the output from the cerebral torus. Sadly, you have destroyed it before it began to predict the worm strikes.'

'Good,' spat Chess, in lame defiance, more frightened than she sounded.

'That will not stop us,' observed Petryx dismissively. She moistened her thin lips before continuing. 'I had the advantage of monitoring the brain's output to you. And then I followed you here. It could not have been easier.'

Chess wrenched back and realized that she would have to cut her own hand off before she would be able to pull free. Only by slipping through the actual substance of the dead hand could she escape its grip.

'You have become very much stronger; it is increasingly difficult to contain you.' The warp began to circle Chess, the sharp, nasal voice jabbing from behind her now. 'The time shift you performed was accomplished; for a beginner. Of course, it was greatly assisted by the fact that Bael had interfered with your flow of time in the first place. But still, a promising first attempt.' The hard lips grazed the nape of Chess's neck. 'Although *far* from perfect.'

Downstairs, the voice crooned, unburdened by the terror above.

Chess shut her eyes, even though she couldn't see anything with them open. It helped her to focus on the space occupied by her trapped left hand. Petryx Ark-turi was nose to nose with her again. Chess could imagine the slit nostrils working, dilating as they tasted the air.

'Your smell is irresistible.' Petryx spoke with pin-like precision. 'You are perfect. There can be no complaint if I allow myself a small feed before our work begins.'

From where Chess imagined the lower half of the warp's face to be, came a noise like the tearing open of a lobster. Chess bit her lips to stop herself from screaming. Something stirred, squelching within the exposed, yet unseen flesh.

Bunching the knuckles of her right hand, Chess drove the uppercut in the direction of the warp's head. The contact was sudden and hard and it banged like metal on metal. She knew that whatever she had struck would have gashed a normal hand. But hers wasn't a normal hand.

I bet you didn't expect *that*, thought Chess, as she heard the warp grunt and stagger back. And boosted by that triumph, she had the confidence to sink into the matrix of space about her left hand, merge with it, and slide herself through the continuum of the grip-switch.

The moment she snatched her hand free, Chess felt the warp's hands on her jacket. In the darkness, both of them were guessing who was where, but Petryx Ark-turi had the advantage; she could smell Chess. However, her grip was clumsy; flailing enough to enable Chess to spin free, but sufficiently heavy to make her stumble as she did so.

Chess had lost all sense of where the door was. She was marooned in the darkness of the laboratory and the primary warp was slowly tasting her way towards her. Only the song of a distant trumpet and the sound of the sniffing broke the silence.

Chess attempted to work out where she had fallen, how she had rotated from the grip-switch and, therefore, where the door would be. But she couldn't be sure; maybe a little to her left, maybe immediately ahead, the way her terror-wide eyes were bulging. From her right, the warp came crawling.

Chess ran, straight into a wooden barrier that struck her diaphragm like a baseball bat. She tipped forwards, arms swimming, heard rather than felt glass smash, and cartwheeled over the top of the workbench. She skittered across the floor, snaring herself on cables and banging off more wood until the crown of her head hit a wall.

For a second, white specks rained through the darkness, dotting the edges of her vision and then Chess realized she had collided with the wall at the *back* of the room. The way out was opposite; the way that she had just come crashing. And creeping towards her came Petryx Ark-turi, assisted by the fresh blood leaking from a cut in Chess's forearm. She was feet away.

'A feed,' croaked the warp, through what remained of her mouth. Bone, flesh and metal clicked wetly in the darkness.

Chess edged along the wall and felt her hand brush against fabric, a cloth of some sort. It whispered to the floor and then she touched glass. That was when Chess remembered that there was someone else in the room; the wretch, her closest, living relative, so close that even its smell was identical to hers.

Petryx was closing on her, panting. Chess plunged a hand into the liquid within the large glass jar and felt the little body spasm against her fingers. She grabbed, feeling folds of fat that were soft as butter, digging her fingers into them however hard the wretch twisted and kicked.

She wrenched the homunculus out of the jar in a spray of fluid and felt it writhe in her grasp, trying to break free. The obese, miniature body was squirming frantically, but her grip was as determined as that of Lemuel's hand.

As Petryx Ark-turi descended on her, Chess offered up her closest living relative. The warp squealed with delight as she homed in on the smell.

Now, Chess ran, dead ahead, groping for the long, wooden work bench, feeling the broken glass under her feet but stopping for nothing, not even when the shrieking began. She didn't know whether the shrieking came out of the dark behind or from inside her own head, because with the shrieking there came a burst of spirits: Behrens, Jones, Red, Klinky, the massive reach of the cerebral torus, the wretch itself. Misery and pain stretched out from the back wall of the laboratory and felt their way into her mind, seeping through her so that she felt she was slowing down even as she ran harder.

The shrieking continued until all the agony stored by the wretch had been returned to Chess. Then she was out; out in the corridor, drenched by daylight, the carpet under her bleeding feet and the wall of darkness pressed up to the mouth of the doorway behind.

Chess's legs were giving way by the time she found the lift doors. She pawed the call button, staining it red, and staggered inside. The doors closed leisurely, as if they occupied a different universe. With a hum and a gentle lurch, the lift began to descend. Chess wanted to cry because that felt like the only way of releasing the pressure inside, but when she keeled back and looked into the wall mirror, the wild, blood-dashed girl opposite stunned her into silence. Her eyes closed and she slumped to the floor.

Trick had been hanging about the crowds that milled across the plaza, watching the Cone that the Bank had told her to watch, the one that a squad of hunters had charged into half an hour ago and then came charging out of, fifteen minutes later. Fury and Pacer had hidden themselves amongst the bodies outside the CREX tower, waiting, anxiously, for Chess to emerge. Hex, the Bank and the others were below the steps at the edge of the plaza, by the road. But this was *her* job. 'To watch out for any more uniformed activity,' the Bank had said. It hadn't stopped her from easing a loose wristwatch from a dopey jack, but, obviously, it was an important job.

It took Trick a minute to realize that the bundle the security guards were dragging through the main entrance was Chess. But when she saw the dishevelled chestnut hair, the torn leather jacket and the blood on Chess's hands and face, Trick's pulse jolted and she was haring across the plaza in search of Fury and Pacer, stopping short only once, when she glimpsed a pale face slip behind a rippling screen of other faces; a face that looked just like Splinter's. But it couldn't have been Splinter's; Trick knew that Splinter wasn't here.

'I'll get the others,' said Pacer as soon as Trick's bright, tattooed face pushed clear of the employees who were in no hurry to return to their offices, although the all-clear had been given twenty minutes ago. Anna ran back to the Cone with Trick to find people walking around Chess and over her, irritably inconvenienced by the blood-stained street rat who was littering the entrance to the tower.

'Someone should clear it up,' Anna heard a bystander complain. She knelt and together with Trick, helped Chess up.

'What have you done to your feet, Chess?' gasped Anna. 'And your arm?'

'What's wrong with her *hand*?' exclaimed a woman with a minute dog and a bright coral coat. A crowd was gathering.

'Identification?' One of the security guards had returned.

'What?' mumbled Chess.

'Identification,' repeated the guard, jutting his little chin forwards.

'She needs a hospital,' announced Anna, surprising the guard with her haughty assurance. 'She's not done anything wrong.'

'Not having ID is doing something wrong,' piped the guard, officiously.

Pacer, the Bank, Hex and a clutch of street rats surged out of the crowd.

'She's going nowhere with you,' said Pacer to the guard, menacingly.

'You want me to call back-up?' squealed the guard. 'You want me to call back-up?'

The Bank gripped the guard's jacket. 'You want me to smack your mash?'

'I just want to go,' whispered Chess to Anna.

For a reason that Chess couldn't see, the crowd began to pull back in a wave. Then she heard the cool purr of a car engine, and the opal eyes and chrome grill of a red Mercedes 280SL cruised to a standstill in front of them. A door slammed and a man with unkempt, peppered locks, three days of stubble and a pair of dark glasses sauntered towards her.

When he was standing in front of the Bank and the security guard, Crazy Boris rubbed his chin, picked at a tooth thoughtfully and then said, 'It doesn't look like the sort of party where they were only throwing cupcakes.'

'Who are you?' demanded the Bank.

'Her granddad,' replied Crazy Boris, without hesitating, even though he wasn't. 'Come on, Chess,' he said. 'It's time to go home.' He shook the guard by the hand. 'Thank you, sir. I'll see how she bears up.'

'She's lost a lot of blood,' cautioned the guard, anxious to display his responsible side to this man with a vaguely familiar face.

'As long as she isn't planning on losing any more in my car, she'll be OK.'

Pacer and Anna put their arms round Chess's waist and helped her to the car.

'How come you turned into the fairy godmother?' queried Anna.

'I just happened to be passing and fancied doing something a little more exciting than herbal tea.'

'It's OK?' Chess asked Boris, as Pacer and Anna prepared to ease her into the car.

'Don't be daft,' and Boris rubbed the back of her head. 'You're more important than the car. And anyway, it matches the paintwork. You'd better come too,' he said to Pacer and Anna. 'She needs you, you're her friends.'

'Friends,' mouthed Chess, and for a moment, she was on a high mountain, watching the dawn break over Surapoor. Then she was sinking into the soft leather which seemed to cushion her with sleepiness. She felt the car begin to roll.

'I have to find Splinter,' she mumbled.

'What about Box?' Pacer was suspicious.

'Box has joined the enemy.' Chess felt her eyes shutting.

'Rubbish,' growled Pacer.

'I saw him,' said Chess wearily, wishing she hadn't.

'You're going nowhere until you're better.' Crazy Boris spoke gently but definitely. 'It's about time someone gave you a break, Chess, for a little while at least. You can't save the universe on your own.' He ignored it when Anna corrected him with '*universes*' and added, 'I'm not keen on the idea of mortal combat, but maybe I could lend a hand by making the tea or something. Perhaps I could choose the soundtrack. Basically, Chess, what I'm saying is that I'd like to help out. You can treat my place like home, although, like I said, if you could just mind the crumbs . . .'

'Home?' Chess shook her head, but she was smiling.

'You could just stay for a bit, until you're fit enough to get yourself back into the state you're in now, if you see what

I mean. It's up to you. Your friends can stay too, it's no problem. Things are a lot more interesting with you guys around. The vegetative brothers never get involved in stuff like this, which is fine from a risk-management point of view, but it's pretty dull.'

'I want to go home.' Anna had pulled the envelope from the back pocket of her jeans and she turned it in her hand. 'Mum and Dad are in bits. They don't know what's going on with me, even though I've been doing it for them too.'

'So, you've finished with . . . well, with all of this?' enquired Boris.

'You must be joking.' Anna ripped open the envelope. 'I'm about to start.'

'Start what?'

'Revenge,' she replied, pushing the neat, black fringe out of her face.

'It really worries me, Fury, when you talk like that,' admitted Crazy Boris, the car swishing away from the Cones.

'I'll come round, once I've checked everything's OK at the wharf.' Pacer leant forwards, trying not to nudge Chess. 'I'll bring Gemma. I think that would help. And you're going to teach me guitar.'

'Well, first you can start listening to some *proper* music.' Boris began to prod the buttons on the car radio and then he took an old-fashioned cassette from the driver's door-well.

'What's that?' Pacer asked Anna.

'A letter,' said Anna, a curious smile playing at the corners of her mouth, 'and this came with it.' She held up a small, clear plastic envelope.

Pacer pushed his nose up to the minute grey rectangle it contained. 'And what's that?'

'A memory chip, I think. Although it's different from any other memory chip I've seen.'

'And what's in the letter?' Pacer wasn't very good at reading but he felt more at home with words on paper than memory chips.

'It says, "Plug me in and dial me up".' She shrugged. 'Nothing else, not even a name.'

Pacer scratched his head. 'The problem is, every time things seem OK, they start to go slash-dot again.'

'What you guys need is a bit of rock and roll. In my experience, which in this field has been extensive, bringing the roof down can really lighten you up.' Crazy Boris pressed the play button, turned the dial and the speakers roared.

'Wow!' whooped Pacer, winding down the window and letting the rush of air clear his head.

'You'll wake Chess,' shouted Anna, even though the vibrant music felt great as it blasted the darkness from her thoughts and raced her spirits away from the aches in her limbs.

The music was screaming, the wind was rushing through the open window, Boris was singing very badly and for the first time in months, Chess felt safe. They had taken on the Twisted Symmetry and won, they had saved more children from the scream rooms than would ever be known and now, when she closed her eyes, she was able to see a face she hadn't even been able to dream of before.

Her drowsy fingers sought the already familiar contours of the chess piece in her pocket and her thoughts were drawn back to a little room in Knott Street, where, for several minutes that were buried beneath the mountainous sediment of time, she had been a little girl in her mother's arms. And, no matter how time heaped itself upon her, nothing could change that or the memory it left. Now, when Chess heard her mother's voice, she could feel her touch and see her face. That was worth everything.

Her mother was sitting in the armchair at Knott Street, singing to her, and Chess was in her arms. A ghost of a smile stole across her pale face and she slept.

CHAPTER 22

An ice wind cut up from the river, shaving the ferrous, clunking hulks of the factory sector, grey and ochre beneath an alabaster sky. Here, where machines stamped and rumbled without rest, where the deep streets were deserted because the giant automata within the sheds worked without human agency, there stood a high silo, once steel-silver, now bleeding rust from the lash of rain and time.

The top of the silo commanded a view over the whole gargantuan clatter of the factories, over the poisoned, industrial wastes to the south, and to the north; the river, the wharf, the Pit and then, climbing to the far horizon until it ripped the belly of the clouds, the aerial jigsaw of the city. And up here, surveying it all, was Splinter.

His eyes watered in the raw wind, his white hair flicked about his face and the tails of his morning coat danced. But Splinter stood still, impervious to the wind with a face so rigid it might have been carved from ivory. He drank in the vastness of the city as if he could be nourished by sight alone, as if his spindly body was able to feed upon everything that his unblinking eyes could drink.

Slowly, his face thawed into a smile that barely revealed the elation which was bursting inside his skin-and-bone chest. He was free. And what a feat of courage and cunning it had been. What a display of ruthless brilliance. And what a disappointment that there was no one to hear the tale. Splinter's face frosted over again. Usually there was Box to gawp at his cleverness. Even Chess did, before she became too obsessed with herself. What use was it, being the King of Rats, if there was no one to celebrate his grand accomplishments?

His fingers crept inside his morning coat and felt cold metal. Out came the battered wedge of silver. He held it up, watching his five faces gradually blot out the entire city. Not a perfect audience. It was nothing more than a piece of silliness; a game. But it was the best in the circumstances. It was a start.

However, it was difficult to know where to begin.

'Why are you so clever?' asked Splinter No. 1.

Splinter smiled ruefully. Flattery was useful against less superior intellects, but he was immune. 'Do you mean, how did I set about catching the Traitor?' he asked modestly.

Splinter No. 1 nodded.

'I spent days creeping about that old bus depot the Committee use as an excuse for their headquarters,' he began. 'Too smart for the old hag and Professor Wheelchair to detect.'

'But you didn't find the Traitor there, did you?' interrupted Splinter No. 2.

Splinter frowned back.

'You needed a bit of luck for that,' added No. 2.

'We all need a bit of luck,' replied Splinter haughtily. 'But I was clever enough to use my luck well.'

He remembered how he had spirited himself into Professor Breslaw's room, hoping to find a clue to Lemuel Sprazkin's whereabouts. Under the solitary hanging light, the desk was still festooned with papers, loose and in stacks. And there it was, a letter, waiting to be posted, and addressed to 'Our Absent Friend, Sky Suite 8, The Second, The Cones'. He hadn't even stayed to work open the envelope, but vanished from Committee HQ that night.

'It was very, very clever, how you broke into the Traitor's laboratory at the Cones,' said Splinter No. 3.

This was better. Splinter much preferred the tone of Nos. 1 and 3. No. 2 was on dangerous ground; the King of Rats was not a person to cross.

'Picking the locks was easy,' he said to No. 3. 'But the tenebrous lamp was a problem.' Splinter had recognized the signature blanket of black from his voracious studies in Balthazar's library.

'What did you do?' asked Splinter No. 4. He had only half a face but he struck the appropriate note of adulation.

Splinter licked his lips. 'By hiding myself in the space above the corridor ceiling and levering up one of the roof tiles a fraction, I could see what happened in the entrance to the Traitor's apartment without being seen myself. Of course, I took the precaution of smearing my skin with engine grease first; a warp's nose can smell what its eyes can't see.'

There was a murmur of admiration from Nos. 1, 3 and 4.

'Chess nearly blew it for you though, didn't she?'

No. 2 still had a lot to learn. Splinter made a mental note that when he wasn't just playing a game, people like Splinter No. 2 would be treated without mercy. He liked that thought.

'I couldn't help choking. I hadn't expected to see *her* there. Typical that her paranoid twitchiness nearly landed me in it.' His voice mellowed as he recalled what happened next. 'She ran from the flat in tears. What did she expect, messing about with a creature like the Traitor? She never listens.'

'Anyway,' he continued, 'once I knew where the lamp was, I could get into Sprazkin's apartment when he left, soon after The Most Selfish Girl in the Universes.'

'Fair comment,' said Splinter No. 4.

'Thank you.'

'But what about the escape route?' asked No. 2.

'I'm coming to that.' It was only a silly game, but Splinter was enjoying himself. 'I found it in the bathroom; a hole smashed through the brick wall to the staircase on the other side. I knew exactly what it was.'

Splinter knew an escape route when he saw one; he was a firm believer in the creed of the emergency exit. From the door at the back of the ledge where he had lived with Chess and Box at the wharf, to his use of the portable vortex during the battle in the factory on Surapoor, he was only ever satisfied where there were more ways out of a place than there were into it.

'By sealing the hole with chipboard lifted from the maintenance store in the Cones, I could watch what Sprazkin did when he found his bolthole blocked.'

'Was it dangerous?' asked No. 1.

'Obviously.' Splinter blinked ice out of his eyes. 'So what?'

He sniffed at the moaning wind. 'I hid in the stairwell that night and waited. And out came the Traitor, very late, when *normal* people should have been sleeping.'

'*You* weren't sleeping,' observed No. 2.

Without hesitation, Splinter said, '*I* am exceptional.'

'Carry on, please.' No. 3 was rapt.

'I saw the Traitor creep up the stairs, onto the roof and up the radio mast and then he disappeared from view. Entirely.'

'But nothing disappears from the King of Rats,' said No. 4.

Splinter eyed the half-reflection suspiciously. Was there a whisper of sarcasm? Disrespect? If there was, he chose to ignore it on this occasion. 'I saw him reappear seconds later. I think he smelt me on his way back, across the roof; probably suspected he was being spied on, but it didn't matter. I knew where his escape route lay. I knew how to catch him.'

For the first time, Splinter No. 5 spoke. 'You knew *fear*.'

Splinter swallowed, his throat numb with cold. He could still hear the General's roar, could still feel his own limbs turn to water. The General had nearly removed Splinter's voicebox along with the rest of his throat when he had returned from the portable vortex without Lemuel Sprazkin. Splinter had had to work very hard, to convince the General that the only way to catch Lemuel was to drive him into his arms and that he, Splinter, knew how to do this. He had gambled on the General's desire for the Traitor being stronger than his desire for Splinter's blood. It was a gamble he had nearly lost. But he pulled it off. He succeeded even in persuading the General to return the portable vortex to him.

'Special steps were required, to capture a creature like the Traitor,' explained Splinter. 'The General ordered a detachment of xenrian gaolers. And a Möbius cell had to be prepared.'

'What's a xenrian gaoler?' asked No. 1.

Splinter sighed. Always, he had to spoon-feed the fools who surrounded him. He was growing tired of his game with the stonedrakes' silver. He would do things differently when it was for real. There would be no questions, and *no* disagreements.

'They look like pillars of blue smoke. They're experts in the detention of pan-dimensional beings. And, before you ask, a Möbius cell is a room that pan-dimensional beings can't escape from.'

'It was your idea to send the hunters in, wasn't it,' prompted No. 3.

'To flush the Traitor out.' Splinter smiled. 'It takes a rat to catch a rat.' All five Splinters smiled back.

Up the stairs and up the radio mast, Lemuel Sprazkin had emerged from the roiling vapours at the edge of the sink hole in a black fedora, black Ulster coat and with a small travelling bag in his hand. 'Of course,' he had sighed, with resignation, when he saw those who were waiting for him, and after two hundred years of hiding, the Traitor was in the vengeful grasp of his greatest mistake.

'Strange,' mused Splinter, 'how dull his eyes were.' They should have been shining with terror, but they were empty; as if something was missing from behind them.

With a swirl of blue mist, the xenrian gaolers had applied the restraining fields to Lemuel's sub-atomic structure and without a word, the gaolers, the General and his most coveted possession departed.

'And so,' Splinter addressed his audience, 'I returned through the gap into which the Traitor had hoped to escape.' But he had lost interest in the reflections. His voice had become a weary drone. 'Didn't even find anything in the laboratory to lift. Wasn't interested. Best to get clear of the General.'

His voice trailed off and he lowered the wedge of silver. Then he looked at it as if surprised to find it in his hand.

'Just a stupid game,' he muttered crossly, and he threw the metal down, onto the silo roof. He deserved to control more than a reflection.

Splinter looked out at the city. Up here, he could look at everyone and everything, without being seen by anyone.

Splinter, all-seeing yet unseen.

Night was coming, the wind blowing icy needles of spindrift out of the darkening sky. They flecked Splinter's morning coat, caught on his eyelashes, furred his thin, white feet. But he didn't move and the north became a frozen firework of orange and blue and green, dashed with the fine sleet that stung his eyes.

Splinter kept staring until the tears drawn by the wind had frosted his cheeks.

He was no longer looking at the city but at a world which stretched away from him in every direction and in every dimension. A world of endless possibilities; a world that could be *his* if he used all that was available to him; if he navigated his way through the coming storm with the skills that only the King of Rats could wield. He would locate the second Omnicon, he would unlock the secrets of the pyramid, he would use his knowledge of the Twisted Symmetry.

And then, he would find his way to the Inquisitors.

Dangerous? Oh yes, dangerous. But how to gain without the risk of loss? And there was the opportunity to gain so much. Then the time would come for the King of Rats to reveal himself.

The silver and its reflections had been dusted out by the silent snow. Night had fallen.

Splinter inclined his head to an imaginary Splinter who faced him.

'Majesty,' he whispered.